1966

1965

*perma*

"The Novel of Juliet" gave Shakespeare his plot for *Romeo and Juliet. Othello* he derived from "The Moor of Venice." "The Cat Cinderella" antedates the more famous Cinderella of the north, and adds horror to its traditional moral. But in addition to providing foundations for better-known tales, Italian writers have created a rich and distinctive national literature. The anonymous author of the lovely stories about St. Francis of Assisi, and Boccaccio, Machiavelli (the same who wrote *The Prince*), Basile, Verga, and Pirandello, Piovene, Moravia and Vittorini—from their different centuries and purposes, each has produced stories which are by any standard great in their warmth and humanity.

P. M. PASINETTI is Professor of Italian at the University of California in Los Angeles. His first novel, just published in Italy, is soon to appear in the United States, and several short stories have also appeared in his native language.

# Great Italian Short Stories

Selected and introduced by
P. M. Pasinetti

LAUREL
EDITION

Published by
DELL PUBLISHING CO., INC.
750 Third Avenue
New York 17, N.Y.

Cover design by John Alcorn

Printed in U.S.A.

ACKNOWLEDGMENTS: The following selections in this anthology are reproduced by permission of the authors, their pub-
lishers, or their agents:

"The Ruby" by Corrado Alvaro, from  Modern Italian Stories
edited by W. J. Strachan. Reprinted by permission of Eyre and
Spottiswoode Ltd., London, and Aldo Garzanti Editore, Milan.

"The Fourth Wife" by Riccardo Bacchelli, © by Riccardo Bacchelli and Arnoldo Mondadori Editore, Milan. From Modern Italian Stories edited by W. J. Strachan. Reprinted by permission
of Eyre and Spottiswoode Ltd., London, and Agenzia Letteraria
Internazionale, Milan.

"Gagliuso" and "The Cat Cinderella" by Giambattista Basile,
from the book The Pentamerone of Giambattista Basile, translated by Benedetto Croce and edited by N. M. Penzer. Published
1933 by E. P. Dutton & Co., Inc. Reprinted by permission of
the publisher, and The Bodley Head, London.

"The First Day, The First Story," "The Third Day, The First
Story," "The Fourth Day, The Fifth Story," and "The Fifth Day,
The Ninth Story" by Giovanni Boccaccio, from The Decameron
by Giovanni Boccaccio, translated by Frances Winwar for The
Limited Editions Club. Copyright, 1930, The Limited Editions
Club, Inc. Copyright, 1958, by Frances Winwar. Reprinted by
permission of The Limited Editions Club and Frances Winwar.

# CONTENTS

# Introduction

### by P. M. PASINETTI

The first of the Italian stories gathered here is about the favorite Italian saint, Francis of Assisi, and his miraculous taming of the wild wolf of Gubbio; the second is the opening story of the most famous Italian collection, Boccaccio's *Decameron,* and it concerns not a saint but a crook, named Ciappelletto, who by a false confession on his deathbed manages to be dubbed Saint Ciappelletto afterward.

The extremes of spirituality and crookedness, of loftiness and ribaldry can be found, for that matter, within the work of one and the same author—in particular, Boccaccio himself. For instance the hero of another story, Masetto da Lamporecchio, with his pretended dumbness and his consequent amatory exploits in a convent of nuns, is no more typical of Boccaccio's characters, than are Isabetta in the pot of basil story or Federigo degli Alberighi in the falcon story, two of the universally proverbial examples of lofty and desperately faithful love.

Indeed the first striking quality of the earlier Italian story-tellers is the variety of types, classes of people, and occurrences which they present, and the equal interest and gusto with which they attend to saint and vagabond, prince and pauper. Story-telling is a broadly popular art. Though it can be compared to illustrative types of painting, it is certainly more popular in quality and function than the other arts which ennoble Italy, for instance civil architecture. In any Italian main street or on the Grand Canal, architecture reflects the taste and needs of aristocratic patrons; story-telling rather reminds us of the market place, the populated *piazza* which is the inheritor of the Roman Forum as the place of business and gossip.

It is useful to recall that the Italian word for short story, *novella,* is related to the idea of novelty and news. A collection of stories is a record of memorable incidents; the classic Italian short story is episodic, anecdotal. Historical or not, its overt assumption is that the author comes up with a worthy piece of news about an actual and memorable event. The event may be recent and the story told for the first time; it may verge on the facetious anecdote as in Bandello's tale about the dead lady and the ape; or it may be furnished with a complicated and adventurous plot. A successful plot may appear in different versions. In fact translations and manipulations of the same story may become so popular as to transcend the boundaries of Italian speech and circulate widely in Europe. My selection of Da Porto's "The Novel of Juliet" and of Giraldi Cintio's "The Moor of Venice" was dictated also by consideration of the Shakespearean connections of those plots; in the same way, Boccaccio's story of Isabetta and the pot of basil may be welcomed by the lover of Keats' poems which it inspired. But to conclude, the over-all characteristics are the pretended veracity and the novelty of the *novelle,* and the variety of subject matter.

That variety may reflect also the authors' wide experience of the world. People like Boccaccio and Bandello lived in many places, talked with people of all stations; they were in a position to gather stories and anecdotes, as travelers and men of the world will do. In selecting illustrations from the work of these writers, however, one has in mind their representativeness not only as mirrors of a society and custodians of a national patrimony of tales, but also, indeed chiefly, as story-tellers, craftsmen, artists. Particularly when the episodes they narrate are simple and even a little childish, what emerges is the narrative quality, the vividness, the plain sense of a life which is being lived with gusto. The merits of style are varied. But even if no one equals Boccaccio, whose elaborate sentences, rhythms and rhymes—for instance in the exemplary falcon story— frequently make his prose a subtle delight in itself, all of the classic Italian narrators may at least be described as competent artisans.

Style reflects, of course, a view of life. What one often discovers here is a quality of clean detachment, of equanimity toward all sorts of material (would we now call it hardboiledness?) which from Homer on is the mark of true narrative. These characteristics may well reflect traits that are typical of an Italian outlook on life and on the human condition, whatever generalizations on countries and people may, in this sense, be worth. Sacchetti's story of the three blind men, for instance, which in different hands could have become quite pathetic or quaintly pitiful, turns out to be neither sad nor comic but simply "natural."

There are occasional flights of fantasy. Fantasy is by no means a minor feature of the Italian arts; in literature it is almost typically mixed with realistic concreteness. This is the case with Basile, the best narrator of the Baroque age; in his bizarre versions of such classic fairy tales as Puss in Boots or Cinderella, the tone is given by the folk-Neapolitan of the milieu, the speech, the imagery.

In my selections I have attempted to give illustrations, however sketchy, from all periods of Italian story-telling. With the rise of journalism after the Renaissance and Baroque ages, at least the most immediately anecdotal quality of Italian narrative finds its outlet in reportage. The brief examples from the eighteenth-century Venetian gazettes of Gaspare Gozzi are cases in point. It is interesting to see how much they have in common with the classic *novella* intended etymologically as news.

And so we come to the modern and contemporary. Continuing in chronological sequence according to year of birth seemed the simplest criterion to follow; but a regional one could also have been applied. Italy reached national unity in the second half of the last century. While this means, on the one hand, that in earlier times Italy had its unifying element in its literary language and generally in its culture (we may say that Italy as an idea is largely a creation of its poets and artists), on the other hand it means that local differentiations have probably remained more decisive there than in most other places. Such differentiations, in Italy as anywhere else, are interesting in literature when they become positive forces and poetic themes. This becomes more definitely apparent after the country's liberation and unification, for in such case a country takes stock of itself also in its inner varieties.

The degrees of regional color are, of course, very different among Italian writers. It is safe to say that Verga and much early Pirandello are inconceivable without their Sicilian background; Matilde Serao's stage is Naples; Italo Svevo's, Trieste. Of the more recent, Palazzeschi is Florentine, and Moravia has increased rather than diminished his local Roman quality. If literature is to be taken also as a reflection of the social and historical scene, in some cases the relationship between the local and the national becomes peculiarly interesting: the regional mind comes into contact, and sometimes into conflict, with the centralized state, whose establishment, in the case of Italy, is relatively so recent; and for this historical reason perhaps Italian fiction offers particularly sharp examples of the universal conflict between individual situations and feelings on the one side, and, on the other, the more or less remote machinery of Government and History: between Us and Them. In stories like Pirandello's "The Medals" and "War" are at least the premises for such a conflict. Only a few of these stories, of course, may be seen from such an obvious historical angle; in most of them the emphasis is on the more universal themes of fiction. Love, as usual, prominently holds its ground: for instance early love in the Nobili selection titled "Idyl," or love and death in two such different stories as the Serao and Comisso selections.

Many of the recent Italian writers have become quite well known in the English-reading world since World War II. In the following pages some of them will be seen in the perspective of previous centuries and some of their qualities will appear to belong to a tradition: Moravia in many of his short stories is in the great anecdotal tradition and aims at fictional characters possessing what he once called a "proverbial" flavor; Bacchelli as a story-writer is in that line too; so is Palazzeschi in a story like "Bistino and the Marquis," with perhaps a social consciousness and irony that go deeper than the gracefully comic surface. Naturally the resources of modern psychological analysis in fiction are added to the traditional narrative forms; this is evident in writers like Svevo or Piovene, both of whom are, incidentally, Northerners and by natural inclination exposed to the main stream of European influences. Awareness of the modern temper, however, is no less intense in Southern writers. Indeed it is among some of them like Alvaro and Vittorini that the contemporary problem of fusing into narrative prose the elements of an essentially lyrical attitude has found some of its most interesting solutions, though the problem is also solved in exemplary manner, and in his own terms, by Comisso, a writer from Venetia. On the whole the panorama of Italian fiction suggests liveliness and promise. The soil for further growth is there, and the materials offered by Italian life, with its variety and fluidity, continually cry out to be used in fiction. For an appropriate rendering of their complexities, however, the proper vehicle is the novel rather than the *novella*.

The present selection is extremely brief in comparison with the span of years it covers; an anthology could have plausibly been compiled with a totally different set of stories. After all a book of this sort is based upon one final criterion, however limited in authority: the taste and responsibility of the anthologist himself.

# GREAT ITALIAN
# SHORT STORIES

# ANONYMOUS

## Fourteenth Century

St. Francis was born in 1182, died in 1226 and was canonized in 1228. His life, first as a wealthy man's son, then as a mystic "wedded to Poverty," as a powerful religious influence, and as the organizer of a great monastic Order, is, of course, one of the most astounding in Christian history. The *Little Flowers of St. Francis* are not a biography of the Saint; they are a series of stories relating his own and his followers' deeds, narrated in the style of the simple, pure believer. The stories were anonymously collected in Italian, freely adapted from an original in Latin, in the earlier part of the fourteenth century. Legend is mixed with history. It has been supposed, for instance, that the wolf of the present selection may be the transformed image of a converted bandit named Lupo, or of some tamed feudal tyrant.

## St. Francis of Assisi Converts the Fierce Wolf of Gubbio

In the days when St. Francis abode in the city of Gubbio, a huge wolf, terrible and fierce, appeared in the neighborhood, and not only devoured animals but men also; in such wise that all the citizens went in great fear of their lives, because ofttimes the wolf came close to the city. And when they went abroad, all men armed themselves as were they

going forth to battle; and even so none who chanced on
the wolf alone could defend himself; and at last it came to
such a pass that for fear of this wolf no man durst leave
the city walls. Wherefore St. Francis had great compassion
for the men of that city, and purposed to issue forth
against that wolf, albeit the citizens, with one accord,
counseled him not to go. But he, making the sign of holy
cross, and putting all his trust in God, set forth from the
city with his companions; but they, fearing to go farther,
St. Francis went his way alone toward the place where the
wolf was. And lo! the said wolf, in the sight of much folk
that had come to behold the miracle, leaped toward St.
Francis with gaping jaws; and St. Francis, drawing nigh,
made to him the sign of most holy cross and called him,
speaking thus, "Come hither, friar wolf; I command thee
in the name of Christ that thou do hurt neither to me nor
to any man." Marvelous to tell! no sooner had St. Francis
made the sign of holy cross than the terrible wolf closed
his jaws and stayed his course; no sooner was the command uttered than he came, gentle as a lamb, and laid
himself at the feet of St. Francis. Then St. Francis speaks
to him thus, "Friar wolf, thou workest much evil in these
parts, and hast wrought grievous ill, destroying and slay-
ing God's creatures without His leave; and not only hast
thou slain and devoured the beasts of the field, but thou
hast dared to destroy and slay men made in the image of
God; wherefore thou art worthy of the gallows as a most
wicked thief and murderer: all folk cry out and murmur
against thee, and all this city is at enmity with thee. But,
friar wolf, fain would I make peace with them and thee, so
that thou injure them no more; and they shall forgive thee
all thy past offenses, and neither man nor dog shall pur-
sue thee more." Now when St. Francis had spoken these
words, the wolf, moving his body and his tail and his ears,
and bowing his head, made signs that he accepted what
had been said, and would abide thereby. Then said St.
Francis, "Friar wolf, since it pleaseth thee to make and observe this peace, I promise to obtain for thee, so long as
thou livest, a continual sustenance from the men of this

city, so that thou shalt no more suffer hunger, for well I ween that thou hast wrought all this evil to satisfy thy hunger. But after I have won this favor for thee, friar wolf, I desire that thou promise me to do hurt neither to man nor beast. Dost thou promise me this?" And the wolf bowed his head and gave clear token that he promised these things. And St. Francis said, "Friar wolf, I desire that thou pledge thy faith to me to keep this promise, that I may have full trust in thee." And when St. Francis held forth his hand to receive this pledge, the wolf lifted up his right paw and gently laid it in the hand of St. Francis, giving him thereby such token of good faith as he could. Then said St. Francis, "Friar wolf, I command thee in the name of Jesus Christ to come with me; fear naught, and we will go and confirm this peace in the name of God." And the wolf, obedient, set forth by his side even as a pet lamb; wherefore, when the men of the city beheld this, they marveled greatly. And anon this miracle was noised about the whole city, and all folk, great and small, men and women, old and young, flocked to the market place to see the wolf with St. Francis. And when all the people were gathered together there, St. Francis stood forth and preached to them, saying among other things, how that for their sins God had suffered such calamities to befall them, and how much more perilous were the flames of hell which the damned must endure everlastingly than was the ravening of a wolf that could only slay the body; and how much more to be feared were the jaws of hell, since that for fear of the mouth of a small beast such multitudes went in fear and trembling. "Turn ye, then, dearest children, to God, and do fitting penance for your sins, and so shall God free you from the wolf in this world and from eternal fire in the world to come." And having made an end of his sermon, St. Francis said, "Hark ye, my brethren, friar wolf, here before you, hath promised and pledged his faith to me never to injure you in anything whatsoever, if you will promise to provide him daily sustenance; and here stand I, a bondsman for him, that he will steadfastly observe this pact of peace." Then the people with one voice promised to feed him all his days. And St. Francis, before all the people, said to the wolf, "And thou, friar wolf, dost promise to observe the conditions of this peace before all this people, and that thou wilt injure neither man nor beast nor any living creature?" And the wolf knelt down and bowed his head, and with gentle movements of tail and body and ears, showed by all possible tokens his will to observe every pact of peace. Says St. Francis, "I desire, friar wolf, that even as thou didst pledge thy faith to me without the city gates to hold fast to thy promise, so here, before all this people, thou shalt renew thy pledge, and promise thou wilt never play me, thy bondsman, false." Then the wolf, lifting up his right paw, placed it in the hand of St. Francis. Whereat, what with this act and the others aforesaid, there was such marvel and rejoicing among all the people—not only at the strangeness of the miracle, but because of the peace made with the wolf— that they all began to cry aloud to heaven, praising and blessing God, who had sent St. Francis to them, by whose merits they had been freed from the cruel wolf. And the said wolf lived two years in Gubbio, and was wont to enter like a tame creature into the houses from door to door, do- ing hurt to no one and none doing hurt to him. And he was kindly fed by the people; and as he went about the city never a dog barked at him. At last, after two years, friar wolf died of old age; whereat the citizens grieved much, for when they beheld him going thus tamely about the city, they remembered better the virtues and holiness of St. Francis.

# GIOVANNI BOCCACCIO

## 1313–1375

The most famous of Italian story-tellers, Giovanni Boccaccio (1313-1375), like many other writers is often recalled for aspects of his work which are relatively
secondary: the bawdiness of some of his stories is proverbial while his great refinement as a literary artist is
neglected. He was also a scholar and a poet; the most
notable of his earlier works is *Filostrato*, a verse narrative on the story of Troilus and Cressida, written in
the *ottava rima*, the beautiful narrative stanza form
which triumphed during the Italian Renaissance and
was used most memorably in English by Byron in *Don
Juan*. The harmoniousness and the subtle rhythms of
his prose are a major feature of Boccaccio's *Decameron*,
from which my four selections are taken. The style reflects the taste and culture of the imaginary story-tellers, a group of young aristocrats (three men and seven
women) who retired into the country to avoid the
dangers of the plague of 1348 and spent a good portion of ten days telling each other tales. And each day
of story-telling ended with a ballad. My selections are
intended, obviously enough, to illustrate the variety of
Boccaccio's sources of inspiration: there are the bawdiness and ribaldry, but there are also outstanding
*gentilesse* and pathos.

## Saint Ciappelletto

It is only proper, dearest ladies, that whatever we do should be rooted in the great and holy name of Him who is the Creator of all things. Therefore, since I must be the first in our story-telling, I shall start with one of His wonders, so that once heard we may rest our faith in Him, the Immutable—may His name be forever praised!

It is evident that, as all worldly things are transient and mortal, they are also replete with trouble, pain and toil within and without, and subject to those infinite dangers which both enmesh and form part of our being and which we could neither endure nor ward off if God's special grace did not lend us strength and foresight. But we must not flatter ourselves that this grace descends upon us through any merit of our own, for it is motivated by His goodness and obtained for us by the intercession of those who were once mortal like ourselves but who have now become eternal with Him, and blessed, by following His commandments while alive. We, who are not bold enough to address our entreaties to the Mighty Presence, petition these saints instead for the things we need, knowing our advocates to be informed of our shortcomings by their own past experience. There is this besides. Though it sometimes happens that out of ignorance of true values we may choose as our intercessor before the Lord one who has been banished from the Presence to eternal exile—for what human sight can penetrate the mystery of the divine mind?—God, from whom nothing is hidden and who abounds in merciful liberality toward us, considers the innocence and not the ignorance of the suppliant. He disregards the graceless state of the banished saint and gives ear to those who entreat him, as though he were still blessed in His Presence . . . all of which will clearly appear from the story I wish to relate—I say clearly, according to man's poor judgment, not God's.

for so long a time, he was almost compelled to say he accepted. They soon came to an agreement. Ciappelletto received the procuration and letters of recommendation from the king, and Musciatto once gone, set out for Burgundy where he was almost unknown. There, contrary to his nature, he began with gentleness and benignity to do what he had to do toward the recovery of the loans, reserving the expedient of violence for the last.

In the meantime, he took lodging in the home of two brothers, Florentines, who used to lend money at interest. For Musciatto's sake they held him in great esteem, when suddenly he fell sick. The two brothers immediately sent for physicians and servants to care for him, and did all in their power to nurse him back to health, but every help was of no avail, for the scoundrel, an old man by now, had moreover burned his candle at both ends and was going from bad to worse. According to the doctors he was suffering from a mortal illness, which caused the brothers no little concern. One day, next to the room where Ciappelletto was lying ill, they began considering the state of affairs.

"What shall we do with the fellow?" said one to the other. "We have the worst of it with him here, for if we were to pack him out of our house while he is so sick, it would stir up reproach against us and adverse criticism for our small wisdom. What would people say, seeing that first we took him in and had him nursed carefully, and then, without his doing anything that could offend us, we suddenly turned him out, sick unto death besides? On the other hand he has been such a bad customer that he won't hear of confessing or taking any sacrament of the church, and if he should die unshriven no holy place would receive his body—he'd be thrown into a ditch like a dog. Then again, even if he did confess, his sins are so many and so dreadful that the result will be the same—there's neither friar nor priest who would or could absolve him. So dying unabsolved, again he'd be flung into a ditch. As it is, the people of this city are always speaking ill of us, what with the sort of business we carry on, which they consider scandalous, and what with their itch to rob us. If what we fear should happen they will raise a rumpus and shout, 'We'll not put up any longer with these damned Lombard dogs—even the church refuses to receive them!' On top of that, they'll run to our houses and they'll not only plunder our goods but even take our lives. Either way we'll have the worst of it if this fellow dies."

Master Ciappelletto who, as we said, was lying near the place where the two were talking things over, had a pretty sharp ear, like most invalids, and could not help hearing what they said of him. Sending for them, he spoke: "I don't want you to have any doubt of my good intentions, nor do I want you to be afraid of coming to harm through me. I heard what you were saying, and I'm positive things would happen as you say if what you discussed comes to pass. But the matter will have quite a different issue, leave it to me. I've played so many dirty tricks during my life on the Lord God that it'd be but a drop in the bucket if I played Him another now that I'm about to die. Look here, I'd like you to go about getting me a good and worthy friar —the best and holiest you can find. Then leave the rest to me and I'll settle your affairs and mine in such a way that all will be well and you'll have every reason to be satisfied."

Although the two brothers had little faith in what he said, they went to a monastery and asked for a wise and holy man to take the last confession of a Lombard who was lying ill at their house. An aged friar of good and sinless life was given them. He was, moreover, learned in Scripture and a very venerable man, for whom all the city folks had very deep and special reverence. The two brothers took him along.

Reaching the room where Ciappelletto was lying ill, the friar sat down beside him, first comforting him with kindly words and then asking him how long it was since he had last confessed.

"Father," answered Ciappelletto, who had not once gone to confession, "it has always been my custom to confess at least once a week, and sometimes much more often. It's true that since I've been ill these last eight days I have not been able to do my holy duty, such is the trouble my sickness has caused me."

"My son," comforted the friar, "you have done well, may you so continue in the future. I can see that I'll have an easy time questioning and listening to you, considering you confess so often."

"Ah, don't say that," said Ciappelletto, "don't say that, good friar! I've never confessed so often or so frequently that I should not make a general confession of all the sins I can remember, from the day I was born to the day I last confessed. Please, then, dear father, question me as particularly in everything as if I had never confessed before. And do not spare me because I am ill. I had much rather punish my body than out of halfheartedness cause the perdition of my soul which my Saviour redeemed with His own precious blood!"

These words were very gratifying to the holy man, who found in them the proof of a well-intentioned mind. Then, after he had lavished much praise on Ciappelletto for his habits, he began to ask whether he had ever sinned in lechery with any woman.

With a sigh Ciappelletto answered: "Ah, my father, I'm afraid to tell you the truth about this, for I might fall into the sin of vainglory."

"Speak in all security," encouraged the friar, "for truth, whether in confession or elsewhere, has never been the cause of sin."

"Well," said Ciappelletto, "since I have your assurance, I'll tell you. I'm still as much a virgin as the day I came out of my mother's body."

"May God bless you!" cried the friar. "How well you have done! And how much more deserving of praise you are, for if you had only wished, you could have had more liberty to do the contrary than we, or all others who are restrained by any rule."

After this he asked if he had ever offended God in the sin of gluttony. Again, with a deep sigh, Ciappelletto said that he had, and many times. For, besides the Lenten fasts that are held yearly by the faithful, he was accustomed to have only bread and water at least three days out of every seven, and he had drunk the water with such avidity and relish, especially on those occasions when he had been weary through prayer and pilgrimages, that no wine-bibber could have equaled him. Often he had even coveted those dainty vegetable salads that women prepare when they go to the country. While eating, too, he had had more enjoyment of it than one should feel who fasted out of devotion, as he did.

"My son," said the friar, "such sins are only natural and slight, and I would not have you burden your conscience with them more than is needful. No matter how holy the man, it often happens that after a long fast he finds pleasure in eating, and also in drinking, after toil."

"Oh, father!" cried Ciappelletto. "Don't tell me this to comfort me! You must know I am conscious that whatever is done in the service of God should be done with a pure and spotless soul. Whoever does otherwise is guilty of sin."

The friar was very much pleased. "I am very glad you believe that in your heart of hearts," he said, "and I also admire your clear and wholesome conscience. But tell me, have you ever been guilty of the sin of avarice, wanting more than your share or keeping what you should not have kept?"

Ciappelletto replied, "My father, I shouldn't want you to have strange notions because I happen to be in the house of these moneylenders. I have nothing to do with such business. Indeed, I came here to rebuke and punish them, and to rescue them from this abominable way of making money. I even think I might have succeeded if God had not visited me with sickness. You must know that my father left me in excellent circumstances, but most of my wealth I gave away after his death, in the service of God. Then, for my livelihood, and also to help Christ's poor, I became a merchant in a small way and hoped to make some profit. But I always went half and half on my gains with God's poor, using my share for my needs and giving them the other. So well has my Maker helped me in this, that I have always succeeded in bettering my condition."

"You have done well," said the friar. "But have you often fallen into wrath?"

"Oh," moaned Ciappelletto. "I must admit I have, very often. But who could help it, to see men doing improper things the livelong day, observing neither God's commandments, nor fearing His judgment? Many times in the course of a day I have wished myself rather dead, than alive to see young men seeking after vanity, cursing and swearing, going to the taverns and neglecting the churches, and sooner following the ways of the world than God's."

Then said the friar: "My son, yours is a righteous wrath, and for my part I could not find it in me to impose a penance on you. But tell me, did wrath, by any chance, ever impel you to commit murder, or speak ill to anyone or do any other wicked deed?"

"Alas, sir," answered Ciappelletto, "and here I've been thinking you a godly man! How can you even speak such words? Why, even if I had had the tiniest little thought of doing any one of the things you mention, do you think I can believe God would have tolerated me so long? Such things only outlaws and wicked men could think of doing, and I have never had occasion to see one without saying, 'Go, may God convert you!' "

"Now tell me, my son," continued the friar, "may God bless you! Did you ever bear false witness, or speak ill of your neighbor, or help yourself to another's property against his will?"

"Never, sir! Yet . . . Yes . . . ," answered Ciappelletto. "I have been guilty of speaking ill. Once I had a neighbor who would do nothing but beat his wife for no good reason in the world, and to such an extent that I once spoke ill of him to the wife's relatives . . . I felt so sorry for the miserable little wretch whom he used to trounce as only God can tell you—and that, whenever he'd had too much of the bottle."

"You say you have been a merchant," said the friar.

"Tell me, did you ever cheat anybody the way merchants do?"

"By my faith, sir, now I think of it, yes," said Ciappelletto, "but I can't tell you exactly except that a fellow once brought me some money he owed me for cloth I had sold him. I put the money into a chest without counting it, and a whole month later I found there were four farthings more than there should have been. So because I never saw the man again I gave them away in charity after I had kept them a year for him."

"That's a trifle," said the friar, "and you were right in doing what you did." Then he asked him many other questions, all of which Ciappelletto answered in the same vein. He was already proceeding to offer him absolution when Ciappelletto interrupted: "Sir, I have still a few other sins I have not confessed."

The friar asked him what they were and he said, "I remember that on a Saturday after dusk I made a servant of mine sweep the house, neglecting to observe the holy Sabbath as I should have."

"Oh, that is a little thing, my son!" the friar comforted.

"Not at all," answered Ciappelletto. "Don't say it is a little thing! The Sabbath is greatly to be honored, for on that day our Lord rose from death to life!"

"Well, now, have you been guilty of anything else?" asked the friar.

"Alas, sir, yes," answered Ciappelletto, "for once I spat unintentionally in the house of God."

The friar smiled and said, "That's nothing to worry about, my son. We, who are pious brothers—why, we spit in it all day long."

"And you do a villainous thing," reproved Ciappelletto. "No place should be kept cleaner than the holy temple, where we offer up sacrifice to God."

In short, Ciappelletto filled his head with many such things. Then he began to sigh and at last to sob aloud, as he knew very well how, when he chose.

"Why, what's the matter, my son?" asked the holy friar.

"Woe!" groaned Ciappelletto. "There is still a sin that

I've never confessed—I was too much ashamed to speak of it . . . and whenever I think of it I fall to weeping as you see. I'm almost certain God will never show me mercy . . ."

"Come, come, my son," said the friar. "What are you saying? If all the sins committed by mankind, or that will be committed while the world lasts—if all these sins, I say, were lodged in one man and he were as repentant and contrite as I see you, so great is God's mercy that if he confessed God would freely forgive him all. So speak in all confidence."

Still weeping bitterly, Ciappelletto said: "Alas, father, mine is a great sin. I can hardly believe God will ever forgive it in me without the help of your prayers."

"Speak with security," the friar urged him, "and I promise to pray God for you."

Ciappelletto still wept and said nothing, while the friar kept on comforting him to speak. But after he had held him in suspense with his weeping for a very long while, he heaved a deep sigh. "Father," he said, "since you promise to pray God for me, I'll tell you. Know, then, that when I was a little boy I once cursed my mother," and having spoken, he sobbed aloud again.

"Oh, my son, and does this seem to you such a dreadful sin?" asked the friar. "Why, men go on cursing God the livelong day, and yet He willingly forgives those who repent. Don't you suppose He will forgive you this? Don't weep, my son! Cheer up! Indeed, even if you had been one of those who nailed Him to the cross, God would forgive you for the contrition you show."

"Woe is me! What are you saying?" cried Ciappelletto. "Too great a sin it is, and too terrible . . . To think I was wicked enough to curse my sweet mother, after she carried me nine months in her body, day and night, and held me about her neck a hundred times or more! Surely this sin will not be forgiven unless you entreat God for me."

Seeing Ciappelletto had nothing more to say, the friar gave him absolution and his blessing, taking him for a very holy man, and firmly believing everything he said was true.

And who would not have believed, hearing a man speak that way, at the point of death? Finally the friar said: "Ciappelletto, with the help of God you will soon be well. Yet if God should be disposed to call your good and blessed soul to Himself, would you wish your body to be buried in our locality?"

"Indeed, sir, yes," replied Ciappelletto. "As a matter of fact I should not want it to be buried anywhere else after you promised to pray God for me. What's more, I've always had a special respect for your order. I pray you, then, when you reach your monastery, please see to it that I get the true body of God which you consecrate on the altar in the morning. For with your permission, I should like to take it, even though I am unworthy. After that, let me have extreme unction, so that even if I have lived a sinner, I may at least die a good Christian."

The holy man said he would gladly do as he wished and commended him for his sentiments. Moreover he promised he himself would see that the consecrated wafer should be brought to him soon.

The two brothers who had been very much afraid Ciappelletto might be deceiving them, had posted themselves near a wooden partition that divided the room where he lay from an adjoining one. As they listened they easily heard and understood what Ciappelletto was telling the friar. Sometimes they were so tempted to laugh on hearing his confession that they almost burst, and they would say to one another: "What a man this must be if neither old age nor sickness, nor fear of death that is staring him in the face, nor even God Himself before whose judgment he expects to be—what a man, if not all these things can serve to turn him from his wickedness or prevent him from dying as great a rogue as he lived!"

Once they had heard him contrive to be accepted in the church for burial, they had no care for anything else. Some time later Ciappelletto received the sacrament, and as he grew worse and worse, was given extreme unction. A little after vespers, the very day he had made his wonderful confession, he gave up the ghost.

The two brothers, commissioning a respectable funeral from his own money, notified the monastery, asking the friars to come that night to keep vigil, according to the custom, and to take the body the following morning. When the good friar who had confessed Ciappelletto heard of his death, he went with the prior of the monastery, had the chapter rung, and convening the brothers, told them what a holy man, to judge by his confession, the deceased had been. Then, with the hope that God might show many miracles through Ciappelletto, he persuaded the brothers to receive the body with the utmost reverence and devotion. The prior and the other credulous friars agreed to it. That evening they gathered in the place where the body was lying and kept a long and solemn vigil over it. Next morning, setting out in their copes and albs, with books in their hands and crosses before them, they went singing to get the body, and amid rejoicing and pomp they bore it to their church, followed by the city population, men and women together.

As soon as the body was deposited in the church the pious friar climbed up into the pulpit and delivered a fine preachment about Ciappelletto's virtues—his life, his fasts, his chastity, his simplicity, innocence and holiness, saying many other marvelous things besides. Among them he mentioned what the weeping Ciappelletto had confessed to him as his greatest sin, and how he, the friar, had hardly been able to make him understand that God would forgive it. From this he turned to rebuke his listeners. "And you, accursed of God," he said, "blaspheme Him and His Mother and all the court of heaven for every little straw you stumble over."

These and other things he said of his loyalty and purity. In short, he managed with his words, listened to with entire faith by the townspeople, to place Ciappelletto so high in their devotion, that the moment the service was over they swarmed to kiss the body's hands and feet. All the clothes were torn from his back, and the man who managed to have a shred of them thought himself fortunate indeed. It was necessary, even, to leave Ciappelletto lying there all day, that everyone might have the chance to visit and see him.

The following night he was buried with great ceremony in a marble vault in one of the chapels. As early as next day people began going to him, lighting tapers and adoring him, making vows, even, and hanging up wax images as a fulfillment of their promises. So widespread was the fame of his sanctity and so great the devotion of the people, that there wasn't a soul in adversity who did not make vows to him rather than to any other saint. They dubbed him Saint Ciappelletto, and so he is known to this day. They even affirm God has revealed many miracles through him, and still does so to favor whatever man commends himself to his graces with devotion.

So lived and died Cepparello da Prato and became a saint, as you have heard. I do not deny it possible for him to be beatified in the presence of God, for although his life was so wicked and evil, he may have shown such contrition in the end that God may have had mercy and received him into His kingdom. But since this is hidden from us I should judge from what we do know, that he ought rather to be in the hands of the devil, in perdition, than in heaven. If it should be that way, we may appreciate the goodness of God toward us in regarding the purity of our faith and not our error whenever we make an intermediary of His enemy, thinking him a friend. And so He grants us our prayer, as if we had indeed resorted to a true saint to plead for us. Therefore that our merry little band may remain safe and sound by His grace in these adversities, let us praise His name, under which we united, and commend ourselves to Him in our needs, in the assurance of being heard.

Here he was silent.

# Masetto da Lamporecchio
## and the Nuns

Loveliest ladies, there are many people foolish enough to believe that, once a girl has a white band tied around her head, and a black cowl hanging down her back, she is no longer a woman, with a woman's desires! As though by becoming a nun, she had turned to stone! If those fools happen to hear anything contrary to their belief, they fly off the handle as though an execrable, unnatural sin had been committed, unmindful of their own personal experience—they whom even license cannot satisfy, and disregarding the great temptations of idleness and brooding. Then, there are also those who believe that a pick and shovel, wretched food and poverty, rid the day-laborer of all desire for physical pleasure, besides making him coarse-witted and dull. But I'd like to show you how greatly they are mistaken, by means of a little story that is in keeping with the given theme, and which I shall now tell you, since the queen has asked me.

There used to be a women's convent in our neighborhood —in fact, it still is standing—which enjoyed a great reputation for holiness. No, I'll not mention its name—far be it from me to detract a jot from its good reputation!

Not so very long ago, when it boasted only eight nuns and the Mother Abbess, all of whom were quite young, there used to be a funny little old fellow who tended their magnificent garden. Somehow, he became dissatisfied with the wages, so settling his accounts with their steward, he went back to Lamporecchio, his home-town. Among others glad to see him was a sturdy, healthy young laborer, a handsome brute of a peasant called Masetto. "Where have you been so long?" he asked.

The old simpleton, whose name was Nuto, told him.

"And what was your work at the convent?" asked Masetto.

"I used to tend a fine, big garden of theirs," replied Nuto, "and I'd also go to the woods sometimes for fagots, and carry water, and do a lot of odd jobs. But those women gave me such stingy wages, I couldn't keep myself in shoe-leather. The worst is, they're all young and full of the devil, and nothing you do suits them. Sometimes, when I was in the vegetable-garden, this one said, 'Put this here,' and another, 'Put that there,' and a third grabbed the spade out of my hand. 'That's no good,' she'd say, until I was so crazy-mad I'd wish the work to the devil, and fly out of the garden. What with one thing and another, I got sick of it and quit—here I am! Before I left, that fellow of a steward begged me that if I came across someone for the job, I should send him over. I said, 'Sure,' but I'll see him in hell first, before I do!"

While Nuto was speaking, Masetto was taken with such a tormenting ambition to be with those nuns, that he could scarcely bear it, especially when he understood from the man's words that it was not at all impossible. But he knew nothing would come of it if he confided in Nuto, and simply cried: "God, you were certainly right to come back! How is it possible for a man to live with a bunch of women? He'd easier live with devils. Why, nine times out of ten, they themselves don't know what they're after!"

Later, when Masetto had had enough of the conversation, he cudgeled his brains for a way to get to the nuns. He knew well enough that he would not be rejected on the grounds of inexperience, for he was as skilled as Nuto in the tasks he mentioned. But he was young and quite an eyeful—there was the rub! However, after thinking a good long time, he hit upon an idea. "The place is quite a way off," he thought. "Nobody knows me there. Suppose I made believe I was dumb, I'd positively be engaged!"

No sooner said than done. Strapping a hatchet on his shoulder, and without revealing where he was going, he went his way, like a tramp, to the convent where, as luck would have it, he stumbled upon the steward himself in the yard. Immediately, Masetto approached him, and making himself understood like a deaf-mute by means of signs and gestures, conveyed the information that he wanted food, for God's sake, in return for which he was willing to chop wood. The steward gladly gave him something to eat, and then laid some logs in front of him, which Nuto had not been able to chop. Masetto cut them up in no time, strong and vigorous as he was. It happened that the steward had to go to the woods, and taking Masetto along with him, set him to cutting up firewood; then, showing him the donkey, he indicated that Masetto was to lead the beast home with the fagots. The deaf-mute acquitted himself nobly, and the steward kept him for some days, to clear up odds and ends of work that had to be done.

One day the abbess came across him, and asked the steward who the fellow was.

"Madam, he's a poor deaf-mute," he informed her, "who came begging here the other day, so I helped him and gave him a few things to do. If he knows anything about gardening, and is willing to stay here, we could certainly use him to our satisfaction, for he's mighty strong and willing to do anything we set him to. What's more, you wouldn't have to worry about his jollying your lasses."

"You're right, indeed," replied the abbess. "Find out if he knows anything about the garden, and try to keep him here. Give him a pair of clods and an old hood. Flatter him, cajole him, and stuff him with good things to eat."

The steward consented, and Masetto, who was not far off, pretending to be busy sweeping the yard, took it all in. "If you put me in there," he said to himself, "I'll do you such gardening as you've never seen in your born days!"

When the steward had assured himself that Masetto could till, he asked him by means of signs whether he was willing to stay. In the same language Masetto answered that he was ready for anything. Accordingly, the steward engaged him, showed him what he had to do, and set him to work in the garden, leaving him alone while he attended to other duties about the convent.

Day in and day out, Masetto was busy about his gardening, and soon the young nuns began teasing and poking fun at him. They even addressed the wickedest little words to him, the way people often do with deaf-mutes, confident that they were not understood. As for the abbess, she did not worry her head about it, under the impression, perhaps, that he was as devoid of tail as of tongue.

One day, as he was taking a rest after a bit of hard work, two little nuns who were walking about the garden, came up to him, and as he made a feint of being fast asleep, looked him over very closely. At that, one of them, bolder than her friend, said: "If I were sure you could keep a secret, I'd tell you something that's often occurred to me, and I think it might help you too."

"Cross my heart," said the other. "Out with it. I promise I'll never breathe a word to a soul."

Then the little wanton began: "I don't know whether you've ever considered how strictly we're kept, so much so, that no man dares come near us, unless it's the steward, who's decrepit, or this dumb fellow here. Now I've been told time and time again, by many women who come to see us, that all the pleasures in the world aren't worth a straw, compared with what a woman feels when she lies with a man. I've often thought of that, and I've wanted to try it out on this mute, since it's out of the question to do it with anyone else. He's perfectly ideal for my purpose, because even if he wished to tell on us, he couldn't, and he wouldn't know how. You see what an overgrown simpleton he is, who's developed in body at the expense of his brains. Well, how does it strike you, sister? I'm anxious to hear."

"God help us!" exclaimed her friend. "What are you saying! Have you forgotten that we've pledged our virginity to the Lord?"

"That's nothing," she said. "There are a thousand things promised Him all day long, and He doesn't get a solitary one. What if we've pledged it to Him? He can find another, plenty of others who would keep their word."

"Yes, and what if we should become pregnant?" asked the other. "What then, sister?"

"You think of trouble before it comes," she rejoined. "Just let it happen, and then we'll worry our heads about it. There are a thousand ways of doing it, so that nobody will know, provided we don't let the cat out of the bag ourselves."

"How shall we go about it?" asked the other nun, who was now more eager than her friend to find out what sort of hobbyhorse man was.

"Let's see, it's near noon, now," she said, "and I think all of the sisters are taking a nap except us. Come, let's look through the garden to see if anyone's around. If not, what's left for us to do, but to take this fellow by the hand and lead him to the shack where he takes shelter from the rain? One of us can slip in with him, while the other stands guard. He's such a fool, he'll do anything we say."

Masetto listened to their discussion, and willing enough to comply, was only waiting for one of them to take the initiative. In the meantime, they had looked all around the place. Reassured that no one could see them from any side of the garden, the first nun went up to Masetto and woke him up. He rose to his feet directly. Soothing and cajoling him with many gestures, she took him by the hand and led him, grinning inanely, to the shack, where he did not need overmuch prompting to do what she desired; afterward, with her wish fulfilled, she gave up her place to the other nun, like the staunch friend she was. Masetto, still playing the idiot, did their bidding. They did not leave the shack, until they had made several trials of how the deaf-mute could gallop, and later, when they talked things over by themselves, they admitted it was indeed a delight as they had heard, and more!

From then on, they took every available moment to go frolicking with the dumb lad. It happened, one day, that a sister, spying on the game from her narrow cell-window, called it to the attention of two others. At first, they were all for reporting the girls to the abbess, but then, suffering a change of mind, they came to an understanding with them, and enjoyed their share of Masetto's prowess. The three remaining nuns joined the ranks at different times, and under other conditions.

Last but not least, while the abbess, as yet unaware of the merry business, was taking a stroll by herself in the garden, she came upon Masetto, stretched under an almond tree, fast asleep, for now even a little work was too much for him, considering the galloping he had to do at night. As he was lying so, the wind blew up the front of his smock, and there he lay, showing his bounties to the world. The abbess gazed, and seeing she was alone, succumbed to the very ardor which had tempted her little nuns. Rousing Masetto, she led him to her cell, where, to the great consternation of the sisters, whose gardener did not show up to work their garden, she kept him several days, tasting over and over again the pleasure she had once condemned in others.

Finally, she released him, and sent him back to his chamber. But she required him so often, and claimed so much more than her own share, that Masetto, the demands for whom were more than he could satisfy, fell to thinking his dumbness might lead to worse mischief, if he kept it up. Accordingly, while he was with the abbess one night, he unloosed his tongue and said: "Madam, I've heard people say one cock is enough for ten hens, but that ten men could hardly toil hard enough to please a single woman. As for me, I've had nine women to work for, and I tell you I can't keep it up for anything in the world. It's come to such a state that, after all my labor, I'm able to accomplish little or nothing. Let me go, then, for God's sake, or try to find some way of setting it to rights again."

The abbess was astounded to hear the dumb man speak, and asked: "What's the meaning of this? I thought you were dumb!"

"Yes, ma'am," said Masetto. "I was indeed dumb, as you say, but not by nature. Sickness took my speech away, and tonight for the first time, it's been given back to me, for which I thank God from the bottom of my heart."

The abbess believed him, and asked what he meant when he said he had nine women to work for. Masetto made himself clear, and she understood from his speech there wasn't a slip of a nun who was not far cannier than herself. She was a prudent woman, however, and without letting him depart, decided to talk the matter over with her nuns, and find some way by which to save her convent's reputation from any gossip in which he might indulge.

At about that time, the steward happened to die, so that after the nuns had made a general confession of their secret doings, they managed with Masetto's consent, to spread the news among the people of the neighborhood, that he had got back his speech after long dumbness, by virtue of the nun's prayers and the grace of the convent's patron-saint, and they appointed him steward in the dead man's place.

However, his duties were so apportioned that he could take care of them with ease. Although, in consequence, he fathered monklets aplenty, the matter was carried on so prudently, that none got wind of it until after the abbess' death, when Masetto was no longer young, and thought of returning wealthy to his home-town. When his wish was known, he had no trouble in putting it into effect.

And so it was that Masetto, who had made his youth pay by using his wits, went back rich in both money and children, for whom he had suffered neither a belly-ache nor a farthing's expense, and settled in the town he had left with only a hatchet on his back. He always used to say that that was the way Christ treated those who adorned His cap with horns.

## The Pot of Basil

Elisa's tale ended and received the king's approval; whereupon Filomena was bidden to begin, who, full of pity for the unhappy Gerbino and his tale, commenced after a heart-rending sigh:

My story, gracious ladies, will not treat of people of such high station as were those of whom Elisa told her story, but perhaps it will not be the less moving. I was reminded of it a little while ago, by the mention of Messina, where the event came to pass.

There once lived in that city three young brothers, all of them merchants, who had been left in the possession of considerable wealth by their father, a man of San Gimignano. They had a sister called Isabetta, a young, very beautiful, sweet and modest girl, whom they had not yet given away in marriage, whatever the reason might be. In one of their shops, these three brothers employed a Pisan youth called Lorenzo, who used to manage all their affairs, and as he was very striking of face and person, he soon exerted a strange fascination over Isabetta, who allowed her eyes to fall upon him, time and time again. Lorenzo, likewise, grew conscious of her love, and abandoning his little flirtations, set his heart entirely upon her. Before very long, matters had progressed to such a degree, that in their passionate love of each other, they did that thing which each of them yearned for above everything.

They kept up their intimacy for a long time, deriving much joy and delight from their love. However, they did not go about it as prudently as they should have done, and one night, while Isabetta was tiptoeing to the place where Lorenzo slept, the eldest of her brothers caught sight of her without her being aware of it. Being a prudent youth, he was moved by a certain sense of honor, and in spite of the pain it gave him to know of it, he bided his time until the following morning, without sign or word, turning over in his mind the proper course to follow.

Then, at daybreak, he told his brothers what he had discovered the night before about Isabetta and Lorenzo, and after talking the matter over at great length with them, decided to let the affair pass over quietly, that no reproach might fall either upon themselves or on their sister; it was wiser to pretend complete ignorance, until such time as they might cast off this shame before it had progressed any farther, and with no harm or injury to themselves.

Abiding by this decision, and jesting and laughing with Lorenzo as they had always done, the three of them pretended to be going to the city for a merry time, and took Lorenzo along with them. They had no sooner reached a lonely and desolate place, than seizing the opportunity, they slew Lorenzo, who was off his guard, and buried him in such a way that no one was any the wiser. Later, on their return to Messina, they spread the rumor that they had sent him somewhere on business, which was readily believed, as they were often accustomed to send him on such trips.

However, when Lorenzo did not return, Isabetta often and insistently questioned her brothers about him, for the long absence was hard for her to bear. Once, while she was so urgently requesting news of him, one of them exclaimed: "What does this mean? What's there between you and Lorenzo, that you ask us about him so often? If you ask any more questions about him, we'll give you the answer you're looking for."

Mournful and sad, fearful and yet ignorant of the truth, the girl continued without asking further, and often in the night, she called upon him piteously and prayed that he might come back to her. Sometimes, with floods of tears, she complained of his long delay, and sadly she waited, expecting him always.

One night, after she had wept much over Lorenzo, who did not return, and had at last cried herself to sleep, he appeared to her in a dream, pale and disheveled, his clothes all torn and rotted with mold. And it seemed to her that he was saying: "O Isabetta, you do nothing but call upon me. You are saddened by my long absence, and with your tears you cruelly accuse me! Know then, that I can never return to earth again, for the last day you looked at me, your brothers murdered me."

Then, pointing out the place where they had buried him, he bade her call on him no more, or expect him; and he disappeared.

Awaking, the girl wept desolately, having faith in the vision. Rising in the morning, and not daring to tell her brothers anything, she determined to go to the place revealed to her, to see whether there were any truth in what had appeared to her in sleep. Asking her brothers' permission to go to the outskirts of the city for her diversion, she set out toward the place as soon as she could, in the company of a woman who had been with her and Lorenzo on other occasions, and knew all that concerned her. There, she cleared away the dead leaves from the earth, and where the mold seemed less hard, she began to dig. Scarcely had she begun, when she came upon the body of her unfortunate lover, still quite unspoiled or corrupted. She knew now for a certainty, that her vision had been true, and was the most wretched of women.

Realizing, however, that this was no place for weeping, she would willingly have carried away the whole body, if only she had been able, and given it more fitting burial; but seeing it could not be, she severed the head from the body, wrapped it in a napkin and laid it in her maid's lap. When the earth had been cast back over the body, she went away unobserved, and returned to her brothers' home.

Shutting herself in her room with the head of her lover, she wept over it long and bitterly, until it was bathed with her tears, kissing it all over a thousand times. Then she took a large and handsome pot, in which people usually plant marjoram and sweet basil, and in it she laid the head, wrapped in a precious cloth. Covering it with earth, she planted above it several sprigs of very beautiful sweet basil of Salerno. With no other water would she nourish it than her tears, or rose-water, or orange-blossom, and would sit always near this pot, brooding over it with her longing, and looking upon it as the treasure-box that hid her Lorenzo. Then after gazing at it a long, long time she would lean over it and weep so persistently, that all the leaves of the basil were dripping with her tears.

What with her long continued care, and what with the richness of the soil, due to the rotting of the head, the basil became more and more beautiful and fragrant. It so happened that Isabetta, who was always behaving in this fashion, was several times surprised by her neighbors.

"We have noticed that every day she behaves in such and such a way," they told her brothers, who had indeed remarked with astonishment how her beauty was wasting away, and how her eyes had almost disappeared from her head with weeping. On hearing what the neighbors told them, and seeing it for themselves, they often scolded her, to no avail, whereupon they had the pot secretly stolen from her. Urgently, insistently she asked for it, but as it was not restored to her, she ceased neither her tears nor her lamenting, until she sickened, still calling for nothing but her pot of basil.

Her brothers wondered greatly at this constant request, and finally their curiosity was aroused to see what was in the pot. The earth emptied out, they came upon the cloth, and in it the head, not yet so wasted but that they could recognize it by the curling hair, to be that of Lorenzo. They marveled at their discovery, and dreaded that the deed might become known, so burying it without more ado, and arranging their affairs to enable their secret departure from Messina, they made off for Naples.

The girl did not cease mourning, still crying for her pot. And weeping, she died. So her unhappy love came to an end. But after a while the story became well-known to many, and one of them composed the song which is sung to this day:

> "Who can the heartless Christian be
> That took my pot away from me?"

# The Falcon

Filomena had already ceased speaking, when the queen, seeing there was no one else left to tell a story but herself and Dioneo, by virtue of his privilege, began, her face aglow with pleasure:

It is now my turn, and I shall acquit myself willingly,

dearest ladies, with a story which somewhat resembles the preceding, so that you may not only know what power your beauty wields in noble hearts, but that you may learn to be the proper donors of your gifts, where gifts are due, without allowing the impulse always to come from Fortune, who, as most often happens, gives not moderately, but with an all too lavish hand.

I'm sure you must all have heard of Coppo di Borghese Domenichi, who was a worshipful man of great authority in our city, and will always be illustrious and worthy of lasting fame, much more for his accomplishments and merits, than for any pride of blood. Well, when he was old and hoary with years, he used to take great pleasure in talking over the past with his neighbors and other men, a thing which he could do better than anyone else, both because of his unfailing memory and the charm of his speech.

Among others of his lovely stories, he used to tell one of a young man, son of Messer Filippo Alberighi, called Federigo, famed above all other Tuscan cavaliers for his prowess in arms and deeds of gallantry. As is always the case with the majority of gentle spirits, he fell in love with a lady called Giovanna, deemed one of the loveliest and most gracious women in Florence; and to gain her favor he held jousts and tournaments, banquets and festivals, made lavish gifts, and spent his money without stint or measure. But Giovanna, whose virtue was a match for her beauty, did not give a thought to all that was done for her, or to the man who did it.

Now while Federigo continued spending his goods with a high hand, and getting nothing in return, his riches dwindled away, as most naturally happens, and soon he was so poor that he had only a little farm left, on the income of which he lived as modestly as possible, and an only falcon, the like of which was nowhere to be found. For all that, his love waxed greater than ever, but seeing that he could no longer maintain his usual elegance in the city, he removed to Campi, where his little estate was situated, and there, without being beholden to anyone, he flew his falcon whenever he could, and bore his poverty with patience.

Meanwhile, with Federigo at such a pass, Monna Giovanna's husband fell ill, and feeling the approach of death, drew up his will. He was a very wealthy man, and naming his son, already grown to boyhood, as his heir, he designated Giovanna, whom he dearly loved, to succeed the lad if he should die without lawful issue; and so he breathed his last.

Giovanna was now a widow. That summer, according to the custom of our women, she went away in the country with her son, settling in one of her cottages, near Federigo's farm. In a short time the boy became friendly with Federigo, and both had great sport together, hunting and flying the hawks. Many a time the lad had seen Federigo's falcon wing its flight upward, and had taken such a singular delight in it, that he wanted it for his own, though he never had courage enough to ask Federigo for it, seeing how much he loved it. At about this time the boy fell sick, much to his mother's grief, who had no other child and cherished him with every fiber of her being. All day long she was at his bedside, comforting him, and many a time she asked him if there was anything he wanted, pleading with him to tell her, and promising that if it could be had, she would surely obtain it for him.

Hearing her make her offer so often, the boy said: "Mother dear, if you can get Federigo's falcon for me, I'm sure I should get well."

The lady hesitated a little at his request, and wondered how to go about it. She was conscious that Federigo had long been in love with her, without having ever received so much as a glance from her, and pondered: "How can I send or go to Federigo and ask him for his falcon, which, from what I hear, is the finest that ever flew, and moreover, is the only thing which gives him a hold on life? And how can I be so selfish as to want to take it away from a poor fellow, who has no other delight left in the world?"

Troubled by her thoughts, and knowing that she had but to ask for the falcon to receive it, she did not know what to say, and without answering her son, remained silent. At last, allowing her love of him to get the upper hand, she determined inwardly to content him at any cost, and not to send for the falcon, but to fetch it herself.

"My son," she said, "be of good cheer and do your best to get well and strong again. I promise that the first thing in the morning I'll go for the falcon myself and bring it back to you."

Filled with happiness, the lad showed a marked improvement that very day.

The following morning, Monna Giovanna, taking another woman with her to keep her company, went to Federigo's house on a visit and sent for him. It was not the season for hawking, nor had he been out for some days past. As it was, he happened to be in his garden, looking after some small chores. On hearing that Monna Giovanna was at the door asking for him, he marveled greatly and hastened to her. With feminine grace she came to greet him, and upon his deep obeisance, she said: "Good day to you, Federigo." Then, "I've come to make up for all the harm you suffered through me," she added, "by placing more love in me than you should have, and I shall begin by dining with you in friendship, with this friend of mine."

Humbly Federigo replied: "Madam, I don't remember ever having suffered any harm through you. On the contrary, you did me such good that if I was ever worth anything, it was due entirely to your virtues and the love I've always borne you. Indeed, though you have come to a poor host, your generous visit is even more dear to me now than it would have been, had I had it in my power to spend my fortune over again."

With these words, he escorted her into his house with great embarrassment, and from there into his garden, where, as he had no one else to entertain her, he said: "Madam, since I have no one to do the honors, this good woman, the wife of that laborer there, will keep you company, while I see that the table is laid."

Not until then, despite his dire poverty, had he been so conscious of the want to which he had been reduced by the inordinate waste of his riches; but that morning when he saw that he had nothing with which to treat the lady for whose sake he had once been bountiful to hosts of men, he awoke with a shock. Up and down the house he wandered, bitterly grieving and almost out of his senses, ransacking the place and cursing himself and the fate which had brought him to such a pass. But no money did he find, nor anything to pawn. Besides, it was getting late. Anxious to do his lady honor, somehow or other, and loth to borrow from his own gardener, or anyone else for that matter, he looked about him perplexed. His eyes fell on his beloved falcon, sitting on its perch in the tiny parlor. It was his last resource. Taking the bird and finding it fat, he thought it would make a worthy dish for so fine a lady, so without another moment's thought, he wrung its neck, and giving it to his small servant girl to pluck and dress, had it put on the spit and promptly broiled.

The table was laid with the whitest of linen, of which he still possessed some; then, rejoining Monna Giovanna in the garden, his face beaming with happiness, he told her that what modest dinner he could furnish, was ready. The lady rose with her friend, and both took their places at table, where, without knowing what banquet was before them, they ate the good falcon in the company of Federigo, who served them with the utmost devotion.

The dinner over, they lingered a while, conversing pleasantly with their host, when Monna Giovanna, thinking the time had come for her to broach the subject of her visit, addressed him graciously: "I don't doubt in the least, Federigo, that you'll marvel at my boldness when I confess the chief reason that brought me here, as you look back upon your past life and my virtue, which perhaps you may have interpreted as cruelty and hardheartedness. Still, had it ever been your lot to have children of your own, to make you understand how great is the love one bears them, I am sure you would half condone my presumption. But though you have none, I, who have one, cannot escape the common laws of motherhood, and following their promptings, I must, despite myself, and contrary to all that is just and proper, ask something of you which I know is the dearest thing you have. And it is nothing to wonder at, for what other delight, what other pastime and consolation has been left you by your evil fortune? It is your falcon I would have. Federigo, your falcon, which my little boy wants so much, that if I don't bring it to him, I greatly fear his present malady will take a turn for the worse, and something terrible may happen. I might even lose him. I beseech you, then, Federigo, not for the love you bear me, for you owe it nothing, but for your own nobility, which you have proved above any other man's, by many worthy deeds—for the sake of that nobility, give me your falcon, that I may say I saved my son's life by your gift, and have him beholden to you for it, for as long as he lives."

When Federigo heard what Monna Giovanna was asking, and saw that it was beyond his power to oblige her, as he had served the bird to her at dinner, tears welled up in his eyes before he could utter a word. At first she believed his grief was caused by the thought of parting with his falcon, rather than by anything else, and was about to tell him that she did not want it; but she forbore, and waited to hear what he had to say.

"Dear lady," said he, drying his tears, "since God willed me to fall in love with you, I've had many an occasion to complain of Fortune, who opposed me in many things; but all were trivial in comparison with what she is making me suffer now! Nevermore can she and I be friends! To think that you came to see me in my poor little cot, where you never deigned to set foot when I was rich, and asked a little gift of me, only to have her make it impossible for me to grant it! Listen, and I shall tell you in a few words why it cannot be.

"When I heard that you, in your graciousness, wished to dine with me, I considered your rank and merit, and thought it would be only seemly and proper to serve you more precious fare, so far as I could afford it, than is generally offered to others. Therefore, thinking of the falcon which you now ask of me, and of its excellence, I deemed it a dish worthy of you, and today you had it, served roasted on a platter. Well-given I thought it, too! But alas! Now I see you wanted it otherwise, and I am so desolate because

I cannot help you, that never may I have another moment's peace." To prove his words, he had her shown the poor bird's feathers, claws and beak.

At first the lady blamed him for having sacrificed so excellent a falcon to entertain a mere woman, but presently she began inwardly admiring the greatness of his spirit, which poverty had not succeeded, nor could ever succeed, in stifling. However, abandoning all hope of obtaining the falcon, and very much concerned about her son's recovery, she left Federigo and returned sadly to the lad's bedside. Whether he was disappointed because he could not have the falcon, or because the natural course of the disease destined him to die, he breathed his last before many days had passed, to his mother's extreme sorrow.

Long she remained in tears and grieving, but as she was still in the prime of youth and immensely wealthy, her brothers urged her again and again to remarry. Though she had no intention of taking another husband, at their insistence she began to dwell on Federigo's fine character, and his most recent proof of generosity by the killing of that marvelous falcon, to honor her, so she said to them: "I'd very gladly remain as I am, if you would let me. But since you insist on my marrying again, I'll have nobody but Federigo degli Alberighi."

They made fun of her, and taunting, said: "You foolish woman! What are you saying? What do you mean by choosing him, when he hasn't a florin to his name?"

"I know very well that it's as you say, my brothers," she said, "but I'd rather have a man in need of wealth, than wealth in need of a man."

Hearing her determination, the brothers, who knew Federigo to be a man of excellence, though poor, bestowed her upon him as she desired, together with her riches. As for Federigo, when he saw himself married to the woman he had so dearly loved, and possessed of so vast a fortune in the bargain, he learned to manage his affairs more wisely, and lived with her happily to the end of his days.

# FRANCO SACCHETTI

## About 1335–1400

A Tuscan of noble family, Franco Sacchetti (*ca.* 1335-
1400) traveled widely as a merchant, and later received
several political and diplomatic appointments from
the *comune* of Florence; hence his knowledge of various
types of people and events. His world is prosaic. It is
not only less poetic but also much more limited than
that of Boccaccio which ranges from the bawdy to the
nobly tragic. His *novelle* (he also wrote poetry) are
usually anecdotes taken from the ordinary life of the
middle class and the "common" people. His narrative
has the immediacy and liveliness of things directly seen
and heard. In different treatments, the material of this
story could have become pathetic, or on the other
hand it could have degenerated into grim slapstick.
The Sacchetti tone is the product of an even, common-
sense grasp of reality.

## Three Blind Men

The neighborhood of San Lorenzo, near Santa Orsa, in
Florence, was the favorite haunt of certain blind mendi-
cants, who were in the habit of rising early to make their
respective rounds. Some took their station at the church of
the Nunziata, some in St. Michael's Gardens, while others
sang songs in the suburbs; all, however, agreed to meet at
St. Laurence's Bell to dine after having made their morning
calls: for the host of said inn wholly devoted himself to

the entertainment of gentlemen of their cloth. It happened that two of the party were sitting together one morning after taking some refreshment, talking over the state of their affairs.

"I first became blind," said one, "about twelve years ago, since which time I have made perhaps a hundred pounds." "Then what an unlucky fellow I am," cried the other, "not to have blinded myself sooner; for I have only saved about twenty." "Why, how long have you been blind?" inquired his companion: to which the latter answered: "Not more than three years."

During this conversation, another beggar of the name of Lazzero da Corneto joined them, saying: "God bless you, my dear brothers!" "What are you, friend?" inquired they. "I am in the dark like you; what is it you were discoursing of?" And they told him.

Lazzero on this said: "Well, I was born blind, and I am now forty-seven years old; if I had saved all the money I got, I should now be one of the richest blind men in all Maremma."

"I can find no one," said the three-years blind, "who has not done better than myself." He soon added in the course of conversation, however: "What is done, is done; let us leave the past to itself, and enter into a new company. I think we three should do very well together; and we might make a common fund. We can sally out together, and take care of one another, should one of us happen to get into straits."

The other two approved of the plan, and they shook hands, and swore a good round oath over the table to play each other fair. The new firm continued for some time; but a person who had happened to overhear the terms they had made, seeing them standing one Wednesday at the gate of San Lorenzo, bestowed upon one of them a farthing, saying: "Divide this shilling among you," a gift which he frequently repeated in the same words. The man who received it at length said: "Faith! I think it feels more like a farthing than a shilling, from its size." "Where is it?" said the others, "do not let us begin to impose upon each other already." "How impose?" replied the man. "I put what I get into the bag, and so do you I hope." Lazzero here observed: "Good faith, my brethren, is a fine thing"; and so the affair stood. Though it first infused suspicions into the whole firm, still they continued to meet, and to unite their spoils every eight days, and to divide them afterward into three parts.

About the middle of August, they resolved as usual to attend the feast of our lady at Pisa, each preparing himself for the journey with his little dog, his money dish, and a correct version of the *Intemerata,* which they sang in every village through which they passed. They arrived at Santa Gonda on the Sabbath, the day fixed for the division of their spoils, and going into an inn, they requested a private room for the evening to settle their accounts. Taking possession of it along with their four-footed guides, with their cane knots in their hands, about the time of going to repose, one of them, called Salvadore, inquired what would be the best time to settle business; it was agreed that this should be done as soon as the whole family was gone to rest.

When the time came, Grazia, the three-years blind, said: "Come, let us sit down, and each count what he has got, and, whoever has most, must make it up to the others." This being understood, they set to work, and having enumerated the whole of their gains, Lazzero said: "I find I have just five shillings and four pence." "And I," continued Salvadore, "have exactly three shillings and two pence." "So far good," cried Grazia, "very good; and I myself have just two shillings." "But how can that be, in the devil's name?" exclaimed the others. "Indeed I cannot tell," answered Grazia. "Cannot tell?" said they; "but you must have some more shillings somewhere; you are playing us false; do you think it is the firm of the wolf and the sheep? Your name is indeed Grazia, but I think it will be disgrazia, a disgrace, sir, to us."

The other replied: "I know not what you mean by that, sir; but if you will recollect, I told you before, that whenever that fellow said he gave me a shilling, I thought it was only a farthing; however, I put it into the bag, such as it was, and I would have you to know that I am just as fair and honorable as yourselves."

"No, you are a perfect Judas," said Salvadore, "and you cheat us in every way you can."

"Then you lie in your throat," replied Grazia; and the next moment they began to shake their fists, and to cuff each other terribly while all their money fell upon the floor. Lazzero hearing the strife begun, took his club, and hazarded some hearty blows in the dark to part them. Feeling the superior effect of the cudgel, both the combatants had recourse to theirs, and they all fell to work, while the whole of their spoils lay scattered on the ground. The action becoming rather warm, the dogs began to take part in it, barking and pulling at their masters to persuade them to desist. Loud was the concert they made amongst them, for their masters, feeling the effect of their teeth, began to return the compliment with their clubs, upon which the dogs howled out still more piteously.

The host, sleeping in the room below, said to his wife: "Surely the demons of confusion must have broken loose above stairs. Did you ever hear such an infernal noise since you were born?" Both of them rose from bed, and taking a light, went forthwith to the room door, calling for admittance. But the blind combatants were too deeply engaged to attend to them, though they heard them knocking all the while. So the host burst open the door. Proceeding to separate the party, he received a pretty smart blow over his face. At this he immediately knocked one of them down, and, seizing the cudgel, began to apply it with so much more precision, swearing all the while, that in a short time, with the help of his wife who screamed and cuffed as women do, he remained master of the field. He ordered the whole party off, but they were scarcely in a condition to move, and one of the dogs seized the landlady's petticoat which tore clean away. The floor was now strewn with the wounded and their spoils, while Lazzero declared to the host that he believed he was a dead man.

"I wish you were," replied the host, "you make such an

infernal noise. So up, and be packing; I will have no such doings in my house."

The blind men in the utmost distress, entreated to be permitted some hours' grace, being beaten black and blue, and their money being dispersed on all sides.

"Money, what money?" cried the host, "you have nearly knocked my eyes out with that huge club."

"I lament that," Lazzero said: "pardon us, my dear sir, for we are all of us as blind as a stone wall."

"That is no reason you should blind me too," said the host; "so get out of my house, you rascals."

"Then be so good as to gather up our money for us, and we will go," said one of them. The host did, collecting about half the original sum. He observed there might, perhaps, be near five shillings, of which he must keep two for their entertainment, leaving one each. He would then, he said, appeal to the vicar for damages against their dogs, which had torn his wife's petticoat, and this would be something more. Great was the lamentation now raised by the blind men, beseeching him, for the love of heaven, not to ruin them utterly, but to take what they could afford to give, and let them go.

"Rogues," said the host, "you must give me something to cure my eyes, or I shall probably be as blind as you. Besides my wife's petticoat cost me ever so much."

In short they were compelled to come to his terms, and give up the whole of the money which had fallen. It amounted to more than half of their profits. They were then obliged to turn out, more dead than alive, well bruised and beaten, so that they cut a still more piteous figure than before, which somewhat helped to replenish their purse as they journeyed along toward Pisa.

Arriving at an inn near Marti, they began to abuse each other afresh, when the host, commiserating their forlorn appearance, inquired who could have used them so?

"Never mind that," they replied, "but bring each of us a pint of wine to wash the remembrance of it away." They had likewise to dress their wounds, and set their broken legs and arms; after which Grazia thus addressed the others:

"Now I will tell the honest truth. I never thrust a thief's hand into the money-bag since we entered into partnership, and broken bones are all the reward I have earned, besides being nearly ruined. But short folly is better than long, and I will even verify the old saying: *uno due e tre, io mi scompagno da te*. I will have nothing more to do with you, and be witness to it, our good host." So he afterward proceeded on his journey to our lady's festival alone, leaving Lazzero and Salvadore to fight their own battles in future. As they were now all of them both lame and blind, great was the harvest which they reaped at our holy lady of Pisa's shrine; and they always considered their engagement as the most fortunate event in the world.

# NICCOLO MACHIAVELLI

## 1469–1527

Machiavelli (1469-1527) is most famous, of course, for *The Prince*, the epoch-making book of advice to the ideal Renaissance ruler on how to obtain and preserve power, on the assumption that man is wicked. He belongs to literary history not only for the originality and forcefulness of his style in *The Prince* and in his many other political and historical writings, but also because he is the author of two plays and a *novella*. One of the plays, *The Mandrake*, hard to produce in times of official prudery, is among the best Italian comedies; the *novella* is presented here in a long overdue new translation. The present translator, Lowry Nelson, Jr., has thus critically evaluated it: "The shortness and concision of the story give it at first glance the appearance of a simple anecdote. And yet certain overtones and stylistic devices create an impression of unexpected depth. One may note, for instance, the droll attempt to convince the reader of its "historical" veracity by casting the narrative as the vision of a *very* holy man. Also, in the pompous, legalistic and self-righteous Pluto one can glimpse a satiric view of earthly monarchs, who by implication are devils in their own right." (*Italian Quarterly*, Spring 1957.)

# The Devil Takes a Wife

In ancient accounts of Florentine history one may read of a certain very holy man (known already by word of mouth), whose manner of life was praised by everyone living at that time. We read how, engrossed in his prayers, he had by their efficacy a vision of the innumerable souls of those wretched mortals who died without God's grace and went to Hell, all or most of whom reproached themselves for no other reason than for having been brought to such misery by taking a wife.

It was this that amazed Minos and Rhadamanthus, and the other judges of Hell. They could not bring themselves to believe these slanders on womankind which were uttered as the truth; yet day after day the accusations increased. When they had presented Pluto with a full and proper account he decided to hold a judicious inquiry in consultation with all the princes of Hell. Then he would take the advice he judged best, either to expose the imposture or to discover the whole truth of the matter. Accordingly, when the council convened, Pluto spoke to this effect:

"Dearly beloved in Hell: though I possess this realm by heavenly ordinance and by fateful and irrevocable fortune (and for this reason I cannot be subjected to any tribunal either in Heaven or on Earth), nonetheless, because those who are most powerful show the greatest prudence in submitting most to the laws and in regarding most highly the judgment of others, I have decided to be advised by you as to how, in a matter that could result in disgrace for our Empire, I should conduct myself. Wherefore, given that every one of the souls of men who come to our realm de-

*Translated by Lowry Nelson, Jr.*

clares the cause to have been his wife and granted that
this seems to us quite impossible, we fear that in rendering
a verdict on the testimony we may be censured for being
too credulous or, in not doing so, for lacking rigor and love
of justice. Observing that the one is a fault of the frivolous
and the other a fault of the unjust, and wishing to escape
the accusation that might proceed from one or the other,
and unable ourself to find a solution, we have convoked
you to the end that you may assist us with your advice and
be the reason that this realm continue, as it has in the
past, to remain above reproach."

All the princes thought the matter exceedingly important and momentous; and, while they all concluded it was
necessary to uncover the truth, they could not agree on
how to go about it. For some thought that just one of
them, and some that several, should be sent to Earth, and
in human shape should find out the truth in person. It
struck many of the others that it could be done without
such inconvenience by inducing certain souls by certain
tortures to reveal it. But when the majority advised that
just one of them be sent, they all came round to that view.
Since no one could be found to volunteer for the undertak-
ing, they decided to resort to lots. The loser was Belfagor
the archdevil (but formerly archangel, before he fell from
Heaven). Though he felt reluctant to accept the assign-
ment, nevertheless, under constraint of Pluto's power, he
agreed to follow the decisions of the council and he bound
himself to those stipulations which they had solemnly set: to
wit, that the one appointed to the task should be granted
forthwith 100,000 ducats, with which he was to depart for
Earth and, in human form, take a wife and live with
her for ten years; then, pretending to die, he was to return and from his own experience give a true account
to his superiors of the burdens and trials of marriage.
Furthermore, it was decreed that during the stated time
he should be subject to all those human discomforts and
ills which result from poverty, imprisonment, disease and
all the other calamities that befall man, unless by deceit
or cunning he were able to escape them. Thereupon Bel-

fagor took the instructions and the money and went off
to Earth.

Having ordered his bands of devils to provide him with
horses and attendants, he entered Florence with a great
show of respectability. He chose that city above all others
for his residence because it seemed to him the most likely
to maintain a person who could handle his money with
all the arts of usury. Under the name Roderick of Castile,
he rented a house in the quarter of Ognissanti. And to
keep people from prying into his circumstances, he told
them he had recently left Spain and gone to Syria, and at
Aleppo had earned all his fortune. From there he had
then departed for Italy to take a wife in surroundings more
civilized and more in keeping with polite society and his
own tastes. Roderick was very handsome and appeared to
be about thirty years old. In a few days he had shown that
he abounded in wealth; and, as he made a show of benevo-
lence and generosity, many noble citizens who had numerous daughters, and little money, offered them to him.
From amongst them all, Roderick chose a very beautiful
girl by the name of Honesta, daughter of Amerigo Donati.
The father had three other daughters, as well as three
grown sons, and the daughters were almost at the age of
marriage. Though he was of a most noble family and
highly regarded in Florence, still, considering the household he maintained and his nobility, he was impoverished.

Roderick had himself a magnificent and resplendent
wedding; nothing desirable on such festive occasions was
omitted. Being subject to all human passions, according to
the orders given him when he left Hell, he began at once
to take delight in the honors and ceremonies of Earth and
to set great store on being praised among men; all of which
cost him no little expense. Besides, he had not lived long
with his lady Honesta before he fell excessively in love with
her. He could not endure to see her sad or vexed. Along
with her nobility and beauty, Lady Honesta had brought
with her into Roderick's house such great pride as Lucifer
never had; and Roderick, who had experienced both, pronounced his wife's to be the greater. And it became greater

by far once she realized the extent of her husband's love. When she found that she could lord it over her husband in all things, she began ordering him about mercilessly and disrespectfully; nor did she hesitate, when he refused her anything, to backbite with low and abusive words. All this for Roderick was the cause of infinite distress. Yet his father-in-law, her brothers, her relations, the marriage bond, and above all his love for her made him have patience.

It would be useless to recount the great expense to which he was put in satisfying her desire to dress in the latest fashion and to follow the fads which our city, according to its confirmed habit, changes continually. In his desire to remain at peace with her, he was forced to help his father-in-law marry off the other daughters, on which he spent a great sum of money. Then, wishing to stay on good terms with her, he had to send one of the brothers to the East with cloth goods, another to the West with silks, and to set up for the third a goldsmithy in Florence. For these enterprises he gave out the greater part of his fortune.

Besides, at Carnival time and on St. John's Day, when the whole city was celebrating according to its ancient custom, and when many of the rich and noble citizens honored each other with elaborate banquets, Lady Honesta, unwilling to be outdone by the other women, desired her Roderick to hold such festivities as would surpass all the others. These things he tolerated for the same reasons; nor would they have seemed burdensome (though in reality they were very much so), if domestic tranquillity had sprung from them and if he had been allowed to await the day of his ruin in peace. But just the opposite occurred. For along with the intolerable expenses, her insolent manner brought him endless distress. There was not a servant or a waiter in his house who could abide her, not for a matter of months but of days. It caused Roderick serious inconvenience in not permitting him to keep a trusted servant who would have regard for his affairs. Not to mention others, there were those devils he had brought with him as attendants, who chose to go back to the fires of Hell rather than live on Earth under the command of that woman.

So, in the midst of such turmoil and agitation, having consumed in excessive spending all his ready money, Roderick began to live on the hope of revenues he expected from both East and West. His credit still good, he issued bills of exchange to keep up his establishment; and since he already had signed and circulated promissory notes, this was soon noticed by those in the same financial plight. While his affairs were already that delicate, news came from both East and West at the same time, to the effect that one of Lady Honesta's brothers had gambled away all of Roderick's funds, and that the other, returning on a ship loaded with his merchandise, wholly uninsured, went to the bottom with it. No sooner was the news out than Roderick's creditors banded together and judged him to be ruined. Unable to reveal their suspicions, since his payments were not yet due, they decided that he should be closely watched, with such vigilance that from one moment to the next he would be unable to escape in secret. As for Roderick, seeing no solution to his trouble and knowing full well his obligations under the edict of Hell, he intended to escape at all costs.

One morning he mounted a horse, and left by way of the Prato gate, near where he lived. No sooner was his departure observed than his creditors raised a hue and cry, and having appealed to the magistrates not only through legal agents but through popular protest, they gave him chase. Roderick had barely gone a mile from the city before he heard the hubbub behind him. Finding himself in such straits, he decided, in order to escape in secret, to turn off the road and try his luck across the fields. But he was hindered from doing so by the great number of ditches that crisscrossed the countryside: and for that reason, unable to continue on horseback, he set out to escape on foot. He left his mount on the road, and crossing field after field covered with vines and canes (which are abundant there), in the neighborhood of Peretola he reached the house of Gianmatteo del Brica, a laborer of

Giovanni del Bene; and by chance he came upon Gianmatteo himself, who was carrying home fodder for his oxen.
He commended himself to him, promising that if he saved
him from the hands of his enemies, who were pursuing
him in order to have him die in prison, he would make him
rich and give him such proofs before leaving that he
would believe him, and if he failed to do so, he was content that Gianmatteo should be the one to turn him over to
his enemies. Though a peasant, Gianmatteo was a man of
courage, and surmising that he could not lose in trying to
save the man, promised to do so. He shoved him onto a
dunghill in front of the house and covered him over with
stalks and other rubbish he had gathered to burn.

Roderick was barely hidden when his pursuers drew up
to a halt. In spite of their intimidations, they failed to
extract from Gianmatteo whether he had seen him or not;
so they went on, and after searching in vain that day and
the next, they returned wearily to Florence. When the
noise had faded away, Gianmatteo brought Roderick out
from his hiding place and asked for the pledge he had
given. "Dear Brother," Roderick replied, "I'm very much
obliged to you and I want to give you full satisfaction. So
that you'll believe I'm capable of it, I'll tell you who I am."
Then he told about himself and about the orders he had
brought with him from Hell and about the wife he had
taken. Also, he told Gianmatteo just how he would make
him rich; in short, thus: when he heard that a certain
woman was possessed by a devil, he would know it to be
Roderick who was inside her; and he would not depart
from her unless Gianmatteo came to exorcise him. In
this way Gianmatteo would be able to ask payment of her
family however he pleased. When they had reached an
agreement, Roderick vanished.

Not many days went by before the news spread around
Florence that a daughter of Messer Ambruogio Amidei,
the wife of Bonaiuto Tebalducci, was possessed by a devil.
Her family did not fail to try all the usual cures: they
placed on her head the head of St. Zenobius and the cloak
of St. John Walbert—at which Roderick only scoffed. To

convince everyone that the girl's trouble was a devil and not some extravagant caprice, he spoke in Latin and debated philosophical questions and revealed the sins of many people, among which those of a friar who kept a woman dressed as a seminarist in his cell for more than four years. These things amazed everybody.

On account of this, Messer Ambruogio lived in misery. Having tried all remedies, he had lost every hope of curing her, when Gianmatteo came to see him and promised to restore the girl's health if he were given 500 florins to buy a farm at Peretola. Messer Ambruogio accepted the offer; whereupon Gianmatteo first had masses said and ceremonies performed to trick things out, and then approached the girl and whispered in her ear: "Roderick, I come here to make you keep your promise." To which Roderick replied: "Very well. But this is not enough to make you rich; and so, when I've left this girl I'll enter into the daughter of King Charles of Naples, and will not be gone without you. He'll then grant you any reward you like. After that you'll give me no more trouble." Having said this, he abandoned the girl, to the delight and amazement of all Florence.

Not long afterward, throughout Italy spread the news of the misfortune of the daughter of King Charles of Naples. No cure was found, and the King, hearing of Gianmatteo, sent to Florence for him. He went to Naples, and after a fake ceremony or two, cured her. But Roderick, before he departed, said: "You see, Gianmatteo, I've kept my promise to make you rich. And now being quits, I'm no longer bound in any way. For that reason you'll be lucky not to meet up with me again; because, just as I've done you a good turn in the past, I'll do you a bad one in the future."

At that, Gianmatteo returned to Florence a very rich man (the King had given him more than 50,000 ducats) and intended to enjoy his wealth in peace, unable to believe that Roderick might think of doing him harm. But his thoughts were soon upset by news he received that the daughter of Louis VII, king of France, was possessed by a devil. It was unsettling to Gianmatteo's peace of mind when he thought of that King's authority and those words Roderick had spoken to him.

Having failed to find a cure for his daughter, and hearing of Gianmatteo's skill, the King sent for him, at first simply by courier. But when Gianmatteo expressed a certain disinclination, the King was compelled to turn to the city fathers, who forced him to obey the summons. When he arrived, dejected, in Paris, Gianmatteo first made it clear to the King that though he had in the past cured women possessed by a devil, it didn't mean he knew how to cure them all; for some devils were so depraved that they feared neither threats nor incantations nor religion. Still, he said he was ready to do what must be done and if he didn't succeed he asked pardon and forgiveness. In reply the King said angrily that if he didn't cure her he'd be hanged. This depressed Gianmatteo's spirits considerably. Still, making the best of it, he had the bedeviled girl come forward; and drawing close to her ear, he humbly commended himself to Roderick, putting him in mind of the good turn done him and of the example of gross ingratitude he would set if he abandoned him in his great need. To that Roderick replied: "Ah, base traitor, so you're rash enough to come into my presence! Do you think you'll be able to boast of having got rich at my hands? I want to show you and everyone else that I can give and take at will." At that, Gianmatteo, seeing no way out for the time being, decided to try his luck some other way. When he had dismissed the bedeviled girl, he said to the King: "Sire, as I told you, there are many devils so wicked that nothing can be done with them; and this is one of those. For that reason, I want to make a last trial, and if it succeeds, both of us will have got our wish; if it doesn't, I'll be in your hands and you will take pity on me because of my innocence. For my purposes I'll have a stage erected in Our Lady Square, large enough to hold all your lords and all the clergy in this city. I'll have the stage draped in cloth of silk and gold. In the middle of it I'll set up an altar. Next Sunday morning I would like you, together with the clergy and all your princes and nobles, to convene there with royal pomp, clad in rich and resplendent costume. After solemn mass is celebrated, I'll have the bedeviled princess brought forward. Besides all of this, in one corner of the Square I would like there to be at least twenty men with trumpets, horns, drums, bagpipes, tambourines, cymbals, and every other kind of noisemaker. When I raise my hat, let them take to their instruments and come toward the stage playing. This, together with certain other secret remedies, will, I think, exorcise this devil."

The King ordered everything to be done at once. When Sunday morning arrived and the stage was full of officials and the Square full of people, after mass had been celebrated the possessed girl was led to the stage by two bishops and many nobles. When Roderick saw so many people gathered together and such magnificence, he was almost taken aback, and said to himself: "What has this base coward thought up? Does he think he can frighten me with this show? Doesn't he know that I'm used to seeing the pomps of Heaven and the furies of Hell? I'll not fail to punish him." When Gianmatteo came up to him and begged him to depart, he said: "Oh, it's a fine thing you've thought up! What do you think you can do with this showy display? Do you think you can escape my power and the King's anger this way? You base scoundrel, I'll have you hanged anyway."

So, what with the one pleading and the other cursing, it seemed to Gianmatteo that he ought not to lose any more time. He signaled with his hat, and the men appointed to make noise took to their instruments, and sounding to high heaven, came toward the stage. At that noise Roderick pricked up his ears. Not knowing what it could be and utterly bewildered, he felt stunned and asked Gianmatteo what was happening. Gianmatteo answered in tones of distress: "Alas, dear Roderick! It's your wife who has come to find you." It was astonishing to witness the sudden change that came over Roderick when he heard his wife's name. He was so overwhelmed that, not pausing to think whether it was possible or reasonable that she should appear, he fled in great fright without answering, leaving the girl free.

At once he set about returning to Hell to give account of his actions, rather than bowing once again to the marriage yoke with all its vexations, its indignities, its perils. And so, Belfagor went back to Hell and gave account of the ills his wife had brought into his house. And Gianmatteo, who knew more about it than the devil, went happily home.

# LUIGI DA PORTO

1485–1529

> Born in 1485 at Vicenza, Da Porto trained himself as
> a courtier at Urbino (the background, incidentally, of
> Castiglione's influential *Book of the Courtier*), and
> later fought valiantly in the service of the Venetian Re-
> public. He died in his native city, not too far from the
> legendary "castles of Romeo and Juliet," in 1529. He
> wrote poetry and *Historical Letters* of some value but
> was made famous only by *The Novel of Juliet,* for
> which, according to the convention of the *novella*, he
> pretends authenticity, inventing a source and provid-
> ing some historical framework. The names of the feud-
> ing families, Montecchi and Cappelletti, he took from
> Dante's *Purgatory* (VI, 106). The story was at once im-
> mensely successful in many languages. I have preferred
> to take Da Porto's early version rather than Bandello's
> later one, based on it. From Bandello, of course,
> through Boaistuau and Brooke, the "story" came to
> Shakespeare.

## The Novel of Juliet

At the period when Bartolommeo della Scala, a gentle and
accomplished prince, presided over the destinies of our native place, a fine and beautiful tract of country, I frequently
remember hearing my father say, that there flourished two
noble, but rival families, whose exasperation against each
other was carried to the utmost extreme. The name of one
of these was the Cappelletti, that of the other the Montec-

chi; and it is believed that the descendants of the latter faction are now residing in Udino, in the persons of Messer Niccolo and Messer Giovanni, who settled there by some strange chance, under the title of Monticoli of Verona. They would appear, however, to have retained little of their ancient splendor and reputation, beyond their courteous manners and demeanor. And although, on perusing several ancient chronicles, I have met with the names of the families, who are mentioned as united in the same cause, I shall merely touch upon their history, as it was told to me in the following words, without deviating from the original authority.

Both families, we are told, were equally powerful and wealthy, abounding in friends and relatives, and highly favored in Verona, under the above mentioned prince. Whether of a private or a public nature, the feud which arose between them was of a very ferocious and fatal character, various partisans on both sides falling victims to its rage. Nor was it, until weary of mutual wrongs, and awed by the repeated commands and entreaties of their prince, that they were induced to enter into such terms as to meet or to address each other peaceably without apprehension of further violence and bloodshed. But daily becoming more reconciled, it happened that a festival was to be given by Messer Antonio, the head of the house of the Cappelletti, a man of gay and joyous character, who made the most magnificent preparations to receive all the chief families in the city. At one of these assemblies there one evening appeared a youth of the Montecchi family, who followed thither some lady whom he was desirous, as lovers often are, of accompanying in person (no less than in mind) upon such occasions of general festivity. He had a noble and commanding person, with elegant and accomplished manners; and he had no sooner withdrawn his mask, screening himself in the character of a wood-nymph, than every eye was turned with admiration on his beauty, which appeared to surpass even that of the most beautiful ladies present. But he more especially attracted the attention of an only daughter of Messer Antonio, whose charms both

because he believed it might be attended with happy results; in which case he would be likely to derive great honor from the heads of both houses, as the means of their reconciliation. In the meanwhile, it being the season of Lent, the fair Juliet, under semblance of going to confession, sought the residence of friar Francesco, and having entered into one of the confessionals made use of by the monks, she inquired for Lorenzo, who hearing her voice, led her along after Romeo into the convent. Then closing the doors of the confessional, he removed an iron grate which had hitherto separated her from her lover, saying: "I have been always glad to see you, my daughter; but you will now be far dearer to me than ever, if you wish to receive Messer Romeo here, as your husband." To which Juliet answered, that there was nothing she so much wished, as that she might lawfully become his wife; and that she had therefore hastened thither, in order that before Heaven and him, she might take those vows which love and honor required, and which the friar must witness, as her trust in him was great.

Then in the presence of the priest, who performed the ceremony under the seal of confession, Romeo espoused the fair young Juliet: and having concluded how they were to meet each other again at night, exchanging a single kiss, they took leave of the friar, who remained in the confessional, awaiting the arrival of penitents. Having thus secretly obtained the object of their wishes, the youthful Romeo and his bride for many days enjoyed the most unalloyed felicity; hoping at the same time for a favorable occasion to become reconciled to her father, in acquainting him with their marriage. But fortune, as if envious of their supreme happiness, just at this time revived the old deadly feud between the houses in such a way, that in a few days, neither of them wishing to yield to the other, the Montecchi and the Cappelletti meeting together, from words proceeded to blows. Desirous to avoid giving any mortal hurts to his sweet wife's relatives, Romeo had the sorrow of beholding his own party either wounded or driven from the streets; and incensed with passion against

Tebaldo Cappelletti, the most formidable of his adversaries, he struck him dead at his feet with a single blow, and put his companions to flight, terrified at the loss of their chief. The homicide had been witnessed by too many to remain long a secret, and the complaint being brought before the prince, the Cappelletti threw the blame exclusively on Romeo, who was sentenced by the council to perpetual banishment from Verona. It is easier for those who truly love to imagine, than it is here to describe, the sensations of the young bride on receiving these tidings. She wept long and bitterly, refusing to hear any consolation; and her grief was deepened by the reflection that she could share it with no one. Romeo, on the other hand, regretted leaving his country on her account alone; and, resolving to take a sorrowful farewell of the object of all his soul's wishes, he had again recourse to the assistance of the friar, who dispatched a faithful follower of Romeo's father to apprise his wife of the time and place of meeting, and thither she eagerly repaired. Retiring together into the confessional, they there wept bitterly over their misfortune. The young bride at length checking her tears, exclaimed in an accent of despair: "I cannot bear to live! What will my life be without you? Oh, let me fly with you; wherever you go I will follow, a faithful and loving servant. I will cast these long tresses away, and by none shall you be served so well, so truly, as by me." "No, never let it be said," replied Romeo, "that you accompanied me in other guise than in that of a cherished and honored bride. Yet were it not that I feel assured that our affairs will soon improve, and that the strife between our two families will very shortly cease, indeed I could not bear, my love, to leave you. We shall not long be divided, and my thoughts, sweet Juliet, will be ever with you. And should we not be quickly restored to each other, it will then be time to fix how we are to meet again." So, after having wept and embraced each other again and again, they tore themselves asunder, his wife entreating that he would remain as near her as possible, and by no means go so far as Rome or Florence.

After concealing himself for some time in the monastery

of friar Lorenzo, Romeo set out more dead than alive for Mantua, but not before he had agreed with the servant of the lady, that he was to be informed through the friar, of every particular that might occur during his absence; and he further instructed the servant, as he valued his protection and rewards, to obey his wife in the minutest things which she might require of him. After her husband had departed, she gave herself up a prey to the deepest grief; a grief so incessant as to leave its traces on her beauty, and attract the attention of her mother. She tenderly loved her daughter, and affectionately inquiring into the cause of her affliction, she merely received vague excuses in reply. "But you are always in tears, my daughter," she continued, "what is it that can affect you thus? tell me, for you are dear to me as my own life, and if it depend upon me, you shall no longer weep." Then imagining that her daughter might probably wish to bestow her hand in marriage, yet be afraid of avowing her wishes, she determined to speak to her husband on the subject; and thus, in the hope of promoting her health and happiness, she pursued the very means that led to her destruction.

She informed Messer Antonio that she had observed, for many days past, that something was preying on their daughter's mind, that she was no longer like the same creature, and that although she had used every means to obtain her confidence as to the source of her affliction, it had been all in vain. She then urged her suspicions that Juliet perhaps wished to marry, but that like a discreet girl, as she certainly was, she was averse to declare her feelings. "So I think, Messer Antonio, we had better, without more delay, make choice for our daughter of a noble husband. Juliet has already completed her eighteenth year, on Saint Euphemia's day; and when they have advanced much beyond this period, the beauty of women, so far from improving, is rather on the wane. Besides," continued her mother, "it is not well to keep girls too long at home, though our Juliet has always been an excellent child. I am aware you have already fixed upon her dower, and we have nothing to do but to select a proper object for her love." Mes-

ser Antonio agreed with his lady, and highly commended
the virtues and the prudence of his daughter. Not many
days afterward, they proposed and entered into a treaty of
marriage between the Count of Lodrone and their daughter. When it was on the point of being concluded, the lady
hoping to surprise her daughter with the agreeable tidings,
bade her now rejoice, for that in a very few days she would
be happily settled in marriage with a noble youth, and that
she must no longer grieve, for it would take place with
her father's consent, and that of all her friends.

On hearing these words, Juliet burst into a flood of
tears, while her mother endeavored to console her with the
hope of being happily settled in life, within the course of
eight days. "You will then become the wife of Count Lodrone; nay, do not weep, for it is really true: will you not
be happy, Juliet, then?" "No, no, my dear mother, I shall
never be happy." "Then what can be the matter with you?
what do you want? Only tell me; I will do anything you
wish." "Then I would wish to die, mother; nothing else is
left me now." Her mother then first became aware that she
was the victim of some deep-seated passion, and saying
little more, she left her. In the evening she related to her
husband what had passed, at which he testified great displeasure, saying that it would be necessary to have the affair examined into, before venturing to proceed further
with the count. And fearful lest any blame might attach
to his family, he soon after sent for Juliet, with the intention of consulting her on the proposed marriage: "It is my
wish, my dear Juliet, to form an honorable connection for
you in marriage. Will you be satisfied with it?" After remaining silent for some moments, his daughter replied:
"No, dear father, I cannot be satisfied." "Am I to suppose
then, that you wish to take the veil, daughter?" "Indeed
I know not what,"—and with these words out gushed a
flood of bitter tears. "But this I know," returned her father,
"you shall give your hand to Count Lodrone; and therefore trouble yourself no further." "Never, never," cried
Juliet, still weeping bitterly. On this Messer Antonio threatened her with his heaviest displeasure, did she again ven-

ture to dispute his will, commanding her immediately to reveal the cause of her unhappiness. And when he could obtain no other reply than sobs and tears, he quitted the apartment in a violent passion, unable to penetrate into her motives, leaving her with her mother alone. The wretched bride had already acquainted the servant, entrusted with their secret, whose name was Pietro, with everything which had passed between herself and her parents, taking him to witness that she would sooner die than become the wife of any lord but Romeo. And this the good Pietro had carefully conveyed through the friar to the ears of the banished man, who had written to her, encouraging her to persevere, and by no means to betray the secret of their love; as he was then taking measures, within less than ten days, to bear her from her father's house. Messer Antonio, and his lady Giovanna, being unable in the meanwhile, either by threats or kindness, to discover their daughter's objections to the marriage, or whether she was attached to another, determined to prosecute their design. "Weep no more, girl," cried her mother, "for married you shall be, though you were to take one of the Montecchi by the hand, which I am sure you will never be compelled to do." Fresh sobs and tears at these words burst from the poor girl, which only served to hasten the preparations for their daughter's nuptials. Her despair was terrible when she heard the day named, and calling upon death to save her, she rushed out of her chamber, and repairing as fast as possible to the convent of the friar, in whom, next to Romeo, she trusted, and from whom she had received tidings of her husband, she revealed to him the cause of her anguish, often interrupted by her tears. She then conjured him, by the friendship and obligations which he owed to Romeo, to assist her in this her utter need. "Alas! of what use can I be," replied the friar, "when your two houses are even now so violently opposed to each other?"—"But I know, father, that you are a learned and experienced man, and you can assist me in many ways if you please. If you should refuse me everything else, at least, however, grant me this. My nuptials are even now preparing in my father's palace; he is now gone out of the city to give orders at the villa on the Mantuan road, whither they are about to carry me, that I may there be compelled to receive the count, without a chance of opposition, as he is to meet me on my arrival at the place. Give me therefore poison, to free me, at once, from the grief and shame of exposing the wife of Romeo to such a scene. Give me poison, or I will myself plunge a dagger into my bosom."

The friar on hearing these desperate intentions, and aware how deeply he was implicated with Romeo, who might become his worst enemy, were he not in some way to obviate the danger, turning to Juliet, said, "You know, my daughter, that I confess a great portion of the people here, and am respected by all; no testament, no reconciliation taking place without my mediation. I am therefore careful of giving rise to any suspicions which might affect me, and should especially wish to conceal my interference in an affair like the present. I would not incur such a scandal for all the treasure in the world. But as I am attached both to yourself and Romeo, I will exert myself in your favor, in such a way as I believe no one ever before did. You must first, however, take a vow that you will never betray to others the secret I now entrust you with."— "Speak, speak boldly, father," cried Juliet, "and give me the poison, for I will inform nobody."—"I will give you no poison," returned the friar: "young and beautiful as you are, it would be too deep a sin. But if you possess courage to execute what I shall propose, I trust I may be able to deliver you safely into the hands of Romeo. You are aware that the family vault of the Cappelletti lies beyond this church, in the cemetery of our convent. Now I will give you a certain powder, which, when you have taken it, will throw you into a deep slumber of eight and forty hours, and during that time you will be to all appearance dead, not even the most skillful physicians being able to detect a spark of life remaining. In this state you will be interred in the vault of the Cappelletti, and at a fitting season I will be in readiness to take you away, and bring you to my own cell, where you can stay until I go, which will not be long, to the chapter; after which, disguised in a monk's dress, I will bear you myself to your husband. But tell me, are you not afraid of being near the corpse of Tebaldo, your cousin, so recently interred in the same place?" With serene and joyful looks the young bride returned, "No, father; for if by such means I can ever reach my Romeo, I would face not this alone, but the terrors of hell itself."—"This is well; let it be done," cried the friar; "but first write with your own hand an exact account of the whole affair to Romeo, lest by any mischance, supposing you dead, he may be impelled by his despair to do some desperate deed; for I am sure he is passionately attached to you. There are always some of my brethren who have occasion to go to Mantua, where your husband resides: let me have your letter to him, and I will send it by a faithful messenger."

Having said this, the good monk, without the interference of whose holy order we find no matters of importance transacted, leaving the lady in the confessional, returned to his cell; but soon came back, bringing a small vase, with the powder in it, saying, "Drink this, mixed with simple water, about midnight, and fear not. In two hours after, it will begin to take effect, and I doubt not but our design will be crowned with success. But haste, and forget not to write the letter as I have directed you, to Romeo, for it is of great importance." Securing the powder, the fair bride hastened joyfully home to her mother, saying, "Truly, dear mother, Friar Lorenzo is one of the best confessors in the world. He has so kindly advised me that I am quite recovered from my late unhappiness." Overjoyed on perceiving her daughter's cheerfulness, the lady Giovanna replied, "And you shall return his kindness, my dear girl, with interest; his poor brethren shall never be in want of alms." Juliet's recovered spirits now banished every suspicion from the mind of her parents, of her previous attachment to another; and they believed that some unhappy incident had given rise to the strange and melancholy disposition they had observed. They would now have been glad to withdraw their promise of bestowing her hand upon the count, but they had already proceeded so far that they could not, without much difficulty, retreat. Her lover was desirous that some one of his friends should see her; and her mother, Lady Giovanna, being somewhat delicate in her health, it was resolved that her daughter, accompanied by two of her aunts, should be carried to the villa, at a short distance from the city, a step to which she made no opposition. She accordingly went; and imagining that her father would, immediately on her arrival, insist upon the marriage, she took care to secure the powder given to her by the friar. At the approach of midnight, calling one of her favorite maids, brought up with her from her childhood, she requested her to bring her a glass of water, observing that she felt very thirsty; and as she drank it in the presence of the maid, and one of her aunts, she exclaimed that her father should never bestow her hand upon the count against her own consent. These simple women, though they had observed her throw the powder into the water, which she said was to refresh her, suspected nothing further, and went to rest. When the servants had retired with the light, her young mistress rose from her bed, dressed herself, and again lay down, composing her decent limbs as if she were never more to rise, with her hands crossed upon her breast, awaiting the dreaded result. In little more than two hours she lay to all appearance dead; and in this state she was discovered the next morning. The maid and her aunt, unable to awake her, feeling that she was already quite cold, and recollecting the powder, the strange expressions she had used, and above all, seeing her dressed, began to scream aloud, supposing her to have poisoned herself. On this, the cries of her own maid, who loved her, were terrible. "True, too true, dear lady, you said that your father should never marry you against your will. Alas! you asked me for the very water which was to occasion your death. Wretch that I am! And have you indeed left me, and left me thus? With my own hands I gave you the fatal cup, which with yours, will have caused the death of your father, your mother, and us all. Ah, why did you not take me with you, who have always so dearly loved you in life!" And saying this she threw herself by the side of her young mistress, embracing her cold form. Messer Antonio hearing a violent uproar, hastened, trembling, to ascertain the cause, and the first object he beheld was his daughter stretched out in her chamber a corpse. Although he believed her gone beyond recovery, when he heard what she had drunk, he immediately sent to Verona for a very experienced physician, who having carefully observed and examined his daughter, declared that she had died of the effects of the poison, more than six hours before.

The wretched father on hearing his worst fears confirmed, was overwhelmed with grief; and the same tiding reaching the distracted mother, suddenly deprived her of all consciousness. When she was at length restored, she tore her hair, and calling upon her daughter's name, filled the air with her shrieks: "She is gone! the only sweet solace of my aged days. Cruel, cruel, thou hast left me without even giving thy poor mother a last farewell! At least I might have drunk thy last words and sighs, and closed thine eyes in peace. Let my women come about me, let them assist me, that I may die! if they have any pity left, they will kill me; far better so to die than of a lingering death of grief. O God, in thy infinite mercy take me away, for my life will be a burden to me now!" Her women then came round her, and bore her to the couch, still weeping, and refusing all the consolation they could offer to her. The body of Juliet was, in the meantime, carried to Verona, and consigned with extraordinary ceremonies, amidst the lamentations of a numerous train of friends and relatives, to the vault, in the cemetery of San Francesco, where the last rites to the dead were discharged.

The friar having occasion to be absent from the city, had, according to his promise, confided Juliet's letter to Romeo to the hands of one of his brethren going to Mantua. On arriving he called several times at the house, without having the good fortune to meet with Romeo, and unwilling to trust such a letter to others, he retained it in his own hands, until Pietro, hearing of the death of Juliet, and not finding the friar in the city, resolved to bear the unhappy tidings to his master. He arrived in Mantua the following night, and meeting with Romeo, who had not yet received the letter from the priest, he related to him, with tears in his eyes, the death of his young bride, whose burial he had himself witnessed. The hue of death stole over the features of Romeo as he proceeded with the sad story; and drawing his sword, he was about to stab himself on the spot, had he not been prevented by force. "It is well," he cried, "but I shall not long survive the lady of my soul, whom I valued more than life. O Juliet, Juliet, it is thy husband who doomed thee to death! I came not, as I promised, to bear thee from thy cruel father, whilst thou, to preserve thy sweet faith unbroken, hast died for me; and shall I, through fear of death, survive alone? No, this shall never be." Then throwing a dark cloak which he wore, over Pietro's shoulders, he cried, "Away, away, leave me!" Romeo closed the doors after him, and preferring every other evil to that of life, only considered the best manner of getting rid of it. At last, he assumed the dress of a peasant, and taking out a species of poison, which he had always carried with him, to use in case of emergency, he placed it under the sleeve of his coat, and immediately set out on his return to Verona. Journeying on with wild and melancholy thoughts, he now defied his fate, hoping to fall by the hands of justice, or to lay himself down in the vault by the side of her he loved, and die.

In this resolution, on the evening of the following day after her interment, he arrived at Verona, without being discovered by anyone. The same night, as soon as the city became hushed, he resorted to the convent of the Frati Minori, where the tombs of the Cappelletti lay. The church was situated in the Cittadella, where the monks at that time resided, although, for some reason, they have since left it for the suburb of San Zeno, now called Santo Bernardino, and the Cittadella was formerly, indeed, inhabited by San Francesco himself. Near the outer walls of this place there were then placed a number of large monuments such as we see round many churches, and beneath one of these was the ancient sepulcher of all the Cappelletti, in which the beautiful bride then lay. Romeo approaching near, not long after midnight, and possessing great strength, removed the heavy covering by force, and with some wooden stakes which he had brought with him, he propped it up to prevent it from closing again, until he wished it; and he then entered the tomb, and replaced the covering. The lamp he carried cast a lurid light around, while his eyes wandered in search of the loved object, which, bursting open the living tomb, he quickly found. He beheld the features of the beautiful Juliet now mingled with a heap of lifeless dust and bones, on which a sudden tide of sorrow sprung into his eyes, and amidst bitter sobs he thus spoke: "O eyes, which while our loves to heaven were dear, shone sweetly upon mine! O sweeter mouth, a thousand and a thousand times so fondly kissed by me alone, and rich in honeyed words! O bosom, in which my whole heart lay treasured up, alas, all closed and mute and cold I find ye now! My hapless wife, what hath love done for thee, but led thee hither? And why so soon two wretched lovers perish? I had not looked for this, when hope and passion first whispered of other things. But I have lived to witness even this": and he pressed his lips to her mouth and bosom, mingling his kisses with his tears. "Walls of the dead," he cried, "why fall yet not around me, and crush me into dust? Yet as death is in the power of all, it is a despicable thing to wish, yet fear it too." Then taking out the poison from under his vest, he thus continued: "By what strange fatality am I brought to die in the sepulcher of my enemies, some of whom this hand hath slain! But as it is pleasant to die near those we love, now, my beloved, let me die!" Then seizing the fatal vial, he poured its whole contents into his frame; and catching the fair body of Juliet in his arms in a wild embrace, "Still so sweet," he cried, "dear limbs, mine, only mine! And if yet thy pure spirit live, my Juliet, let it look from its seat of bliss to witness and forgive my cruel death; as I could not delighted live with thee, it is not forbidden me with thee to die": and winding his arms about her, he awaited his final doom. The hour was now arrived when, the vital powers of the slumbering lady reviving, and subduing the icy coldness of the poison, she would awake. Thus straitly folded in the last embraces of Romeo, she suddenly recovered her senses, and uttering a deep sigh, she cried: "Alas! where am I? in whose arms, whose kisses? Oh, unbind me, wretch that I am! Base friar, is it thus you keep your word to Romeo, thus lead me to his arms?" Great was her husband's surprise to feel Juliet alive in his embrace. Recalling the idea of Pygmalion, "Do you know me, sweet wife?" he cried. "It is your love, your Romeo; hither come to die with you. I came alone and secretly from Mantua, to find your place of rest." Finding herself within the sepulcher, and in the arms of Romeo, Juliet would not at first give credit to her senses; but springing out of his arms, gazed a moment eagerly on his face, and the next fell on his neck with a torrent of tears and kisses: "Oh, Romeo, Romeo, what madness brings you hither? Were not my letters which I sent you by the friar enough to tell you of my feigned death, and that I should shortly be restored to you?" The wretched youth, aware of the whole calamity, then gave loose to his despair: "Beyond all other griefs that lovers ever bore, Romeo, thy lot has been! My life, my soul, I never had thy letters!" And he told her the piteous tale, which he had heard from the lips of her servant, and that concluding she was dead, he had hastened to keep her company, and had already drunk the deadly draught. At these last words, his unhappy bride uttering a wild scream, began to beat her breast and tear her hair, and then in a state of distraction, she threw herself by the side of Romeo, already lying on the ground, and pouring over him a deluge of tears, imprinted her last kisses on his lips. All pale and trembling, she cried: "Oh, my Romeo! will you die in my sight, and I too the occasion of your death? Must I live even a moment after you? Ah, would that I could give my life for yours! Would that I alone might die!" In a faint and dying tone her husband replied: "If my love and truth were ever dear to you, my Juliet, live, for my sake, live; for it is sweet to know that you will then be often thinking of him who now dies for you, with his eyes still fixed on yours." "Die! yes! you die for the death which in me was only feigned! What therefore should I do for this your real, cruel death? I only grieve that I have no means of accompanying you, and hate myself that I must linger on earth till I obtain them. But it shall not be long before the wretch who caused your death, shall follow you": and uttering these words with pain, she swooned away upon his body. On again reviving, she felt she was catching the last breath which now came thick and fast from the breast of her husband.

Friar Lorenzo, in the meanwhile, aware of the supposed death and of the interment of Juliet, and knowing that the termination of her slumber was near, proceeded with a faithful companion, about an hour before sunrise to the monument. On approaching the place he heard her sobs and cries, and saw the light of a lamp through an aperture in the sepulcher. Surprised at this, he imagined that Juliet must have secreted the light in the monument, and awaking and finding no one there, had thus begun to weep and bewail herself. But on opening the sepulcher with the help of his companion, he beheld the weeping and distracted Juliet holding her dying husband in her arms, on which he immediately said: "What! did you think, my daughter, I should leave you here to die?" To which she only answered with another burst of sorrow: "No! away! I only fear lest I should be made to live. Away, and close our sepulcher over our heads; here let me die. Or, in the name of pity, lend me a dagger, that I may strike it into my bosom, and escape from my woes. Ah, cruel father! well hast thou fulfilled thy promise, well delivered to Romeo his letters, and wed me, and borne me safely to him! See, he is lying dead in my arms": and she repeated the fatal tale. Thunderstruck at these words, the friar gazed upon the dying Romeo, exclaiming with horror: "My friend, my Romeo! alas! what chance hath torn thee from us? Thy Juliet calls thee, Romeo, look up and hope. Thou art lying in her beauteous bosom, and wilt not speak." On hearing her loved name, he raised his languid eyes, heavy with death, and fixing them on her for a short space, closed them again. The next moment, turning himself round upon his face, in a last struggle, he expired.

Thus wretchedly fell the noble youth, long lamented over by his fair bride, till on the approach of day, the friar tenderly inquired what she would wish to do? "To be left and to die where I am," was the reply. "Do not, daughter, say this, but come with me; for though I scarcely know in what way to proceed, I can perhaps find means of obtaining a refuge for you in some monastery, where you may address your prayers to heaven for your own and for your husband's sake." "I desire you to do nothing for me," replied Juliet; "except this one thing, which I trust, for the sake of his memory," pointing to the body of Romeo, "you will do. Never breathe a syllable to anyone living of our unhappy death, that our bodies may rest here together forever in peace. And should our sad loves come to light, I pray you will beseech both our parents to permit our remains to continue mingled together in this sepulcher, as in love and in death we were still one." Then turned again toward the body of Romeo, whose head she held sustained upon her lap, and whose eyes she had just closed, bathing his cold features with her tears, she addressed him as if he had been in life: "What shall I now do, my dear lord, since you have deserted me? What can I do but follow you? for nothing else is left me: death itself shall not keep me from you." Having said this, and feeling the full weight of her irreparable loss in the death of her noble husband, resolute to die, she drew in her breath, and retaining it for some time, suddenly uttered a loud shriek, and fell dead by her lover's side. The friar perceiving that she was indeed dead, was seized with such a degree of terror and surprise, that, unable to come to any resolution, he sat down with his companion in the sepulcher, bewailing the destiny of the lovers. At this time some of the officers of the police, being in search of a notorious robber, arrived at the spot; and perceiving a light, and the sound of voices, they straightway ran to the place, and seizing upon the priests, inquired into their business. Friar Lorenzo recognizing some of these men, was overpowered with shame and fear; but assuming a lofty voice, exclaimed: "Back, sirs, I am not the man you take me for. What you are in want of, you must search for elsewhere." Their conductor then came forward, saying: "We wish to be informed why the monument of the Cappelletti is thus violated by night, when a young lady of the family has been so recently interred here? And were I not acquainted with your excellent character, friar Lorenzo, I should say you had come hither to despoil the dead." The priests having extinguished the lamp, then replied: "We shall not render an account of our business to you; it is not your affair." "That is true," replied the other; "but I must report it to the prince." The friar, with a feeling of despair, then cried out: "Say what you please"; and closing up the entrance into the tomb, he went into the church with his companion.

The morning was somewhat advanced, when the friars disengaged themselves from the officers, one of whom soon related to the Cappelletti, the whole of this strange affair. They, knowing that friar Lorenzo had been very intimate with Romeo, brought him before the prince, entreating, that if there were no other means, he might be compelled by torture, to confess his reason for opening the sepulcher of the Cappelletti. The prince having placed him under a strict guard, proceeded to interrogate him, wherefore he had visited the tomb of the Cappelletti, as he was resolved to discover the truth. "I will confess every thing very freely," exclaimed the friar. "I was the confessor of the daughter of Messer Antonio, lately deceased in so very strange a manner. I loved her for her worth, and being compelled to be absent at the time of her interment, I went to offer up certain prayers over her remains, which when nine times repeated by my beads, have power to liberate her spirit from the pangs of purgatory. And because few appreciate or understand such matters, the wretches assert that I went there for the purpose of despoiling the body. But I trust I am better known. This poor gown and girdle are enough for me; and I would not take a mite from all the treasures of the earth, much less the shrouds of the departed. They do me great wrong to suspect me of this crime." The prince would have been satisfied with this explanation, had it not been for the interference of other monks, who, jealous of the friar, and hearing that he had been found in the monument, examined further, and found the dead body of Romeo, a fact which was immediately made known to the prince, while still speaking to the friar. This appeared incredible to everyone present, and excited the utmost amazement through the city. The friar, then, aware that it would be in vain further to conceal his knowledge of the affair, fell at the feet of his excellency, crying: "Pardon, oh pardon, most noble prince! I have said what is not truth, yet neither for any evil purpose, nor for love of gain have I said it, but to preserve my faith entire, which I promised to two deceased and unhappy lovers." On this, the friar was compelled to repeat the whole of the preceding tale. The prince, moved almost to tears as he listened, set out with a vast train of people to the monument of the family, and having ordered the bodies of the lovers to be placed in the church of San Francesco, he summoned their fathers and friends to attend. There was now a fresh burst of sorrow springing from a double source. Although the parties had been the bitterest enemies, they embraced one another in tears: and the scene before them suddenly wrought that change in their hearts and feelings, which neither the threats of their prince, nor the prayers of their friends, had been able to accomplish. Their hatred became extinguished in the mingled blood of their unhappy children. A noble monument was erected to their memory, on which was inscribed the occasion of their death; and their bodies were entombed together with great splendor and solemnity, and wept over, no less by their friends and relatives, than by the whole afflicted city. Such a fearful close had the loves of Romeo and Juliet; such as you have heard, and as it was related to me by Pellegrino da Verona.

But whither art thou now fled, sweet piety and faith in woman? What living instance could we boast of that truth, proved unto death, shown by Juliet to her Romeo? Can it be, that her praises shall not soon be sung by the most eloquent and gifted tongues? How many are there, who in these times, instead of falling by the side of their departed lovers, would have turned their thoughts only to obtaining others? For if I now behold them capable, against every obligation of fidelity and true service, of rejecting those who once were dear to them, when they become oppressed by fortune, what are we to believe their conduct would be, after their death? Unfortunate are the lovers of this age, who can never flatter themselves, either by long devoted service, or by yielding up their very lives, that their ladies will consent to die with them. They are rather on the other hand assured that they are no further objects of regard, than inasmuch as they devote themselves altogether to the good will and pleasure of their ladies.

# MATTEO BANDELLO

## 1485–1561

Bandello represents one variety of that loosely defined type, the man of the Renaissance. Besides being a writer of *novelle,* he was a friar, and a man of the world. As a boy he saw Leonardo da Vinci paint, in the Milan monastery of which Bandello's uncle was the prior. For some time after becoming a monk himself, he wandered through Italy following that same uncle, who had become "General" of the Dominican Order. In Rome he frequented the *salon* of Imperia, a celebrated courtesan; in Naples, as he relates, Queen Beatrice of Aragon cured him of an apparently mortal illness by means of a potion containing emerald powder. After a Renaissance courtier's career in Milan and Mantua, he lived in France where he was formally appointed bishop of Agen in 1550, and died in 1561. His 214 stories are generally presented as accounts of true happenings; each is preceded by a dedication which places it in a definite time and place perspective. They reveal a knowledge of many social levels apparently acquired from hearsay; they are the recordings of a well-traveled and curious man. Some are bawdy; some, like the chosen example, are mere pleasant trifles.

## The Dead Lady and the Ape

In the time of Lodovico Sforza, the unfortunate Duke of Milan, there was kept, among other living curiosities in the ducal palace, a large and beautiful ape, whose amusing yet harmless manners, full of practical jests and witticisms, had long obtained for him the liberty of going at large. Such indeed was his reputation for prudence and good conduct, that he was not merely permitted the range of the whole palace, but frequently visited the outskirts, in the vicinity of Maine, of Cusano, and San Giovanni, and was not unfrequently seen conversing with some friend upon the walls. In fact most people were eager to show their respect for him by presenting him with fruits and other dainties, no less from regard to his ducal patron, than to his own intrinsic merits. The singular pleasure he afforded to all classes of society, by his happy talents of various kinds, was always a sufficient passport from place to place. But his favorite resort, among many others, was the house of an ancient gentlewoman, situated in the parish of San Giovanni, upon the walls; where he cultivated the society of her two sons, one of whom in particular, though at the head of a family, invariably received his monkey guest in the most amiable manner, making him as much at home as if he had been the lady's favorite lap-dog. These young men, perceiving their aged mother amused with the animal's unequaled exhibitions of his art, vied with each other in paying the most gratifying attentions to his monkeyship; and would certainly, had he not happened to have been ducal property, either have purchased or stolen him, merely out of regard to their mother. The whole household, likewise, received orders to treat him with the same invariable kindness and respect, studying what appeared most agreeable to his taste, so as to give him an affection for the old lady's house. This last motive weighed so greatly with his apeship, that he almost deserted his other neighbors, in order to enjoy more of the society of these very agreeable friends; although he was careful to return to his own ducal residence at the castle in the evening. During this time the aged lady becoming very infirm, no longer left her chamber, where she was affectionately attended by her whole family, who supplied her with every alleviation in the power of medical advice to bestow. Thither, occasionally, our facetious hero was also introduced for the purpose of awakening a smile on the wan features of the patient, by his strange and amusing manners, receiving some delicate morsels in return from the poor lady's own hand. As he possessed a natural taste, in common with most of his race, for every kind of sweets, he was in the habit of besieging the old lady's room with great perseverance and assiduity, feasting upon the best confectionery with far higher zest than the poor patient herself. Worn out at length, by long infirmities and age, she soon after departed this world, having first with becoming piety confessed herself, and received the holy sacraments of our church, with the communion and extreme unction at the final close.

While the funeral ceremonies were preparing, and the last offices rendered to the deceased, the monkey appeared to pay remarkable attention to all that was going forward. The corpse being dressed, and placed on the funeral bier, the holy sisterhood then attended with the usual ceremonies, offering up hymns and aves to the Virgin for the soul of the deceased. The body was afterward borne to the parish church not far distant, not unobserved by the monkey, who watched the procession depart. But he soon turned his attention to the state of things around him; and after feasting on the cake and wine, being a little elevated, he began to empty the boxes and drawers, and examine the contents. Having observed the deceased in her last habiliments, and the form of her headdress when she was laid out, the facetious ape immediately began to array himself in the cast-off garments, exactly in the manner he had witnessed; and so perfect was the resemblance, that when he had covered himself up in bed, the physician himself would have been puzzled to detect the cheat. Here the false patient lay, when the domestics entered the chamber; and suddenly perceiving the monkey thus dexterously laid out, they ran back in the utmost terror and surprise, believing that they had really seen either the corpse or the spirit of the deceased. After recovering sufficient presence of mind to speak, they declared, as they hoped to be saved, that they had seen their mistress reposing upon her sick couch as usual. On the return of the two brothers with their friends and relatives from church, they directly resolved to ascend in a body into the sick chamber; and night already approaching, they all felt, in spite of their affected indifference, an unpleasant sensation on entering the room. Drawing near the bedside, they not only fancied they saw and heard a person breathe, but observing the coverings move, as if the patient were about to spring from the couch, they retreated with the utmost precipitation and alarm. When they had recovered their spirits a little, the guests requested that a priest might be sent for, to whom, on his arrival, they proceeded to explain the case. On hearing the nature of it, the good friar, being of a truly prudent and pious turn, dispatched a person back for his clerk, with orders to bring him the large ivory crucifix, and the illuminated psalter. These, with the help of holy water, the wafer, and the priest's stole, were judged a sufficient match for the devices of the Evil One; and thus armed, repeating the seven psalms, with due ejaculations to the Virgin, they once more ascended the stairs, the clerk, in obedience to the friar, bearing the huge ivory crucifix at their head. He had previously exhorted the brothers to have no fears for the final salvation of their parent, as the number and excellence of her confessions were an effectual preservative against the most diabolical efforts of the adversary. He maintained that there was not the least cause for alarm, for what the servants had beheld were merely Satanic illusions, which he had frequently been in the habit of dispelling with singular success; and that having made use of his exorcisms, he would then bless the house, and with the Lord's help, lay such a curse upon the bad spirits, as would deprive them of the least inclination to return.

When they arrived at the chamber-door, all the guests, in spite of these encouraging exhortations and the sprinkling of holy water, drew back, while the bold friar ordered his clerk to advance in the name of the Lord; which he did, followed only by his superior. Approaching the sick bed, they perceived Monna Bertuccia, our facetious ape, laid out as we have said, in perfect personification of the deceased. After mumbling some prayers and flourishing the cross in vain, for some time, they began to entertain doubts of their success, though at the same time they felt ashamed to retreat. So sprinkling the holy water with a more liberal hand, crying: *"Asperges me, domine; asperges me";* they complimented the ape with a portion of it in his face. Expecting upon this to be next saluted with a blow of the huge cross, he suddenly began to grin and chatter in so horrible a manner, that the sacred vessel fell from the priest's hands, and the clerk at the same time dropping the crucifix, they both fled together. Such was their haste, that they stumbled, one over the other, down the stairs, the priest falling upon his clerk, when they reached the bottom.

On hearing the sudden crash, and the terrified exclamations of the good friar, *"Jesus, Jesus, Domine, adjuva me,"* the brothers, followed by the rest of the party, rushed toward the spot, eagerly inquiring what dreadful accident had occurred. Both of the holy personages gazed on the guests, without being able to mutter a word; but their pallid looks spoke volumes sufficient to answer all demands. The poor clerk fainted away, no less from excess of fear than from the terrible fall he had just received. Having obliged both to partake of some restoratives, the priest at length summoned courage enough to say: "It is true, my dear children, I have indeed seen your poor departed mother in the form of a fierce demon"; when just as he had finished these words, the cause of all their disturbance, desirous of securing the remnants of the feast, was heard approaching at a pretty brisk and clattering pace down the unlucky stairs. Without giving any of the party time to discover a fresh place of refuge, or even to prepare their minds for his reception, he bounced suddenly into the room, armed cap-à-pie, in the fearful petticoats of the deceased. His head was dressed to a nicety exactly in the same manner as the old lady's, and his whole body very decently arrayed in her late habiliments. He placed himself in the midst of the company, all of whom stood rooted to the spot, silent and awe-stricken, awaiting the dreadful

urned her love; and their affection was so mutual that, ough the parents of the lady strove all they could to in- er to take another husband, she consented to marry or; and they lived in such harmony and peace in altho that no word ever passed between them that was ectionate and kind.

w it happened that the Signoria of Venice made a in the troops whom they used to maintain in us, and they appointed the Moor commander of the soldiers whom they dispatched there. Joyful was the Moor at the honor proffered him, such dignity being only conferred on men of noble rank and well-tried faith, and who had displayed bravery in arms. Yet his pleasure was lessened when he reflected on the length and dangers of the voyage, fearing that Disdemona would be pained at his absence. But Disdemona, who had no other happiness in the world than the Moor, and who rejoiced to witness the testimony to his valor her husband had received from so powerful and noble a Republic, was all impatient that he should embark with his troops, and longed to accompany him to so honorable a post. And all the more it vexed her to see the Moor so troubled; and not knowing what could be the reason, one day, when they were at dinner, she said to him: "How it is, O Moor, that when so honorable a post has been conferred on you by the Signoria, you are so melancholy?"

The Moor answered Disdemona: "My pleasure at the honor I have received is disturbed by the love I bear you; for I see that of necessity one of two things must happen: either that I take you with me to encounter the perils of the sea, or, to save you from this danger, I must leave you here in Venice. The first could not be otherwise than serious to me, for all the toil you would have to bear and every danger that might befall you would cause me extreme anxiety and pain. Yet, were I to leave you behind me, I should be hateful to myself, since in parting from you I should part from my own life."

Disdemona, on hearing this, replied: "My husband, what thoughts are these that wander through your mind? Why let such things disturb you? I will accompany you wherever you go, were I to pass through fire in a night-s͏ as now to cross the water in a safe and well-provide͏ if indeed there are toils and perils to encounter, ͏ share them with you. And in truth I should think ͏ loved me little to leave me here in Venice, denying me͏ bear you company, or could believe that I would rath͏ bide in safety here than share the dangers that await you. Prepare then for the voyage with all the happiness which the dignity of the post you hold deserves."

The Moor, in the fullness of his joy, threw his arms around his wife's neck, and with an affectionate kiss exclaimed: "God keep us long in such love, dear wife!" Then speedily donning his armor, and having prepared everything for his expedition, he embarked on board the galley with his wife and all his troops, and, setting sail, they pursued their voyage, and with a perfectly tranquil sea arrived safely at Cyprus.

Now among the soldiery there was an Ensign, a man of handsome figure, but of the most depraved nature in the world. This man was in great favor with the Moor, who had not the slightest idea of his wickedness; for, despite the malice lurking in his heart, he cloaked with proud and valorous speech and with a specious presence the villainy of his soul with such art that he was to all outward show another Hector or Achilles. This man had likewise taken with him his wife to Cyprus, a young, and fair, and virtuous lady; and being of Italian birth she was much loved by Disdemona, who spent the greater part of every day with her.

In the same Company there was a certain Captain of a troop, to whom the Moor was much attached; he often went to the Moor's house, and dined with him and his wife. And Disdemona, knowing how much her husband valued him, showed him proofs of the greatest kindness, for which the Moor was grateful. Now the wicked Ensign, regardless of the faith that he had pledged his wife, no less than of the friendship, fidelity, and obligation which he owed the Moor, fell passionately in love with

Disdemona, and bent all his thoughts to satisfy his lust; yet he dared not declare his passion openly, fearing that, should the Moor perceive it, he would at once kill him. He therefore sought in various ways, and with secret guile, to betray his passion to the lady; but she, whose every wish was centered in the Moor, had no thought for this Ensign more than for any other man; and all the means he tried to gain her love had no more effect than if he had not tried them. But the Ensign imagined that the cause of his ill success was that Disdemona loved the Captain of the troop, and he pondered how to remove him from her sight. The love which he had borne the lady now changed into the bitterest hate, and, having failed in his purpose, he devoted all his thoughts to plot the death of the Captain of the troop and to divert the affection of the Moor from Disdemona. After revolving in his mind various schemes, all alike wicked, he at length resolved to accuse her of unfaithfulness to her husband, and to represent the Captain as her paramour. But knowing the singular love the Moor bore to Disdemona, and the friendship which he had for the Captain, he was well aware that, unless he practiced an artful fraud upon the Moor, it were impossible to make him give ear to either accusation; wherefore he resolved to wait until time and circumstance should open a path for him to engage in his foul project.

Not long afterward it happened that the Captain, having drawn his sword upon a soldier of the guard, and struck him, the Moor deprived him of his rank; at that Disdemona was deeply grieved, and endeavored again and again to reconcile her husband to the man. This the Moor told the wicked Ensign, and how his wife importuned him so much about the Captain that he feared he should be forced at last to receive him back in service. On this hint the Ensign resolved to act, and began to work his web of intrigue. "Perhaps," he said, "the lady Disdemona may have good reason to look kindly on him."

"And why?" said the Moor.

"I would not step between man and wife," replied the Ensign, "but let your eyes be witness to themselves."

In vain the Moor went on to question the officer. He would proceed no further; nevertheless, his words left a sharp, stinging thorn in the Moor's heart, who could think of nothing else. He tried to guess their meaning and was lost in melancholy. And one day, when his wife had been endeavoring to pacify his anger toward the Captain, and prayed him not to be unmindful of ancient services and friendship for one small fault, especially since peace had been made between the Captain and the soldier he had struck, the Moor was angered, and exclaimed: "Great cause have you, Disdemona, to care so anxiously about this man! Is he a brother, or your kinsman, that he should be so near your heart?"

The lady, with all gentleness and humility, replied: "Be not angered, my dear lord; I have no other cause to bid me speak than sorrow that I see you lose so dear a friend as, by your own words, this Captain has been to you; nor has he done so grave a fault that you should bear him so much enmity. But you Moors are of so hot a nature that every little trifle moves you to anger and revenge."

Still more enraged at these words, the Moor replied: "I could bring proofs—by heaven it mocks belief! But for the wrongs I have endured revenge must satisfy my wrath."

Disdemona, in astonishment and fright, seeing her husband's anger kindled against her so contrary to his custom, said with humbleness: "None save a good intent has led me to speak of that with you, my lord; but to give cause no longer for offense, I'll never speak a word more on the subject."

The Moor, observing the earnestness with which his wife again pleaded for the Captain, guessed that the words spoken by the Ensign meant that she was in love with him; and in deep melancholy he went to seek that villain and induce him to speak more openly of what he knew. Then the Ensign, who was bent upon injuring the unhappy lady, after feigning at first great reluctance to say anything that might displease the Moor, at length pretended to yield to his entreaties, and said: "I can't deny turned her love; and their affection was so mutual that, although the parents of the lady strove all they could to induce her to take another husband, she consented to marry the Moor; and they lived in such harmony and peace in Venice that no word ever passed between them that was not affectionate and kind.

Now it happened that the Signoria of Venice made a change in the troops whom they used to maintain in Cyprus, and they appointed the Moor commander of the soldiers whom they dispatched there. Joyful was the Moor at the honor proffered him, such dignity being only conferred on men of noble rank and well-tried faith, and who had displayed bravery in arms. Yet his pleasure was lessened when he reflected on the length and dangers of the voyage, fearing that Disdemona would be pained at his absence. But Disdemona, who had no other happiness in the world than the Moor, and who rejoiced to witness the testimony to his valor her husband had received from so powerful and noble a Republic, was all impatient that he should embark with his troops, and longed to accompany him to so honorable a post. And all the more it vexed her to see the Moor so troubled; and not knowing what could be the reason, one day, when they were at dinner, she said to him: "How it is, O Moor, that when so honorable a post has been conferred on you by the Signoria, you are so melancholy?"

The Moor answered Disdemona: "My pleasure at the honor I have received is disturbed by the love I bear you; for I see that of necessity one of two things must happen: either that I take you with me to encounter the perils of the sea, or, to save you from this danger, I must leave you here in Venice. The first could not be otherwise than serious to me, for all the toil you would have to bear and every danger that might befall you would cause me extreme anxiety and pain. Yet, were I to leave you behind me, I should be hateful to myself, since in parting from you I should part from my own life."

Disdemona, on hearing this, replied: "My husband, what thoughts are these that wander through your mind? Why let such things disturb you? I will accompany you where-ever you go, were I to pass through fire in a night-shirt, as now to cross the water in a safe and well-provided ship; if indeed there are toils and perils to encounter, I will share them with you. And in truth I should think you loved me little to leave me here in Venice, denying me to bear you company, or could believe that I would rather bide in safety here than share the dangers that await you. Prepare then for the voyage with all the happiness which the dignity of the post you hold deserves."

The Moor, in the fullness of his joy, threw his arms around his wife's neck, and with an affectionate kiss ex-claimed: "God keep us long in such love, dear wife!" Then speedily donning his armor, and having prepared every-thing for his expedition, he embarked on board the galley with his wife and all his troops, and, setting sail, they pursued their voyage, and with a perfectly tranquil sea arrived safely at Cyprus.

Now among the soldiery there was an Ensign, a man of handsome figure, but of the most depraved nature in the world. This man was in great favor with the Moor, who had not the slightest idea of his wickedness; for, despite the malice lurking in his heart, he cloaked with proud and valorous speech and with a specious presence the villainy of his soul with such art that he was to all outward show another Hector or Achilles. This man had likewise taken with him his wife to Cyprus, a young, and fair, and virtu-ous lady; and being of Italian birth she was much loved by Disdemona, who spent the greater part of every day with her.

In the same Company there was a certain Captain of a troop, to whom the Moor was much attached; he often went to the Moor's house, and dined with him and his wife. And Disdemona, knowing how much her husband valued him, showed him proofs of the greatest kindness, for which the Moor was grateful. Now the wicked En-sign, regardless of the faith that he had pledged his wife, no less than of the friendship, fidelity, and obligation which he owed the Moor, fell passionately in love with it pains me to the soul to be so forced to say what must be to you more painful than any other thing; but since you will it so, and the regard I owe your honor compels me to confess the truth, I will no longer refuse to satisfy your questions and my duty. Know, then, that for no other reason is your lady vexed to see the Captain in disfavor than the pleasure that she has in his company whenever he comes to your house, and all the more since she has taken an aversion to your blackness."

These words pierced the Moor's heart to the roots; but in order to know more (although he had already suspected the truth of the Ensign's words) he replied, with a fierce glance: "I can hardly hold this hand from plucking out that tongue of yours, so bold, that it dares to speak such slander of my wife."

"Captain," replied the Ensign, "I looked for such reward for these my faithful offices—none else; but since my duty, and the jealous care I bear your honor, have carried me so far, I do repeat, so stands the truth as you have heard it from these lips; and if the lady Disdemona has, with a false show of love for you, blinded your eyes to what you should have seen, this is no argument but that I speak the truth. The Captain himself said it to me, like one whose happiness is incomplete until he can declare it to another; and, but that I feared your anger, I should have given him, when he said it to me, his merited reward, and slain him. But since informing you of what concerns you more than any other man brings me so undeserved a recompense, I wish I had held my peace, since silence might have spared me your displeasure."

Then the Moor, burning with indignation and anguish, said: "Make you these eyes self-witnesses of what you tell, or on your life I'll make you wish you had been born without a tongue."

"An easy task it would have been," replied the villain, "when he used to visit at your house; but now that you have banished him, not for just cause, but for mere frivolous pretext, it will necessarily be awkward, for although I believe that he makes love to Disdemona whenever you give him the opportunity, now that he knows you hate him, he must do it much more cautiously than he did before. Still, I do not forgo the hope to make you witness of that which you will not credit from my lips."

So they parted. The wretched Moor, struck to the heart as by a barbed dart, returned to his home, and awaited the day when the Ensign should disclose to him the truth which was to make him miserable to the end of his days. But the evil-minded Ensign was, on his part, not less troubled by the chastity which he knew the lady Disdemona observed inviolate; and it seemed to him impossible to discover a means to make the Moor believe what he had falsely told him. Turning the matter over in his thoughts in various ways, the villain resolved on a new deed of guilt.

Disdemona often used to go, as I have already said, to visit the Ensign's wife, and remained with her a good part of the day. Now, the Ensign observed that she carried about with her a handkerchief, which he knew the Moor had given her, finely embroidered in the Moorish fashion, and which was precious to Disdemona, nor less so to the Moor. Then he conceived the plan of taking this handkerchief from her secretly, and thus laying the snare for her final ruin. The Ensign had a little daughter, a child three years of age, who was much loved by Disdemona, and one day, when the unhappy lady had gone to pay a visit at the house of this vile man, he took the little child up in his arms and carried her to Disdemona, who took her and pressed her to her bosom; while at the same instant this traitor, who had extreme dexterity of hand, drew the handkerchief from her sash so cunningly that she did not notice him, and overjoyed he took his leave of her.

Disdemona, ignorant of what had happened, returned home, and, busy with other thoughts, forgot the handkerchief. But a few days afterwards, looking for it and not finding it, she was in alarm, lest the Moor should ask her for it, as he often used to do. Meanwhile, the wicked Ensign, seizing a fit opportunity, went to the Captain of the troop, and with crafty malice left the handkerchief at the head of his bed so that he did not discover the trick until the following morning. When he got out of bed, the handkerchief fell upon the floor, and he set his foot upon it. Since he could not imagine how it had come into his house, and because he knew it belonged to Disdemona, he resolved to give it to her. Waiting until the Moor had gone from home, he went to the back door and knocked. It seemed as if Fortune conspired with the Ensign to work the death of the unhappy Disdemona. Just at that time the Moor returned home, and hearing a knocking at the back door, he went to the window, and in a rage exclaimed: "Who knocks there?" The Captain, hearing the Moor's voice, and fearing lest he should come downstairs and attack him, took to flight without answering a word. The Moor went down, and opening the door hastened into the street and looked about, but in vain. Then, returning into the house in great anger, he demanded of his wife who it was that had knocked at the door. Disdemona replied, as was true, that she did not know; but the Moor said: "It seemed to me the Captain."

"I don't know," answered Disdemona, "whether it was he or another person."

The Moor restrained his fury, great as it was, wishing to do nothing before consulting the Ensign, to whom he hastened. He told him all that had passed, praying him to gather from the Captain all he could respecting the affair. The Ensign, overjoyed at the occurrence, promised the Moor to do as he requested, and one day he took occasion to speak with the Captain when the Moor was so placed that he could see them as they conversed. While talking to him of every other subject but Disdemona, he kept laughing all the time aloud, and, feigning astonishment, he made various movements with his head and hands, as if listening to some tale of marvel. As soon as the Moor saw the Captain depart, he went up to the Ensign to hear what he had said to him. After long entreaty, the Ensign at length said: "He has hidden from me nothing, and has told me that he has been taking his pleasure with your wife every time you have made it possible for him by being away from the house; and that on the last occasion she gave him this handkerchief which you presented to her when you married her."

The Moor thanked the Ensign, and it seemed to him now that if he should find Disdemona not to have the handkerchief, clearly all must be as the Ensign had told him. One day, therefore, after dinner, in conversation with his wife on various subjects, he asked her for the handkerchief. The unhappy lady, who had been in great fear of this, grew red as fire at this demand; and to hide the scarlet of her cheeks, which was closely noted by the Moor, she ran to a chest and pretended to seek the handkerchief, and after hunting for it a long time, she said: "I don't know how it is, I cannot find it; can you perhaps have taken it?"

"If I had taken it," said the Moor, "why should I ask you for it? But you will look better another time."

On leaving the room, the Moor fell to meditating how he should put his wife to death, and likewise the Captain of the troop, so that their death should not be laid to his charge. And as he ruminated over this day and night, he could not prevent his wife's observing that he was not the same toward her as he had used to be; and she said to him again and again: "What is the matter? What troubles you? How come it that you, who were the most lighthearted man in the world, are now so melancholy?"

The Moor found various reasons in reply to his wife's questioning, but she was not satisfied, and although conscious that she had given the Moor no cause, by act or deed, to be so troubled, yet she feared that he might have grown wearied of her. She would say to the Ensign's wife: "I don't know what to say to the Moor; he used to be all love toward me; but within these few days he has become another man; and much I fear that I shall prove a warning to young girls not to marry against the wishes of their parents, and that the Italian ladies may learn from me not to marry a man whom Nature, and Heaven, and way of living, disjoined from us. But as I know the Moor is on such terms of friendship with your husband,

and communicates to him all his affairs, I pray you, if you have heard from him anything of which you may give me warning, don't fail to help me." And as she said this, she wept bitterly.

The Ensign's wife, who knew the whole truth (her husband wishing to make use of her to compass the death of Disdemona), but could never consent to such a project, dared not, from fear of her husband, disclose a single circumstance. All she said was: "Beware not to give any cause of suspicion to your husband, and show to him by every means your fidelity and love." "Indeed I do so," replied Disdemona, "but it is all of no avail."

Meanwhile the Moor sought further proof of that which he would have liked not to prove, and he prayed the Ensign to contrive that he might see the handkerchief in the possession of the Captain. This was a difficult matter for the wicked Ensign; nevertheless, he promised to use every means to satisfy the Moor of the truth of what he said.

Now, the Captain had a woman at home who worked the most marvelous embroidery upon lawn, and seeing the handkerchief, which belonged to the Moor's wife, she resolved, before it was returned to her, to work one like it. As she was engaged in this task, the Ensign observed her standing at a window, where she could be seen by all the passers-by in the street, and he pointed her out to the Moor, who was now perfectly convinced of his wife's guilt. Then he arranged with the Ensign to slay Disdemona and the Captain of the troop, treating them as it seemed they both deserved. And the Moor prayed the Ensign that he would kill the Captain, promising eternal gratitude to him. But the Ensign at first refused to undertake so dangerous a task, the Captain being a man of skill and courage. At length, after much entreaty and rich payment, the Moor prevailed on him to promise to attempt the deed.

Having formed this resolution, the Ensign went out one dark night, sword in hand, met the Captain on his way out of the house of a courtesan with whom he used to take his pleasure, and struck him a blow on the right thigh which cut off his leg and felled him to the earth. Then the Ensign was on the point of putting an end to his life, when the Captain, who was a courageous man and used to the sight of blood and death, drew his sword, and, wounded as he was, kept up his defense, exclaiming with a loud voice: "I'm murdered!" Therefore the Ensign, hearing people running up with some of the soldiers who were lodged thereabouts, took to his heels to avoid being caught; then turning about again, he joined the crowd, pretending to have been attracted by the noise. When he saw the Captain's severed leg, he judged that the blow must, at all events, end his life; and while in his heart he rejoiced at this, he yet feigned to pity the Captain as if he had been his brother.

The next morning the tidings of this affair spread through the whole city, and reached the ears of Disdemona; so that she, who was kindhearted and little dreamed that any ill would betide her, evinced the greatest grief at the calamity. This served but to confirm the Moor's suspicions; and he went to look for the Ensign, and said to him: "Do you know that my wife is in such grief at the Captain's accident that she is on the verge of going mad?"

"And what could you expect, since he is her very soul?" replied the Ensign.

"Soul, indeed," exclaimed the Moor, "I'll draw the soul out of her body; call me no man if I fail to shut the world upon this wretch."

Then they consulted of one means and another—poison and daggers—to kill the woman, but could resolve on neither of the two. Finally the Ensign said: "A plan comes to my mind, which will give you satisfaction and raise no suspicion. It is this: the house in which you live is very old, and the ceiling of your chamber has many cracks; I propose we take a stocking, filled with sand, and beat Disdemona with it till she dies, so that her body will bear no signs of beatings. When she is dead we can pull down a portion of the ceiling, and break the woman's head, pretending that a falling rafter had killed her; in this way, suspicion can not rest on you, since all men will impute her death to accident."

This cruel counsel pleased the Moor, and he only waited for a fitting time to execute the plot. One night, when he and Disdemona had retired to bed, the Ensign, whom the Moor had concealed in a closet which opened into the chamber, raised a noise in the closet, according to a concerted plan; on hearing it, the Moor at once said to his wife: "Did you hear that noise?"

"I heard it," she replied.

"Rise," said the Moor, "and see what it is."

The unhappy Disdemona rose from bed, and the instant she approached the closet, out rushed the Ensign, and being strong and of stout nerve, he beat her cruelly with the bag of sand across her back; so that the woman fell to the ground, hardly able to draw her breath. With the little voice she had left, she called upon the Moor for help. But the Moor, leaping from bed, exclaimed: "You wickedest of women, now has your falseness found its just reward, the recompense to wives who, counterfeiting love, place horns upon their husbands' brows."

The wretched lady, hearing these words, and feeling that she was near her end (for the Ensign had given her another blow), appealed to the justice of Heaven, since justice here had failed her, in proof of her fidelity and truth; and as she was calling God to help her, the wicked Ensign inflicted a third blow, under which she sank lifeless to the floor.

Then the Ensign and the Moor, after laying Disdemona on the bed and breaking her head, pulled down part of the ceiling of the chamber, as they had arranged; and the Moor began to call aloud for help, exclaiming that the house was falling. Hearing the uproar, the neighbors all came running up, and there found Disdemona lying dead beneath a rafter—a sight which, from the good life of that poor lady, did fill all hearts with sorrow.

On the following day Disdemona was buried, followed to the grave by the universal grief of the people. But God, the just regarder of all hearts, willed not that so wicked a deed should go unpunished. In fact, the Moor, who had once loved the woman more than his very eyes, seeing himself now without her, began to feel such desire for her that he went wandering about as one bereft of reason, searching in every part of the house. And reflecting in his thoughts that the Ensign had been the cause that he had lost, with Disdemona, all the sweetness in life, and himself as well, he conceived so deep a hatred for that wicked man he could not bear to set eyes on him, and had it not been for his fear of the inviolable justice of the Signoria of Venice, he would have slain him openly. But unable to do this with impunity, he deprived him of his rank, and would not allow him to remain in his Company, so that a deadly enmity arose between the two.

The Ensign, that wickedest of all bad men, now turned his thoughts to injuring the Moor. He sought out the Captain, whose wound was by this time healed so that he went about with a wooden leg in place of the one that had been cut off. The Ensign said to him: "The time has come for you to be avenged for your lost limb; and if you will come with me to Venice, I'll tell you who the male-factor is, whom I dare not mention to you here for many reasons; and I will bring you proofs."

The Captain of the troop, whose anger returned fiercely, but without knowing why, thanked the Ensign, and went with him to Venice. On arriving there the Ensign told him that it was the Moor who had cut off his leg, on account of the suspicion he had formed that he had lain with Disdemona; and for that reason he had killed her, and then spread the report that the ceiling had fallen. Hearing this, the Captain accused the Moor to the Signoria, both of having cut off his leg and killed the woman, and called the Ensign to witness the truth of what he said. The Ensign declared both charges to be true, for the Moor had disclosed to him the whole plot, and had tried to persuade him to perpetrate both crimes, and having afterward killed his wife out of the bestial jealousy he had conceived, he had narrated to him the manner in which he had perpetrated her death.

The Signoria of Venice, when they heard of the cruelty inflicted by a Barbarian upon a lady of their city, commanded that the Moor's arms should be pinioned in Cyprus, and he be brought to Venice, where, with many tortures, they sought to draw from him the truth. But the Moor, bearing with unyielding courage all the torment, denied the whole charge so resolutely that no confession could be drawn from him. Although by his constancy and firmness he escaped death, he was confined for several days in prison and then condemned to perpetual banishment. Eventually he was slain by the kinsfolk of Disdemona, as he merited. The Ensign returned to his own country, and, following his custom, he accused one of his companions of having sought to persuade him to kill an enemy of his, who was a man of noble rank; whereupon this person was arrested, and put to the torture. But when he denied the truth of what his accuser had declared, the Ensign himself was likewise tortured to make him prove the truth of his accusations. He was tortured so that his body ruptured, and he was removed from prison and taken home, where he died a miserable death. So did God avenge the innocence of Disdemona. And all these events as I have told them here were narrated by the Ensign's wife, who was privy to the whole, after his death.

# GIAMBATTISTA BASILE

## 1575–1632

Born in Naples in 1575, Basile was a soldier in Venice,
a courtier at Mantua where the local Gonzaga ruler
made him a count, and finally a feudal governor in
various places in the south of Italy. In the last of these
posts he died in 1632. His signed work comprises a
large, conventional and forgotten literary production
which he signed with his own name, while glory came
to him from compositions in the Neapolitan dialect
published as Gian Alesio Abbatutis, an anagram of
his name. His major work, called in the vernacular *Lo
cunto de li cunti,* is better known as *Pentameron* (i.e.,
half-*Decameron*). There he collected fairy tales as they
were told around Naples, not in the spirit of what we
would call a cultural anthropologist but rather with
the participation and gusto of an artist possessing an
exceptional sense for the fantastic manipulation of language. His tone is a mixture of fantasy and realism,
of the baroque and the folksy. As in Boccaccio, whom
in this sense he parodies, there is a frame to his five
(against Boccaccio's ten) days of story-telling: the
forty-nine tales are narrated in turn, to the prince of
Camporotondo, by ten old and ugly women. I am
presenting here the extremely unusual Basile version
of the Cinderella story, while Gagliuso is recognizably
Puss-in-Boots, who also has had other literary treatments (Perrault in France, Tieck in Germany).

# Gagliuso

Ingratitude, my masters, is a rusty nail which, driven into the tree of courtesy, makes it wither; it is a broken sewer which saps and undermines the foundations of affection; it is a lump of soot which, falling into the pot of friendship, spoils its smell and flavor: as you may see and prove in many instances and of which I will show you a rough outline in the story I am about to tell you.

There was once in my own city of Naples, an old beggar, so weak, poor and wretched, so bare and destitute and without the shadow of a groat in the shadows of his purse, that he went about as naked as a louse. When the hour came when he was called upon to shake out the sacks of life to make whatever remained fall to the ground, he called his two sons Oraziello and Gagliuso to him, and spoke to them as follows: "I have now been summoned according to the contract, to pay my debt to nature, and believe me, as you are Christians, I should be well pleased to quit this Mandracchio of troubles, this den of worry, if it were not that I must leave you on the bare ground, big as the church of Santa Chiara, at the five roads of Melito, and without a ducat, clean as the barber's basin, nimble as police agents, dry as a plum stone, without so much as a fly can bear on its foot, and if you were to run a hundred miles no farthing would come to you. Fortune has driven me to where the three dogs foul and I have nothing left except my life. But as you see me, so will I write myself, for I have always, as you know, yawned and made crosses, and gone to bed without candles. Nevertheless, I still wish to leave you some sign of my affection at my death. Therefore you, Oraziello, who are my firstborn, take that sieve which hangs on the wall, and so earn your bread with it; and you, who are a stay-at-home, take the cat and don't either of you forget your father." Thus speaking, he broke into sobs, and after a little while said, "Good-by, for it is night."

Oraziello saw to it that his father was buried by charity, and then taking the sieve went searching here and there to find a way of earning his living, and the more he searched the more he earned. But Gagliuso, taking the cat, bewailed himself, "Now look what kind of a legacy my father has left me! I've not enough to live on myself, and now I shall have to feed two. Why should I have this miserable heritage? It would have been better to have gone without it!"

The cat, hearing this whining lamentation said to him, "You are complaining too soon, and you've more luck than wits! You don't know your good fortune, for I am able to make you rich, if I put myself to it."

Gagliuso took hope and thanked his catship, and stroking his back three or four times, earnestly recommended himself to him.

The cat took pity on him, and went every morning, when the Sun angles for the shades of Night with the bait of daylight on his golden hook, either to the beach at Chiaia or to the Fish Rock, and fixing his eye on some magnificent mullet and some fine goldfish, hooked it in and carried them to the King. When he gave them to him he said, "Lord Gagliuso, the devoted slave of Your Highness, craves your indulgence and with all due respect sends you this fish. Humble presents to powerful princes." And the King, with the pleasant smile usually bestowed on them who bring presents, said, "Tell this gentleman, whom I do not know, that I thank him with all my heart."

At another time the cat ran off to where they were shooting, to the Marshes or to Astroni, and when the fowlers had brought down some orioles, blackbirds or bluetits, he gathered them up and carried them to the King with the same message. He repeated this game so often, that at last the King said to him one day, "I feel greatly obliged to this Lord Gagliuso, and should like to know him so that I can repay him the kindness he has shown me." And the cat answered, "Lord Gagliuso's one desire is to place his life and blood at the service of your throne; tomorrow, without fail, when the Sun has set a match to the gleanings from the fields of the air, he will come to make obeisance to you."

When morning came, however, the cat approached the King: "Sire, Lord Gagliuso sends me to excuse him for not coming, but this night some of his servants have robbed him and made off, leaving him without even a shirt to his back." When the King heard this, he at once sent clothes and linen from his own wardrobe to Gagliuso, who after two hours appeared at the palace, accompanied by the cat.

The King showed him a thousand civilities, bidding him sit down beside him and offering him a splendid banquet. All the time he was eating, however, Gagliuso kept turning to the cat and saying, "Now pussy, you be careful about those rags of mine, or they'll get lost"; and the cat answered, "Be quiet, hold your peace, don't talk of such beggarly trifles"; and when the King asked if he desired anything, the cat answered for him, that he had a sudden desire for a lemon. The King, therefore, sent to the garden for a basketful. Gagliuso, after a while, went back to the old song about his rags and tatters, and the cat again told him to keep his mouth shut, wherefore the king once more asked what he needed, and the cat promptly brought forward another excuse to cover Gagliuso's lack of manners. At last, when they had finished eating and had discoursed on various topics, Gagliuso took his leave.

As soon as the cat remained alone with the King, he took upon himself to describe Gagliuso's intelligence and judgment, and above all the great wealth that he possessed in his lands round Rome and in Lombardy, and by reason of which he was worthy to ally himself with a crowned king. The King asked what was the extent of his riches, and the cat answered that it was impossible to count up the movables, the immovables and all the chattels of this excessively rich person, for he did not even know himself how much he possessed. If, however, the King wanted information about him, he had only to send someone to accompany him out of the kingdom, so that he could prove to them that there was no wealth to equal his master's in the whole world.

The King commanded some of his trusty servants to follow on the cat's tracks and procure detailed information about the matter. The cat then, with the excuse of obtaining refreshment for them by the wayside at the different stopping-places, ran ahead of them, as soon as they were outside the kingdom, and whenever he met any flocks of sheep, herds of oxen and troops of horses, he said to the shepherds and keepers, "Hola, be on your guard, for there is a band of brigands who want to pillage all that is to be found in these fields. If you want to protect yourselves from their fury and be left unharmed, say that everything belongs to Lord Gagliuso, and they won't touch a hair of your heads." And the same thing did he say at all the farms that he passed, so that wherever the King's people arrived, they found the bagpipes tuned, for everyone told them that all that could be seen belonged to the Lord Gagliuso. Tired at last of asking the same question and hearing the same answer, they returned to the King, bringing back seas and mountains of tales of the immense riches of Lord Gagliuso.

On hearing this, the King promised a rich reward to the cat if he should bring off a match between his daughter and Gagliuso. The cat, playing shuttle between them, finally arranged the marriage. So Gagliuso came, and the King entrusted him with his daughter and a large dowry. After an entire month of feastings and rejoicings, Gagliuso said that he wanted to conduct his bride to his estates, so the King accompanied them to the frontiers, and then they went on toward Lombardy, where by the cat's advice Gagliuso bought land and property and became a powerful lord.

Now, when Gagliuso saw himself so fabulously rich, he could hardly stop thanking the cat, saying that he owed his life and greatness to him and to his good offices, and that the wit of a cat had brought him greater blessings than the cleverness of his father. Therefore, he could do whatever he wished and could dispose at will of his life and all his property, and he promised him, that when he died (may it be a hundred years hence!) he would have him embalmed and placed inside a golden cage and kept in his own room.

Scarcely three days after this bragging, the cat pretended to be dead and lay stretched out full length on the ground. When Gagliuso's wife saw him, she cried out, "O husband, see what a tragic misfortune! the cat is dead!" "The devil die with him!" answered Gagliuso; "rather he than we." "What shall we do with him?" asked the wife, and he: "Take him by the paws and throw him out of the window!"

When the cat heard this fine gratitude which he was far from expecting, he jumped to his four feet and cried, "This is all the reward for the lice I've freed you from? This is the 'thousand thanks' for the rags I lifted from your back that were only fit to hang spindles on? Is this the return you make for all I have done for you, for having fed you, tattered, torn, ragged, miserable and lousy beggar that you were! This is what happens to anyone who tries to wash a donkey's head! Go, and a curse be on everything that I have done for you, for you're not worth spitting on! A fine golden cage have you prepared for me! and a fine tomb have you allotted me! One gives service, work, toil and sweat, and this is all the reward! Woe is he who boils his pots for others' hopes! The philosopher spoke well when he said, 'Who goes to bed an ass, wakes up an ass!' In short, who works most must expect least. But fine words and ill deeds deceive both fools and wise men!"

So saying he shook his head and ran toward the door, and although Gagliuso with the lung of humility tried to pacify him, there was no way of making him turn back. He went on running, without turning his head, and muttering:

God keep you from the rich man poor grown
And from the beggar who now does riches own.

# The Cat Cinderella

In the sea of malice, envy always exchanges ruptures for bladders, and when she hopes to see others drowned, finds herself under water or dashed to pieces against a rock. This happened to certain envious girls whose story I intend to tell you.

There was once, therefore, a Prince who was a widower, and he had a daughter so dear to him that he saw with no other eyes but hers. He gave her an excellent teacher of sewing, who taught her chain-work, openwork, fringes and hems and showed her more love than was possible to describe. The father, however, shortly remarried, and his wife was an evil, malicious, bad-tempered woman who began at once to hate her stepdaughter and threw sour looks, wry faces and scowling glances on her enough to make her jump with fright. The poor child was always complaining to her governess of her stepmother's ill-treatment, finishing up with "O would to God that you could be my little mother, who are so kind and loving to me," and she so often repeated this song to her that she put a wasp in her ear and, at last, tempted by the devil, her teacher ended by saying, "If you must follow this madcap idea, I will be a mother to you and you shall be the apple of my eye." She was going on with the prologue, when Zezolla (as the girl was called) interrupted her by saying, "Forgive my taking the words out of your mouth. I know you love me well, mum's the word, and *sufficit;* teach me the way, for I am new; you write and I will sign." "Well, then," answered her governess, "listen carefully; keep your ears open and you shall always enjoy the whitest bread from the finest flour. When your father leaves the house, tell your stepmother that you would like one of those old dresses that are kept in the big chest in the closet, to save the one you now have on. As she always wants to see you in rags and tatters, she will open the chest and say, 'Hold the lid.' You must hold it while she is rummaging inside and then suddenly let it fall so that it breaks her neck. After that, you know well that your father would even coin false money to please you, so when he fondles you, beg him to take me for his wife, and then you shall be happy and the mistress even of my life."

When Zezolla had heard the plan, every hour seemed a thousand years until she had carried out her governess's advice in every particular. When the period of mourning for her stepmother was over, she began to sound her father about marrying her governess. At first the Prince took it as a joke, but Zezolla so often struck with the flat that at last she thrust with the point, and he gave away to the persuasive words of his daughter. He therefore married Carmosina, the governess, with great celebrations.

Now, while this couple were enjoying themselves, Zezolla was standing at a balcony of her house, when a dove flew on to the wall and said to her, "If ever you desire anything, send to ask for it from the dove of the fairies of the Island of Sardinia, and you will at once have it."

For five or six days the new stepmother lavished every sort of caress on Zezolla, making her take the best seat at table, giving her the best titbits, and dressing her in the finest clothes. But after a little time the service that Zezolla had done her was forgotten, and banished from her memory (how sorry is the mind that has an evil mistress!) and she began to push forward six daughters of her own that she had kept in hiding till then, and so worked on her husband that they won his good graces and he let his own daughter slip out of his heart. So that, a loser today and a pauper tomorrow, Zezolla was finally brought to such a pass that she fell from the *salon* to the kitchen, from the canopy to the grate, from splendid silks and gold to dishclouts, from scepters to spits; not only did she change her state, but also her name, and was no longer called Zezolla, but "Cat Cinderella."

Now it happened that the Prince was forced to go to Sardinia on important affairs of State, and before he left he asked one by one of his six stepdaughters, Imperia, Colomba, Fiorella, Diamante, Colombina, and Pascarella, what they wanted him to bring back for them on his return. One asked for a splendid gown, another for a headdress, one for cosmetics for the face, and another games to pass the time; one one thing and one another. At last, and almost to make fun of her, he asked his daughter, "And you! what would you like?" and she answered, "Nothing, except commend me to the dove of the fairies and beg them to send me something; and if you forget, may it be impossible for you to go forward or back. Bear in mind what I say: thy intent, thy reward."

The Prince went away, transacted his affairs in Sardinia, and bought the things his stepdaughters had asked for, but Zezolla went quite out of his mind. But when they were embarked with the sails ready unfurled, it was found impossible to make the vessel leave the harbor: it seemed as if it were detained by a sea-lamprey. The captain of the ship, who was almost in despair, dropped off to sleep with weariness and in his dreams a fairy appeared to him who said, "Do you know why you cannot leave the harbor? Because the Prince who is with you has broken his promise to his daughter, remembering all the others except his own flesh and blood." As soon as he woke up the captain told his dream to the Prince, who was overcome with confusion at his omission. He went to the grotto of the fairies, and commending his daughter to them, begged that they should send her some gift.

Behold, out of the grotto there came a young girl, beautiful as a gonfalon, who bade him thank his daughter for her kind remembrances and tell her to be of good cheer for love of her. With these words, she gave him a date tree, a spade and a golden can with a silken napkin; the date tree for planting and the other articles to keep and cultivate it.

The Prince, surprised at this present, took leave of the fairy and turned toward his own land. When he arrived, he gave his stepdaughters the things they had asked for, and lastly he handed the fairy's present to his own daughter. Zezolla nearly jumped out of her skin with joy and planted the date tree in a fine pot, watering it every day and then drying it with the silken napkin.

As a result of these attentions, within four days the date tree grew to the size of a woman, and a fairy came out who said to the girl, "What do you want?" Zezolla answered that she would like sometimes to leave the house without the sisters knowing it. The fairy replied, "Whenever you want this, come to the plant and say:

> O my golden date tree,
> With golden spade I've dug thee,
> With golden can I've watered thee,
> With silken napkin dried thee,
> Strip thyself and robe thou me,

Then when you want to undress, change the last line and say: Strip thou me and robe thou thee."

One day it happened to be a feast-day, and the governess's daughters went out of the house in a procession all fluttering, bedaubed and painted, all ribbons, bells and gewgaws, all flowers and perfumes, roses and posies. Zezolla then ran to the plant and uttered the words the fairy had taught her, and at once she was decked out like a queen, seated on a white horse with twelve smartly attired pages. She too went where the sisters had gone, and though they did not recognize her, they felt their mouths water at the beauty of this lovely dove.

As luck would have it, the King came to this same place and was quite bewitched by the extraordinary loveliness of Zezolla. He ordered his most trusty attendant to find out about this fair creature, who she was and where she lived. The servant at once began to dog her footsteps, but she, noticing the trap, threw down a handful of crowns that she had obtained for that purpose from the date tree. The servant, fired by the desire for these glittering pieces, forgot to follow the palfrey and stopped to pick up the money, whilst she, at a bound, reached the house and quickly undressed in the way the fairy had told her. Those six harpies, her sisters, soon returned, and to vex and mortify her, described at length all the fine things that they had seen at the feast.

The servant in the meantime had returned to the King and had told him about the crowns, whereupon the King was furious, and angrily told him that he had sold his pleasure for a few paltry coins and that at the next feast he was at all costs to discover who this lovely girl was and where nested so fair a bird.

When the next feast-day came, the sisters went out, all bedecked and bedizened, leaving the despised Zezolla by the hearth. But she at once ran to the date tree and uttered the same words as before, and behold a band of maidens came out, one with the mirror and one with the flask of pumpkin water, one with the curling-tongs and another with the rouge, one with the comb and another with the pins, one with the dresses and one with the necklace and earrings. They all placed themselves round her and made her as beautiful as a sun and then mounted her in a coach with six horses accompanied by footmen and pages in livery. She drove to the same place as before and kindled envy in the hearts of the sisters and flames in the breast of the King.

This time too, when she went away, the servant followed her, but so that he should not catch her up, she threw down a handful of pearls and jewels, which this trusty fellow was unable to resist pecking at, since they were not things to let slip. In this way Zezolla had time to reach home and undress herself as usual. The servant, quite stunned, went back to the King, who said, "By the soul of your departed, if you don't find that girl again, I'll give you a most thorough beating and as many kicks on your seat as you have hairs in your beard."

On the next feast day, when the sisters had already started off, Zezolla went up to the date tree. She repeated the magic spell and was again magnificently dressed and placed in a golden coach with so many attendants around it that it looked as if she were a courtesan arrested in the public promenade and surrounded by police agents. After having excited the envy and wonder of her sisters, she left, followed by the King's servant, who this time fastened himself to the carriage by double thread. Zezolla, seeing that he was always at her side, cried, "Drive on," and the coach set off at such a gallop that in her agitation she let slip from her foot the richest and prettiest patten you could imagine.

The servant, not being able to catch up the carriage, which was now flying along, picked up the patten and carried it to the King, telling him what had happened. The King took it in his hands and broke out into these words: "If the foundation is so fair, what must be the mansion? Oh, lovely candlestick which holds the candle that consumes me! Oh, tripod of the lovely cauldron in which my life is boiling! Oh, beauteous corks attached to the fishing-line of Love with which he has caught this soul! Behold, I embrace and enfold you, and if I cannot reach the plant, I worship the roots; if I cannot possess the capitals, I kiss the base: you first imprisoned a white foot, now you have ensnared a stricken heart. Through you, she who sways my life was taller by a span and a half; through you, my life grows by that much in sweetness so long as I keep you in my possession."

The King having said this called a secretary and ordered out the trumpeters and tantarara, and had it proclaimed that all the women in the land were to come to a festival and banquet which he had determined to give. On the appointed day, my goodness, what an eating and feasting there was! Where did all the tarts and cakes come from? Where all the stews and rissoles? all the macaroni and graviuoli which were enough to stuff an entire army? The women were all there, of every kind and quality, of high degree and low degree, the rich and the poor, old and young, the well-favored and the ill-favored. When they had all thoroughly worked their jaws, the King spoke the proficiat and started to try the patten on his guests, one by one, to see whom it fitted to a hair, so that he could find by the shape of the slipper the one whom he was seeking.

But he could find no foot to fit it, so that he was on the point of despair.

Nevertheless, he ordered a general silence and said, "Come back tomorrow to fast with me, but as you love me well, do not leave behind a single woman, whoever she may be!" The Prince then said, "I have a daughter, but she always stays to mind the hearth, for she is a sorry, worthless creature, not fit to take her place at the table where you eat." The King answered, "Let her be at the top of the list, for such is my wish."

So they all went away, and came back the next day, and Zezolla came with Carmosina's daughters. As soon as the King saw her, he thought she was the one he wanted, but he hid his thoughts. After the banquet came the trial of the patten. The moment it came near Zezolla's foot, it darted forward of itself to shoe that painted Lover's egg, as the iron flies to the magnet. The King then took Zezolla in his arms and led her to the canopy, where he put a crown on her head and ordered everyone to make obeisance to her as to their queen. The sisters, livid with envy and unable to bear the torment of their breaking hearts, crept quietly home to their mother, confessing in spite of themselves that:

He is mad who would oppose the stars.

# GASPARE GOZZI

## 1713-1786

A Venetian of an impoverished noble family, Count Gaspare Gozzi (1713-1786) lived mainly by his intellectual and literary activities which ranged from writing poetry to dealing with practical problems of education. While his brother Carlo is best known as a writer of fantasy plays (*Turandot* among others), Gaspare emerged as a journalist. His *Gazzetta Veneta* and his *Osservatore* were in some ways Italian, or Venetian, counterparts to Addison's *Spectator*. They contained information of all sorts, including free advertisements, and have remained well known especially for their character sketches, and for the stories drawn apparently from daily life. The latter are legitimately to be considered within the tradition of the Italian *novella* as incident and as real or fictitious "pieces of news."

## Three Stories About Venetian Women

### 1. WOMEN IN ARMS

I don't know whether it's the influence of the stars or some other cause that disposes women nowadays to take up arms. But ever since the day they unwigged the orator in the Calle del Forno, the women of this neighborhood have

*Translated by Lowry Nelson, Jr.*

been tirelessly at it, just like those female warriors Brada-
mante and Marfisa. A few days ago some men stopped on
the Fondamenta dei Frari, the sort who, by the sound—or
rather noise—of bagpipes and a trumpet that seemed to
shatter the air, first entice people to look out their doors
and windows, and then set to dancing a muzzled bear that
shows on the whole more inclination to sleep than to hop
about and cut capers. Be that as it may, what with the rus-
tics playing and the bear dancing like a creature condemned
to hang, a large crowd of onlookers gathered and stood
around enjoying the spectacle. Then, I don't know how or
why, two of them, after an exchange of words, pulled out
knives and would have gone further if the people there
had not immediately separated them and led them off in
opposite directions. That precaution was a great relief to
them both, since they had shown the proper courage and
yet got off without a scratch.

Both of the adversaries had wives, and they, on hearing
something of what had happened, ran immediately to the
place from which the bear and the merriment had since
departed. On seeing each other and recognizing themselves
to be enemies as wives of hostile husbands, they began to
tongue-lash each other, and lash by lash they grew so
heated that for every verbal wound, they managed, one
way and another, to add a slap here and a slap there. As
their fury mounted they tried various weapons, such as
teeth and nails, biting and scratching each other with the
fury of the possessed. At the height of their struggle, as
the bystanders egged them on, all of a sudden a little
woman appeared, shouting breathlessly as she ran: "Oh
what a shame to our sex! Who knows what they'll say
about us now that in public, for all to see, we beat each
other like men? Sisters, beloved sisters, fellow sisters, stop!
Don't disgrace yourselves in public. Remember the decency
proper to women. In God's name, calm yourselves." Then,
along with these soothing and moral exhortations, the
philosopheress now amongst them dealt the one a full-
handed slap and the other, in a flash, a backhanded swat,

so quickly that the two of them heard the prudent words and felt the thunder-and-lightning blows almost at one and the same time. Great laughter arose from the bystanders who had seen and heard everything; and the two enemies were so astonished they didn't know what to say, while the third woman renewed her harangue with hand raised to repeat her maneuver.

The two of them stammered, at a loss to know what to say in the presence of so determined a woman, who, as if she were the Tables of the Law or even Jurisprudence itself, undertook to inform them that they had gravely erred and should put away anger. In fact, she decreed that on the next day all three of them should meet at a certain time under the portico that abuts on the Fondamenta dei Frari, with a jug of wine, three fine glasses and a linen cloth, to make a treaty of peace and a clean breast of their anger. The two women went off grumbling and fuming.

Yet when the time came next day, behold the bringer of peace and the other two, so serene in countenance that they hardly seemed the same women as the day before. After listening to a brief discourse from the eloquent lady, they passed the glasses round. Between swallows and sips one would actually turn to the other and say: "You know, I hold nothing against you, and to show you that I don't, take this," and she would kiss her. "Still, you must forgive me if I say that you did not behave like the sensible woman I thought you were . . ." for this, that or the other reason. "God knows I'm fond of you," the other would say, and plant a sticky kiss on her cheek, "but you shouldn't have done . . ." thus and so. The third, who was mediatrix of peace, kissing neither of them but only the jug, swore that they were both crazy.

What with drinking and chattering, they went on for more than two hours. But seeing that crowds of people were collecting around them—and more to the point, that the jug was emptied of its liquid—just as if they had not yet exchanged a single word and as if much still remained unsaid, they embraced affectionately and promised to confide all the rest in greater comfort and at a more appropriate time. So they parted for the moment, taking leave with great reluctance.

## 2. THREE SWEETHEARTS' REVENGE

In a certain place which I shall not name, but which is not far from here, an incident occurred not long ago that deserves a place in these pages. There was a young man about nineteen years old, endowed by nature with all the beauties and graces of youth, in whose face a certain touch of manliness suffused a complexion like a woman's, and whose glance was so gentle, though at the same time a trifle brusque, that it would pierce the heart of any girl who looked at him. His body was as shapely as any ever seen: erect, with sinewy calves that narrowed toward the ankles without losing proportion and strength; besides, his hair was curly and blond like spun gold: in short, he resembled the handsome Adonis whom Venus loved in ancient times. Nor was he any less loved by a local girl of his own station, who had eyes only for him and who seemed lifeless the days she didn't look upon him; and she in turn was loved by him, in so far as it is possible to love women.

But, as usually happens, wherever there is beauty, there are many competitors in loving it. As a matter of fact, two other girls of the same age had also fallen in love with the young man, and each managed separately to declare her affection for him, and the young man, who was good-natured and felt pity for the misery of others, lent a kindly ear to all their talk, and felt no wish to deprive them of hope and thus allow two such charming girls to perish. So he would converse now with one and now with the other, and would offer comforting words and hold out the hope of having him. These intrigues could hardly remain hidden from the first of the love-stricken girls. She bitterly upbraided the young man for his unfaithfulness and cruelty, not without shedding a tear or two, mingled with many a sob. The young man, feeling sorry for her, replied that she was his only love, and promised her that she was the only one who could ever be his wife, adding that the other two were shameless and wild in the way they chased and wheedled him, and that he visited them on occasion only for the purpose of giving them no cause to spy out his true love and then to tattle in public. So, with fine words and many vows, he reassured his sweetheart, who for that day remained satisfied.

But once jealousy has begun to muddle the brain, however much it seems that in the lover's presence and while he is talking the heart begins to achieve its first tranquillity, such an impression can only be false and the root of suspicion remains to sprout and send forth a thousand surmises. Accordingly, the girl began to imagine things, and could not tolerate his going now and then to visit either of her two rivals. So she decided to cast about for a way to discover the truth, and could hit upon none better than to make friends with the other two, and so determine more closely whatever the truth might be.

To be brief, she did just that, and in a few days she had gained such familiarity with them that she began to talk about that love of hers, and she was so skillful that she soon brought their secrets out into the open. Thus in no time, they both informed her that he had promised to marry them, and that he had told each of them that the others were silly and tiresome and that he visited them only to avoid scandal and gossip. How resentful they were can better be imagined than expressed. Still, they all agreed in wanting to be witnesses of the truth, and after consulting together, they decided that one of them should cajole him into talking with her in a secret room, while the others stood hidden near by, within earshot. The first girl did not wish to be the one to lure him, so one of the other two undertook to lay the trap. Then they went their several ways.

In a few days the plot was ripe, and by evening the young man was at the house of the girl who had invited him.

With a little lamp she led him into a room and closed the door, while the other two girls, unseen, stood in a passage-way to listen. The girl who was with him began to complain bitterly that he loved two others; and he answered her fervently, swearing that they were brainless creatures, that they dogged his tracks, but that she was his only delight. To gain her confidence more easily, he catalogued the defects of the other two, calling them lopsided and squint-eyed, belaboring them with words as much as he could.

How great was the fury of the two girls in hiding, my pen shrinks from describing. I shall say only that they sprang forth like two serpents, crying "Traitor! You told us the very same about the girl you're talking to now." The poor fellow, powerless to open his mouth, was standing there like a statue, when the three girls, raging like Bacchantes, their eyes rolling, and muttering in frenzy, threw themselves on him with nails bared, scratching and biting—so wildly that he lost all power to defend himself, and finally the storm and fury went to such lengths that an accursed pair of scissors . . . But must I describe such awful tragedies? If the poor young man ever manages to survive the assault, he will have gained a soprano's voice.

## 3. THE GIRL AND THE LAWYER

In a certain city—one of those under the protection of Venice, that mother of cities—lives a noble and ancient family which, from the vicissitudes of fortune, is no longer rich in land nor in those goods that are the admiration of men; but on the other hand, in that family flourishes celebrated virtue and that gentility which it inherited from its ancestors. The family consists of three brothers and a number of sisters, all of whom, wishing to compensate for the riches that blind fortune has denied them, have embellished their courteous manners with various talents for playing and singing and other pleasant accomplishments, and have thus made themselves agreeable in company. It would seem, indeed, that fortune shows a certain hostility and invincible opposition toward those she sees most gifted with qualities of the spirit. For, not content to be niggardly in the favors she bestows on this well-mannered family, she saw to it that almost all the brothers and sisters in the family were born with some bodily defect; and not only those living, but everybody in that family, according to the accounts of the local elders, sustained some misfortune of the kind. Right thinking people do not generally attribute such things to a failing in the person afflicted; rather they are very careful never to speak of it and consider mentioning it a crude impoliteness and an unworthy subject for mockery.

But, to take up the story, I should say that all three of these fine brothers, attending to their affairs, hold nothing quite so dear as making sure that what substance they possess be stretched in such a way that the end of their income always reaches to the beginning of the new year, while they always avoid the appearances and masks of grandeur, so that their affairs remain stable. For this reason, two of them, though everyone would think well of them and receive them in their houses, live mostly by themselves, not caring for company or conversation; and the third, younger than the others, out of a desire to see his family maintain a position in the world and have a friendly circle of their own, goes about a good deal and frequents the same places as everyone else. Being often scolded by his brothers on that account, he would defend himself by saying that solitude makes others forget the man immersed and buried in it, and that since men live in mutual dependence, it was necessary to know each other. So, continuing in the same manner that he described, he would often be found in those places frequented by the men of the city, and he was, for the politeness of his manners, generally beloved and respected there.

It happened one day that as he was sitting in a coffee house and conversing with a number of gentlemen there, there entered a lawyer who in his profession is one of the most talented and famous in that city; but partly by temperament and partly out of a desire to make people laugh, he takes pleasure in needling and teasing others, perhaps more vigorously than politeness or kindness of spirit would allow. Once the lawyer had arrived and once he had set eyes on the young man in the midst of great company, he said: "Sir, for some time now I've wanted to hear from your lips whether in your family there is indeed a will, an instrument or some other document of *fidei commissum* or primogeniture whereby your bodies continue to inherit some deformity or other." The young man, who heard the discourse end much differently from what he had at first imagined, and who heard the company round about laugh at the malice of those words, first blushed and then, feeling no little shame in his heart, answered: "Sir, I have not, so far as I know, offended you, nor do I intend to do so; therefore, I beg you, from now on, to refrain from attacking me with words, since it could happen that I might feel in a bad humor from having eaten poorly and might make you repent of your boldness."

"Much obliged," said the lawyer at once. "You give me good advice, and I shall not address you either today or tomorrow or the day after or ever again, because you will always be in a bad humor since it is well known that you never eat well. Much obliged, much obliged for the advice."

All the bystanders laughed at the harsh retort, though inwardly it displeased many of them, since human nature is such that it is impossible to refrain from laughing at a spontaneous thrust at someone else, though the thruster is not inwardly applauded.

The young man, mortified and saddened, left the coffee house, and when he reached home he just sat at table that day, full of melancholy, and did not have the heart to eat a single bite. His brothers noticed his condition and asked him what was the matter; he told them at last, loudly bemoaning the sharp tongue that had insulted him without reason or cause. The two brothers who had often warned him to live in retirement, decided not only that there was no reason for them to regret the matter, but they almost rejoiced that it had happened to teach him a lesson, and instead of comforting him, they scolded him for his manner of living, and they decided to keep quiet about the whole thing. That resolve did not please one of the sisters at all, since she was full of spirit and vivacity. So she began to object: "What harm does our family do anyone if we live happily with what God has given us? Are we to blame and do we have to suffer derision and taunts from a tongue that lashes both good and bad without distinction? If we manage to bear up under our own calamities, I don't ask that we be praised for that; but I for one don't wish it to bring us blame and derision. And I am really surprised that, instead of condemning someone else's boldness, you blame your own brother for another's wrong. Oh! Shall we let ourselves be spat at because we are neither very rich nor so very well made as ballet dancers? I swear to you that all by myself I'll make the lawyer see the error of his ways." Having said that, she fell silent, and all the others also fell silent in the belief that everything would end merely in words.

But the girl, who was inwardly boiling with understandable resentment, did not forget her promise on the following day. At a certain hour she put on a little dress and a thin silk kerchief which covered her face, and with a maid also in disguise, went off to a place much frequented, where the lawyer was usually to be found. Once she arrived, then, and had singled out her adversary, who was there in the midst of a crowd of people making sharp remarks and laughing, she went up to him and, like a sudden flash of lightning from the heavens, threw her veil aside, exposing her face, and reached out and seized his hat and wig and tossed them away. Then, without hesitation, she began slapping and pummeling him, striking his cheeks and head with such fury and violence that he no longer knew where he was. At last, when she thought she had done enough and that all the bystanders had turned to watch the scuffle, she said to him: "Sir, these are the will, the instruments and the documents of *fidei commissum* and primogeniture of our family: you are a lawyer, read them and examine them at your leisure, since I leave them with you."

And having said that, she went about her business, without further words, leaving her adversary in a state of embarrassment to retrieve his hat and wig from the mud, with all the people standing around laughing at what had happened.

# GIOVANNI VERGA

## 1840–1922

Of a well-to-do Sicilian family, Verga was born in 1840 and conformed to pattern by leaving his island and spending long periods of time "on the continent," in Florence and Milan. The results of his contacts with social and literary fashions are reflected in some of his early novels "of passion," such as *A Sinner* and *Royal Tigress*. He found his more proper speech and themes when in his later works he turned to his native Sicily and to the poetic observation of the humble. That is what gave us the major Verga of the great novels, *I Malavoglia* ("The House by the Medlar Tree") and *Mastro Don Gesualdo*, and of many Sicilian short stories, two classic examples of which are offered here. The two Sicilian novels had been intended as the early steps of a large cyclical work of fiction on the theme, among others, of social ascent; the project was never realized and Verga's silence during the last decades of his life possibly indicated disharmony with the prevalent literary fashions. He died in 1922, and the full revaluation of his work is a relatively recent event.

## The She-wolf

She was tall, thin; she had the firm and vigorous breasts of the olive-skinned—and yet she was no longer young; she was pale, as if always plagued by malaria, and in that pallor, two enormous eyes, and fresh red lips which devoured you.

In the village they called her the She-wolf, because she never had enough—of anything. The women made the sign of the cross when they saw her pass, alone as a wild bitch, prowling about suspiciously like a famished wolf; with her red lips she sucked the blood of their sons and husbands in a flash, and pulled them behind her skirt with a single glance of those devilish eyes, even if they were before the altar of Saint Agrippina. Fortunately, the She-wolf never went to church, not at Easter, not at Christmas, not to hear Mass, not for confession.—Father Angiolino of Saint Mary of Jesus, a true servant of God, had lost his soul on account of her.

Maricchia, a good girl, poor thing, cried in secret because she was the She-wolf's daughter, and no one would marry her, though, like every other girl in the village, she had her fine linen in a chest and her good land under the sun.

One day the She-wolf fell in love with a handsome young man who had just returned from the service and was mowing hay with her in the fields of the notary; and she fell in love in the strongest sense of the word, feeling the flesh afire beneath her clothes; and staring him in the eyes, she suffered the thirst one has in the hot hours of June, deep in the plain. But he went on mowing undisturbed, his nose bent over the swaths.

"What's wrong, Pina?" he would ask.

In the immense fields, where you heard only the crackling flight of the grasshoppers, as the sun hammered down overhead, the She-wolf gathered bundle after bundle, and sheaf after sheaf, never tiring, never straightening up for an instant, never raising the flask to her lips, just to remain at the heels of Nanni, who mowed and mowed and asked from time to time:

"What is it you want, Pina?"

One evening she told him, while the men were dozing on the threshing floor, tired after the long day, and the dogs were howling in the vast, dark countryside.

"It's you I want. You who're beautiful as the sun and sweet as honey. I want you!"

"And I want your daughter, instead, who's a maid," answered Nanni laughing.

The She-wolf thrust her hands into her hair, scratching her temples, without saying a word, and walked away. And she did not appear at the threshing floor any more. But she saw Nanni again in October, when they were making olive oil, for he was working near her house, and the creaking of the press kept her awake all night.

"Get the sack of olives," she said to her daughter, "and come with me."

Nanni was pushing olives under the millstone with a shovel, shouting "Ohee" to the mule, to keep it from stopping.

"You want my daughter Maricchia?" Pina asked him.

"What'll you give your daughter Maricchia?" answered Nanni.

"She has all her father's things, and I'll give her my house too; as for me, all I need is a little corner in the kitchen, enough for a straw mattress."

"If that's the way it is, we can talk about it at Christmas," said Nanni.

Nanni was all greasy and filthy, spattered with oil and fermented olives, and Maricchia didn't want him at any price. But her mother grabbed her by the hair before the fireplace, muttering between her teeth:

"If you don't take him, I'll kill you!"

The She-wolf was almost sick, and the people were saying that when the devil gets old he becomes a hermit. She no longer roamed here and there, no longer lingered at the doorway, with those bewitched eyes. Whenever she fixed them on his face, those eyes of hers, her son-in-law began to laugh and pulled out the scapular of the Virgin to cross himself. Maricchia stayed at home nursing the babies, and her mother went into the fields to work with the men, and just like a man too, weeding, hoeing, feeding the animals, pruning the vines, despite the northeast and levantine winds of January or the August sirocco, when the mules' heads drooped and the men slept face down along the wall, on the north side. "In those hours between nones and vespers when no good woman goes roving around," [1] Pina was the only living soul to be seen wandering in the countryside, over the burning stones of the paths, through the scorched stubble of the immense fields that became lost in the suffocating heat, far, far away toward the foggy Etna, where the sky was heavy on the horizon.

"Wake up!" said the She-wolf to Nanni, who was sleeping in the ditch, along the dusty hedge, his head on his arms. "Wake up. I've brought you some wine to cool your throat."

Nanni opened his drowsy eyes wide, still half asleep, and finding her standing before him, pale, with her arrogant breasts and her coal-black eyes, he stretched out his hands gropingly.

"No! no good woman goes roving around in the hours between nones and vespers!" sobbed Nanni, throwing his head back into the dry grass of the ditch, deep, deep, his nails in his scalp. "Go away! go away! don't come to the threshing floor again!"

The She-wolf was going away, in fact, retying her superb tresses, her gaze bent fixedly before her as she moved through the hot stubble, her eyes as black as coal.

But she came to the threshing floor again, and more than once, and Nanni did not complain. On the contrary, when she was late, in the hours between nones and vespers, he would go and wait for her at the top of the white, deserted path, with his forehead bathed in sweat; and he would thrust his hands into his hair, and repeat every time:

"Go away! go away! don't come to the threshing floor again!"

Maricchia cried night and day, and glared at her mother, her eyes burning with tears and jealousy, like a young she-

---

[1] An old Sicilian proverb, which refers to the hours of the early afternoon, when the Sicilian countryside lies motionless under a scorching sun and no person would dare walk on the roads. Those hours are traditionally believed to be under the spell of malignant spirits.

wolf herself, every time she saw her come, mute and pale, from the fields.

"Vile, vile mother!" she said to her. "Vile mother!"

"Shut up!"

"Thief! Thief!"

"Shut up!"

"I'll go to the Sergeant, I will!"

"Go ahead!"

And she really did go, with her babies in her arms, fearing nothing, and without shedding a tear, like a madwoman, because now she too loved that husband who had been forced on her, greasy and filthy, spattered with oil and fermented olives.

The Sergeant sent for Nanni; he threatened him even with jail and the gallows. Nanni began to sob and tear his hair; he didn't deny anything, he didn't try to clear himself.

"It's the temptation!" he said. "It's the temptation of hell!"

He threw himself at the Sergeant's feet begging to be sent to jail.

"For God's sake, Sergeant, take me out of this hell! Have me killed, put me in jail; don't let me see her again, never! never!"

"No!" answered the She-wolf instead, to the Sergeant. "I kept a little corner in the kitchen to sleep in, when I gave him my house as dowry. It's my house. I don't intend to leave it."

Shortly afterward, Nanni was kicked in the chest by a mule and was at the point of death, but the priest refused to bring him the Sacrament if the She-wolf did not go out of the house. The She-wolf left, and then her son-in-law could also prepare to leave like a good Christian; he confessed and received communion with such signs of repentance and contrition that all the neighbors and the curious wept before the dying man's bed.—And it would have been better for him to die that day, before the devil came back to tempt him again and creep into his body and soul, when he got well.

"Leave me alone!" he told the She-wolf. "For God's sake,

leave me in peace! I've seen death with my own eyes! Poor Maricchia is desperate. Now the whole town knows about it! If I don't see you it's better for both of us . . ."

And he would have liked to gouge his eyes out not to see those of the She-wolf, for whenever they peered into his, they made him lose his body and soul. He did not know what to do to free himself from the spell. He paid for Masses for the souls in purgatory and asked the priest and the Sergeant for help. At Easter he went to confession, and in penance he publicly licked more than four feet of pavement, crawling on the pebbles in front of the church—and then, as the She-wolf came to tempt him again:

"Listen!" he said to her. "Don't come to the threshing floor again; if you do, I swear to God, I'll kill you!"

"Kill me," answered the She-wolf, "I don't care; I can't stand it without you."

As he saw her from the distance, in the green wheat fields, Nanni stopped hoeing the vineyard, and went to pull the ax from the elm. The She-wolf saw him come, pale and wild-eyed, with the ax glistening in the sun, but she did not fall back a single step, did not lower her eyes; she continued toward him, her hands laden with red poppies, her black eyes devouring him.

"Ah! damn your soul!" stammered Nanni.

## *Ieli*

Ieli, the horsekeeper, was thirteen when he met Don Alfonso, the rich boy, but was so small that he didn't come up to the belly of Bianca, the old mare who carried the herd's bell. You could always see him straight and still on the edge of a cliff or squatting on a big rock, here and there, on the hills or on the plain, wherever his animals were grazing.

His friend, Don Alfonso, while in the country on his summer vacation, went to see him every day that God sent to Tebidi,[1] and the two shared the good things of the little baron and the barley bread of the herd boy, or the fruit stolen from the neighbor. At first Ieli called the rich boy "Your Excellency," as people do in Sicily, but after they had a good fight, they became very close friends. Ieli taught his friend how to climb up to the magpies' nests, at the top of the walnut trees higher than the bell tower of Licodia, how to hit a sparrow in flight with a stone, or how to mount with a running jump on the bare backs of the yet-untamed mares, grabbing by the mane the first that passed within reach, without being scared by the unbroken colts' angry neighing and desperate leaping.

Ah, the wonderful chases over the mown fields, manes in the wind! the beautiful days of April, when the wind piled up the green grass into waves and the mares neighed in the pastures! the beautiful summer afternoons, when the whitish countryside lay silent under the hazy sky, and the grasshoppers crackled among the clods, as if the stubble were catching fire! the beautiful winter sky through the naked branches of the almond tree that shivered in the north wind, and the path that sounded frozen under the horses' hoofs, and the skylarks that sang high up in the warmth, in the blue! the beautiful summer evenings that came up very slowly, like fog, the good smell of the hay in which you sank your elbows, and the melancholy humming of the evening insects, and those two notes of Ieli's pipe, always the same—ee-oo! ee-oo! ee-oo!—that made you think of faraway things: of the fiesta of Saint John, of Christmas Eve, of the dawn of a picnic day, of all those big events gone by, which seemed sad so far away, making you look up, your eyes wet, as if all the stars that were lighting themselves in the sky rained into your heart and flooded it!

But Ieli didn't suffer from that melancholy; he squatted on the ridge, his cheeks puffed out, all intent on his playing

---

[1] The name of a group of houses and of the farm land surrounding them, in the region that lies west of Vizzini, where most of the present story is set. Tebidi was owned by Verga's family.

—ee-oo! ee-oo! ee-oo!— Then he rounded up the herd by yelling and throwing stones and drove it into the stable, beyond Poggio Alla Croce.

Panting, he went up the slope on the far side of the valley, at times shouting to his friend Alfonso:

"Call the dog; hey, call the dog!"—or: "Throw a stone at Zaino,[2] who's acting up and playing around with the bushes in the valley and is coming along much too slowly" —or: "Tomorrow morning bring me a needle, one of Lia's."

He knew how to do all kinds of things with a needle; and he had a little bundle of rags in his canvas sack to patch his pants or the sleeves of his jacket when necessary; he also knew how to weave braids of horse hair, and he washed with the clay of the valley the kerchief he wore around his neck when it was cold. In short, as long as he had his sack on his shoulder he needed nobody in the world, whether he was in the woods of Resecone or lost deep in the plains of Caltagirone. Lia used to say:

"See Ieli? He's always been alone in the fields, as if one of his mares had brought him into the world, and that's why he knows how to do everything with his own hands."

As a matter of fact, it was true that Ieli needed no one, but all the people at the farm would have been glad to do things for him, since he was a helpful boy and there was always a chance of getting something from him. Lia baked him bread, out of Christian charity, and he repaid her with well-made little wicker baskets to carry eggs in, cane winders, and other trifles.

"We act like his animals," said Lia, "that scratch each other's necks."

At Tebidi they all knew him since he was a baby, when you couldn't see him among the tails of the horses that were grazing on the Piano Del Lettighiere; and he had grown up under their eyes, you might say, though nobody ever saw

[2] The name of a chestnut colt. Words that are used as names of animals in the original have generally been left in Italian, but when they refer only to the animal's colt, they have been translated.

him, and he was always wandering here and there with his
herd. "He rained down from the sky, and the earth picked
him up," as the saying goes; really one of those who have
neither home nor family.

His mother was working at Vizzini and saw him only
once a year, when he went to Saint John's fair with the
colts; and the day she died they came to call him—one
Saturday night—and on Monday Ieli went back to the herd,
so that he didn't even lose the day's pay; but the poor boy
had come back so upset that at times he let the colts break
into the wheat fields.

"Hey, Ieli!" *massaro* Agrippino shouted at him from the
threshing floor. "You want an extra good taste of my whip,
you son-of-a-bitch?"

Ieli started running after the scattered colts and drove
them dejectedly toward the hill. But his mother was always
before his eyes, her head wrapped in a white kerchief, and
not able to speak any more.

His father herded cows at Ragoleti, beyond Licodia,
"where you could mow malaria," said the peasants of the
neighborhood; but in malaria country the pastures are rich,
and cows don't catch the fever. So Ieli stayed in the fields
all year long, either at Donferrante, or at the Commenda, or
in the Valle Del Iacitano, and the hunters or the travelers
who took the short cuts would always see him here and
there, like a dog without a master.

He didn't suffer from all of this, because he was used to
staying with the horses that walked along step by step in
front of him nibbling the clover, and with the birds that
swirled around him in flocks, for the whole time the sun was
making its slow, slow journey, till the shadows grew long
and then vanished; he had the time to watch the clouds pile
up little by little and picture mountains and valleys; he
knew how the wind blows when it brings a storm and what
the color of the clouds is when it's about to snow. Everything had its look and its meaning, and there were always
things to see and things to listen to, every hour of the day.
So toward sunset, when Ieli started playing on his pipe of
elder-wood, the black mare would draw near, listlessly

chewing clover, and would stand looking at him with her big, pensive eyes.

The one place where he suffered a little melancholy was on the desert lands of Passanitello, where neither a bush nor a shrub grows and in the hot months not a bird flies overhead. The horses gathered together in a circle to make shade for one another, with their heads drooping, and on the long days of the threshing, that great silent light rained down always the same and suffocatingly hot for sixteen hours.

But where feed was abundant and the horses liked to linger, the boy would busy himself in some other way. He made reed cages for crickets, pipes with carvings on them, and little rush baskets, using a few twigs; he could set up a little hut, when the north wind drove the long files of crows through the valley, or when the cicadas beat their wings in the sun that scorched the stubble; he roasted acorns from the oak grove in the embers of sumac branches, as if they were chestnuts, or toasted his big slices of bread when they began to get hairy with mold—for when he was at Passanitello in the winter, the roads were so bad that fifteen days would pass without a living soul going by.

Don Alfonso, who was kept in cotton by his parents, envied his friend Ieli the canvas sack where he kept all his things: his bread, his onions, his little flask of wine, his kerchief for the cold, his little bundle of rags with his thread and needles, his tin box with flint and tinder; he envied him also the haughty speckled mare, that animal with the tuft of hair sticking out on her forehead, who had mean eyes and swelled her nostrils like a surly mastiff when anybody wanted to mount her. Instead she let Ieli mount her and scratch her ears, which were especially sensitive, and she kept sniffing him to listen to what he had to tell her.

"Leave that mare alone," Ieli advised, "she's not bad, but she doesn't know you."

After Scordu, the man from Buccheri,[3] led away the Calabrian mare that he had bought at Saint John's fair with the agreement that they would keep her in the herd until vintage

---

[3] A large village about twenty-five miles west of Syracuse.

time, the chestnut colt, left an orphan, didn't want to quiet down, and ran around on the cliffs of the mountain, with long lamenting neighs and his nostrils in the wind. Ieli ran after him, calling him with loud shouts, and the colt stopped to listen, his neck stretched tight and his ears restless, lashing his flanks with his tail.

"It's because they took his mother away from him, and he doesn't know what he's doing any more," observed Ieli. "Now he'll have to be watched, because he's liable to let himself fall over the cliff. It's like me, when my mother died I couldn't see straight any more."

Then, after the colt began to sniff the clover and take a couple of bites halfheartedly:

"See? Little by little he's beginning to forget all about her. —But he'll be sold too. Horses are made to be sold, like lambs are born to be butchered, and clouds bring the rain. Only the birds have nothing to do but sing and fly all day."

Ideas didn't come to him clear and straight one after the other, for there had rarely been anybody for him to talk to, and so he was never in a hurry to dig them out and disentangle them from the back of his mind, where he was used to letting them sprout and grow until they came forward little by little, like the buds on the branches under the sun.

"The birds, too," he added, "have to hunt up food, and when snow covers the ground they die."

Then he thought it over awhile:

"You're like the birds; but when winter comes you can sit by the fire without doing anything."

Don Alfonso, however, answered that he went to school, to learn. Then Ieli opened his eyes wide and was all ears when the rich boy started reading, and he looked at the book and at him suspiciously, listening with that slight winking of the eyelids that shows intensity of attention in those animals that come nearest to man. He liked poetry, which caressed his ears with the harmony of an incomprehensible song, and sometimes he knitted his brow and pointed his chin, and a lot of work seemed to be going on inside him; then he would nod yes, yes, with a cunning smile, and he would scratch his head. When the rich boy started writing to show how many things he knew how to do, Ieli would have stayed there for whole days to watch him, and suddenly a look of suspicion would escape him. He couldn't understand how one could repeat on paper those very words he had said, or that Don Alfonso had said, and even those things that had never come out of his mouth at all, so that he ended by drawing back incredulously with his cunning smile.

Any new idea that knocked on his head to get in made him suspicious, and he seemed to sniff at it with the savage mistrust of his speckled mare. But he showed no surprise at anything in the world: if somebody had told him that in town horses rode in carriages, he would have remained impassive, with that mask of oriental indifference which is the dignity of the Sicilian peasant. He seemed to entrench himself instinctively in his ignorance, as if it were the strength of poverty. Every time he found himself short of answers, he repeated, with that obstinate smile that was intended to be sly:

"I don't know anything about it. I'm poor."

He had asked his friend Alfonso to write Mara's name for him on a piece of paper he had found, God knows where, for he picked up everything he saw on the ground, and he had put it in his little bundle of rags. One day, after having been silent for a while looking here and there deep in thought, he said very seriously:

"I've got a girl friend."

Alfonso, even though he knew how to read, opened his eyes wide.

"Yes," repeated Ieli. "Mara, the daughter of *massaro* Agrippino, who used to live here and who lives at Marineo now, in that big house on the plain, that you can see from the Piano Del Lettighiere, up there."

"Then you're going to get married?"

"Yes, when I'm grown up and make four *onze* a year. Mara doesn't know anything about it yet."

"Why haven't you told her?"

Ieli shook his head and became lost in thought. Then he unwrapped his little bundle of rags and spread out the paper he had had Alfonso write for him.

"It really does say 'Mara'; Don Gesualdo the field watchman read it, and Brother Cola too, when he came down to collect broad beans for the monastery.

"Anybody who knows how to write," he observed then, "is like one who keeps words in his tinder box, and can carry them in his pocket, and even send them here and there."

"What are you going to do with that piece of paper now, when you don't know how to read?" Alfonso asked him.

Ieli shrugged his shoulders, but continued to wrap up carefully in his little bundle of rags the piece of paper with the writing on it.

He had known Mara since she was small, and they had begun by beating each other up, when they had met in the valley while picking blackberries in the wedges of bramble. The little girl, knowing she was "on her own ground," had grabbed Ieli by the collar as if he were a thief. For a while they pounded each other on the back, one blow for you and one for me, as the cooper does on the hoops of the barrels, but when they grew tired they began to calm down little by little, still clutching each other by the hair.

"Who are you?" Mara asked him.

And since Ieli, who was the wilder of the two, didn't say who he was—

"I'm Mara, the daughter of *massaro* Agrippino, who's the watchman of all these fields here."

Then Ieli let go his hold without saying anything, and the little girl started picking up the blackberries that she had dropped on the ground, peeking now and then at her opponent with curiosity.

"On the other side of the bridge, in the hedge of the vegetable field," added the little girl, "there are lots of big blackberries and the chickens eat them."

Meanwhile, Ieli was slinking away very softly, and Mara, after she had followed him with her eyes as far as she could see him in the oak grove, also turned and ran home as fast as her legs could carry her.

But from that day on they started to become tame and get used to each other. Mara would go to spin hemp on the parapet of the little bridge, and Ieli would slowly drive the herd toward the foot of Poggio Del Bandito. At first he kept his distance, circling around her, looking at her suspiciously from afar, and little by little he kept going closer with the cautious movements of a dog used to stones. When at last they happened to be side by side, they remained silent for hours, Ieli attentively watching the intricate work of the knitting Mara's mother had assigned to her, or she looking at him while he carved fine zigzags on sticks of almond wood. Then they went off, one in this direction, the other in that, without saying a word, and soon as she was in sight of her home, the little girl began to run, making her skirt go high up on her little red legs.

Then when the prickly pears were ripe, they spent their time in the thick of the cactus bushes, peeling prickly pears all day long. They wandered together under the century-old walnut trees, and Ieli knocked down so many walnuts that they fell thick as hail; the little girl worked hard picking up as many as she could, shouting with pleasure, and then she fled away swiftly, holding out the two corners of her apron and wobbling like a little old woman.

During the winter Mara didn't dare stick her nose out, the weather was so cold. At times, toward evening, you could see the smoke of the little fires of sumac wood that Ieli was making in the Piano Del Lettighiere, or on Poggio Di Macca, in order not to freeze to death like those titmice he found in the morning behind a stone or a clod of earth. Even the horses enjoyed swinging their tails a little around the fire, and they huddled together to keep warmer.

With March, skylarks came back to the plain, sparrows to the roofs, leaves and nest to the hedges; Mara began to go for walks with Ieli again, in the soft grass, among the flowering bushes, under the trees that were still bare but were starting to show dots of green. Ieli plunged into the thorny scrub like a bloodhound, to root out the nests of the blackbirds who looked at him in bewilderment with their little eyes of peppercorn. Inside their shirts the two children often carried almost naked baby rabbits, freshly taken from their holes, but with their long ears already uneasy; they ran around the fields following the horses, going into the stubble behind the reapers, step for step with the herd, stopping every time a mare stopped to crop a mouthful of grass. In the evening, when they came to the little bridge, they left each other, one in this direction, the other in that, without saying good-by.

So they spent the whole summer. Meanwhile, the sun was beginning to set behind Poggio Alla Croce, and the robins went after it toward the mountain, following it through the cactus bushes, as darkness was coming. The grasshoppers and the cicadas were not heard any more, and in that hour something like a great melancholy spread through the air.

At that time to Ieli's hut came his father, the cowherd, who had caught malaria at Ragoleti, and could hardly hold himself up on the donkey that was carrying him. Ieli lit a fire immediately and ran to "The Houses" to get him some eggs.

"You'd better put some straw by the fire," his father said, "I feel the fever coming back."

The chills of the fever were so strong that Menu, buried under his big cloak, the donkey's saddlebag, and Ieli's sack, shook like the leaves in November, in front of that huge blaze of branches which made his face look as white as a dead man's. The peasants from the farm came to ask him:

"How do you feel, Menu?"

The poor man answered only with a whine, like that of a suckling pup.

"It's the kind of malaria that kills you better than a gunshot," said his friends, warming their hands at the fire.

They sent for the doctor too, but it was all a waste of money, for the disease was one of those simple and familiar ones that even a boy would know how to cure, and if the fever hadn't been one of those that kill you anyhow, quinine would have cured it right away. Menu had spent a fortune buying quinine, but it was like throwing it down a well.

"Take some good strong eucalyptus tea, which doesn't cost anything," suggested *massaro* Agrippino, "and if it doesn't help any more than the quinine, at least you won't ruin yourself by spending money."

He took the eucalyptus tea also, but the fever kept coming back, and it was even more violent. Ieli helped his father as well as he could. Every morning before going away with the colts, he left him the tea ready in a bowl, a bundle of branches within reach, eggs in the hot ashes, and he came back early in the evening with more firewood for the night, and a small flask of wine and some mutton that he had run as far as Licodia to buy. The poor boy did everything carefully and well, like a good housewife, and his father, following him with tired eyes as Ieli did the little chores here and there in the hut, smiled now and then, thinking that the boy would be able to take care of himself when left alone.

On the days the fever stopped for a few hours, Menu got up, his features all distorted and his head wrapped up tight in a kerchief, and he waited for Ieli at the doorway, while the sun was still warm. As Ieli dropped the bundle of firewood at the doorway and put the flask and the eggs on the table, his father said to him:

"Put the eucalyptus on to boil for tonight"—or: "When I'm gone remember that Aunt Agatha's keeping your mother's gold for you."

And Ieli nodded yes.

"It's no use," repeated *massaro* Agrippino each time he came back to see Menu. "By now your blood is all infected."

Menu listened without batting an eye, his face whiter than his cap.

He didn't get out of bed anymore. Ieli began to cry when he wasn't strong enough to help him turn from one side to the other; little by little Menu couldn't even speak any more. The last words he said to his boy were:

"When I'm dead go to the owner of the cows at Ragoleti and have him give you the three *onze* and the twelve *tu-*

*moli*⁴ of wheat that he owes me for my work from May until now."

"No," answered Ieli, "it's only two and a half *onze,* because you left the cows more than a month ago, and we have to be fair with the master in figuring out the salary."

"That's right!" said Menu, half closing his eyes.

"Now I'm really alone in the world like a lost colt that the wolves can eat!" thought Ieli when they had taken his father to the cemetery of Licodia.

Mara also had come to see the house of the dead man, with that morbid curiosity that frightening things arouse.

"See how I'm left?" Ieli said to her. The little girl stepped back startled, fearing that he would make her go into the house where the dead man had been.

Ieli went to get his father's money, and then he left with his herd for Passanitello, where the grass was already tall on the fallow land, and the feed was abundant; so the colts stayed there to graze for a long time.

Meanwhile, Ieli had grown up—and Mara must have grown too, he often thought to himself as he played his pipe; and when he returned to Tebidi, after a long time, driving the mares very slowly in front of him on the slippery paths of the Fontana Dello Zio Cosimo, he kept searching with his eyes for the little bridge in the valley and the hut in the Valle Del Iacitano, and the roofs of "The Big Houses" where the pigeons were always flapping their wings.

But at that time the master had fired *massaro* Agrippino, and Mara's whole family was moving away. Ieli found the girl, big now and rather pretty, at the door of the courtyard, keeping an eye on her things while they were being loaded on the cart. Now the empty room seemed darker and smokier than usual. The table, the bed, the chest of drawers, and the images of the Virgin and of Saint John, and even the nails to hang the gourds with the seeds, had left marks on the walls where they had been for so many years.

"We're moving away," Mara said as she saw him looking

---

⁴ The *tumolo* was a Sicilian measure of grain equivalent to about forty pounds.

around. "We're moving down to Marineo where that big house is, on the plain."

Ieli began to help *massaro* Agrippino and Lia load the cart, and when there was nothing left to carry out of the room, he went to sit with Mara on the edge of the watering trough.

"Even houses," he said to her when he had seen the last hamper piled on the cart, "even houses, when you take their things away from them, don't seem the same any more."

"At Marineo," answered Mara, "my mother said we'll have a room that's nicer and as big as the cheese house."

"Now that you'll be away I don't ever want to come here again, because it'll seem like winter's back, seeing the door closed."

"At Marineo, though, we'll find other people, Pudda the Redhead and the field watchman's daughter; we'll have fun; at harvest time more than eighty reapers will come with bagpipes and there'll be dancing on the threshing floor."

*Massaro* Agrippino and his wife had started out with the cart, and Mara ran gaily behind, carrying the basket with the pigeons. Ieli followed her as far as the little bridge, and when Mara was about to disappear in the valley, he called after her:

"Mara! Oh! Mara!"

"What do you want?" she said.

He no longer knew what he wanted.

"What're you going to do here all alone?" the girl asked then.

"I'll stay with the colts."

Mara went skipping away, and he remained there motionless as long as he could hear the noise of the cart that bounced on the stones. The sun was touching the high rocks of Poggio Alla Croce, the gray foliage of the olive trees faded gradually in the twilight, and in the vast countryside, far, far away, you could hear nothing but the bell of Bianca in the widening silence.

After going to Marineo, where there were new people and so much to do at vintage time, Mara forgot all about him; but Ieli was always thinking of her, because he didn't have anything else to do in the long days he spent watching the tails of his animals. Now he no longer had any reason to go down into the valley, beyond the little bridge, and he was not seen at the farm again. So for a long time he didn't know that Mara had gotten engaged—so much water had passed and passed meanwhile under the little bridge. He only saw the girl again the day of the fiesta of Saint John, when he went to the fair to sell the colts: a fiesta that turned completely to poison for him and made him lose his bread, because of an accident that happened to one of his master's colts, God save us!

The day of the fair [5] the factor had been waiting for the colt since dawn, walking up and down in his shiny boots behind the rumps of the horses and the mules which were arranged in rows on both sides of the highroad. The fair was already almost over and still there was no sign of Ieli and his animals around the curve of the highroad.

On the scorched slopes of Calvario and Mulino A Vento there still remained a few small flocks of sheep, huddled together in circles with their muzzles to the ground and their eyes lifeless, and a few yoke of oxen with long hair, the kind that you sell to pay the rent of the farms; they were waiting motionless under the broiling sun. There below, toward the valley, the bell of Saint John's sounded High Mass, accompanied by the long crackling of firecrackers. Then the fairground seemed to quiver, and a loud cry ran through the town, lingering among the peddlers' awnings that were spread along the Salita Dei Galli, going down the streets and then seeming to return from the valley where the church was. *Viva San Giovanni!* [6]

[5] This fair takes place on the 24th of June, St. John's Day, at Vizzini, which is a small town on the Iblei Mountains, about thirty miles west of Syracuse. The names of places occurring in this section of the story are either points near Vizzini or streets in the town.

[6] "Long live Saint John!"

"Damn it!" screamed the factor. "That bastard of an Ieli will make me miss the fair!"

The sheep lifted their muzzles in wonder and began bleating all together, and the oxen took a few steps slowly, looking around with big, intent eyes.

The factor was furious because the rent for the "big fields" was due that day, "as Saint John arrives under the elm" [7] the contract said, and the money from the sale of the colts had been counted on to complete the sum. Meanwhile, there were as many colts, horses, and mules as God had made, all groomed and shiny, and decorated with tufts and tassels and little bells, swishing their tails to while away the time and turning their heads toward everyone who passed, as if waiting for some kind soul willing to buy them.

"He must have gone to sleep somewhere, that bastard!" the factor kept shouting. "And he leaves me stuck with the colts!"

Instead, Ieli had walked all night so that the colts would arrive at the fairground fresh, and would be able to get a good place when they arrived, and he had reached the Piano Del Corvo when the *Three Kings* [8] had not yet gone down and were shining on Monte Arturo with their arms crossed. Along the road, carts and people on horseback going to the fiesta passed continuously; so Ieli kept his eyes wide open to make sure that the colts, scared by the unusual traffic, didn't scatter, but went together along the edge of the road behind Bianca, who walked calmly straight ahead, the bell on her neck. From time to time, when the road ran over the crest of the hills, even way up there you could hear the bell of Saint John's, so that also in the darkness and silence of the countryside the fiesta was in the air; and all along the highroad, far, far off, as far as there were people on foot or on horseback going to Vizzini, you could hear the cry: *Viva San Giovanni!* And rockets rose straight and shining behind

[7] The procession of Saint John. The elm refers to a specific location of the kind used in old rural contracts.

[8] Three stars of the constellation of Orion.

the mountains of Canziria and they were like the stars that rain down in August.

"It's like Christmas Eve," Ieli was saying to the boy who helped him drive the herd, "when all the farmhouses are lit up and the people are celebrating, and here and there you can see bonfires all over the countryside."

The boy was half asleep, slowly pushing ahead one leg after the other, and didn't answer; but Ieli, who felt all his blood stirred by that bell, couldn't stay quiet, as if each one of those rockets sliding silent and shining on the darkness behind the mountain burst from his soul.

"Mara must have gone to Saint John's fiesta too," he said, "because she goes every year."

And not caring that Alfio, the boy, didn't answer—

"You don't know? Mara's so tall now that she's even bigger than her mother who brought her into the world, and when I saw her again I couldn't believe she was the same girl I used to go with to pick prickly pears and knock down walnuts."

And he began to sing out loud all the songs he knew.

"Hey, Alfio, are you asleep?" he shouted when he had finished. "Watch out that Bianca keeps following you, watch out!"

"No, I'm not asleep," answered Alfio with a hoarse voice.

"See the Puddara [9] winking at us up there above Granvilla, as if rockets were being shot off at Santa Domenica too? It can't be long before daybreak, but we'll get to the fair in time to find a good place. Hey, my good Morellino! You'll have a new halter, with red tassels, for the fair! and you too, Stellato!"

And he went on talking to each of the colts, so that they would take heart hearing his voice in the dark. But he felt sad that Stellato and Morellino were going to the fair to be sold.

"When they're sold they'll go away with their new master, and we won't see them in the herd any more, just as it's been

[9] The Sicilian name of the Pleiades.

with Mara after she went away to Marineo.—Her father's doing very well down there at Marineo; when I went to see them they put in front of me bread, wine, cheese, and any other food you could think of, because he's almost the factor, and he's got the keys to everything, and I could have eaten the whole farm if I'd wanted to. Mara almost didn't know me any more, it'd been so long since she'd seen me, and she began to shout:—'Oh look, it's Ieli, the horse-keeper, the one from Tebidi!'—It's like when you come back from far away; and if you only see the tip of a mountain you recognize right away the place where you grew up. Lia didn't want me to use *tu* with Mara any more, now that she's big, because people who don't know talk easily.[10] But Mara laughed, and she was all red in the face as if she'd been putting bread in the oven that very minute; she spread out the tablecloth and set the table and she didn't seem the same any more.—'Do you still remember Tebidi?'—I asked her as soon as Lia had gone to draw some fresh wine from the barrel.—'Yes, sure, I remember,' she said to me. 'At Tebidi there was the bell and the bell tower that looked like the handle of a saltcellar, and they rang the bell from the platform, and there were two stone cats that purred on the gate of the garden.'—I felt them here inside, all those things, as she was saying them. Mara looked at me from head to foot, all eyes, and said over and over again—'You're sure big now!' and she also began to laugh and hit me here on the head."

So Ieli, the horsekeeper, lost his bread, because just at that moment a carriage suddenly came along, which hadn't been heard before, since it had been climbing step by step up the steep grade, and when it had reached the level it had begun to trot with a terrific cracking of whips and jingling of bells, as if the devil were driving it. The colts, frightened,

[10] *Tu* is the familiar form of address in Italian and was considered a sign of intimacy. If an unmarried girl and a young man addressed each other with *tu,* people thought that they were at least engaged to be married, and as a result the girl would have no other suitors.

scattered in a flash, as if there were an earthquake, and it took a lot of calling and shouting and ohee, ohee, ohee's! by Ieli and the boy before they could gather them around Bianca, who was listlessly trotting away, the bell on her neck.

As soon as Ieli had counted his animals, he noticed that Stellato was missing, and he thrust his hands into his hair, because at that spot the road ran along the ravine, and it was in the ravine that Stellato broke his back—a colt that was worth twelve *onze,* like twelve angels of paradise! Weeping and shouting, Ieli called the colt—ahoo! ahoo! ahoo!—for it was still dark. Stellato finally answered from the bottom of the ravine with a painful neighing, as if he could speak, poor animal!

"Oh, *mamma mia!"* Ieli and the boy were screaming. "Oh, how terrible, how terrible, *mamma mia!"*

The travelers who were going to the fiesta, hearing them cry like that in the darkness, asked what they had lost; and then, when they found out what it was all about, continued on their way.

Stellato was lying motionless where he had fallen, with his legs in the air, and while Ieli was feeling him all over, crying and speaking to him as if the colt could understand, the poor animal lifted his neck painfully and turned his head toward him, and you could hear the panting, broken by convulsions.

"He must have broken something!" whined Ieli, desperate because he couldn't see a thing in the dark; and the colt, as inert as a stone, let his head fall down again heavily. Alfio, who had remained on the road to look after the herd, had been the first one to calm down and had taken his bread out of his sack.

Now the sky had grown whitish, and the mountains all around seemed to rise one by one, black and tall. From the curve in the highroad you could begin to see the town, with Monte Del Calvario and Monte Del Mulino A Vento outlined against the pale light of dawn; they were still hazy and speckled by white blotches of sheep, and as the oxen, grazing atop the mountain in the blue, moved here and there, it seemed that the profile of the mountain itself became animated and swarmed with life. From the bottom of the ravine the bell could no longer be heard; the travelers were rarer, and those few who passed were in a hurry to get to the fair. Poor Ieli didn't know which saint to turn to, in that solitude: Alfio, by himself, couldn't help him at all, so he slowly nibbled his piece of bread.

Finally, the factor was seen, coming on his mule, hurrying toward them, shouting and swearing in the distance as he saw the animals stopped on the road; so that Alfio ran up the hill as fast as his legs could carry him. But Ieli didn't move from the side of Stellato. The factor left the mule on the road and went down into the ravine and tried to help the colt get up, pulling him by the tail.

"Leave him alone!" said Ieli, white in the face as if he had been the one to break his back. "Leave him alone! Don't you see that he can't move, poor animal?"

Stellato, in fact, at every movement and every effort they had him make, gave a death rattle, as if he were a Christian.[11] The factor vented his rage by kicking and beating Ieli and let go a stream of curses that burned the ears of all the saints and angels in paradise. Alfio, a little reassured by this time, had gone back to the road, in order not to leave the animals unguarded, and he kept trying to clear himself by saying:

"It isn't my fault. I was up front with Bianca."

"There's nothing we can do here," said the factor at last, when he realized that it was all a waste of time. "All we can get out of him is the hide, as long as it's good."

Ieli began shaking like a leaf when he saw the factor go and pull the shotgun from the saddle of the mule.

"Get out of the way, you good-for-nothing!" the factor howled at him. "I don't know who's stopping me from leaving you dead on the ground with that colt who was worth a lot more than you, in spite of the stinking baptism that thief of a priest gave you!"

Stellato, who couldn't move, turned only his head, his

[11] In Sicily, a human being in general.

eyes wide and staring as if he had understood everything, and his hair curled in waves along his ribs and it seemed that a shiver ran under it. And so the factor killed Stellato on the spot to get the hide, at least, and Ieli seemed to feel inside himself the dull noise made by the shot fired at close range into the live flesh.

"Now, if you want a piece of advice," the factor told him, "don't try to come to the master for the money he owes you, because he'd sure pay you, but good!"

The factor went away with Alfio, and with the other colts, who cropped grass from the edge of the road and didn't even turn to see where Stellato remained. And Stellato remained alone in the ravine, waiting for somebody to come and skin him, his eyes still wide open and his four legs stretched out—lucky he, who at last didn't suffer any more. Ieli, now that he had seen how the factor had aimed at the colt and fired the shot in cold blood while the poor animal turned his head painfully as if he were human, stopped crying and sat there on a stone, staring fixedly at Stellato until the men came to get the hide.

Now he could go wherever he pleased, to enjoy the fiesta or stay in the square all day, to see the rich men in the café, anything he liked, because he didn't have bread, or a roof over his head any more, and he had to look for a master, if anyone wanted him after the accident with Stellato.

That's the way the world goes: while Ieli, with his sack on his shoulder and his staff in his hand, went looking for a master, the band played gaily in the square, with plumes in their hats, in the middle of a crowd of white caps as thick as flies, and the rich men sat in the café enjoying it all. Everybody was dressed up, like the animals of the fair, and in a corner of the square there was a woman with a short skirt and flesh-colored stockings that made her legs look bare, and she was pounding a big drum in front of a large painted sheet on which you could see a massacre of Christians, with blood flowing in torrents; and in the crowd that was watching openmouthed, there was *massaro* Cola too, who knew Ieli from the time he was at Passanitello, and he said that he would find him a master, because Isidoro Macca was looking for a swineherd.

"But don't say anything about Stellato," *massaro* Cola warned him. "An accident like that can happen to anybody in this world; but it's better not to talk about it."

So they went in search of Macca, who was at the dance, and while *massaro* Cola went to talk to him, Ieli waited on the street, in the middle of the crowd that was looking in from the door of the shop. In the shabby room there were lots of people jumping around and enjoying themselves, all excited and red in the face, and making a terrific noise pounding their big shoes on the brick floor, and you couldn't even hear the *ron-ron* of the double bass; and as soon as one piece, costing a *grano*, was finished, they raised their finger as a sign that they wanted another, and the double-bass player, to keep a count, made an X on the wall with charcoal, and started all over again.

"Those people spend money without thinking," Ieli was saying to himself, "so they must have their pockets full, and they're not in difficulty like me, left without a master, since they sweat and wear themselves out jumping around as if they were paid for it!"

*Massaro* Cola came back saying that Macca didn't need anybody. Then Ieli turned his back and went away dejected.

Mara lived near Saint Anthony's, where the houses climb up the mountain facing the valley of Canziria, which is all green with cactus, and has mill wheels foaming below in the torrent; but Ieli didn't have the courage to go over there now, after he hadn't even been wanted as a swineherd, and as he wandered around in the middle of the crowd that bumped and pushed him without paying any attention to him, he felt more alone than when he was with the colts on the desert lands of Passanitello, and he felt like crying.

He finally met *massaro* Agrippino, who was walking around in the square with his arms hanging down, enjoying the fiesta, and who began shouting after him: "Hey! Ieli! Hey!" And he took him home. Mara was all dressed up, with long earrings beating against her cheeks, and her ring-laden hands on her belly, waiting at the doorway for it to get dark, to go and see the fireworks.

"Oh!" said Mara. "You've come for the fiesta of Saint John too?"

Ieli didn't dare go in because he was badly dressed; but *massaro* Agrippino pushed him by the shoulders, telling him that they weren't seeing each other for the first time, and all of them knew he had come to the fair with his master's colts. Lia poured him a big glass of wine, and they took him along with the women and other friends of the neighborhood, to go and see how the town was all lit up.

When they got to the square, Ieli was openmouthed with wonder; it was all a sea of fire as when the stubbles are burning, because of the large number of rockets the faithful lit in front of the Saint, who, all black under the silver canopy, was enjoying it all from the entrance to Rosario.[12] The faithful were coming and going among the flames like so many devils, and there was even a woman with her clothes all loose and in disorder, her hair disheveled and her eyes bulging out of her head, who was lighting rockets too, and a priest with his gown flying in the air, without a hat, who seemed to be obsessed by devotion.

"That's the son of *massaro* Neri, the factor of Salonia; he spends more than ten *lire* for rockets!" said Lia, nodding toward a young man who was going around the square holding in his hands two rockets at a time, like candles, so that all the women devoured him with their eyes, and shouted to him: *Viva San Giovanni!*

"His father's rich and owns more than twenty head of cattle," added *massaro* Agrippino.

Mara also knew that he had carried the big banner in the procession, and had held it as straight as a pole—he was such a strong and good-looking young man.

*Massaro* Neri's son seemed to hear this talk and to light his rockets for Mara, whirling about her; in fact, after the

---

[12] The name of a section of Vizzini.

fireworks he joined them and took them to the dance and to the *Cosmorama*, where you could see the old world and the new, and he paid for everyone, of course, even for Ieli, who walked behind the group like a dog without a master to see *massaro* Neri's son dance with Mara, who twirled around and curtsied like a turtledove, prettily holding out one corner of her apron. *Massaro* Neri's son capered like a colt, so that Lia wept with joy, and *massaro* Agrippino nodded yes, yes, all was going well.

Finally, when they were tired, they walked here and there on the Promenade, carried along by the crowd as if they were in a raging river, and they went to see the illuminated pictures, in which Saint John's head was being cut off—a sight that would have moved even the Turks to pity [13]—and under the ax Saint John kicked like a wild buck. Close by, the band played under a big wooden umbrella that was all lit up, and in the square the crowd was so thick that never before had so many Christians been seen at a fair.

Mara walked arm in arm with *massaro* Neri's son, like a rich girl, and whispered in his ear and laughed and seemed to be having a lot of fun. Ieli was dead tired, and fell asleep sitting on the sidewalk until the first explosions of the fireworks woke him up. At that moment Mara was still at the side of *massaro* Neri's son, leaning against him with her two hands clasped on his shoulder, and in the light of the colored fireworks she looked all white and then all red. When the last rockets fled into the sky in one big bunch, *massaro* Neri's son, whose face looked green, turned toward her and kissed her.

Ieli didn't say anything, but at that moment the whole fiesta, which he had enjoyed until then, changed to poison for him, and he again began to think of all his troubles, which he had forgotten—that he was without a master, and no longer knew what to do or where to go, and no longer

[13] In Sicily and in other parts of Italy the word *Turco* ("Turk") often indicates a non-Christian in general and a man of cruel nature in particular.

had bread, or a roof over his head—in short, that it would be better to go and throw himself into the ravine, like Stellato, whom the dogs were eating by now.

In the meantime, around him people were gay. Mara and her girl friends skipped and sang along the stony little road while they were going back home.

"Good night! Good night!" the friends kept saying as they separated along the way.

Mara said good night, and seemed to be singing, there was so much happiness in her voice; and *massaro* Neri's son seemed to go completely wild and never want to leave her, while *massaro* Agrippino and Lia argued as they opened the door of the house. No one paid any attention to Ieli; only *massaro* Agrippino remembered that he was there, and asked him:

"And now where'll you go?"

"I don't know," said Ieli.

"Tomorrow come and see me and I'll help you find a job. Tonight, go back to the square where we were listening to the band; you'll find some room on a bench, and as for sleeping in the open, you must be used to it."

He was used to it all right, but what hurt him most was that Mara didn't say anything to him, and left him just like that at the doorway, like a tramp; so that he told her about it the next day, as soon as he could find her alone in the house for a moment:

"Oh, Mara! How you forget your friends!"

"Oh, it's you, Ieli!" said Mara. "No, I haven't forgotten you. But I was so tired after the fireworks!"

"Do you love *massaro* Neri's son at least?" he asked, turning his staff over and over in his hands.

"What are you talking about?" answered Mara bluntly. "My mother's right in the next room and can hear everything."

*Massaro* Agrippino found him a job as shepherd at Salonia, where *massaro* Neri was the factor; but since Ieli was new to this kind of work, he had to be satisfied with a very poor salary.

Now he was busy tending his sheep, and learning how to make cheese, and *ricotta*,[14] and *caciocavallo*,[15] and all the other products of the herd; but when chattering in the courtyard in the evening with the other shepherds and peasants while the women shelled broad beans for the soup, if they started speaking of *massaro* Neri's son, who was going to marry *massaro* Agrippino's Mara, Ieli didn't say anything more and didn't even dare open his mouth. Once, when the field watchman made fun of him by saying that Mara had dropped him after everyone had said that they were going to be husband and wife, Ieli, who was busy watching the pot in which the milk was boiling, answered, as he slowly and carefully stirred in the rennet:

"Mara's prettier now that she's grown up, she's like a rich young lady."

Since he was patient and a hard worker, he quickly learned everything about his job better than one who had been born to it, and since he was used to staying with animals, he loved his sheep as if they were his own children; the "disease," therefore, didn't cause such a slaughter at Salonia, and the herd prospered so that it was a pleasure for *massaro* Neri every time he came to the farm, and as a result, at the beginning of the following year, he decided to induce the owner to raise Ieli's salary, and so Ieli now got almost as much as he had been earning as horsekeeper. And it was money well spent, for Ieli never counted the miles and miles he covered looking for better pastures for his animals, and when the sheep gave birth or were sick he took them to the pasture in the saddlebags of his little donkey, and carried in his arms the lambs, who bleated in his face with their noses out of the sack, and suckled his ears.

In the famous snowstorm on Saint Lucy's night, more than three feet of snow fell in the Lago Morto at Salonia, and all around for miles and miles, as day came you couldn't see anything else in the whole countryside.—*Mas-*

[14] A type of cottage cheese made by heating the curd that is left after cheese has been extracted.

[15] A special kind of full-cream cheese made in southern Italy.

*saro* Neri would have been ruined that time, as were so many others in the region, if Ieli hadn't gotten up three or four times during the night to chase the sheep around in the corral, so that the poor animals shook the snow off and didn't get buried like so many in the near-by herds—at least that's what *massaro* Agrippino said when he came to take a look at the little field of broad beans he had at Salonia, and he also said that the other story about *massaro* Neri's son marrying his daughter Mara wasn't true at all, for Mara had anything but that on her mind.

"But people said they were supposed to get married at Christmas!" said Ieli.

"It's not true at all, they weren't supposed to marry anybody! It's all just gossip of envious people who stick their noses in somebody else's business," answered *massaro* Agrippino.

But, after *massaro* Agrippino had gone, the field watchman, who knew all about it because he had heard the talk in the square when he went to town on Sunday, told how it really was: they weren't going to get married because *massaro* Neri's son had found out that *massaro* Agrippino's Mara was carrying on with Don Alfonso, the rich young man, who had known Mara since she was a little girl; and *massaro* Neri had said that he wanted his son to be honorable like his father, and the only kind of horns he wanted in his house were those of his oxen.[16]

Ieli was there too, seated with the others in a circle, having lunch, and at that moment was slicing bread. He didn't say anything, but he lost his appetite for the whole day.

While he was driving the sheep to pasture, he began to think of Mara again, when she was a little girl and they spent the whole day together and walked in the Valle Del Iacitano and on Poggio Alla Croce, and she watched him

[16] In Italy people say that cuckolds "wear horns." This expression was already very common in Boccaccio and in the writers of the Italian Renaissance and passed to English Renaissance literature through their works. In our time Italians apply it also to wives of unfaithful husbands.

with her chin in the air as he climbed up to get the nests at the tops of the trees; and he also thought of Don Alfonso who used to come and see him from the near-by villa, and they would lie flat on their stomachs in the grass to tease the crickets in the nests, with a little twig. Sitting on the edge of a brook, his arms around his knees, for hours and hours he kept turning over in his mind all these things, and the high walnut trees at Tebidi, and the thick bushes of the valleys, and the slopes of the hills green with sumacs, and the gray olive trees that covered the valley like fog, and the red roof of the big house, and the bell tower, "that looked like the handle of a saltcellar" among the orange trees of the garden.—Here the countryside spread out before him barren, desolate, speckled with scorched grass, fading silently into the faraway suffocating heat.

In the spring, as soon as the broad-bean pods began to bend down with weight, Mara came to Salonia with her father and mother and the boy and the little donkey, to pick the beans, and they all came to sleep at the farm for the two or three days the harvest lasted. So Ieli saw the girl morning and evening, and they often sat side by side on the little wall of the sheepfold, talking together, while the boy counted the sheep.

"It's like being at Tebidi," said Mara, "when we were small, and used to be together on the little bridge of the path."

Ieli remembered it all too, although he didn't say anything, because he had always been sensible and a boy of few words.

When the harvest was over, the evening before she left Mara came to say good-by to the young man, while he was making *ricotta* and was intent on skimming the whey with the ladle.

"I'll say good-by now," she said, "because tomorrow we're going back to Vizzini."

"How did the broad beans go?"

"Bad! The rust ate them all up this year."

"We didn't have enough rain," said Ieli. "Just think, we had to kill even the ewe lambs because they didn't have anything to eat; all over Salonia there weren't even two inches of grass."

"But it doesn't make much difference to you. You always have your salary, good crops or bad!"

"Yes, it's true," he said, "but I hate to hand those poor animals over to the butcher."

"Remember when you came for the fiesta of Saint John, and you didn't have a master?"

"Yes, I remember."

"It was my father who found you a job here, with *massaro* Neri."

"And you, why didn't you marry *massaro* Neri's son?"

"Because it wasn't the will of God . . . My father's been unlucky," she went on after a while. "Since we went to Marineo everything has gone wrong, the broad beans, the wheat, that piece of vineyard we have up there. Then my brother had to go into the service, and we lost a mule that was worth forty *onze*."

"I know," answered Ieli, "the bay mule!"

"Now that we've lost so many things, who'd want to marry me?"

Mara was breaking a little prune shoot to pieces while she was talking, her chin on her breast and her eyes low, and she nudged Ieli's elbow a little with her own, as if by accident. But Ieli didn't say anything, his eyes on the churn; so she went on:

"At Tebidi they used to say we were going to be husband and wife someday, remember?"

"Yes," said Ieli, and put the ladle down on the edge of the churn. "But I'm a poor shepherd and couldn't dream of marrying a *massaro's* daughter, like you."

Mara remained silent for a little while, and then she said:

"If you love me, I'd be glad to marry you."

"Really?"

"Yes, really."

"And what will *massaro* Agrippino say?"

"My father says you know your job now, and you're not one of those who squander their salary but you make two pennies out of one, and you hardly eat in order not to use up the bread, so someday you'll have sheep of your own and you'll get rich."

"In that case," concluded Ieli, "I'll be glad to marry you too."

"Here!" Mara said to him after it became dark, and the sheep were quieting down little by little. "If you want a kiss now, I'll give it to you since we're going to be husband and wife."

Ieli took it meekly, and not knowing what to say, added:

"I've always loved you, even when you wanted to leave me for *massaro* Neri's son . . ." But he didn't have the heart to talk about the other one.

"See? We were meant for each other!" concluded Mara.

In fact, *massaro* Agrippino said yes, and Lia hurriedly put together a new jacket and a pair of velveteen pants for her son-in-law.

Mara was as beautiful and fresh as a rose, with a white mantilla that looked like the Easter Lamb, and an amber necklace that made her neck look white; so Ieli, going along the street at her side, walked straight and stiff, all dressed up in new wool and velveteen, and didn't dare blow his nose with his red silk handkerchief, not to call people's attention to him; but the neighbors and all those who knew the story of Don Alfonso laughed in his face. When Mara said "I will," and the priest, making a big sign of the cross, gave her to him as a wife, Ieli led her home, and he felt as if he had been given all the gold of the Madonna and all the land his eyes had seen.

"Now that we are husband and wife," he said to her when they got home, sitting opposite her and making himself very small, "now that we are husband and wife, I can tell you that I can't believe that you wanted me . . . when you could have had so many others better than I am . . . as beautiful as you are! . . ."

The poor man couldn't say anything else to her, and could hardly fit in his new clothes, so happy was he to see Mara arranging and touching everything and being the mistress of the house. So he didn't know how to tear himself away from the door to go back to Salonia; when Monday came, he lingered around as he arranged his bags, his cloak, and his umbrella of oilcloth on the packsaddle of the little donkey.

"You should come to Salonia too!" he said to his wife, who was watching him from the threshold. "You should come with me."

But the woman began to laugh, and answered that she wasn't born to be a shepherdess, and there was no reason for her to go to Salonia.

In fact, Mara wasn't born to be a shepherdess, and she wasn't used to the north wind of January when your hands stiffen on the staff and your fingernails seem to be falling out, and to the furious rainstorms when the water goes through to your bones, and to the suffocating dust of the roads when the sheep move along under the burning sun, and to the hard bed on the ground and to the moldy bread, and to the long silent and solitary days when in the scorched countryside you can see nothing but a rare sun-blackened peasant driving his little donkey silently ahead of him on the white, endless road. At least Ieli knew that Mara was warm under the covers, or spinning by the fire together with her neighbors, or that she was enjoying the sun on the balcony, while he was coming back from the pastures tired and thirsty, or drenched with rain, or when the wind drove the snow into his hut and put out the fire of sumac wood. Every month Mara went to get his salary from the master, and she was neither without eggs in the chicken coop, nor without oil in the lantern, nor without wine in the flask.

Twice a month Ieli went to see her, and she waited for him on the balcony with her spindle in her hand; then when he had tied the donkey in the stable and had taken off the saddlebags and put the feed in the manger, and had set the firewood in the shed in the yard, or put away whatever else he was carrying into the kitchen, Mara helped him hang his cloak on the nail and take off his drenched leggings in front of the fire, and poured him wine while the soup boiled gaily; and quiet and considerate like a good housewife she set the table, while she was talking to him of this and that, of the hen that was brooding, of the cloth she had on her loom, of the calf they were raising, without forgetting a single one of the little chores of the household, so that Ieli felt like a king there.

But on Saint Barbara's night he went home at an unusual hour, when all the lights were out in the little street, and the clock in the town was striking midnight. It was a night for wolves, and the wolf had gone into Ieli's house while he stayed out in the rain and wind for the love of his salary and of the master's mare, who was sick and needed the farrier right away. He knocked and stormed at the door, calling aloud for Mara, while the water poured down on him from the roof gutter and came out at his heels. His wife finally came to open the door and began to give him a tongue-lashing as if she had been the one to run around the fields in that bad weather, and she had such a look on her face that he asked:

"What's wrong? What's the matter?"

"The matter is that you scared me coming at this hour! Do you think this is an hour for Christians? Tomorrow I'll be sick."

"Go to bed, I'll light the fire myself."

"No, I've got to go and get some wood."

"I'll go."

"No, I say!"

When Mara came back with the wood in her arms, Ieli said:

"Why did you open the door to the courtyard? Wasn't there any more wood in the kitchen?"

"No, I went to get it from the shed."

She let herself be kissed, very coldly, and turned her head the other way.

"His wife lets him get drenched outside the door," said the neighbors, "when there's another bird inside!"

But Ieli didn't know that he was a cuckold, nor did the others take the trouble to tell him, since he didn't seem to care at all, and had taken the woman as she was, after *massaro* Neri's son had jilted her because he knew the story of Don Alfonso. Instead, Ieli was happy and content in his disgrace, and grew as fat as a pig, "for horns are thin, but keep the house fat!"

Finally one day, the herd boy told him to his face, when they were wrangling over some cheese that had been stolen by shaving off a piece at a time:

"Now that Don Alfonso has taken your wife, you think you're his brother-in-law, and you've become so conceited that you think you're a crowned king, with those horns on your head."

The factor and the field watchman expected to see blood flow at these words; instead, Ieli kept quiet as if it were none of his business, and he had such an idiotic look on his face that the horns suited him very well.

It was getting close to Easter now, so the factor sent the farm hands to confession, hoping that for fear of God they wouldn't steal any more. Ieli also went, and coming out of the church he looked for the boy with whom he had had words, and threw his arms around his neck saying:

"The father confessor told me to forgive you; but I'm not angry with you about what you told me; and if you don't shave pieces of cheese off any more, I won't care at all about what you said to me when you were angry."

It was from that moment on that they called him Golden Horns, and the nickname stuck with him and all his family even after he washed those horns in blood.

Mara had gone to confession too, and came back from church all huddled up in her mantilla, her eyes low, so that she looked like Saint Mary Magdalene. When Ieli, waiting for her in silence on the balcony, saw her come like that, and it was clear that she had the Sacrament inside her, he, as pale as death, kept looking her over from head to foot, as if he were seeing her for the first time, or as if they had changed her, his Mara, and he didn't even dare lift his eyes to her while she spread out the tablecloth and put the bowls on the table, calmly and neatly as usual.

Then after having thought about it awhile, he asked her coldly:

"Is it true you're carrying on with Don Alfonso?"

Mara fixed her beautiful, limpid eyes on his face and made the sign of the cross:

"Why do you want to make me sin on this holy day?" she exclaimed.

"No! I still don't want to believe it . . . because Don Alfonso and I were always together when we were boys, and not a single day passed that he didn't come to Tebidi . . . just like two brothers. . . . Then he's rich and has money by the shovelful, and if he wanted women he could get married because he's got bread and everything else."

Mara was losing her temper and began to give him such a tongue-lashing that he didn't raise his nose from his plate any more.

Finally, so that the food they were eating didn't turn to poison, Mara changed the subject and asked if he had thought of having someone hoe the flax they had sown in the broad-bean field.

"Yes," answered Ieli, "and the flax will be good."

"In that case," said Mara, "this winter, I'll make you two new shirts to keep you warm."

In short, Ieli simply didn't understand what "cuckold" means, and didn't know what jealousy was; every new thing was slow getting into his head, and this one was so big that it really had a devil of a time getting in especially when he saw his Mara before him, so beautiful and white and neat, and she herself had wanted him, and he loved her so much, and had thought of her for such a long time, for so many years, since he was a boy, so that when they had told him she wanted to marry somebody else he hadn't felt like eating or drinking the whole day.—And even when he thought of Don Alfonso, he couldn't believe that such a dirty trick was possible; he still could see him at Tebidi, with his kind eyes and his smiling little mouth coming to bring sweets and white bread, so long ago—such a dirty trick! And since he hadn't seen him any more, for he was a poor shepherd who stayed in the country the whole year round, he always remembered him that way.

But for the first time that, unfortunately, he saw Don Alfonso again, now a full-grown man, Ieli felt as if he had

had a blow in the stomach. How big and handsome he had become! With that gold chain on his vest, and the velvet jacket, and that smooth beard that seemed to be of gold too. Not conceited either; in fact, he slapped Ieli on the shoulder calling him by his first name. He had come with the owner of the farm and a group of friends for a picnic in the country at shearing time; and unexpectedly Mara had come too, under the pretext that she was pregnant and had a craving for fresh *ricotta*.

It was a beautiful, warm day in the golden fields with the flowering hedges and the long green rows of vines. The sheep were gamboling and bleating with pleasure at feeling themselves freed from all that wool, and in the kitchen the women were making a big fire to cook all the things that the owner had brought for dinner. Meanwhile, the rich men who were waiting had gone into the shade under the carob trees, and were having someone play the tambourines and bagpipes, and those who wanted to danced with the women of the farm.

Ieli, while he was shearing the sheep, felt something gnaw inside him, without knowing why, like a thorn, a driven nail, a pair of fine shears that worked around inside him bit by bit, worse than poison. The owner had ordered that they kill two kids, and the year-old wether, and some chickens and a turkey. In short, he wanted to do things in a big way, without stinting, so that he would make a good show in front of his friends; and while all those animals cried out in pain, and the kids screamed under the knife, Ieli felt his knees shake, and at times it seemed to him that the wool he was shearing and the grass, in which the sheep were gamboling, were aflame with blood.

"Don't go!" he said to Mara, when Don Alfonso was calling her to come and dance with the others. "Don't go, Mara!"

"Why not?"

"I don't want you to go. Don't go!"

"Don't you hear them calling me?"

He said nothing more; he had become dark and gloomy

like a gathering storm, while he was bent over the sheep he was shearing. Mara shrugged her shoulders and went to dance. She was flushed and gay, her black eyes looked like two stars, and when she laughed you could see her white teeth, and all the gold she was wearing beat and glistened on her cheeks and breast, and she looked just like the Madonna. All at once Ieli straightened up, the long shears in his fist, so white in the face, as white as his father, the cowherd, had once been, when he shook with fever by the fire in the hut. He looked at Don Alfonso—his fine curly beard, and the velvet jacket and the gold chain on his vest—who was taking Mara's hand and inviting her to dance; he saw him reach out with his arm, as if to press her to his chest, and she was letting him do it—then, God forgive him, he lost his head, and cut Don Alfonso's throat with a single stroke, just like a kid's.

Later, while they were leading him before the judge, bound, broken, without having dared offer the least resistance:

"What!" he said. "I shouldn't even have killed him? . . . But he'd taken Mara! . . ."

# GUIDO NOBILI

## 1850–1916

Guido Nobili (1850-1916) was a Florentine lawyer, not a professional writer. He left a novel and much material of a generally autobiographical character, the best of which was rediscovered and collected in 1942 by the Tuscan critic Pietro Pancrazi and published, under the title *Memorie lontane*, by the firm of Felice Le Monnier in Florence, one of the most respected and historically most important of Italian publishing houses. The present section from that book has appeared in isolation in Italian short-story anthologies and even in a screen version (as part of Blasetti's *Times Gone By*). I have chosen it not only because of its obvious charm but because from the point of view of both social milieu and narrative treatment it turns out to represent a *genre* which is sadly rare in modern Italian writing.

## *Idyl*

To tell the truth, I was not very pleased that the young ladies had made their appearance; I had a dislike for girls, because to me they seemed downright sick. With them you couldn't compete in running or jumping contests; for recreation they had only the silliest little games in which speed or agility or strength didn't matter. As far as I could

*Translated by Lowry Nelson, Jr.*

see, there was no use in talking with girls at all. I had no idea what things to talk about with them; and then, the way they played dumb, or teased, or acted silly, struck me as sinister, all the more so because there could be no decisive resort to blows as among boys. And above all, what made the company of girls most abhorrent to me was that I found them all, more or less, given to deceit and lying. If I had been able to follow my impulses, and if my upbringing had not restrained me, I would gladly have torn those hateful dolls from their necks and, twirling and tossing them in the air, finally smashed them to bits.

To me dolls were a phobia, like a red cloth to a bull; and all those endearing little words that good girls are in the habit of pronouncing over those plaster heads seemed to me such idiocy that I was unable to fathom it. And then, too, screams and screeches over a grasshopper! Fainting spells over a frog! Oh those girls! But by now the little ladies had infiltrated our group, and out of courtesy I had to tolerate them.

Among the boys who frequented the Square, of those I remember, there was the Marchese Emilio Pucci, who had many a falling-out with his tutor; now and then the Marchese Carlo Ginori would be there, chained also to a tutor who was rather stern; the Commendatore Edoardo Philipson, who in those days was not yet a Commendatore but showed even then all the good qualities that would make him one; also, a certain Pugi would come, whom I have seen since as a cavalry colonel, and these last two lived on Independence Square near me; there was Guglielmo Vestrini, and there were many others besides, to mention all of whom would take too much time.

Among the young ladies who used to come were two daughters of the Minister of State of the last government, His Excellency Landucci, a Miss Trollope (whose surname is world-famous), and others, all of the best and most respectable families.

Many of these regulars came each day, stayed inconspicuously for a while, and then left as others began to appear. In this way, without introductions, without formalities, friendships were formed which have lasted over the years. After ten minutes of social acceptance, one was addressed in the familiar form, and no one objected to this intimacy. The reader will forgive me if I have dwelt longer than I should on this side of the story, which may seem to him rather beside the point. But it was essential to know this, for shortly the sun will rise.

"What? The sun will rise?" someone may say. "Why bring the sun into it?"

Let him be patient and he will soon enough have a full accounting.

To that gathering everybody tried to bring some sort of trifle or trinket that might engross or amuse his friends; puzzles, for instance—that is, those knots made of two pieces of metal, which if you know how and have the patience you can disentangle. Some one of us, whose name I don't recall, obviously full of imagination, attracted our attention in order to show us the red fire he had invented. He had powdered some brick, wrapped it in a piece of paper, and setting it afire, announced that it should give off a red flame. Who knows what other disappointments, more serious, the poor fellow must have encountered in his world later on!

One evening, just before sunset, one of the boys of our band had brought some Pharaoh's Serpents which he lit on a bench. I had never seen anything like it, because at home, in spite of the New Freedom, fireworks, gunpowder, and anything that might have caused personal injury or fire danger, had been strictly forbidden me, almost as if I were being kept under a state of siege.

Between Serpents one of my friends pointed out to me a girl about my age, and said, "Look at that girl buzzing around us; she's curious to see too. She's awfully pretty."

His bright remark, "She's awfully pretty," made me feel rather hostile toward him, because I could find no reason within me to admire beauty or ugliness in human shape. I thought whatever was good was beautiful; ugliness, then, was wickedness, and that girl, I thought, must be goodness in person, since to me she looked like one of those delicate images of angels or seraphim. It was something vague, which reminded me at the same time of Jesus, the Madonna, Paradise, wreaths of flowers, sunrise, fragrant odors, rainbows, and I felt unhappy that the circle crowding about the bench kept her from seeing. And so I said to my friend, "Let's make room for her and you go ask her to come over here. She must be well-bred, she dresses very nicely."

"You go. I want to see the next Serpent," he replied rather ungraciously.

Having noticed that we were talking about her, she averted her enormous eyes, and ran off turning the rope she was jumping; and running hither and yon capriciously like a dragonfly, she came to a halt over there near a bench on which sat a little boy, a scowling rascal, who nevertheless resembled her.

I say he resembled her, but let's agree. They were brother and sister—that was clear enough. Yet they resembled each other the way one day resembles another, just because they are both days and children of the same year, with the same possibility of difference that exists between a fair day and a foul.

While intent on the sparkling Pharaoh's Serpents, we suddenly heard from the direction of Via San Carlo the pounding of horse's hoofs and the quick clatter of carriage wheels: it was a runaway horse. Coming straight for the Square, the animal in its blind frenzy failed to see the chains that stood in its path and smashed right into them; and in falling to the ground it utterly ruined the carriage it was dragging behind.

Hearing everyone shout and all that confusion, we children instinctively drew together, full of fear, and closed ranks as if we had been a school of fish; and by instinct of self-preservation even the pretty girl dropped her jumping rope and, protectively hugging her brother to her breast, scarcely smaller than she, fearfully took refuge among us.

Those who had been brought by their tutors to partake of some heart-easing refreshment, and those who had been brought by their governesses for a drink somewhere, and those whose houses were on the Square, all were immediately sent for. Since my friend who owned the fireworks was unable to find his nurse (who perhaps had gone off to seek comfort from some sergeant of the near-by fort), I brought him home for a breather, and he secretly made me a present of a Serpent, which I hid in the darkest corner of my room.

Next day I was not given permission to go to the Square, since the Order of the Day, to use the military expression, included me in prescribing a ride through the Cascine.

There was absolutely nothing I found more tedious and more disagreeable than carriage-rides through the Cascine. My mother, my grandfather and I went off to the Cascine, silent and listless. First we went up and down, and then we went down and up, along the drives. We greeted lots of people in the other carriages, and we were greeted in turn. Then the carriage stopped in the Square near the brass band (that band I hated so because it deafened me to the pit of my stomach), and after we had listened to something or other, our pair of horses drew us along the Arno as far as the Pegaseo, where all three of us, together with our servant Leopoldo who followed (and whom I would have taken into my confidence in conversation but for the constraint of the occasion), got out and walked two or three hundred yards toward the city. Then we got into the carriage again and at last headed home to get ready for dinner. The only pleasant memory I have of those excursions was the appearance of rabbits which might either be dashing for the meadows or standing their ground in the middle of the street. Then, if the latter should happen, I was allowed to abandon the rigid composure that had been taught me as the customary behavior of those who rode in carriages, and to look out on the road between the coachman and the servant who were careful to notify me when the rabbit came into view.

That day Basilio was no longer in our service. Not only had he been sent away from our house, but also the Barone Ricasoli, who had been his protector, had chased him out of Tuscany, because, as head of the provisional government, he was in a position to know for a fact that Basilio was an Austrian spy.

Why was it that Basilio had done us no harm, since he knew all about the perilous conspiracies in our house? "His love for the maid," said Uncle Nicola; "that must have saved us. To avoid leaving her, he must have stolen his reward for spying by gobbling it all up, leaving us alone. Our family, then, owes a debt to love, if only to show it our gratitude."

Apart from the annoyance of those hours of immobility, carriage-rides caused me the torture of "getting ready," an unchanging ritual which the maid forced me to undergo. When we went to the Cascine or to the theater, I had to change all my clothes and allow my ears and neck to be washed with great quantities of suds. And that gave rise to bitter quarrels with Teresa, because her nails scratched me or because my ears got full of water or because soap got in my eyes. While I was undergoing this scouring, I might well have served as the model for that delightful statue of the "bad boy" which made the Florentine sculptor Foscardi famous in London.

Fortunately this "getting ready" with a vengeance was not a daily occurrence, since they seldom took me to the theater; and as for the Cascine, one day I would go with my mother, and another day Aunt Maddalena would go with my cousin Carlo, and then, when it was my mother's turn again, she would take my brother Aldo with her. So, counting rainy and windy days, all that squealing and carrying on, as Teresa would say, became at least bearable.

On that very day, when it came time to change my shirt, it was discovered that one cuff had only half of a gold cufflink with just a bit of the chain left dangling from the buttonhole; but the chain was broken and the little bar was gone.

"Oh, what a thing to happen! Just think what mother will say!" we said to each other, Teresa and I; and the shadow of the switch flashed before my mind's eye.

"Where can you have lost that piece of cufflink?" Teresa asked me. "Did you have it this morning?"

I didn't recall that I'd given it any notice, but it occurred to me that the day before, in the midst of all the confusion over the runaway horse, the friend who was standing next to me had, out of fright, seized me forcibly by the sleeve in an effort to draw me toward him, and might very well have broken my cufflink chain, and the little piece of it might have fallen to the ground, and could possibly be there still, if, hidden in the gravel, it had not caught someone's eye. I shared my surmise with Teresa, and begged her to go look.

"You go. Do you think I can go to the Square this way with my cap and apron on, and without a hat? I'd have to ask permission and go change my clothes. You go."

After Teresa had agreed to provide my excuse for going to the Square without permission, I put on my cap, slipped out the door and ran to the bench where the fireworks had been the day before.

The gravel on the Square had been put there only a few days before; it was therefore still quite thick and I had to scratch here and there to see if that little cufflink bar would show itself. While I was hunched over, intent on my search, I observed out of the corner of my eye the arrival from Via Barbano of that girl, along with her brother and her mother. The three of them went and sat down on a bench just a short distance away.

"Here come those awful people," I said to myself. "You can't ever go about your own business without being bothered by something."

My annoyance at being seen looking for something derived in particular from my idea of propriety: it seemed to me humiliating to be seen grubbing for lost objects, whether gold or not, in the middle of a square like a street sweeper. A gentleman, so I thought, is degraded when he bends over in a humiliating posture like this, because, though a gentleman may possibly lose something, he certainly doesn't look for it; at most he may put up notices on the corner of buildings asking people to retrieve it, while here I am rooting in the dirt.

And to escape the glances of the three seated on the

bench, without standing up I turned my back on them and continued my search.

I heard the rhythmic clatter of the girl who had begun to jump the rope. I heard her go off and then return, only to stop near me. She was watching me two paces behind my back. Since I was quite incapable of holding that bent posture forever, I rose up in great annoyance and turned to look. With a smile that I found charming, she asked me in French whether I had lost something.

Never in my life had I heard such lovely harmony as in that voice; I felt in it the touch of a caress, in a way rather like my father's voice when he would spring a surprise on me and say, "This evening we're going to see the puppets." And I felt all this inside me, despite her having addressed me in French.

I was studying French at the time; but as for speaking it, that was a horse of a different color, since I hadn't had much practice. Besides, that French language is so slippery it eludes the thick tongues of us descendants of the Etruscans. I've always felt just how French ought to be pronounced; but that terrible *u*—before you can get it out in proper French fashion, you have to make an enormous effort to screw up your lips to the proper aperture. By living in France I've reached the point of being able to think, and even to dream, in French; but whenever I've had to speak it, it's always been a trial, so much so that in comparison towing a barge strikes me as simple and pleasant work. Many Tuscans, in fact almost all of them, speak French, but it's not the French that I hear inside of me; our tongues grow thick and stupid when they have to sputter French. Every time I've come back to Italy, even the customs inspector, the barbarous customs inspector, has seemed amiable, since with him I could throw off the weight that held my tongue in check while abroad, and could once again speak quickly and freely without calculation and without hesitancy in Italian, which is a language so hard to write well but so easy and flowing to speak.

Being caught at close quarters and with no warning by the pretty creature, I had to avoid cutting a bad figure and threw myself headlong into French; and to make the best of it I answered that I had lost a little gold cufflink. To say "cufflink," since I didn't trust the word that came to mind, I told her that what I had lost was a gold *button*.

She called her brother over to help me (it was then that I heard he was called Giacomo), and all three of us set about patiently hunting. A while later even their mother got up from the bench and came over to us.

I was now hoping inwardly that we wouldn't find the cufflink, since I would look awfully silly if we unearthed that minute little piece of gold which I was hunting as if it were the most precious of jewels.

Just then, the mother pointed to the ground under the bench and spoke to her daughter in a different language, which was not French at all, and the daughter, following her mother's directions, drew out from under the bench the little gold bar we were looking for.

I thanked them all, rather awkwardly; and I was going toward home when the family carriage stopped at the door, just at the moment when my grandfather and mother were coming out of the doorway.

I went right up to them, and before they began to question me, I showed my mother the little piece of cufflink, which then the servant was told to hand over to Teresa, who by the way stood at the first-floor window, anxious perhaps to see what turn my discomfiture over the lost cufflink might take.

I was the last to get into the carriage, and I saw all three of my new acquaintances standing near by to watch our departure. Before the horses began to pull away, the little girl waved good-by to me and flashed a farewell with her eyes, and I raised my cap in answer. My mother turned to look at them and could not help exclaiming, "What a beautiful child! She's an absolute wonder. I've never in my life seen the like. Who are they?" she asked me, since I had waved to them.

With a touch of surliness I answered, "I don't know them, but they're the ones who helped me find my cufflink. That girl isn't really as pretty as you say: her nose and forehead are all in a straight line. When she was still a baby they must have knocked her face against a wall to make her profile straight like that."

"You poor child, you'll never be an artist. That is a Greek profile, one of the purest, the most classic, the sort that until now I had seen only on ancient statues and never on a living person."

My mother was an artist; she painted portraits in oils, and so she knew all about lines. But I hadn't exactly made that remark because it was the truth; rather, more than anything else, it was to dispel a fear that I actually liked the girl.

I must confess the truth of the matter, that that profile was something new to me, and that it reminded me vaguely of a papier-mâché mask I once owned, and for that reason it had seemed to me a defect.

I should explain that what embarrassed me most in relations with the female sex, and what drove me, almost with criminal slyness, to hide them, was the fear of being teased by my uncles who found in everything an occasion and an excuse to have fun at my expense. If they were to say "Look! Look! Our Micio is in love!" I would die of shame.

To be a lover, according to the notion I had formed, meant to be someone who went around lame in the head, who made himself look ridiculous with the oddities of sighing and writing verses, only to go at night to play the guitar under his beloved's window and have buckets of water thrown on his head.

It seemed to me that if a lover allowed his fancy to go beyond all limits and if he publicly showed his oddity, he must certainly find himself the laughingstock of street-urchins, as were in those days *So' Cesare bombò* and "The Stump," a certain Orlandini who drowned himself in the Giardino dei Semplici. For that reason, I never let myself be caught admiring feminine graces, so as to avoid incurring, even by mistake, the taunts of anyone.

For the time being, human vanity had been paid its due with the excursion to the Cascine, and the following day, which was fine and clear, I was free to go visit my friends in the Square. I was the first to arrive.

After a while, the foreign girl arrived with her brother Giacomo. I kept rather to myself, but when I saw that they were coming in my direction I went out to greet them, darting a glance at the windows of my house for fear that someone might see me on good terms with a pretty girl.

We shook hands just as if we had been grown-ups, and then gradually we moved away from that corner of the Square and walked toward the one opposite, thus eluding the line of vision from my house, where I was fearful of mocking and teasing.

Children's friendships are quickly formed; in fifteen minutes we had become as intimate as if we had known each other for years. I was at once very glad, since she, in contrast to her brother Giacomo who remained closemouthed, told me with charming gaiety that she would be very happy to speak Italian just for practice.

You can imagine how glad I was to escape the torture of speaking French. Only then did I feel *myself*, and leader of the conversation as well, capable of showing off my usual tricks.

"You aren't Italian, are you? What country do you come from?" I asked.

"We're Greek," she answered affably.

At that moment I admired my mother's insight, and the profile of my new friend struck me as divine.

"What are your names?"

"His name is Giacomo, and mine is Matilde Elizabeth; but most of the time my family calls me Filli. And what's your name?"

"My name is Guido, but at home they call me *Micio*."

"*Miccio*? What does *Miccio* mean in Italian?"

"In Italian *Miccio* would mean 'donkey'; but my name is pronounced *Micio*, which means, well, 'kitten.'"

And changing the subject, I added, "Yesterday when my mother saw you, she said that you were very pretty."

"And you don't think so?"

Oh, oh! I was at once caught in a dilemma. How could I extricate myself? If I say yes, that she is pretty, I thought to myself, she may think I'm in love with her, and never in my life will I fall in love. If I say no, it would be rude, a coarse gesture I don't care to make and which she doesn't deserve. And to gain time to think up an answer that would save the situation, I looked for a moment into her eyes.

What it was I saw deep in those violet eyes, I don't know; I had the impression, looking into them, that my neck began to stretch and my throat to arch backward; I felt something like what I imagine the nightingale feels under the gaze of the serpent. To break the spell I shook myself, and could not help saying, "You're not pretty, you're beautiful!" And then, with a spin, a jump, a silly laugh, I ran off and circled round her at a distance. She spread out her rope and came toward me jumping, with Giacomo beside her, and the three of us then ran to the corner of Via Barbano, where the usual crowd had begun to gather.

I found that among the arrivals there was a certain commotion. The day before, in my absence, a border dispute had arisen between them and the gang of boys from the other corner. Because one of our crowd had happened to land over there, they had stopped him and told him that they considered us Germans and that they would give us all the next day to abandon our usual corner of the Square, and for the time being they would allow us to retreat to the south, half the Square away.

"But that's bullying," some one of us said. "If anybody's German, they are. We're Italian."

"Let's wait for them," said another, "and give them a good fight."

"Really? Is that another of your bright ideas? If we make an uproar in the Square, we won't be sent here any more."

"Let's tell the patrol," I suggested.

This proposal was accepted as the most practical.

When we spied two municipal guards, who were listlessly circling the Square, we went up to them in a group and explained our difficulty. But with that stolid listlessness which was, is, and always will be the essential nature of all municipal guards, they answered us sententiously: "The Square is for everybody; no one has the right to chase you away." Then, like sloths, they continued on their way.

So we were back where we had started.

That day none of my family took a drive in the Cascine because Pasha, one of our horses, had driven a nail in his hoof, and so my grandfather was quite alone in taking his constitutional around the Square. I saw him, stopped him, and told him about the threat that hung over us.

"Go home and you'll be better off," he answered.

I pretended to be convinced, but to me it would have seemed a dreadful act of cowardice to abandon my friends in danger; so I left him to continue on his way, pretended to go toward home, and then went back to throw in my lot with the others, who in the meantime had increased in numbers. At that moment, from the direction of Via San Francesco we could hear the approaching sound of thumping drums and crashing sheets of iron, all of which put us on guard against the enemy who would take the field in full warlike array. At long last, the mob of ragged urchins entered the Square in formation two abreast and came to a halt around a flagpole, which had been stuck in the ground right in front of our house for heaven knows what public holiday to come. At the base of the flagpole there was still a heap of stones and bits of mortar thrown up from underground during the digging.

We felt, to tell the truth, utterly dismayed; we gazed on the danger with no plan of action, having already abandoned any hope of legal defense.

It seemed to me that the bullying that threatened us was outrageous, so much so that I thought it impossible those boys would attack us since we had done them no harm; still, the shouts and insults they hurled at us convinced me that matters were serious, and I advised Filli and her brother to go home. But I was not heeded.

Without any real reason, without any exact purpose, but as a spontaneous impulse, I left my band of friends and

calmly walked toward the troop armed with wooden rifles
and tin sabers. I took even greater courage because on the
terrace of my house were a number of people. I wanted to
talk with the leader of those fanatics to make them quietly
see the light. When they saw me come toward them, they
ceased their clamor; then, just when I had got near them,
they suddenly started to run away, and only three or four
of the bigger ones stood their ground and began to aim
stones and bits of mortar at me. As I turned toward the
balcony where some of my family were, a stone hit me at
the temple, and though I didn't entirely lose consciousness,
my sight clouded over, my ears began to buzz, and I fell
to the ground.

Much later I saw the very same scene in the famous trio
from *I Lombardi*. When I was lifted up off the ground, my
grandfather supported me on one side, and on the other the
excellent Filli, who was weeping desperate tears and holding her handkerchief against my temple wound from which
a profusion of blood trickled. They took me home, where
before I arrived everyone had been in a state of agitation
over what had happened.

I was bandaged. After two hours I no longer felt any
pain at all; I was as good as new. But I had incurred parental discipline, and was sentenced to two days on bread
and water shut up in my room for having disobeyed my
grandfather who had enjoined me to return home—to
which was added the provocation of deplorable conduct,
deplorable because it was rowdy and common.

Imprisonment weighed on me to some degree; but it was
counterbalanced by the happy fortune of not going to
school. It was the bread and water that gave me pause.

I was confined; and my brother Aldo and my cousin
Carlo, who with a sardonic smile on their lips had witnessed the execution of the sentence, would come every
now and then, out of a desire to tease me, and scratch at
my door and compose doggerel about me. Once, while my
room was being cleaned, I was able to catch hold of one
of them and give him a slap or two. Hearing his cries, my
father arrived on the scene and then and there extended my

term of imprisonment, as if I were a hardened offender, by three more days.

But the bread and water were not of strict observance, since Teresa, in league perhaps with my mother, and perhaps even with my father, would bring me secretly (so she said) everything that was served at table.

To tell the truth, even with the advantage of not going to school, being pent up was a great tribulation, and my only comfort was the pretty canary in my room that sang all day long, and for which I had hoarded melon seeds to give to it.

On the second day I was in prison my mother came to deliver a sermon. First of all, she told me that my father, in view of my extreme rowdiness and the scandal of my ill-breeding in public at the risk of my life, had decided to shut me up in Volterra.

"In prison?" I asked anxiously.

"No, not in prison; but in a college, where they'll dress you up like a priest."

I started to smile, since it struck me as a curious idea to be dressed up like a priest. Heaven only knows, I thought in a flash, what tricks and what jerks on my tunic Aldo and Carlo would inflict on me.

"But are you such a bad boy, then, such a lost soul? You just don't have any feelings; you even snicker at the threat of leaving your father, your mother, your whole family?"

"Aw," I said, twisting my mouth and with tears in my eyes, "if papa wants to send me to Volterra what can I do about it? He's the one who decides. I got hit in the head with a stone by some boys I never did any harm to. I take the punishment you give me without complaining. Is it my fault then if you want to send me away even to Volterra?"

My mother cut me short; tears were coming to her eyes too. She got up and went out, not saying another word; only, just before she closed the door, as if to clear herself, she tossed a phrase at me, which seemed to me at the time out of place: "I'm sorry, my boy, that you have so little heart."

It was a legend that had grown up about me at home,

that I had little heart. That is a story in itself. Once, some time before, I had been taken to the Teatro alla Pergola, where Verdi's opera *Il Trovatore* was being performed. At that age I was interested not in the music but in the action of the opera; indeed, I deplored the fact that the performers sang instead of speaking their lines, thus preventing me from making head or tail of the plot.

It was the custom among people of rank not to remain in the theater until the very end of the performance. Long before the end of the last act they would leave their stalls and go to the foyer, where they would wait until the doorman announced that the carriage of such-and-such a family was at the entrance. Only peasants would wait until the very end of the performance, not good families. But that evening I was interested to know how the opera would finish, and while they were stuffing me into my cape I asked my father earnestly just how the Trovatore finally ended up.

"They'll kill him in a minute or two, and it's all over," he replied.

"Well, now I understand!" I told myself. "We're leaving before the end, so that I won't be here to watch the slaughter."

"But tell me," I asked again, "do they kill a Trovatore every night?"

My mother, who heard the question, was dumbfounded. "What?" she said. "Did he think, standing there so calmly, with such composure, that that man would *really* have to be killed, and he goes home without a care? But he's a monster of a child, a little Nero. He has no heart!"

The episode was made known in the family, and that evening on the dinner menu one of my uncles had them write, in place of roast swifts, roast Trovatori.

Was I bad at heart? No one knew how to judge my state of mind: that was the long and short of it. I had thought—because I was utterly incapable of allowing that my father might say something that was not true—I had thought that that Trovatore had to be killed. But there he was, calmly singing. Everybody seemed quite unaffected watching him hasten toward his death. My father and my mother showed no sign of concern. Out of the whole audience why should I be the one to rise up, I who had so many times felt upset when in the country I had heard my mother order, with the mastery of a tyrant, a capon's neck to be wrung?

But there was another act, much more serious, inscribed against me in the family blackbook. I had shed blood; unfortunately, innocent blood, as I discovered later.

Uncle Cesare had made me a present of a fine white Paduan hen, with splendid head-feathers that hung down over its eyes. As soon as we had reached our country house in Impruneta, I let the hen out so that it could enjoy its freedom. A black old barnyard cock came over at once, seized the head-feathers, tore them off and stamped on them. I chased it away, but soon after it began the outrage all over again. To protect my poor hen, I took up a stone and threw it at that wretched animal, which, hit by mere chance at the head, went rolling on the ground and, clawing the air as if it were knitting, finally breathed its last.

After committing this slaughter, I was so taken aback that I didn't know but what I should head for the woods. But already the crime had been discovered; there were too many witnesses against me. I underwent the punishment I had earned; and the reputation of being a bad boy without heart stuck to me.

When my mother had left me in my prison, I opened the window. My room was on the second floor, and I set about watching the sparrows that came and went in flocks, alighting on a laburnum bush in front of the stable, on which in other days I used to drape limed strings in an attempt to snare them. Then I turned my gaze toward the Philipsons' garden; beyond that garden stretched out the houses on Via Barbano, all of which I could see very well, even as far as the first floor and even just a bit of their little gardens. At the top of a broad marble staircase in one of those houses, a lady was sitting on a wicker chair doing needlepoint. While I was watching her to discover whether the furious fluttering of her hands around that green muff was a game or a chore, a little girl appeared on the threshold of the house. It was Filli. I recognized her at once.

I was at a loss to know how to make her see me. First I clapped my hands several times, but she continued to talk with her mother without showing any awareness of me. Then I tried whistling, but whistling too was useless. And then I lost patience and, cupping my hands, began to call to her as loudly as I could.

She turned, saw, and recognized me. She pointed me out to her mother and they both waved. But I had to draw in at once, because someone was approaching my prison. The door opened. It was my father.

"What's wrong that you have to shout?" he asked benignly.

"I was saying hello to a friend of mine over there," and I pointed in that direction. But he took no notice. He told me to sit down to hear what he had to say. "You would still have to stay shut up another day, but thanks to your mother's intercession, I'm letting you out. But, make no mistake, if the same spectacles happen again, off you go to Volterra. On the double!"

And he opened the door for me, and I slipped through with all the haste of a finch that sees a stick of its cage broken. My brother and cousin welcomed me with that same mocking smile with which they had greeted me when they saw me being locked up. But without rancor we all went off together to the stable to see Pasha, who was very ill because of his leg and who at that moment had just been visited by the veterinary.

Before dinner I wanted to go up to my room again to see if I could spy Filli; but I found the garden deserted and the glass doors shut. Thinking she might be in the Square, I went to the front windows. I was unable to see her there either, and in fact I could see neither friends nor enemies.

I found out from my brother and cousin that there had been some disagreement between my uncles and my father on my account. I discovered that my uncles thought I had done right in confronting those little urchins and that the

Square had returned to a state of calm because the local magistrate himself, when he was informed, had ordered the police to be very vigilant, and the rowdy boys had been banished. But also, unfortunately, our own good friends had thinned out because they were afraid that the disturbances might begin again.

The tape was still on the wound at my temple, and I was ashamed to show myself in public with that patch on my face. But I had to go to school, and that forced me to expose myself to view, along with the lesser annoyance of telling what had happened, which, according to my opinion at the time, did not make me cut a very good figure since I had been picked up off the ground by my grandfather and by a girl, as if I were a wet rag.

When I encountered Filli again I was all healed; you could see only the redness of the scar. Filli was with her mother and brother, and all three of them made a lot of me, as if I had escaped a great danger of which I was unaware. They were walking homeward, and, deviating a bit from the Square, I accompanied them to their door. When we arrived, her mother invited me in, and Filli, with gentle constraint, insisted, because her father had expressed a desire to meet me.

To tell the truth, I was a little frightened at this insistence, first of all, because entering someone else's house without being authorized by my family seemed to me something that might revive the idea of Volterra; secondly, because a father, even Filli's, inspired me with awe, as did all fathers, after the manner of the Eternal Father. But I failed to make out a case, and went in.

This father of Filli's was employed by a bank and also wrote. He spoke neither Italian nor French. On his head he wore a fez with a long tassel of black silk. He had lost an eye, his face was dark reddish, with mustache and black pomaded hair, and he had a bull neck. When he came into the room and was told who I was, he made a long discourse in Greek, and drawing me to him, caressed my head. Filli acted as interpreter and translated for me all that her father had said: to wit, that he was glad to meet a little boy worthy of the fatherland of Garibaldi who all by himself had been able to confront a gang of little aggressors.

As soon as I could, to avoid trouble, I ran to take refuge in my own house; but at heart I was uneasy, because in receiving that praise worthy of a hero I felt like a thief. Indeed, where is my daring? I asked myself; in what way did I show courage in that affair? I got hit on the head by a rock; but if I had known beforehand that those ragamuffins were going to throw stones, I feel it in my heart that I would not have gone out to meet them. If I advanced in their direction it was not to challenge them, since I had calculated that they would not be so treacherous as to attack me. Heaven knows how many heroes must have been in my boots! As I was leaving Filli's house, she saw me to the door and whispered to me, "We've been in town shopping, but now Giacomo and I will go back to the Square every now and then. Try to be there; I like being with you."

I toured all the rooms in my house so that everyone would see me and no one could suspect that of my own free will I had gone into someone else's house; then I returned to the Square. Filli was there jumping rope.

We sat down on a bench and I asked her why not come tomorrow, which was Sunday, to eleven o'clock mass at St. Mark's Church, where my mother was taking me; and I asked her which church she went to.

"But," she replied, "I don't go to your church; I'm Orthodox."

If someone at that moment had squeezed my heart, I would not have had so painful a feeling as I had at that news. I earnestly set about discovering how my religion differed from hers, because it was a question of knowing whether or not Filli would go to Hell for not being a regular Christian.

"But do you believe in God?" I asked her anxiously.

"Of course I do."

"And do you believe in Jesus?"

"I love Jesus dearly."

"And don't you believe in the Virgin?"

"How could anyone not believe in the good Mother of Jesus?"

I had forgotten the Holy Ghost; but I was to be excused for this, because I had never had occasion to invoke Him on my account.

"Well then, how are our religions different?"

"I really don't understand," said Filli, looking sadly into my eyes. "Maybe because our priests don't obey the Pope as yours do."

"Yes, that must be it."

When we said good-by I was in a melancholy mood. The idea that my good and pretty friend would have to go to Hell tormented my soul. I would like to have been well practiced in matters of religion in order to illumine her mind, save her soul, so that we would meet again in Paradise.

Up there in Paradise, how we would run, Filli and I! Without fear of Volterra, without the switch, and all day long together!

I went to see Aunt Luigia, who was the specialist in religious affairs at home; with the most circumspect diplomacy I questioned her on the subject that was so close to my heart.

"Tell me, Aunt," I began, "in what way is our religion different from the Orthodox?"

"In that it is different: ours is true and theirs is false."

"How do you tell true religions from false ones?"

"What an absurdity! There is only one true religion, which is ours, and all the rest are false."

I saw that we wouldn't sink to the bottom of things that way. Maybe not even Aunt knew about these differences and was just trying to extricate herself as best she could. Then I pressed her with subjects a bit nearer the heart of things.

"Well, it's this way. I have a friend I love very much, but he's Orthodox because that's his mother's and father's religion. Is it his fault that that's his religion? Even if he lived all his life like an altar saint would he have to go to Hell?"

"There is no help for it, he has to go to Hell."

This sharp verdict resounded in my soul like a death-dealing blow. I broke off further discussion with my aunt, and in utter dejection left her.

Saving Filli's soul became an obsession to me. I would like to have been a preacher; I would have wished for a miracle, just to rescue her from the pains of Hell.

One of those evenings, when I had got into bed and was thinking over the doleful prospects of Filli's soul, an idea flashed through my mind, a resolution. I extinguished the night-light so that "He who sees all and is in every place" might not catch me in the dark at what I was about to do. I took down the little picture of the Virgin I had at the head of my bed. I knelt down and, bringing the image close to my mouth as if I were speaking into her ear, I said to her more or less the following: "Dear Mary, most reasonable of the Saints, listen graciously to my prayer. It isn't a prayer for myself. It isn't a prayer in Latin like all the others. It's a private one of my own. But I beg you to listen to it and lift a heavy weight of sorrow from my heart. I know a girl, with whom I am not in love, but for whom I have a brotherly affection. But the poor thing—it's not her fault since she is Orthodox—will have to go to Hell. I'd like you to ask your Son, who loves you so well, to spare this innocent girl such suffering. Or, if it isn't possible to do otherwise, ask Him at least to allow me, if I behave well all my life, to give her my place in Paradise, and to go in her place to Hell."

I was trembling as I made this invocation. I thought I saw the Devil happily rubbing his hands in the certainty of being able sooner or later to snatch my soul. But I was resolute in this sacrifice, and it seemed to me that the Blessed Virgin ought not to look askance at it, since Filli, so lovely and charming, would have been a more beautiful ornament in Paradise than I could have been, all full of jumps and somersaults; and I would have trampled often enough the flowerbeds up there as I had done in our garden down here.

"Tell me, Aunt Luigia," I asked the next morning, "what

would God think of somebody offering to go to Hell in place of somebody else?"

"He'd pack them both off to Hell."

"Really? Even if Mary or Jesus asked Him to make the change?"

"What do they matter in comparison with the will of God?"

This disconcerting answer plunged me again into a state of confusion, and distressed me so that I left my aunt, took refuge in my room; and turning to the little picture of the Madonna, I looked at her lovingly, unable to say a word.

What with this upset in my innermost thoughts, things at school went badly; indeed, disastrously.

In spite of my aversion to school, up to that time I had not been among the most worthless pupils. But it was a serious drawback that the teacher himself was almost as much of a donkey as I. That school undertook a pretentious program; among other things, they taught philosophy and physics. Philosophy was the drivel that the teacher was able gropingly to extract from Taurino's treatise on logic. And as for physics, it was a clutter of nonsense we pupils were made to ingurgitate.

"Bodies," said the teacher in one of the first classes of physics, "adhere to the earth only because of the pressure exerted by the atmosphere above them. If you pumped all the air out of a room, the centrifugal force which derives from the rotation of the earth, in the absence of the opposing force of atmospheric pressure, would drive all the furniture to the ceiling."

"What a fine joke," I thought, "to play on some guest at the house in Impruneta, if I had an air pump like that."

"Man," said the teacher on another occasion in dealing with optics, "because of the special construction of the eye, perceives images upside down; it is by habit that he manages to see these images right side up. So it is that savages, who have never before seen a rising balloon, see it the first time upside down."

And these heterodox utterances concerning physical laws

were just the thing to repeat at home. Most of the time no one paid any attention to me; but one evening my father was listening to me and had me repeat what I had just said. Then he looked at me wryly and exclaimed, "Who in heaven's name made you swallow that bottleful of twaddle?"

"The teacher!"

"The teacher? Go on! I'll drop over myself and look into this. Lord knows what you've misunderstood."

"I'm telling you; it was the teacher who said it."

"That's enough, I say; that's enough. We shall see."

My father had said he would go and ask for an explanation; but I didn't like the idea much since in practice I already valued the aphorism "Let sleeping dogs lie." Who knows what might come of that interview, all the more since I was beginning to doubt whether I really had understood the lessons, even though I still heard echoing in my ears this or that word the teacher had used in teaching us those delightful aberrations of physics.

It was just about that time that my father received a letter from the teacher, containing two complaints. The first, that I had become careless about my studies; and the second, that the father of one of my schoolfellows had come to complain that I had made a deal with his son, selling him an explosive in exchange for a Japanese porcelain figurine that stuck out its tongue when you jiggled it, and that with this explosive my schoolfellow had succeeded in setting on fire a curtain in his room, causing great damage and frightening the whole family.

When I heard these weighty charges I felt miserable, because they were all quite true, and again I saw the specter of Volterra and the inseparable priest's garb rise before my eyes.

As for my studies, I had not done my homework because I was immersed in the questions of theology that concerned Filli. As for the explosive, this is the way things had happened. I had told one of my fellow pupils what a splendid thing the Pharoah's Serpents were, and confided in him that one of them had been given to me and that I guarded it jealously. He began asking me how you went about lighting this prodigious contraption; then, what the Serpent was like that emerged from the flame; and finally, he pressed me to make him a present of it. But I refused. He kept returning to the attack, trying to persuade me to hand it over, and one day he said, pulling out a tiny statue of colored porcelain hardly as big as a finger that stuck out its tongue when you jiggled it, "Look, if you promise to bring me the Pharoah's Serpent, I'll give you this toy of mine."

I was seduced by his offer, and the exchange was made. I would never have imagined that that idiot would then have set fire to a curtain.

"Tomorrow," said my father waving the teacher's letter, "you will not go to school; you will stay in your room. I will go to school in your place. Now give me that porcelain trinket, since that boy, as a minor, had no right to dispose of anything, supposing, though not granting, that he didn't pilfer from his father's parlor something that didn't belong to him."

"I don't have it any more."

"What do you mean you don't have it any more? What did you do with it?"

At this point I felt the impulse to tell a lie and say that the trinket was broken or that I had looked for it without finding it again; but lies were repugnant to me by nature, and I declared that I had given it away.

"To whom?"

*Dear Jesus, Holy Mary, rescue me,* I said inwardly without answering my father, *help me because I'm deep in trouble. I didn't think I was doing anything bad. One of you give me your hand and lift me out of this awful predicament.*

"Well, whom did you give the thing to?"

"To a girl," I replied, trembling.

"And did this puppet stick out its tongue?"

"It did."

"Go to bed," my father commanded, hiding in a frown the smile that had come upon him, perhaps from observing my abashed monkey-face; "tomorrow I'll see the teacher and we'll decide what's to be done with you."

The change from formal to intimate address was in him a sort of barometric gauge of his state of mind, kindly or stern, in my regard.

If my father had insisted that I give him that porcelain trinket and had ordered me to go ask it back from Filli, I would certainly have preferred to throw myself from the balcony rather than obey him.

It's true that children don't really understand much; but it's just as true that no one takes much trouble to help them understand. What was so improper about that swap between two boys? My friend was delighted to have the Pharoah's Serpent, and I was delighted to accept in return that little ceramic figurine. What difference could I possibly see between us and the much-praised merchants of Florence who had gained such an *honor'ble* reputation for themselves and for their city? Just this, that he went and set fire to the curtain! If this hadn't happened, all the trouble would have been avoided.

I had been so happy to make Filli a present of the Japanese figurine that stuck out its tongue. She had laughed so when she saw it. Her eyes had sparkled with gratitude when I offered it to her. All this had been for me a boundless pleasure, which I then had to pay for in large measures of fright, all because of that simpleton who made a bonfire of the curtain in his room.

There was no escaping the mocking jibes of Uncle Cesare. The way things were at home, you might have thought that in making that trade with my friend I had throttled him. Uncle Cesare would say to me in a nasal voice, "Light of my life, let's make a deal" or "Tell me, little Isaac, do you have any shekels? Where did you put the measuring rod?"; and on and on.

It often happens that we see a black future, that we find ourselves in great anxiety over pending events, and then nothing occurs; everything that had troubled us vanishes into nothing, like the fog that had been mistaken for a storm. My father's outing to see the teacher made me tremble for the consequences, which I was incapable even of anticipating. I knew that I would be judged guilty, that I would not feel the lack of unpleasantness. By this time I thought of myself as a poor rabbit frustrated at every turn, whether it takes to the hills or to the valley, to the garden or to the woods, whether it stands still or runs. Nevertheless, things turned out unexpectedly well.

"You know what?" my father said the next evening. "You're not going back to school. We're going to the country very soon, and next November you will go to the Charity School. Meanwhile your mother will teach you. That's what we have decided."

Well! What could have happened? I wondered. But this means freedom, life, at least for a while!

I went to tell my brother and cousin about my not going to school any more. Looking at me enviously, they asked me what I'd done to get such splendid results, since they too wanted to try the experiment. But since I had understood nothing of this miracle, I could hardly show them the road to take, especially since they went to a different school.

Teresa let me know confidentially that my father had told my mother that he had given the teacher a verbal drubbing, and for that reason it was no longer possible to send me to that school.

"So I was right, then," I said to myself; "I wasn't a blockhead not to understand." All the better now that, as a reward, all this free time has come upon me like rain from heaven.

"Look, look, Master Guido, there in the Square is your friend with his pretty little sister looking at the sky through a telescope." That is what Teresa, who had gone to close the parlor blinds, said to me one evening after dinner.

I ran to look; it was true. Passing the telescope from one to the other, they were looking upward in ecstasy. I looked up at the sky here and there, but I saw nothing unusual that would call for any special use of a telescope; my lively curiosity, therefore, pricked me to learn the cause of such rapt attention directed toward the sky. I got permission from my mother and ran into the Square to meet them.

"Look there," said Filli with her silver voice; "put this

tube to your eye and you'll see what a present papa has given Giacomo. For me he bought a box of oil paints so that I can paint flowers."

The telescope was in fact a fine kaleidoscope, rather a large one. In my time I had received many gadgets and toys; but I had never seen the likes of that. All that riot of colors that change constantly inside the tube delighted me, and if I had not been well brought up I would have enjoyed the spectacle all by myself.

When I handed the tube back to Giacomo, Filli asked what time it was.

"Listen. Right now they're striking the hour at the Palazzo Vecchio."

Filli listened carefully for the number of strokes and then turning to Giacomo, said, "Go on home. You have to take your medicine. Go, and come back soon. Leave your toy here with us; we'll wait for you here."

I took the tube from Giacomo's hand and he went slowly off toward home. Filli and I sat down on a bench.

"You know?" said Filli, breaking the silence, "papa and mama said you were very handsome and that you had an intelligent face."

This I had hardly expected to hear, and it troubled me greatly. I would like to have answered as she had done when I told her what my mother thought about her. But to say "What do *you* think?" would open the way to declarations I didn't want to make; and I didn't want to do so because for me they were the Unknown, which frightened me more than the dark, and I thought I'd get out of it by answering with an empty phrase.

"All men are handsome, or so I've heard tell."

"But not as handsome as you," Filli answered readily.

It was getting complicated. I felt like a chick in oakum. I didn't know what attitude to take; I would have needed an hour of concentration to find the right word for the situation I was in. And I was at a loss to do anything except put the kaleidoscope to my eye in a quick gesture that was meant to conceal the idiotic expression I felt I had on my face.

Filli said nothing, nor did I. But we couldn't stay that way forever, especially since I found myself looking, but not seeing, into the hole of the toy.

"How do we get back down to earth?" I said to myself as I turned the kaleidoscope. "How can I properly end this conversation with Filli?"

"Filli, if only you could see what a wonderful combination of colors! How nice it would be if only you could see. How can we manage it?"

"Hold the tube as tightly as you can, and hand it very slowly over to me."

"Then you come from the left."

I held the tube tightly to my eye, while Filli came cautiously nearer. When she was right next to my cheek and I felt her breath, she gave me a kiss!

I leapt up as if I had been touched with a branding iron. The surprise for me right then and there was so great that if I had been a dog I'm sure that without thinking I would have lunged and nipped her. In a flash I was looking at her with a scowl, as if she had impudently taken liberties with me; but on seeing her smiling and calm, looking at me with her two sparkling stars, I pulled a wry grimace, and to get more quickly to the bottom of a situation I found so bewildering, I hastily took up the kaleidoscope again and looked into the hole.

"You gave my arm a little push and the pretty pattern disappeared," I said, gurgling my words. "It still looks nice, but not the way it did."

"Oh, show it to me if it looks nice."

I hardly knew how I would manage to look her in the face again. Inside I felt the sort of tingling of a shiver which you feel at that age when you've had a fright or been in danger. At the place on my cheek (I still remember it) where Filli had kissed me, I felt the same sensation you feel on being touched by a jellyfish. Giacomo's return extricated me, all the more since he brought orders from her mother that she had to go home and change her dress to go visiting.

Though still rather embarrassed, I had begun to breathe

again, and I walked them as far as their corner. Filli seemed not even to remember what had happened between us. When we were on the point of saying good-by, as I was handing over the kaleidoscope to Giacomo and thanking him for the pleasure he had given me with that toy, Filli asked, "Don't you like Giacomo? He likes you a lot."

"Of course I like Giacomo," and as I said it I shook him by the hand.

"And don't you like me, then?"

"Very much," I answered, "very much."

My legs almost buckled on account of my feeling. I nodded to both of them; I raised my hat in farewell and then went my way, almost staggering; and I entered my house moonstruck.

My mother and brother were on the terrace, and I was sure they must have seen from up there everything that had happened; but I was reassured when I approached them since neither one took any suspicious notice of me.

I went to look at myself in the mirror, because it was fixed in my mind that the impress of Filli's kiss must be visible. There was nothing to see; but thinking back on that kiss I felt a pleasure that vaguely reminded me of the sweet sensation I had felt before when I had gone to bed shivering and had begun to relax in a well-warmed bed.

"What can it be," I wondered; "is the kiss of a pretty girl like the bite of a mad dog that begins to hurt only later? Am I in love? But as far as I know, boys don't fall in love."

The conversation that evening happened to turn to Dante. Uncle Cesare was saying, "There is nothing more tedious than the *Divine Comedy*. What a bore! And, you know, I've swallowed it whole, out of a sense of duty, twice in my life. But I had to give up trying it a third time, because after the second reading I was leaking bile, and I had to take a cure to get well."

Uncle Niccolò, on the other hand, had only praise for Dante. "I fully understand," he said, "that the *Divine Comedy* is not the sort of thing you can read straight through like a newspaper; but if you make a special study of it and consult the commentators, you finally come to appreciate its worth."

"No matter how you look at it," Uncle Cesare repeated, "Dante, even as a man, must not have been a very likable fellow. It's a fact that they sent him into exile, and at the court of Can Grande della Scala they tried to get rid of him by playing pranks, boring a hole in his chamberpot, and at table they piled up at his feet the bones of the whole dinner, as if to throw in his face how much he had eaten."

"But," remarked Uncle Niccolò, "can you be charging him with bad manners as a guest?"

"For me just one slip is enough to make him a square peg," insisted Uncle Cesare, "and that happened at the age of nine when he fell in love with Beatrice."

"Good heavens!" I said to myself, and my heart shriveled. "So all this talk about Dante was got up to take a secret dig at me? I know these uncles!"

I was mistaken. The discussion continued for a while, then slowly subsided without anyone ever looking in my direction. Only one thing in this discussion of Dante made me sad, and that was the news that boys were capable of falling in love at the age of nine; and, as a matter of fact, I had a sort of feeling about Filli that I had never before in my whole life experienced.

I hardly ate anything for dinner, an unusual thing for me. Besides—even more serious, never before witnessed till that moment—I had failed to finish my dish of whipped cream and sugar wafers. This drew my father's attention upon me, and turning to my mother, by whose side I sat at dinner, he said in a worried voice, "That boy is up to no good; he's hardly eaten a thing and his face looks as green as an unripe plum. Take a look at his tongue. He must have gobbled up a bowl of jujubes."

"After you've eaten, your tongue gives no sign of indigestion," broke in Uncle Niccolò who served as our doctor.

"Well then, without going into the matter," my father added, "tomorrow he must be given an ounce of castor oil."

I was not allowed to protest, and that evening the castor oil was expeditiously got ready to be administered the next morning. When I went to bed I felt hungry. I was unable to fall asleep, and succumbed to a sort of reverie. "I'm really in love," I thought. "I have the feeling that I'd like to be able to kiss Filli's cheek, just as she kissed mine. That's all there is to it. I give in. I'm in love."

And thereupon, giving free rein to my imagination, I fancied it late at night with lovely moonlight. I imagined myself in the middle of Via Barbano, singing to her, in a fine reedy voice, a love-ballad, accompanying myself on the guitar.

"So now I feel the need of a guitar," I confronted myself. "Well, that's it. There's no doubt about it, this madness could hardly be conceived except in a lover. But what could I actually say to Filli in a reedy voice accompanied by a guitar? I'd need a ballad, and written in poetry. How do you write poetry? I don't know the method at all, and I don't have the recipe for writing poetry. I'd have to have Uncle Niccolò teach me, since he knows how. But would I be foolhardy enough to do such a thing at the risk of bringing my whole calamity out into the open? If it were easy, everybody would write poetry, while they praise real poets to the skies. If poetry were writing the first line longer or shorter than the second, they wouldn't make so much of it all. There must be some secret to it that I actually possess but don't know how to go about seizing. 'Oh Filli mine, my pretty glow.' This must be a line of poetry; I feel it is but I don't know why."

In the midst of these divagations I fell asleep with my insides gurgling from hunger.

The next morning I had a fight with Teresa because I wanted something to eat and refused to take the castor oil. I defended my position by saying that if you were hungry you had nothing wrong with your stomach and there was no need for a purge, and I had almost convinced her of the idea. But before she would take the responsibility on herself in my father's absence, she went to consult Uncle Niccolò. Teresa returned with my uncle who decided that I had to take the oil since it was well known that indigestion is most often characterized, so he said, by a false hunger. The sacrifice had to be made, a first and serious sacrifice for love: I submitted to swallowing the oil.

I felt a burning desire to return Filli's kiss; but a doubt, a gnawing doubt kept me in a state of agitation. I had heard (it was whispered in my ear) that there were men *who do women wrong,* and I was afraid, not knowing the details of such chicanery, that if I followed this impulse I would be setting myself on the primrose path; and I would have made any sacrifice at all rather than incur guilt in the eyes of poor Filli, who had now become my fixed and concentrated thought.

While my mother was being combed in the morning, I sometimes sat near her on a little bench, and taking hold of the long black tresses that touched the floor, I delighted in drawing apart the double locks in which long hair usually falls. And this time, while Teresa was pulling the comb through her hair, I made conversation with my mother, putting her often enough in serious discomfiture as she replied to the questions I proposed.

That morning I waited on purpose until Teresa had gone, then I threw out this question: "If God doesn't want there to be other religions, why does he allow children to be born to people married in false religions?"

"Oh, this morning I hardly feel like arguing," my mother answered in some embarrassment. "Once children are born, even under those conditions, it's a sign that this is God's will. Doesn't that seem clear to you?"

"Can children be born without any marriage at all?"

"Listen, Micio, if you don't leave me now, so much the worse for you," she said, somewhat annoyed. "These are matters that ought not to interest you. It's a bother to have a boy as talkative and prying as you are."

"I ask only because I was curious to know how the wet-nurse of Aunt Maddalena was able to have a baby without having a husband."

"You are so naughty. Who told you all this?"

"I was there when the wet-nurse agent said to Aunt Maddalena: 'Take her, she's unmarried. She has a good character, and this way you won't be annoyed by having a husband around the house, and you'll pay less. She was betrayed by a rascal who promised to marry her, and then it was discovered he already had a wife. But she's a good girl, believe me.' "

"People so often talk without taking the children into account. But what has all this to do with you? Micio, why should you be interested in it?"

"Why, because I wanted to know how you make children. If *you* made some, it must be a thing proper people do."

By this time I was thrusting below the waist, as they say in fencing, and my mother had a hard time extricating herself wisely and without arousing my suspicions. She had no other choice than to continue conversation on the subject I had brought up.

"You'll know all this much better when you get married. There's time enough. But if you insist on knowing, on condition that you tell no one, I'll explain it to you in all confidence, since it's wrong for children to know certain things. When a man and a woman are in love and kiss each other, often, but not always, a baby is the result.

With this formula, my mother had the impression that she'd finally brought the conversation to an end; but she was mistaken because she was unaware of the aim of my inquiry. I pressed forward: "Well then, why do you always want me to kiss my girl cousins when they come to visit?"

"Because you can't possibly be in love with each other. But that's enough for now. You've said enough foolishness and you've made me say more than enough. Out you go! I want to finish dressing."

She took me by the hand, walked me to the door and put me out of the room.

"Well then," I ruminated, "I was not wrong in being careful with Filli. Just think what a risk she ran with me, the poor thing, all because of her innocence! It's lucky I'm thoughtful and that I knew something, however confused, about it; otherwise, heaven knows what I might have brought down upon us. There was the possibility of seeing her father come in a fury to look for my father, and then, at least Volterra!" Just thinking about it gave me goose pimples. You can imagine the scandal, the mischief and mocking of my uncles if I had produced a child! It's a good thing I was careful, and that way I remain. Still, it would have been a nice plaything for me to have a child of my own flesh and blood. I would have taken it to the country house at Impruneta; I would have taught it how to drag crabs from their holes in the brooks without getting bitten; I would have taught it how to climb trees to pick fruit. And since it would be mine, when it was bad I would whip it. But let's not get caught up in our imagination; it's better, much better to be free of the whole business.

A long season of rain and storm intervened at that time and kept Filli and me from meeting in the Square. I was careful to look for her in the garden, but her windows were shut and the drapes kept my gaze from penetrating into her rooms. I would run to the terrace window in the hope she would be walking that way; but I had to open the window, and then the doors began to bang on account of the wind, and everybody would run to see who had been careless enough to open the window to the storm. The longer I went without seeing Filli, the more my agitation and my thoughts about her grew.

I was very pleased when they had a suit with long trousers made for me at the tailor's. Until then I had been fitted at the seamstress. And I was overjoyed at the long trousers, because that more virile apparel seemed to me to make my condition as a lover more defensible and more reasonable, a condition which, even in my own thoughts, I had by this time accepted.

It was my father who had chosen the suit and also the style, and everything was well managed. But it was my mother who had bought the cap, and in the matter of masculine dress she was always archaic. Even with its brim flattened, it was a cap that vaguely suggested the kind French priests wear.

When I had tried on the whole suit and the cap, Uncle

Cesare, on seeing me, said at once, "Oh, look at Stilts in long trousers! With that cap of yours you look like a Bible distributor."

I went to look in the mirror alone, and I felt that the whole outfit gave me a distinguished air. Only the cap gave me trouble in setting it at a proper and attractive angle; and turning it this way and that, I found the best way was to set it a bit down over my ears, aslant, as they used to say then.

When my mother saw me, the first thing she said was, "Look how he's set his cap. He looks just like a journalist!" In those days, however new and free they were, the reputation of journalists had not yet been set as high as it deserved. Not wanting Filli to take me for a journalist when she saw me, I put my cap on in such a way that it hung down over my eyes.

"What a way to wear your hat!" my father exclaimed when he saw me. "In long trousers and with your hat on your nose, they'll take you for Mr. Caterina."

I have no idea who this Mr. Caterina was; he must have been a buffoon of the time. As for me, I was terrified of being a buffoon, and to avoid being taken for one I pulled my cap up, leaving my forehead almost clear.

"Look! Here comes Cipistione!" said Uncle Guglielmo when he saw me with my cap to the back. Cipistione was the nickname of a scion of good family, known all over Florence, but who had the foible of getting drunk. When he was in such a state, he wore his cap on the nape of his neck. I remember once as I was strolling with my father, this Cipistione undertook to justify his failing, arguing that it wasn't wine that had a bad effect, but rather cream and that sort of thing. "If I go out to dinner," he said, "all I need is a little cream, a dessert with whipped cream, and I'm sick on the spot; so much so, they have to carry me home as if I were drunk."

"Drink less cream, then, whipped or unwhipped," advised my father.

"Really, now! A person who doesn't do justice to what is offered him at dinner is guilty of discourtesy."

So my cap was not to be worn toward the back either, to

avoid confusion with Cipistione. How then should it be worn?

I went to my mother with the idea that she, the artist, would find the most esthetic position for the cap. She put it squarely on my head, drew back two or three paces as if eyeing the effect produced by the final brushstrokes on a painting, and then said, "There! You can go now; it looks quite all right. You look like an Englishman."

I encountered Uncle Niccolò who was just returning home. The moment he saw the cap on my head he began silently to gaze on it. Then he said, "Walk carefully, or else you'll spill everything."

"What will I spill?"

"You look like a hodcarrier hoisting a load of mortar up a ladder. How is it you don't know how to put a cap on?"

To make an end of the matter, since I had exhausted all the possible slants and angles, I had to get used to putting on my cap just the way it seemed to go. I was sorry not to be able to be sure about the position of my cap, since I wanted to make my appearance before Filli in such a way that everything would impress her, and I would take pleasure from it. But I had to accept things as they were, hoping that chance would make up for the failure of so many attempts.

Good weather returned and with it, hopes of seeing Filli again. One day, when from the window I had seen her in the Square, I got permission to go out. I put on my new suit and the famous cap, and went into the garden to pick a gardenia, which I then hid in my pocket only to put in my buttonhole once I had shut the gate behind me and made sure well in advance that I would not meet anyone from home.

I made my appearance on the Square with the gardenia in my buttonhole. I was a bit constrained in walking because my long trousers, which I was not yet used to, kept catching at my underwear, and because I was rather excited at seeing Filli again.

Filli, who was jumping rope as usual, came toward me without recognizing me; so I halted, and when she drew near, in a state of wonderment, she dropped the rope on the ground and ran to embrace me.

Particularly because I was enclosed in that new box of a suit, I recall that at that first encounter, against my every wish, I was terribly cold toward her; and all the more so, because I was afraid she would take it into her head again to give me a kiss. I now knew what fearful consequences that might have. Silently, I took both her hands in mine, pressed them tightly and drank from her eyes the gentleness that emanated from them.

"How well you look dressed up like a man! You're splendid. Why, look! You've even brought me a flower, and that's a real delight since last night I dreamt of you and I imagined that you filled my lap with roses."

I was sorry it was a single flower I was giving her. I would like to have had an armful of roses, but at that time of year they weren't blooming in our garden. I would have stripped it anyway to bring her some.

"You cut such a fine figure dressed up like a man," she said, taking up where she had left off, and putting the gardenia on her bosom. "I think you look like Byron."

I didn't know who this Byron was. I was afraid he might be some Cipistione or Mr. Caterina in her country. So I asked her timidly, "And who is this Byron?"

"An extremely handsome man, an English poet who did so much for my country. We have a picture of him at home; I'll show you how much you look like him."

"Is that all?" I thought. "That means that I have my cap on a level, since mama said when I was trying it on that I looked like an Englishman."

"You brought me a flower. So you knew it was my birthday! This evening at six o'clock I'll be ten years old."

"I didn't know, and I'm sorry not to have known. I would have brought you a lot of flowers." I would have stolen them from the garden, as I did the gardenia, I thought to myself.

"Come with me," said Filli, taking me by the hand. "You see there? There is my mother sitting on the bench with

Giacomo. She has something to say to you. We were here waiting for you."

"What does she want to say to me," I wondered. "With all these fathers and mothers in between, the moments of gladness I enjoy with Filli are always short and clouded with apprehension."

Filli's mother greeted me with a gracious smile and desired me to sit next to her, while Filli remained standing in front of us.

"This evening Filli will end the year at six o'clock, and at that time we shall drink a toast to her in champagne and eat some pastry; and since she has always told me that you are a great friend of hers, we invite you to our house. May we count on your being there?"

"Thank you very much. I'll try hard to be there, but I have to get permission from my parents," I answered rather timidly.

"If you think it's all right, go right now and ask permission. Filli's father likes you a great deal, too; it would be a pleasure for him if you came."

I got up a bit abstractedly, nodded to the lady; and at a slow pace, with Filli beside me, I went in the direction of home.

"Will you come? Tell me you'll come. Oblige me, since I like you so much."

At this point I cast off any afterthought, and with the resolution of a man, of which I hardly thought myself capable, I answered, "But I like you too, very much, a lot more than you can imagine. My every thought is about you; you have captured my whole soul. But I find it painful to think that while so many older than we are have some hope in their attachments, our extreme youth allows us none."

At this speech of mine, or near-speech, when for the first time I opened my heart to Filli without concealment and without reticence, she began to cry. I stopped, looked at her and realized that her tears did not drop from the corners of her eyes, but instead they tumbled in a veritable little fountain from the midpoint of her eyelids; and I thought that that different way of releasing tears must be a special Greek characteristic.

"But Filli, dear Filli, don't cry. I don't think I said anything that should bring you to this. Don't cry, because if you make me cry too, in the midst of my sorrow I won't know, as you do, how to be gracious and endearing. When I cry I shriek as loud as a braying donkey, and then your mother will come running, and my parents too. Then how could we explain all this fuss?"

Filli entered the hallway of my house. I dried her tears with my handkerchief. I didn't kiss her, though I felt drawn to do so. Yet I did clasp her to me for a moment, and then said, "You'll see, this evening I'll come to your house."

"Swear that you will."

With me promising had always been just the same as swearing, but under those conditions, beside myself with emotion, I didn't shun the solemnity of an oath. And when we said good-by I repeated, "I've sworn that I'd come; and you can count on it that whatever may happen to me, I'll be at your house before six. But you must promise me you won't cry any more because your tears make me as sad or sadder than seeing a poor man die of hunger. I won't return to the Square. Wait for me in your house at six. Now you can tell your mother that I've got permission."

I had done the right thing by Filli. I had thrown myself into it recklessly. But now the serious moment had arrived to ask and to gain that permission. According to the custom at my house, if people were not known by family relation the inclination was against them and they were not visited. The families had to be exclusively of the innermost circle of Florence, or at least they had to have had an ancestor at the First Crusade; the Second Crusade was already a bit suspect. Imagine, then, Filli's family, who were foreigners from God knows where, and it was not known why they had come to Florence. Then, too, it is an inveterate habit in the discipline of all families to refuse children all requests, even the most trivial and innocent, out of a show of authority.

I asked if my father were at home, and they said he was out. I asked Teresa where my mother was, and she told me she was painting.

"At this hour?"

"It's a quarter to five. What time did you think it was?"

Just an hour and a quarter before six. I still had time to think. But the trouble was that if I went myself and my mother forbade me to go out, I would then have lacked the courage to take a decisive step. So I confided in my brother Aldo and my cousin Carlo the invitation I had received, and charged them with going for me to ask permission of my mother.

They went, full of good will, and I waited for them with a palpitating heart, down on the ground floor.

They took so long in coming back that it seemed to me an age. At last they reappeared and my brother Aldo gave me a reply that didn't leave much to hope for.

"Mama said for you to go up yourself, because she doesn't understand a thing."

I would like to have given them both what for.

"What did you tell her?"

"One thing and another."

"Then how could she not understand?"

I went up the stairs and, full of daring, appeared before her, leaving it to her to speak first.

"Aldo and Carlo were here to say that you were invited out to dinner this evening."

"But I didn't say to dinner! I said that I had been invited to eat pastry here in Via Barbano at six o'clock, to celebrate the birthday of one of my boy friends."

"Just as you say. But it's rather late in the day, and without your father's approval I don't feel I have the authority to send you to the houses of people we don't know. Go get undressed, dear. That will be best all round."

I was frozen on the spot. I looked at the clock on the mantel; it showed five twenty-five. I was speechless and incapable of decision when my mother, reading my discomfiture on my face, continued, "If your father came in, I'd plead with him to allow your request; but as a matter of fact, he said we shouldn't expect him for dinner this evening, since he would be late."

I saw that my mother was sorry to refuse me, but this was not what weighed on me. So I suddenly turned on my heels and went out. And she, fearing from my behavior an act of rebellion, called Teresa and told her to guard the entrance without being seen; and I became aware of this surveillance. I looked at another clock: it showed twenty minutes to six! At this point I called my brother and cousin, led them into the garden and told them, "I said I was going, and I am going. I can't leave by the street door because Teresa is there on the beat. Near the stable on Via delle Officine I noticed that the door is locked. But I want to go even if I have to walk on red-hot stakes. I've thought up a way that nobody could suspect. While I'm gone you be sure to do what you can for me and I'll be grateful."

And thereupon, leaving the two of them agape, I climbed up an ilex tree in the part of the garden near the Philipsons, scrambled onto the wall and catching hold of a tree on the other side, slid down into the garden, across which I sprinted unseen. By the same maneuver I managed to climb onto the wall of Filli's garden, and from there, since there were no trees, I jumped to the ground and ran at once to rap on the panes of that long window at which I had gazed so often from my room.

My arrival was a great occasion. It was all of five minutes to six. Even Filli's father said a lot of things in his own language to congratulate me, and I gathered that he would like Giacomo to be as prompt as I.

When we had seated ourselves in a circle, the bottle of champagne was uncorked and at the stroke of six we clinked glasses and drank Filli's health, each of us expressing the most joyous wishes. Those few moments gave me such happiness that I've never forgotten them, and if I half close my eyes I can still see the room, the light blue of the walls, the round table, the goblets, and everything returns as if it rose up before me. I relished those few mo-

ments in the true spirit of a philosopher; for if the hang-
man had been just outside the door ready to deprive me of
my head, instead of the storm brewing for me at home, he
would not have been able to cast a shadow on the joy I
felt in my heart for having kept the promise I had made
to Filli and for being with her, in her house, among her
family who made so much of me.

I wanted to hurry my departure and return the way I
had come, hoping to reach the garden before dinner time.
But what with Filli and one thing and another, it turned
out that I was incapable of warding off entreaties and
stayed late; indeed, it had grown dark. Besides, the champagne had started a certain bubbling inside me, so that
at that moment, now that I wore long trousers, I was not
afraid to stand up to my father if he should take it into
his head to whip me.

A serious difficulty arose, really serious. In jumping from
Filli's wall I had felt a certain something that held me back
somewhat in the leap; and it must have been a hook stuck
in the wall that caught my trousers, and tore them a hand-
breadth in the back.

"If it's not one thing, it's another," I said to myself.
"The tear can be mended. I'll certainly have a lot to account for at home."

When I was able to get away, they obliged me to go out
the street door, and at the corner, as I caught sight of my
house, I suddenly began to see things with less presumption
than just a moment before. The realities were borne in on
me, and I felt a glimmer of fear.

At the gate there were three asses which came every evening to bring milk for Aunt Luigia. "So," I thought, "it's
open," and quickly I slipped through. At the service entrance the driver was receiving money for the milk from the
servant, and I, furtive as a mole, slipped between them into
the house.

"Here he is, here he is! The young master has come
back!" Leopoldo began to shout. "Teresa, tell the mistress not to fret; the young master has come back home."

Instead of going up to the second floor I took refuge in the basement to see how things were, but the cook knew nothing. The servants' hall was empty, even though the light was always lit. Then I flew to the stairway that went up to my grandfather's apartment; but there, too, all was silent. I saw, however, that his light shone through, and surmised that my grandfather was there. On tiptoe, not making the least noise, I looked from the dark into the room and saw my grandfather sitting in an armchair, writing, with great piles of silver in front of him.

I was about to turn back when I heard in the distance a door open, and the voice of my father who was looking for me in a rage.

"Where is that rascal? Where has he hidden himself? It's soon enough for him to begin with women! If I catch him I'll geld him like a tomcat."

I really didn't have a very clear notion of what gelding was, but it was sufficient to recall how the same word had been used in describing the operation performed on chestnuts before roasting to put me in distress. I had no idea how to escape the peril, but since I realized from his tone of voice that my father was really furious, I got down on all fours and slithered like a snake behind my grandfather's armchair (he was rather deaf) and slipped under his bed unseen. There, all curled up, I tremblingly awaited the course of events.

But everything for the moment had returned to silence. After a bit the farther door opened again and I recognized the voice of Uncle Cesare who was jokingly calling out "Micio" as if he were calling the cat.

"Come out, little one, there's tripe for you."

But I wasn't in a mood for jokes. I was mistrustful, having heard what a rage my father was in; so I stayed put, curled up under the bed.

Suddenly my father and Uncle Cesare came into grandfather's room.

"Have you seen Micio?" asked Uncle Cesare.

"No, I haven't seen him. Why? What has happened?"

"He's hidden himself in the house," my father answered,

"or else he's escaped outside. We can't find him. He's up to his usual tricks."

"Well, what has he done?"

"You saw, didn't you, that the rascal wasn't at dinner? Well, he went off to have a snack at the house of a girl his own age; but the girl is a prodigious beauty. He went over the garden wall like a lovesick cat."

"Well, it's true enough that the litter of cats grow up to catch mice," said my grandfather, turning toward my father. "But then, for such a piece of foolishness, there's no reason to scare the poor child this way."

"But we're doing it more as a joke than anything." It was my father speaking.

"We felt we had to find him," added Uncle Cesare, "to know whether or not he had eaten. We've sent Leopoldo to see if he's gone out again to the Square. But, you know, now that I think of it, Ferdinando, where can he have hidden himself? In the coach house! He must certainly be in the stable."

"You're right. Let's go look."

And at that they went off, promising my grandfather they would do me no harm.

I couldn't stay forever under my grandfather's bed, but I didn't know how to go about returning to the world of the living. It was clear I had to return and as soon as possible, either for the sake of relieving my mother of worry or to avoid hardening my father and thwarting in him those benign feelings which he might have had toward me and which I had heard with my own ears from under the bed. I thought I'd go back the way I came and then slip as quietly as possible into my bed, giving up dinner for that evening.

I had put on my new cap again, which had been all crumpled up under my back. With great prudence I had turned my head around to where my legs had been and I was all ready to leave, when I heard my grandfather getting up from his armchair. He walked around the table a bit and then I heard him open his strongbox. From the jingle of coins I realized he was putting them into little bags for

storage in the safe, when one of the *scudi* fell to the floor.
I saw it slither on the floor and then roll right for me and
stop barely an inch from my face.

"Now if he comes to pick up the coin he'll find me for
sure," I thought. And to remedy the situation, something
very stupid occurred to me. I quickly seized the coin with
the idea of sending it skittering into the middle of the room,
but my uncomfortable posture spoiled the game and the
coin came back, landing flat as if it had fallen from the sky.

My grandfather, whom I couldn't see but who was
surely keeping his eye on the bed, unable to bend over on
account of his weak back, caught sight of the *scudo* which,
absolved from obeying the physical laws of the universe,
was rolling about the room on its own. Then he seized the
bell cord to call the servants.

Leopoldo ran in.

"Do you see? A *scudo* dropped on the floor. Pick it up
for me. Something strange happened: the coin went under
the bed, and after a moment it came back here all by itself, as if it had flown."

Like all faithful and beloved retainers, Leopoldo understood things in an entirely different way. From the cane-
rack he took out a stick and with it began to scrape under
the bed in an attempt to draw forth the coin.

"No, no," said my grandfather. "Don't you see it? The
coin is right there on the floor near the table."

But Leopoldo, with the blockheadedness of a faithful and
beloved retainer, went on poking with the stick, striking
me on the nose so hard that I let out a cry.

"The devil! There's somebody there!"

And then I slid out, all dusty, my nose bleeding, and, in
my hand, the cap, so white with dust that it looked as if it
had been picked off a rubbish heap.

"The little master!" exclaimed Leopoldo in amazement.
"I'm sorry, I must have hurt you."

My grandfather was at first taken aback; then he began
to laugh, and so did I.

"There's not much to laugh about, my little man; there's
not much to laugh about! I've heard bad accounts of your

conduct. When did you crawl under the bed? Leopoldo, go tell them the child is in my room. They've been looking for him a long time."

My grandfather would have liked to adopt a parental tone; but he had laughed, and he could no longer command the necessary tone of voice. Therefore, he said to me good-naturedly, "Look at the state you're in. It would seem that Leopoldo seldom takes the trouble to sweep under the bed."

Everybody ran to grandfather's room, including Aldo and Carlo whose mouths were stretched from ear to ear from laughing, my uncles and my father, my mother, and the servants. Everybody came. Even the cook! I seemed to be a "Jesus Smitten" exhibited to the multitudes, all the more since even blood was not wanting; I was blowing it from my nose into a handkerchief, all because of the blow from Leopoldo's stick.

Everyone wanted to have his say. There was no dearth of reproaches: the crumpled hat passed from hand to hand, accompanied by a chorus of rebuke; nor did Teresa fail to see the tear in my trousers. I was silent and looked at the floor. But I was thinking of Filli.

Uncle Cesare was moved by my wretched state, and acted in the manner of policemen who, to save someone from the fury of the crowd, arrest him. With a stern look he took me by the arm, had them make way, and conducted me down the secret stairway that led to the kitchen. In the servants' hall he had something prepared for me to eat. Then he put me to bed, and I fell at once into a lethargic sleep on account of the champagne I had drunk, and also the nervous wear and tear from so many and varied emotions.

Very early in the morning, Teresa came to wake me. Setting my breakfast on the bureau, she said to me, "Today you must get dressed quickly and have breakfast in your room because at nine the whole caboodle leaves for the house at Impr23a."

"My uncles too? And my grandfather? Are they coming to the country too?"

"Your grandfather's staying in Florence, and your uncle's are too. They'll come in a day or so. In the meantime we're setting off. Come now. Hurry up, because it's not long till nine. Now, I'll take your torn trousers; I'll put them away and mend them in the country. But you're a regular lout. How did you manage to do what you did, put the family in a fit that way last night? We went out looking for you all over the Square and in the streets. Oh, if I were your father I'd treat you like a jailbird!"

"And where do you come in? What does it matter to you?"

"What does it matter to me? Of course it matters to me! Why, when you were in bed I had half a mind to give you a couple . . ."

I got dressed like an automaton. I swallowed my breakfast as if it were medicine; my bitter insides constricted my throat. I had to leave. There was not even time enough to say good-by to Filli. I was thinking of her tears the day before. And now I had to leave like a boor, without seeing her again, without saying good-by.

"What a curse love is, and this love especially!" I thought. "Other lovers at least write to each other, while we are going to be separated, and until November when school opens again we won't be able to see one another. The poor thing will take it into her head to jump rope around my house. She'll look for me and I won't be there. She'll think I'm sick, and she won't have the courage to ask for news of me, and she'll cry. She'll cry as she did yesterday, and I'll be far away and won't be able to dry her tears. Good Lord, have pity on her."

At this point Teresa returned, and she already had her hat on her head.

"Hurry, Master Guido, the carriage is ready. It's at the door."

It was my duty to say good morning to my father, mother and grandfather. I went to their rooms; but my parents had already gone down to say good morning and take leave of my grandfather, and I caught up with them there. I learned there that my father would come to the country that evening; and to tell the truth, that made me glad, since

I was afraid that on the way he might take up again the events of the night before.

After the ceremony of saying good morning and good-by, I went back to my room to take a look at Filli's windows. They were closed and I could see no one. By now the bitter cup of separation was ready, and I could not avoid bringing it to my lips. To cut short my agonies, I went to sit in the carriage where Teresa and my brother Aldo were already sitting, and the only thing we were waiting for to set off was my mother's arrival. In this brief interval, Uncle Cesare came to the carriage window, joked with my brother and me, and then helped my mother get in. As he closed the window, he said, to tease me, "You see, Micio? You are going off to have a good time, while your poor uncle must stay in Florence to do his homework."

The carriage set off, and I craned my neck to catch sight of the Square in the foolish hope of seeing Filli. When we turned into Via Sant' Apollonia and the Square faded from view, I felt a lump in my throat, my mouth contorted into a grimace, and I began to shed torrents of tears.

My mother was surprised, and asked me, "What's there to cry about now?"

"I'm sorry Uncle isn't coming with us to have a good time," I replied between sobs, and again I began so convulsively to cry that I choked up.

"There, there; I understand. It's your uncle. Come over here, right next to me. Rest your head on me and give me your hand. Don't think about anything. With a character like that, poor boy, you'll have your share of trouble in this world."

# MATILDE SERAO

## 1856–1927

Born in Greece, the daughter of a Neapolitan exile, Matilde Serao (1856-1927) was trained in Italy as an elementary school teacher. Later she was employed by the state telegraph company. Her intimate acquaintance with both milieux, and with many others, is evident in her novels and stories. Serao is not a stylist but rather a reporter; during much of her life, she practiced journalism. With her husband Eduardo Scarfoglio, one of the leading journalists of the time, she founded the *Corriere di Roma* and the *Corriere di Napoli;* much of her success with the latter newspaper is credited to her creation of a society column. She later edited with her husband *Il Mattino,* which is still the leading newspaper in Naples. After her separation from Scarfoglio she founded and edited *Il Giorno.* Her fiction and her reportage, though not great literature, often portray the large Neapolitan scene with vividness and competence, long before the "picturesque" Italian South became fashionable through film "neorealism." My selection reflects the variety of her social experience, her keen instinct for social characterization; and the *palazzo,* the large apartment building with a central courtyard, is the appropriate background for her varied view of life and society.

## Giovannino or Death

At ten-thirty that particular Sunday the sacristan of Holy Apostles parish went to the doorway of the old Neapolitan church and began vigorously to ring a large and noisy silver bell. Leaning against the post of the heavy old oak door, the sacristan pulled the bell, making it ring out loud and unremitting: it served to warn the faithful in Via Gerolomini, in the quarter Grotta della Marra in Vertecoeli, in Holy Apostles Square, in Le Gradelle, that high Mass would soon begin, the solemn celebration of Pentecost. Suddenly the bell stopped ringing; but the sacristan continued to stand near the door, repeating every few minutes to the deserted square: "Step right in; Mass is just beginning."

Yet the merchant women who paced back and forth in front of the closed windows of their shops, the housewives who went to take another look at the kitchen where the big piece of meat was simmering in tomato sauce, the affluent ladies who were still submitting to the hairdresser, failed to make haste: before high Mass began the sacristan would have to ring three times. Only a few lower-class women began to arrive with their new percale dresses and their silver combs set in gleaming masses of hair, hauling their children behind them. The sacristan, utterly disregarding these nobodies, went on monotonously repeating, to the echo of the square, "Step right in; Mass is just beginning."

In the palazzo number two in Holy Apostles Square on that holiday morning, activity began to intensify. It was a large ocher building with a broad ill-paved courtyard which the coachmen and stable boys of the Princess of Santobuono were filling with puddles of dirty water as they curried the horses, washed the carriages and polished the harnesses; and from the inner rooms opening on the courtyard

*Translated by Lowry Nelson, Jr.*

emanated a pervasive and penetrating stable smell. The cabriolet of the Princess of Santobuono stood almost ready amid the noise of the coachmen and stable boys, the clatter of the horses which were soon to leave, to go down twenty paces, turn at San Giovanni a Carbonara, call for the Princess who lived in a fortress-like mansion, and take her to Mass. The stairway of palazzo number two in Holy Apostles Square was quite filthy. There was no doorman, and the inhabitants, floor by floor, were in charge of cleaning. It happened that donna Orsolina, who lived on the second floor, was five months pregnant again that year, and her four little ones gave neither her nor the maid Mariagrazia a moment of peace. On that particular Sunday donna Orsolina could no longer button her black woolen dress which had worn thin and was hideously short in front: red and pale by turns, with tears in her eyes, she cursed the moment when, instead of becoming a maiden aunt, she had conceived a wild and silly passion for Ciccio, the postal employee.

Across the way the Ranaudos were calmly getting ready for Mass. Donna Peppina Ranaudo, fifty by now, large, fat, broader than she was tall, with the rosy childish face of a chubby woman who has never had children, her head now continually losing hair, was having her wide twill shoes put on by her maid Concetta; while don Alfonso Ranaudo, her husband, employee at the lottery and great hunter before the Lord, veteran of Pomigliano d'Arco, where he had gone at three that morning in search of quail and whence he had returned at ten, having gone on foot all the way, was removing his velveteen jacket and getting ready to put on his black beaver coat. The old husband and wife, childless, happy, tranquil, content not to have children, glanced at each other smilingly with a serene sparkle in their eyes. On the third floor, to the left, another happy couple were getting ready to go to Mass: don Vincenzo Manetta, a thin old man, tall and white, with a gaunt face and a beaked nose, thin white mustaches and legs as slender as sticks, don Vincenzo Manetta, retired court clerk, angry at being retired and passionately interested in the history of old

Naples, to the point of copying out whole passages from certain documents and then thinking himself the author; donna Elisabetta Manetta, a good woman who had married late, at the age of forty-five, whose complexion remained delicate though yellowed like a spinster's, and who persisted in the habit of dyeing her hair with Zempt coloring so that it varied in hue from dark red to light brown to dark violet, though mostly it remained a greenish color, the color of dark bog weeds. And don Vincenzo Manetta, methodical, meticulous, a trifle petulant, was thumping the floor with his cane.

"Elisa, the sacristan has rung twice."

"Once, once," said donna Elisa patiently, pulling short black lace gloves over her pudgy yellowish hands.

"Elisa, do you want to get there too late?"

"I'm looking for my rosary."

"Elisa, what about the keys?"

"I have them in my pocket."

"Elisa, what about the cat?"

"He's shut up in the coal closet."

Meanwhile the sacristan had begun to ring again. Now it was only ten minutes before the sung Mass would begin. In the third-floor apartment to the right, a large apartment of twelve rooms, there was a loud slamming of doors and bustle back and forth, and a woman's strident voice shouted: "Chiarina, Chiarina!"

"Who is it?" responded a voice from a little room whose door was closed.

"It's rung twice for Mass," shouted the voice of donna Gabriella, as she fastened a gold chain bracelet that hung heavily.

"All right," answered the little voice of Chiarina from her room.

"You want to get there too late, don't you?" shouted donna Gabriella, fastening another gold bracelet of interlocking rings, big and massive. "Do you want to lose your soul to boot?"

"Everyone's soul is his own affair," answered Chiarina's voice, now shrill, from behind the door.

"Listen, just listen who has the courage to speak!" screamed donna Gabriella, while trying in vain to clip on heavy gold earrings covered with pearls and diamonds.

"Can't I even speak now?" shrieked the girl still in her room.

"You ought to be ashamed, in love with that ragamuffin Giovannino. Ragamuffin, ragamuffin, that's all he is!"

"It's none of your business," said Chiarina, showing her dark thin face through a crack in the door.

"What do you mean it's none of my business? I'm your mother, you know. I give the orders!"

"No you don't. You're not my mother; so you don't give the orders," Chiarina retorted, appearing in petticoat and bodice.

Donna Gabriella, large, fat, with a ruddy complexion that powder failed to make pale, suffocating in her black satin corset, turned purple.

"I'll show you who gives the orders!"

Chiarina went toward her a step or two and said calmly, "You know that it's either Giovannino or death."

And returning to her room to finish dressing, she slammed the door. Donna Gabriella was almost on the point of running after her, but she restrained herself to avoid sending even more blood to her head. Sitting down and waving her black hat covered with feathers, in whose velvet bow she had stuck a big diamond brooch, she tried to calm herself. In the bedroom, which was furnished with the large brass double bed on which donna Gabriella slept her widow's sleep, a great mahogany wardrobe fronted by a large looking glass, two massive mahogany chests of drawers topped with white marble, and an ample dressing table covered in gray marble, there was still the Sunday morning disorder of Neapolitan houses when everybody gets up later than usual. On the dressing table lay a great many open boxes of leather or velvet from which donna Gabriella had extracted the heavy jewels with which she had adorned herself; some of the boxes were made of rough white wood on which three or four numbers were written in red ink. Donna Gabriella, who was always hot (being large and fat, she held herself in to reduce her waist a bit), breathed with the help of a black satin fan, common enough, but fastened to her body by an uncommonly heavy gold chain. At this point Carminella the maid appeared in the room. Carminella had already been to six o'clock Mass, being very devout and dedicated to the "spiritual life," dressed as she was in black, like a nun, with a white kerchief around her neck. She was a pale and silent creature, with a hesitant glance, a penitent air, and she worked only to get into God's good graces and sighed contritely when rebuked.

"This girl will be the death of me," donna Gabriella said to Carminella by way of observation.

"Offer up these tribulations to the Almighty at St. Clare's," murmured Carminella.

"The Almighty could do me the favor of putting her head to rights," donna Gabriella grumbled, "but it's harder than granite."

"They are our sins too," the pious Carminella insisted.

Chiarina had come out of her room, all dressed, with her hat on, pulling on an old glove. Her black woolen dress was old too, and the black beaver hat had been worn all winter. Donna Gabriella took in her stepdaughter at a glance and frowned.

"Why did you put those old things on?"

"They're not old yet."

"That's what you think. You could put on the light dress and the between-seasons hat I had made for you."

"That dress is too big for me."

"No it isn't. And if it were too big for you, couldn't it be refitted?"

"Tomorrow."

"Chiarina, go put it on," said donna Gabriella.

"It's too late."

"I'll wait, but you must put on that dress, or they'll say I send you out like a ragamuffin because you're my stepdaughter."

"If that were the only thing they said!" muttered Chiarina.

"What are they saying? What can those wicked tongues be saying? Don't they know how much you cost me? Don't they know that I spend my life's blood to support you and dress you like a carriage lady?"

"Your life's blood?" asked Chiarina ironically.

"Of course; and if you weren't an ingrate, a thankless ragamuffin, if your people had not been haughty and beggarly, like your father, and as your silly mother must have been, you would say so too."

The dark girl paled; her eyes sparkled and her gentle red lips trembled in anger. "Listen to me, donna Gabriella," she said quietly, "it's all right if you want to insult me, I have to bear it, since it's God's will; if you want to insult my dear dead father, I have to bear that too, since he made the awful mistake of marrying you and suffered purgatory on earth; but for you to offend the holy memory of my mother, when you are not worthy to kiss the ground she walked on, this, by all that's holy, I will not bear. You say my mother was a beggar? She was a lady, do you hear? The dresses she put on were bought at the store; the jewels she wore were in her family; she was so good that when she went out everyone said to her 'God bless you,' do you hear? What are you? You're a beggar who's come up in the world; you have poor people's money and you make loans to them at a hundred and twenty per cent; you wear dresses that dishonest maids steal from princesses and you wear jewels pawned at your shop; and when people see you pass by they curse your hard heart. Don't mention my mother, donna Gabriella. She is in heaven; and the Almighty has made this the devil's own place for you."

"Is this the reason you don't want to put on the dress?" asked donna Gabriella, overcome with anger, while outside the sacristan of Holy Apostles Church rang for the third time. Carminella, terrified, made the sign of the cross over and over again.

"I don't have to tell you," replied Chiarina stubbornly.

"But I know why you don't want to put on the dress," shrieked the fat pawnbroker. "Most likely your lover told you not to."

"Well, what if he did?" asked Chiarina boldly.

"That yellow-faced, green-faced, third-rate weakling: now *he* gives the orders and acts jealous!"

"Yes, yes, what if he did?" repeated Chiarina, whose quivering emotion became intensified.

"I want you to put on the new dress at once."

"No."

"Chiarina, don't make me do anything rash."

"Go to the madhouse."

She turned to go into her room, but donna Gabriella rushed up to her and, with her large hand encased in a red leather glove, she slapped her on both cheeks. One of the heavy gold bracelets stung Chiarina's slender neck, and she began to weep and cry out desperately.

"Be quiet!" said donna Gabriella in a low hoarse voice.

"No, no!" Chiarina shrieked, so the whole palazzo could hear her.

"Be quiet, be quiet!"

But the girl, seized by an ungovernable attack of nerves, began to scream as if she were having a fit. On the second-floor landing donna Orsolina, who was closing the door and herding out her flock of children, pale, tired, her stomach already quite big, was mumbling as she counted out the money needed to pay for seats in church.

"Get married, girls; get married. You'll see what happens then!"

And she was upset that her children, attracted by Chiarina's shrieks, no longer wanted to go to church.

Leaning placidly on the arm of her husband don Alfonso Ranaudo and supporting her bulk on the other side by means of a cane, donna Peppina descended the stairs shaking her balding head which bore a hat unmistakably designed for spring, though it was at least six springs old.

"They're always doing that, from morning to night," she said, chuckling.

"Beating girls does them good: they're like wool," responded don Alfonso, who was a man of proverbs and vast good humor.

More slowly, don Vincenzo Manetta, the court clerk

whom a vindictive government had forced to retire, was
descending from the third floor with his wife donna Elisabetta on his arm.

"Elisa, did you bring the missal?"

"Of course."

"Why is donna Chiarina screaming?"

"Her stepmother must have beaten her."

"Ah youth, youth!"

On the fourth floor all the students who lived on the left
had stuck their heads out the courtyard windows; on the
right the high-school English teacher, blessed with five
sisters, all more or less old, had appeared behind the windowpanes in nightcap and slippers. And in the courtyard
the coachman of the Princess of Santobuono, looking upward, hummed:

> Papa's against it and mama is too.
> What shall we do? Oh what shall we do?

while his cheeky stable boy sang in full voice:

> Ain't got no money, ain't got none;
> So what's to be done, so what's to be done?

All convulsed, donna Gabriella tried to compose her
countenance as she too went down to Mass followed by
Carminella who had put on a black veil over her dull black
hair. She had shut up Chiarina at home and carried off the
keys, and pretended as she went down not to hear the loud
weeping and sobbing. Those who were at the windows, on
the balconies of the courtyard, and on the stairway, fell
silent as she passed by; she was trembling from the effort
not to hear that weeping, that lamentation heard by everyone. But she knew, she knew full well, in spite of the smiles
with which she had been greeted by the five sisters of the
English teacher—obligatory smiles, since the teacher owed
her two hundred and twenty lire, and was bled white by
payment of the interest alone so that he could never reduce
the principal—in spite of those forced smiles, she knew that

the old spinsters felt pity for the poor girl shut up at home, weeping out her cruel fate on the floor. Donna Gabriella knew that the students on the fourth story, who had pawned watches and gold rings at her shop, greeted her only to mock her. Donna Gabriella, going down the second-floor flight of stairs, had heard, farther down, donna Elisabetta Manetta saying to her husband, "But doesn't she have a guardian?" and the husband, a man of the law—a magistrate, as he would say, not without adding in all seriousness the epithet "of the greatest integrity"—the husband who replied, "The guardian, my dear Elisa, could intervene . . ." Donna Gabriella had seen the mocking smiles of the coachman and the groom of the house of Santobuono. She felt that they all despised her, hated her; she felt that all of them were in sympathy with her stepdaughter, still weeping in piercing and penetrating sobs that troubled the calm, silent air of the spring morning. Only donna Orsolina, trying in vain to keep her flock of children in step, only donna Orsolina, whom she met at the entrance, gave her a humble, almost obsequious greeting. At every new birth, donna Orsolina contracted new indebtedness with donna Gabriella: her little treasure of gold objects, fine linen, shiny utensils, was on deposit at the shop of donna Gabriella, who was always threatening to offer everything for sale. Donna Orsolina, poor creature, was not even able to pay to renew the pawn, she found herself so securely in the clutches of respectable poverty. So when she met the strong fat pawnbroker, she would bow her head, turn pale, and greet her with a trembling voice. But donna Gabriella knew full well that beneath that humility stirred a dull, vague hatred, the hatred of the hopelessly oppressed. How relieved she was, the pawnbroker loaded with gold and jewels, when she went out the door, crossed the square in twenty steps, and entered the church in which the organ was already booming for solemn Mass. She was happy when she knelt beside the great altar in the beautiful old church filled with the faithful. Donna Orsolina rose from her knees, plumped down on a chair, prayed fervently, while her children sat there overcome by the music, silent, a little ashamed. Don Vincenzo Manetta had laid a colored handkerchief on the floor and had rested one of his knees on it, his hands folded over the knob of his cane, his head resting on his hands, his hat on the seat next to him, and now and then he would say to his wife:

"Elisa, the rosary for souls in purgatory."

"I've said it."

"Elisa, the *devotion* to St. Andrew Avellino for a holy death."

"I'll say it now."

"Elisa, don't forget the sixty glorias."

Sitting side by side, donna Peppina and don Alfonso Ranaudo smiled at each other, smiled at the genuflections of the priests performing the solemn Mass, smiled at the censer-swinging of the acolytes. A hissing sound issued from the dry lips of the devout Carminella who was praying rapidly, mechanically. Only donna Gabriella, still upset, still in hot anger, incensed at the others, was trying in vain to pray, finding consolation at least in contemplating her bracelets, in feeling her rings under the leather of her gloves, in feeling on her thick ears the weight of her earrings made of gold, pearls and diamonds. The others had tranquil hearts, or hearts humbly begging serenity, or hearts contrite from innocent sorrow; but her heart, in its vexation, found solace only in resembling a jeweler's window, sparkling, offensive and merciless, in which every jewel is either a tear or a drop of blood.

All the while Chiarina, prostrate on the floor, shut up in the house, still wept and sobbed. But her nervous shock vented itself and gradually subsided. She got up from the floor, adjusted her dress and smoothed her hair. She was a pleasant, goodhearted creature, with a dark expressive face, sparkling gray eyes, and a delicate shape; a nervous, sensitive creature, susceptible to tears and smiles, with an unconquerable will. In ten minutes she was quite calm, able to go out on a balcony which, like the others on each floor, overlooked the courtyard where the inhabitants of the other palazzo Santobuono, which faced the courtyard along one side, also drew their water at the well. She went to the well as if to draw water; but all of a sudden at an adjoining window which also looked out on the well, a young man appeared. The balcony and the window were on the same level, but they had the well between them, not to mention a litter of rope, pulleys, iron chains and buckets: even by stretching, it was impossible to touch hands and it was entirely possible to fall in the well. Yet it was quite simple to carry on a conversation. Everybody could look out, from the entrance and from the courtyard up to the fourth floor: many would have been able to hear. But at that moment they were all at Mass, and there was an immense quiet, an immense silence in the courtyard, from top to bottom. The two young people looked at each other with such intensity and in such silence that it sufficed for the most loving words. The young man, blond, pale, tall, spoke in a low voice, looking around every now and then as if afraid, while the dark girl looked and smiled at him without speaking, overcome with emotion.

"You didn't go to Mass," said Giovannino.

"No," she said.

"Why?"

"I didn't want to go."

"Tell the truth: did donna Gabriella punish you?"

"No, no."

"Tell the truth, Chiarina," and his voice became more fervent, more pressing.

"We had a quarrel," she whispered, blushing, unable to lie.

"Why did you quarrel?"

"Because I love you."

"Do you really love me, really, really?"

"Giovannino, you know I do."

"I know nothing," he murmured, pretending to doubt.

"Do you know what I said again today to my stepmother?" she exclaimed, suddenly aroused. "For the hundredth time I told her: either Giovannino or death. Donna Gabriella can't stand to hear that word and she slapped me."

"Did she hurt you?" he asked softly, turning pale.

"A little, but it doesn't matter," she answered proudly.

"Poor Clara, poor Clara!" he said, as if he were talking to himself.

"Why do you pity me? Don't pity me," she exclaimed, almost beside herself.

They fell silent. A deep coolness arose from the open well over which their young heads were poised, and a deep silence continued to envelop them. Chiarina mounted a coil of wet rope, as if to draw near her beloved. Two or three of the teacher's sisters had appeared behind the windowpanes, had smiled on seeing the young couple and had discreetly withdrawn. One of the students was smoking a pipe, shaking his head, as if to say that he understood and conceded such things.

"We can't go on like this," said the handsome Giovannino all of a sudden.

"Not like this," echoed Chiarina.

"What can we do?"

"Go away together," said the girl.

"And do what?" he asked, shaken and disturbed.

"Get married."

"Without money?"

"Without money."

"It's too desperate a thing to do," he replied, shaking his head in the manner of a handsome indolent young man who knows life and fears its violence.

"Where there is love there is everything. Do you love me?"

"Very much, Clara, very much."

"Well then, we have no need for money. Let's run away."

"Without money you can do nothing."

"You're a coward," she said indignantly.

"My pretty Clara, you're joking," he said laughingly.

"I'm not joking; I am not. You're afraid, you have to have money, you don't know what it is to love, you're a coward."

"I adore you, Clara."

"No."

"I swear to you on my soul, Clara, that I adore you."

"No."

But the third denial was weaker. She looked into the young man's eyes and surrendered.

"You're right," she said.

"Let's think of something else, because we can't go on living like this," he repeated once more, as if tortured incessantly by the problem of existence.

"I don't know, Giovannino. This stepmother is cruel."

"As cruel as that? Wouldn't it be possible to get the best of her?"

"I wouldn't even try," she said, twisting her lips in disdain. "I cannot humiliate myself."

"It's not humiliating; it's as if she were your mother."

"God keep my mother!" she exclaimed, crossing herself.

"Why don't you ever want me to speak to her?" he went on, as if pursuing a train of thought. "Do you want me to speak to her?"

"It would do no good."

"Who knows?"

"She's a vile woman; she appreciates nothing but money."

"Money's a fine thing," he observed, "next to love."

"I don't think she has ever loved anyone," retorted Chiarina, still indignant.

"She might love you if you wanted her to."

"Why should I want her to if she slaps me and shuts me up at home? I'm shut in like a criminal. And if she comes back now and finds us talking, she'll beat me again, you'll see."

"I'll go away then."

"No, no, Giovannino," she pleaded, "don't go away, don't go away."

Her voice was so passionate, and so passionate her gaze, that her love turned him pale.

"She's not coming yet," she murmured without ceasing to look into her lover's eyes. "She's not coming yet—and what does it matter if she does come?"

"Give me your hand, Chiarina," he whispered, magnetized by love.

"I can't; it's too far," and she arched her body, stretching forward. "I can't. I can't," she exclaimed again, almost in tears.

"I'll talk with your stepmother, Clara," he began again persistently.

"What will you say to her, if she doesn't chase you away?"

"She won't chase me away, you'll see. I don't know what I'll say to her. I'll tell her the truth. That we're in love . . ."

"And that we would rather die than be separated," she added simply.

"Don't think about death. I'll tell her that I'm poor enough, but that no one could love you more or better than I; that I hope to better myself and rise above this obscure poverty, with the help of your love."

"She's an evil woman," she murmured uneasily. "She won't believe you."

"I'll try anyway," he said. "I can't watch you suffer any more; I suffer too much."

They looked at each other, caught in the drama of their thwarted love. Meanwhile, in the old church of the Holy Apostles the solemn Mass in celebration of Pentecost had come to an end. The first arrival at the palazzo was the empty carriage of the Princess of Santobuono, which had escorted the lady back to her great house on Via San Giovanni a Carbonara: the Princess had left the church before the others. The coachman climbed down from the box and, looking upward, grinned when he saw the two lovers and slowly began taking off his livery. Then came the Manettas; the former clerk had on his arm the woman he gallantly called his "lady." They also saw the two lovers who were now smiling at each other in silence.

"Elisa?"

"Yes?"

"Do you remember when we saw each other at Santa Maria Capua Vetere?"

"I remember."

"Elisa, do you remember that you weren't happy to leave?"

"I remember."

"Haven't you been better off here in Naples?"

"Yes."

"God be praised!" said the good clerk.

The Ranaudos came more slowly; they smiled maternally and paternally when they saw the two lovers.

"The slaps did no good at all," chuckled donna Peppina on the broad terrace that looked out on the courtyard.

"Love at a distance is hardly love," sang don Alfonso, who prided himself on having an extraordinary voice.

The Manettas and the Ranaudos slowly ascended the staircase, while the fourth-floor residents appeared at the windows and on the balconies. Oblivious, the two lovers kept looking into each other's eyes.

"You must tell me again for the last time that you love me, Chiarina."

"Again for the last time? Always; I love you always."

"Give me your hand, Clara."

She set about piling up the coils of rope to make herself tall enough to reach up to him. At this point poor donna Orsolina appeared in the courtyard, hauling her children behind her and aware that donna Gabriella was on her heels. Donna Orsolina looked up, saw the lovers and the danger they ran of being surprised; and in spite of her rejoicing, she produced a loud cough, a cough that called, that warned, that tried to save. At that moment the two young people had just triumphantly succeeded in touching fingers, for all to see, on that warm spring morning, happy for that little innocent favor—in the midst of the silent or abstracted smiles of all those people pretending not to see. On entering, donna Gabriella saw too. But the indulgent, compassionate silence of those poor or old or unhappy or ailing people, of those good and loving people who looked on and tenderly forgave, overcame even the scorn in that hard heart that knew neither how to pray nor to forgive.

## II

Sitting in her room near the little balcony, Chiarina tried in vain to beguile her impatience while waiting. Her soul was profoundly disturbed. Mechanically she had tried to pray, saying a rosary in order to put her life at one with the Virgin, because it was the hour of decision; but the beads of the circlet remained motionless in her hands and her lips closed on the holy words of prayer: the rosary lay in her lap, disregarded. To distract herself, she had tried to work a bit, crocheting some of her lace for the yellow-gold brocade furniture in the living room, but she was unable to carry on even that mechanical occupation. Time seemed to her interminably long that summer afternoon. Hadn't it already been two hours since Giovanni Affaitati had arrived and was seated in the living room with donna Gabriella, trying to overcome the stepmother's stubborn cruelty? It had been all of two hours; and Chiarina, alone in her room, not daring to enter the living room, not daring to call anyone, overwrought by her imaginings and even more by the silence and loneliness, listened intently for the sound of steps or the slam of a closing door. Nothing. Indeed, for a long time, she had instinctively, with a vague fear of greater evil, kept Giovannino from speaking with her stepmother. But the young man insisted, asserting that that was the only way of salvation, and one day, with out telling her anything, he wrote a letter to donna Gabriella, asking to be received. Strange to say, the stepmother consented at once and even with a show of courtesy. At eight that evening the two women dined in silence: their meals were always silent if they were not interrupted by angry arguments.

"Your sweetheart has written to me," said donna Gabriella all of a sudden.

"Oh!" said the girl, trying to quell a pang of fear. "What does he want?"

"He wants to talk to me. He's coming tomorrow."

Silence again. The stepmother had spoken dryly, but without anger: she gave the impression of not wanting to be questioned further. Chiarina out of pride said nothing more. But it was a restless, feverish night for her, a night of wakeful sleep full of dreams that seemed reality, of reality that seemed dreams. She would at one moment turn cold from unspeakable fear, at another the sweetest hope would set her blood on fire. She could find no peace. When, at three in the afternoon, she heard the bell, she had an impulse to send Giovannino away, almost to tell him to escape. But she remained motionless in her room, overcome by the nervous shock that allowed her to do nothing. Time seemed all the while interminable. But what, then, was Giovannino saying at such length to the obstinate stepmother? Perhaps, as was probable, she would not allow herself to be persuaded, and then, perhaps, Giovannino was beseeching her, beseeching her not to force unhappiness upon two hearts that loved each other. Why did he plead with that cruel woman? Chiarina would never have pleaded with her, never; she was too proud. She would prefer any kind of sorrow to the humiliation of pleading. The girl looked out into the street to calm her agitation, to master her gloomy thoughts. Her glance rested on the alleyway of Le Gradelle, where a laundress was ironing in the doorway of her shop, while every now and then maternally nudging with her foot a wicker basket in which her baby was napping: at that rocking the little one would close its eyes, appeased, and the mother would apply vigorous strokes of the iron to a steaming shirt front. A penetrating smell of preserved tomatoes came from the balconies of donna Peppina Ranaudo's apartment. The indolent fat lady would emerge every now and then on the balcony and with a ladle stir the preserves drying in the July sun. A loud buzzing of flies; and from San Giovanni a Carbonara the voice of a lemon vendor commending in melancholy accents his fresh lemons. Chiarina felt as if she were sleepwalking: she leaned her head against the green slats of the blind, without seeing what was going on below in the street, without hearing the voices or the words of the street urchins or the vendors or the animals. And strangely enough, her excitement was without hope: she thought that no good could come of that interview between Giovannino and donna Gabriella. She was waiting anxiously, but for evil, for treachery, for new tortures inflicted on her love: she expected nothing good from that woman. All her resentment toward her stepmother was rekindled by the state of agitation her nerves had been in for twenty hours. From that woman she had never derived a single benefit, never; she was the cause of all her torments, all her tears, all the dark hours of her life. How could she possibly do good to her now? She expected evil, but an unknown evil, a strange evil, an evil she had never suffered before. Fear had finally overcome all her other emotions: stiff on the chair, her head lowered on her breast, her eyes saw nothing. She awaited that unknown danger, and the minutes that still ticked by had begun finally to seem fatal to her. From behind, a low voice called her:

"Donna Chiarina!"

"What do you want?" she asked Carminella, from deep in her reverie.

"Your mother wants to see you in the living room."

Chiarina looked at the pious Carminella. Her face was greener than usual and her line-thin lips were dry from anger. The girl did not respond and did not move.

"Donna Chiarina, your mother wants you in the living room."

"Is she alone?" the girl asked.

"No, ma'am; she has company," answered the bigot maliciously, "and she wants you."

"All right. Tell her I'm coming."

Mechanically Chiarina touched the rosary, kissed a small faded photograph of her mother which she kept on a little table, looked at herself in the mirror without really seeing, and went in the direction of the living room. Donna Gabriella, dressed in a white robe covered with the lace she had bought from the Duchess of Episcopio's maid, was seated on the large divan upholstered in the usual yellow brocade. That white robe made her seem enormous, and heightened even more the brick-red coloring of her fat cheeks. On her ear lobes donna Gabriella wore two splendid solitary diamonds. On her great bare arms almost up to the elbow and on her big red fingers which seemed swollen, there was a sparkling mass of bracelets and jeweled rings. On her breast a heavy gold chain mingled with the lace of her robe. Her fan, which she fluttered methodically, failed to mitigate the ruddy color of her large face. Donna Gabriella's eyes glittered.

Sitting in a yellow chair, modestly dressed but with a natural elegance, his fine blond hair curled, was Giovannino Affaitati, pale but calm. The two of them appeared unruffled and contented as they watched Chiarina approach tentatively, without looking at them, feeling her heart beating in her throat.

"Come here, Chiarina my dear," said donna Gabriella with unaccustomed gentleness.

Again, for no reason in the world, Chiarina was seized with fright and began to tremble. Watching her and smiling, Giovannino also invited her to come near.

"Come here, Chiarina," repeated the stepmother with tenderness in her voice.

The girl approached in silence: her little white thin hand trembling feverishly was seized by the big red seemingly swollen hands of her stepmother.

"My wish has been to make you happy," said donna Gabriella, pronouncing the words slowly, "since that seems to be God's will, and don Giovannino here is, I find, a proper young man. I want to treat you better than a mother would. God willing, and in His own time, you will be married. Give me a kiss."

On the girl's delicate cheek the stepmother planted her big smacking lips; Chiarina also performed the act of kissing. But her lips did not move, and hot silent tears trickled down her face, her neck and the bodice of her dress. Giovannino, calm, blissful, was looking at his fiancée.

"Call me mama," said the softened Gabriella to the girl. She did not answer, but continued to weep silently.

"Call me mama," she repeated humbly, almost in tears.

"Mama, mama," the girl burst out in shrieks, sobbing desperately.

When the pious Carminella, with those thin and purple lips of hers that stretched as she spoke, with those evasive and deceptive glances, went about telling everybody, in palazzo Santobuono, in the little square of the Holy Apostles, in the alleyway of Le Gradelle, there was a universal wave of satisfaction in spite of the hissing sarcastic tone of the maid, in spite of her treacherous and ambiguous silences. The continuing spectacle of that constant, indomitable, unhappy love had softened the hearts of all the neighbors, had given them a sense of great compassion.

"Donna Gabriella has made a holy decision," said the plump goodhearted donna Peppina Ranaudo, while bargaining at the landing for a basket of peaches to make the preserve known in Naples as *percocata*.

"No one is holy in the presence of God," replied the bigot, making the sign of the cross and going off.

Yet everywhere, on all sides, in spite of her insinuations, in spite of the harshness of her sour voice, she found that people would smile at this good fortune, at this prospective marriage.

"Listen, Carminè," replied donna Orsolina, who could stand no more on account of the discomfort of being pregnant in the summer, without money and without the strength to work, "listen, I must tell you that it gives me as much pleasure as if she were my own daughter. Marriage is slavery, I know; but it's what we all must come to . . ."

"Not all of us, not all of us," retorted the bigoted maid sourly.

"It's all chance," muttered donna Orsolina good-naturedly, since she felt the need to get along with everybody. "Now and then it just happens that way. . . ."

Even the old maids on the fourth floor, the teacher's sisters, expressed their satisfaction, greeting Chiarina with a festive air from behind the windowpanes of their balconies. She would lower her head and blush. Everyone she met now, on the stairs, in the courtyard, on the street, shared in her joy, greeting her with animation, presenting her with mysterious congratulations, squeezing her hands, embracing her, asking her when the "goodies would be eaten." Don Vincenzo and donna Elisa Manetta stopped her one day under the entrance arch, as the stepmother went on ahead, to tell her how their marriage had gone, a marriage between old people, which they recounted as if it were an idyl, interrupting each other to tell tender old stories. Even the coachman of the Princess of Santobuono saluted her one day with his whip and with a certain air of chivalrous gallantry and phrases full of compliments, offered himself and his carriage to take the wedding party of Chiarina and Giovannino to the church and town hall. Even the sly sacristan of the parish church of the Holy Apostles said to Chiarina one Sunday on the threshold of the church that he had had three masses said, without her knowing, for her happiness now that her stepmother's will was conforming to the grace of God. Even the laundress in the alleyway of Le Gradelle, one morning when she saw Chiarina appear on her little balcony, planted a vehement blow of her iron on the steaming shirt front and shouted happily: "Love, O love!"

Chiarina felt surrounded by this wave of tenderness and she would lower her head, overcome with emotion but not wanting to seem so. She felt inside a great confusion of happiness, always saddened, however, by an inescapable feeling of mistrust. Still, everything should now be sweetness for her. Giovannino Affaitati, in his capacity as official suitor, was allowed to write to her whenever he liked and to expect a reply; he visited her house Thursday and Sunday evenings, remaining three or four hours; if the girl was going out, he was informed and would be there on the street as if by chance, and he would join the two ladies, without any remark on the part of donna Gabriella, and would accompany them wherever they went; if the two ladies went to the theater, he was their gentleman-in-waiting, carrying the case with the eyeglass, helping them off with their shawls and cloaks, staying modestly in the back of the box. Actually, donna Gabriella was always present at all conversations between the two lovers, and never left them for a moment alone; but this is also one of the local customs, nor did the two of them think of complaining. What did it matter if she was there! They would sit in the dining room, around an oval table; in the center was a lamp covered with a large shade. Chiarina would be crocheting industriously, partly to master the nervous trembling that shook her hands;

donna Gabriella, in her pink or her blue robe, loaded down with gold and large gems, would flutter a large black fan glittering with silver sequins; Giovannino would make cigarettes and then smoke them slowly, silently. Actually, they were evenings full of sweetness. Chiarina felt during them a suspension of that sense of bitter mistrust that was spoiling all her joy: Giovannino's glance surrounded her with an atmosphere of tenderness; Giovannino's voice, breaking the silence now and then, caressed her like a lover's breathing. When he spoke in his low seductive tones, she would unintentionally stop working, her hands motionless, while the blood rose to warm her cheeks. The stepmother, from the day she had given her momentous consent, continued to be unusually polite. It seemed that all of a sudden, as if by magic, Giovannino Affaitati had succeeded in quelling that deep hatred, that deep resentment which had set one woman against the other, that the same spell had overcome the hard heart of the one and the proud heart of the other. Those evenings Giovannino Affaitati did not have permission to come up, the two women spent together; but Chiarina was always a bit nervous and donna Gabriella yawned, neglecting to flutter her fan to make her jewels sparkle. At a certain point in the evening a soft thin whistling could be heard in the little square of the Holy Apostles. Chiarina would start up.

"There he is," the girl would whisper to herself.

"There he is," donna Gabriella would say out loud.

It was Giovannino passing by at that hour on his way to spend some time at the café near the St. Januarius Gate, where at one time, word had it, the best Neapolitan ices were made, and where a crowd of burghers, employees and small landowners, priests and lottery addicts gathered. Giovannino whistled to make himself heard; and the amorous meaning of the whistle was: "Here I am, I love you, don't forget!"

Chiarina's mind would hang in suspense.

"Where would he be going now?" the stepmother would ask after a while.

"To the café," the girl would answer calmly.

"To spend money," grumbled donna Gabriella.

Chiarina would look her straight in the face, but without saying anything. The girl had kept her old pride intact; and she refrained from saying that Giovannino would not be going to spend money at the café, if she, the stepmother, had given him permission to come up more evenings; she did not tell her that because it would have seemed like asking favors, and she had no desire to ask favors of her stepmother. Naturally, her thankfulness for the happy hours she spent had tamed in Chiarina's heart that fervently youthful anger she felt toward her stepmother; but the remembrance of her father's sufferings, the remembrance of her own, was not yet obliterated. She simply did not want to ask anything of her. If she had misjudged her stepmother, if she had been unjust toward that woman, the girl wanted to be undeceived—naturally. But to ask a favor, a kindness —never. She had shut herself up within her own sensitive, extremely stubborn character, given to emotion but not to easy forgetfulness. Donna Gabriella, annoyed, would rap her fan against the chair arm. Finally, vexed by that silent face of Chiarina's that moved not a muscle, she would call Carminella. The maid would be dozing while at prayer in the kitchen.

"Let's say the holy rosary," donna Gabriella would mumble without getting up from the easy chair in which she was ensconced.

The maid would take a chair, kneel down on the bare floor, put her elbows on the straw seat and her head on her hands; then she would begin to say the Mystery. Donna Gabriella would listen attentively, moving her lips slightly, as if she too were saying the words. Chiarina would stop working and set her hook and thread on the marble-covered table, then put her hand in front of her eyes as if she were concentrating on the prayer.

". . . *Fructus ventri tui, Jesu*," the pious maid would end monotonously.

"*Sancta Maria*," the two women would carry on, finishing the *Ave*, donna Gabriella out loud, Chiarina under her breath.

When they came to the beautiful Litanies of the Virgin,

Chiarina would also get down on her knees, leaning against a chair like Carminella. Only donna Gabriella would remain seated, scarcely able to kneel on account of her bulk; but she would bend forward a bit out of respect, as it were. Sometimes while they were saying the Litanies that whistling could again be heard, soft and thin, coming from Holy Apostles Square. It was Giovannino Affaitati returning from the café and greeting his beloved before going in: "Here I am, I love you, don't forget!"

Only Chiarina's back, bent at prayer, could be seen to start. Donna Gabriella, in distraction, would stop saying the Litanies. And the maid Carminella, who was on to all this, would raise her voice, in admonition, in annoyance, praying as if she were hurling insults. She would go off in a huff at the end of the rosary, and begin to say it again, alone, in the kitchen, because that first time, in the midst of all those *temptations,* was of no value in her opinion either to the soul or to the body.

And so it was that Giovannino Affaitati began to visit Chiarina at home three times a week instead of two: it came, naturally, as a great consolation to the girl in love, and aroused no objection from her stepmother. Giovannino behaved properly: he spoke little and then in a low voice; he always asked permission to smoke; he observed, especially toward the stepmother, such courteous manners that this fat ferocious woman, pimply and covered with gold, seemed enchanted. Then, on occasion, Giovannino would venture to talk about the future with Chiarina; she would listen to him blissfully as if the sweetest music were echoing in her ears. Before answering she would raise her eyes fearfully and look toward her stepmother; then she would answer in a low voice, always timidly. One evening they were talking about trousseaus, cloth, muslin, whatever is needed to make a shirt or a skirt on the sewing machine.

"A shirt would take me two days," reckoned Chiarina, animated by the topic. "A skirt would take me only one day."

"It would take you longer, it would take you longer," interposed the stepmother.

"Rest assured, Clara, it would take you longer," Giovannino remarked with a smile, knocking the white ash off his cigarette.

Pleasant talk. The next morning Chiarina saw the porter who did the heavy work bring in two large bolts, one of the finest holland, one of good muslin. In bliss, the girl felt the holland to test its fineness and stroked the muslin to make the starch fall out, when she noticed something and turned pale. The two bolts bore a stamp, a curious stamp: she realized immediately that they came from her stepmother's pawnshop. She turned pale and trembled: those things belonged to unfortunate people who had pawned them because of poverty and had never been able to redeem them. Bolts of tears and blood, like the furniture of sorrow from a repossession, like a set of pots and pans pawned and never redeemed, like donna Gabriella's own clothing, like the jewels and gold she wore. Tears and blood of poor people, like all things. At this point her stepmother appeared.

"Will this be enough?" she asked, spreading the holland and the muslin to see the light through it.

"Yes, I think it will be enough," the girl muttered in confusion. Then, after a great effort, she added, "Thank you."

"What do you mean? I asked if it was enough; I have other things, holland, muslin, linen, many bolts, the agency is full of them. These ragamuffins keep pawning them. It's good stuff, though. Let's measure it."

And they set about measuring it in silence. Chiarina felt a pang in her heart, an incurable pang. That evening when Giovannino came she was even quieter than usual; but the stepmother, to show off her munificence, had the holland and muslin brought out although part of it had already been cut. Giovannino admired its quality, asked its value, then turned to his fiancée:

"Chiarina, did you thank our good mother for the gift she's given us?"

"Yes, I thanked her," murmured the girl without lifting her eyes from her work.

"And I thank you too, good kind mother," said Giovannino in his seductive voice. Donna Gabriella fanned herself in ecstasy. Then, called away, she left the room. And Chiarina, speaking rapidly in a whisper, said to Giovannino, "Did you know? It's cloth from the shop."

"Well? What of it?" he asked in surprise.

"It's been pawned, I tell you," she insisted fearfully.

"Yes, I realize. What of it?" he repeated calmly.

At that moment the girl suffered cruelly; but her stepmother was returning and she dared say nothing more. The next day everyone in the palazzo was talking about donna Gabriella's generosity in giving Chiarina a trousseau fit for the daughter of a princess. But the girl, disappointed, discouraged, had not been able to sleep a wink the whole night. Toward morning she had fallen asleep uneasily, dreaming that she had on a fantastic shirt of tears and a fantastic skirt of blood, and that donna Gabriella and Giovannino laughed at it long and loud. It took many days to overcome her scruples; and the disillusionment remained painfully in her heart. She worked now at the sewing machine, even in the evening: its clatter distracted her from unpleasant thoughts. Sometimes she was so absorbed in her work that her stepmother and Giovannino would converse without her even noticing. He addressed the large woman, mincing in her girl's robe, with a deep respect that flattered her, and he had a certain air of attentiveness in listening to her that also flattered the large red and puffy woman. But when Chiarina lifted her eyes, Giovannino would look again at his fiancée with such tenderness that she felt ready to die of love, and he spoke to her with such gentleness that she would stop working, overwhelmed, and the sewing machine would come to a halt. They now talked often about their future house: that is, Giovannino would sketch a fine bedroom, with a great glittering brass bed, made to order by Angelo Pesce, with a carved mahogany wardrobe fronted by a big looking glass.

"You need a mahogany dressing table with a gray marble top," suggested donna Gabriella maternally.

"Yes, a dressing table too, and a nice chaise longue at the foot of the bed, since that's fashionable now," Giovannino added.

When she heard these delightful plans, Chiarina, who loved Giovannino more and more, would lose herself in the happiest of dreams. Her marriage day meant liberation for her, a complete and natural forgetting of the painful past, the beginning of a serene new life at the side of her beloved, just the two of them alone, holding hands in joy and in sorrow: she would be free, free, at his side forever, divided in the flesh only by death, but reunited *beyond*, since she really believed. If the day would only come soon when she would leave the house where she had suffered so much to go with her husband to their house where she would be the happiest of women. This is what the religious, lovesick girl dreamt of. But one evening, while Giovannino was talking about a fine image of the Virgin, the Madonna di Valle di Pompei, that should be hung on the wall of their bedroom, Chiarina stopped working and ventured to ask: "What about the living room?"

"What living room?" interposed her stepmother in surprise.

"The living room where visitors are received," said the girl, on the point of trembling.

"Isn't mine good enough? I think it's elegant, all in yellow brocade; it's like new. Then too, I see hardly anyone; it will always be for your use."

"Oh," breathed the girl in quick reaction.

Her sweet dream of freedom, of solitude, had vanished—cruelly vanished forever. Giovannino, his eyes downcast, remained silent. That evening the stepmother never moved for a moment from her easy chair. Chiarina worked rapidly, a bit nervously, often breaking the thread and the needle on the machine. When Giovannino got up to leave, she resolutely got up too and followed him outside the door. There she stopped him. They were alone. The moon shone on the landing, the stairs and the courtyard.

"Did you hear what my stepmother said?" she asked, fidgeting with the doorlock.

"What did she say?" he asked in annoyance.

"That we don't need a living room. Will we live with her, then?"

"That's the way it looks."

"Why?"

"Because we have no money, dear girl," he said, stroking her hair gently.

She took another tack.

"Then do we have to live on her charity?"

"What charity? She's our mother; she has money and she doesn't know what to do with it. She has only you: it's her duty to give you what you need to live on."

"You ought to work, Giovannino; you ought to provide my support. I only want to eat bread, but yours, not hers, Giovannino."

"I'll do just that, my dear; that's exactly what I'll do: I'll try to work and earn something. Right now, you realize, work is hard to find. I'll think of something."

"Promise me you'll find something," she pleaded.

"I promise. But it will be hard at first; we'll have to make this do. We'll be all right, you'll see."

"But after, at least after, promise me again that we'll go away, that we won't live off her charity," she implored him.

"Don't say such naughty exaggerated words; you're just a bit extreme, you know. When you don't have money, you have to be reasonable. I'll promise you whatever you want; don't worry."

They left each other discontented. Donna Gabriella was standing in the dining room as if she were waiting impatiently for her stepdaughter's return.

With a slight frown she confined herself to saying, "You took a long time."

"I'm sorry, I'm sorry," said the girl, bursting into tears.

And those tears stayed in her heart, in spite of her outburst. She couldn't reconcile herself to the idea of living in her stepmother's house, eating her charity bread, which so many times had been thrown in her face as given out of charity; she couldn't tolerate the idea, for herself or for Giovannino or for their new family's pride. Meanwhile, wherever she went she heard people speak well of donna Gabriella, a saintly woman, who after giving her stepdaughter the trousseau of a princess was now getting ready a splendid apartment, granting her nothing less than the living room in yellow-gold brocade. True; but Chiarina could find no way to console herself. So every evening, with a certain anxiety, she would ask Giovannino whether he had been looking, whether he had made progress. He would answer vaguely, telling her of a job with the railway, but it was necessary to have influence with the director general; of a position with the city lighting company as a regular employee, a municipal business, but one had to know the mayor and the department head. In a vague way she allowed herself to be satisfied with little, yet she understood that he was not looking seriously, that he told her those things only to comfort and deceive her. And she would then insist, insist with some warmth, until he shrugged his shoulders in annoyance. Now, on the other hand, he would often talk business with Chiarina's stepmother. At first he had made cautious inquiries, as if it were a distant matter, and she had answered inconclusively. But then, little by little she had begun to explain her affairs openly and to talk with him about the dark and dismal world of pawnshops. Chiarina listened in surprise; now and then she would look fearfully at Giovannino, as if she wanted to make certain it was actually he and not someone else who went on about those dismal matters.

"The *office*," donna Gabriella would say when she wanted to mention the pawnshop.

"The *office*," Giovannino would echo when he wanted to mention the pawnshop, with an air of mysterious compunction.

They didn't dare yet to call it by its harsh name. But now they talked about it at length every evening, in spite of the expression of suffering that would cross Chiarina's face every time they started on the subject. Donna Gabriella complained bitterly that those witches who brought things to be pawned for someone else who was ashamed to enter the shop would demand too high a consideration: one lira for every ten.

"When you come right down to it, what sort of work do these ugly creatures do?" said donna Gabriella, almost in anger. "They stand there waiting for timid poor people who haven't the courage to come into the *office*, they take from them, as nicely as you please, a clock, for instance, and just for that they get maybe three lire above the price of thirty."

"A real racket," Giovannino agreed, in his charmingly modulated voice.

"And nothing can be done, do you see? Nothing can be done about it. True, at first even I worked as a small-time pawnbroker, sparing lots of people the shame of going into the *office*; but I always did it honestly, keeping only half a lira for every ten. But with God's help and the protection of the Virgin, I made so many deals that it actually amounted to the same! . . ."

"You've always been a fine upstanding woman," exclaimed Giovannino, full of emotion and looking at her with admiration.

Chiarina would tremble now and then, as if she were hearing things intolerable to her. But then her mind became confused and she would no longer hear, sensing the distant noise of words, feeling a kind of aching pain, a dull but continual pain. One evening, in order to explain something to Giovannino more clearly, donna Gabriella went to get the books of the pawnshop. The lovers were left alone.

"Why are you doing this, Giovannino? Why are you doing this?" the girl asked feverishly, completely at a loss.

"It's good to know as much as you can," he said calmly, throwing away his cigarette.

She made no reply. He had absolute power over her; she adored him as if he were a god, but a god who could make her cry as easily as laugh. She suffered on his account, but obedient, subdued, she made no reply. All evening long, donna Gabriella and Giovannino sat bending over the large dirty books, pondering the cruel machinery that allows the pawnbroker always to be perfectly sure of his capital, to exact usurious interest, and finally to confiscate an item three times as valuable as the capital risked: the cruel machinery that makes it nearly impossible for someone who has pawned something ever to get it back.

"Eighty times out of a hundred it happens that the item

becomes ours," donna Gabriella concluded triumphantly, shutting her large and dirty books.

"It's splendid, splendid," murmured Giovannino lost in thought.

And in spite of the pleading glances from his fiancée, he asked donna Gabriella to lend him those books just for the next day, which was a Sunday, since she had no need for them: he wanted to make a study of them; he was looking at new things, and it was just possible he might be able to give her some better piece of advice. When on his way out he went over to clasp his fiancée's hand, he found it cold.

"What's wrong, Chiarina?" he asked her in a low voice.

"I'm suffering; you make me suffer," she replied, almost fainting.

"Don't be silly; let me handle it. You'll see."

But from then on, their dialogues of love were very short. The whole evening (Giovannino now came every evening, without any objection from the stepmother) was spent in talking about the pawnshop, the items, the interest, the pawn ticket or the container for which another charge was added: that is, about the whole black procession of black words that encompass this torment of the poor. Giovannino spoke of it without repugnance, indeed, with composure: he had understood everything at once, had become expert, gave practical advice; donna Gabriella looked at him with a tender glance. And in secret one day Giovannino went around ten o'clock to the pawnshop where donna Gabriella sat in state and stayed there until twelve. He took to going there every day, but kept the poor innocent Chiarina in the dark. He, Giovannino, with his bewitching glance, his gentle voice, became such a hard bargainer, such a devious and rapacious amasser of money, of half lire and lire, that donna Gabriella was in ecstasy. Now, before going to the shop the fat pawnbroker fitted herself out in her best dresses and showiest hats; she tightened herself in the breast to the point of suffocation, always wearing four or five thousand lire worth of jewels, and she even bought some Rossetter to dye her hair. Chiarina would watch her leave every morning and follow her with her eyes, seized as she was by an uncontrollable tremor of fear; sometimes she would wait for her at the window at two in the afternoon, nervous, troubled, not knowing why, trembling with impatience. Indeed, from the living room balcony that looked out on the Square, one day she saw her returning escorted by Giovannino. She drew back, bewildered but as yet unaware.

Her stepmother came up alone. "I met Giovannino," she said quickly, "and I had him walk with me part of the way."

"Oh," said Chiarina.

But that evening the secret of Giovannino's work at the pawnshop came out, since the large fat pawnbroker said laughingly to her stepdaughter's fiancé:

"Giovannino, remember that man who wanted to pawn the nickel watch?"

"If I hadn't been there, you would have done it," replied Giovannino, undismayed yet not turning toward Chiarina.

"You're right; I've seen how sharp you are: you were born to be a pawnbroker."

The girl got up suddenly and left the room. The two remained silent for a while, looking at each other. The first to speak, and with composure, was Giovannino; but now and then something like a tremor clouded his voice. Chiarina did not reappear.

"Carminella, what is Chiarina doing?" donna Gabriella asked the maid whom she had summoned.

"She's saying her prayers," the bigot answered dryly, taking in both of them in a single sullen glance, and then went out.

Yet, after a while Chiarina reappeared. She paused stiffly at the doorway:

"Mother!" she said in a voice much changed. "Mother!"

"What is it?"

"Will you let me say something to Giovannino?"

"Of course."

"It has to be secret, if you don't mind. I'd like him to come here."

"Can't you say it in front of her?" said Giovannino, trying to avoid the interview.

"I'm sorry, I can't, Giovannino. Please excuse me, Mother, but I have to talk in secret," Chiarina insisted, her voice betraying emotion.

"Go on, go on, Giovannino; make her happy," said donna Gabriella with an air of motherly protectiveness.

"Just as you say," he said, bowing.

Chiarina took him by the hand and led him out on the little balcony near the open well where they had had so many delightful conversations when their love found so much to hinder it. It was a dark night. A vast coolness rose up from the open well: they were there beside it, among those wet coils of rope that covered the floor. Down below, on the second-floor balcony, the maid of the excellent plump donna Peppina Ranaudo was laboriously drawing up a bucket of water by the light of a flickering candle, singing to herself. Chiarina was still holding her fiancé's hand convulsively tight.

"Do you really have the heart to do that?" she asked anxiously.

"Heart to do what?"

"How can *you, you,* my dearest, have anything to do with a business like that? It's so shameless, so cruel."

"Don't exaggerate, Chiarina."

"Don't you know that it's a business of tears and blood? Don't you know that everyone hates us for it, and that the curses of the poor fall on us?"

"Don't exaggerate."

"Don't you know that my poor father died from the disgust, the horror he felt for it?"

"Don't exaggerate."

"Don't you realize that I'll die from the sorrow I feel?"

"People don't die from such little causes," he murmured, smiling in the shadows.

"Oh my dearest, my dearest," she cried, wringing her hands, "how can you do this and love me too?"

"Calm down, Clara, calm down," he said in fear.

And he took up her hands, in the dark, and caressed them; in a whisper he spoke vague words to her, as if to benumb her pain. She listened, still trembling, gradually calming down; he touched, now, on more practical, more positive matters.

"My dear girl, you yourself urged me to find work so that we wouldn't have to live off the charity of your stepmother. I've looked, as you saw, I've looked for a long time, and I haven't found anything: it's all a matter of luck and backing. But so many deserving people, better than I, are out on the street. I haven't found anything. Then I thought I might make myself useful to your stepmother. Do you think it hasn't cost me a lot? I've suffered, but I've borne up out of love for you, not to have you live off charity . . ."

She sobbed in the shadows.

"Don't cry, Clara; there's no reason to cry. Of course it's not a very nice profession; but I'd do anything for you. Even your stepmother, believe me, is a good woman. She's acted very well toward us. What can you complain of? And her interests, you know, my dear girl, are our interests too. Don't you realize, silly girl, that we will inherit it from her? Then too, if there are people who have to pawn their possessions, someone has to do it, isn't that true?"

"Don't say such things," she murmured, exhausted.

"I won't, then. But the matter of looking after our interests, my dear, you can't blame me for that. You know the only thing that makes me afraid? It's that your stepmother might remarry. Then we'd be in a fine fix!"

She looked at him in the shadows.

"But I don't really think she will," he added at once to mute the effect of his words. "She's already well along in years. She's a good woman if you take her in the right spirit. Are you calm now?"

"Yes."

"Do you love me?"

". . . Yes."

"Do you believe that I love you very very much?"

". . . Yes."

"Will you give me a kiss?"

It was the first time he had asked. She took a step backward, and leaning against the well, said, "No!"

"You're a naughty girl; but you'll give me one another time," he said, laughing a little to hide his embarrassment.

They went in at once. But the girl said she was tired and wanted to go to bed. To tell the truth, from that evening on she could no longer sleep; her excitable nature, heightened by pain and by love, gave her no peace. At night she would light the lamp again, pace up and down her room, write, and then tear up the tormented letters that flowed from her pen, addressed to Giovannino. She would douse her head in a basin of cold water to calm herself: an icy shiver would come over her. At times on the other side of the door she would hear light steps. It was Carminella who slept near by and who would come barefoot to eavesdrop.

"Miss?"

"Yes?"

"Don't you feel well?"

"Yes; but I can't sleep."

"Say your prayers."

"I said them."

"Say them again."

"It's no use, Carminella, it's no use."

"Commend yourself to the Virgin."

"She has forgotten me."

"Don't talk that way."

"Good night."

"Good night. God keep you."

During the daytime too Carminella was always around her, showing her attentions she had never shown before. And when she went out all the tenants of palazzo Santobuono would surround her and call her "the bride." The girl would smile, like someone suffering from chills and fever, at those inquiring about her feverish condition. At times, when Carminella accompanied her, it would be the maid who would answer with customary Neapolitan familiarity:

"God willing, there'll be a marriage."

Carminella would now try to draw the girl often to church, and she, who could find no peace at any hour of the day, would go willingly. The chill inside the church soothed the burning in her head, and prayer would gather up the tangled threads of her thought. Yes, she would go to church often, morning and evening, especially to vespers. Carminella always kept close to her, as if she were always wanting to tell her something; but the girl would look at her with so lost an expression that she would seem to swallow her words and then fall silent. They went to vespers every evening: the hour was gentle and sweet, and the women's singing was melancholy; so much so that, melting with emotion, the girl would start to weep. Her strength now was giving way wearily, in the presence of deep disillusionment, in the presence of that deep and bitter sorrow that had fallen on her in the fullness of love. One of those evenings she felt so ill that she was on the point of fainting. She turned very pale.

"Let's leave," she said to Carminella.

"The service isn't over," answered the maid, frightened.

"If I stay here another minute I'll faint."

Resentfully the bigot stood up and slowly followed her mistress, as if she wanted to force her to slacken her pace. But Chiarina, impatient, nervous, turned round.

"Do you have the key?" she asked.

"Well, I don't know . . ."

"You must have it; give it to me."

Automatically the maid gave it to her and the girl started to run ahead, anxious to be home so that she might throw herself on her bed as if she were about to die. As in a dream, the maid found no way of quickening her pace to reach the girl. Chiarina quickly opened the door of the house, but from the waiting room a sound of voices struck her ear, a sound of voices that made her pale face turn livid. She had the strength to go forward, to pull aside, gradually, the yellow brocade curtains, to see her fiancé gently kissing the lips of her stepmother. A horrible high-pitched scream, barely human in sound, pierced the apartment. It was heard everywhere, and summoned the peaceable inhabitants of palazzo Santobuono. It was a scream they will never be able to forget. Then people heard a furious running through the apartment, a slamming of doors, pleading, desperate calls from two voices. The door of the little balcony, violently opened, smashed a broken pane, and in the evening light a shadow appeared at the edge of the well.

At the sound of screaming, all windows, all landings lit up. Donna Gabriella was shrieking from the little balcony, shrieking:

"She's thrown herself down the well! She's thrown herself down the well!"

The well-man came in ten minutes. Carminella had gone to look for him; he was still asleep, since he worked from midnight on underground. He was a tall strong man, wearing shirt and trousers, barefoot, with a certain way of blinking his eyes. Down in the courtyard the coachmen and stable boys tied a thick rope around his waist and he began the descent. Immense silence. Carminella, on her knees at the third-floor landing, prayed fervently, and all the rest, perhaps, prayed too. The stepmother's head had sunk to the cold iron of the railing while Giovannino still looked down fixedly.

"Easy!" said a voice from the depths that seemed hoarse to the coachmen.

The well-man had reached bottom. After three or four minutes he tugged vigorously: and the coachmen and stable boys began to pull. It was heavy. He was bringing up the body. At one point donna Peppina Ranaudo, who was sobbing, cried out: "Is she dead or alive?"

"Dead!" answered the hoarse labored voice.

And from all sides, from the first to the top floor, in the street, in the alleyways, came groans, weeping, sobbing.

"Dead, dead, dead!"

# ITALO SVEVO

## 1861–1928

Italo Svevo, whose real name was Ettore Schmitz, symbolized in his chosen pen-name a mixed Italian and middle-European origin and cultural tradition ("Svevo" means "Swabian"). This origin, and the fact that his background was the city of Trieste, account both for a European, rather than a local Italian quality in his art, and for the fact that its recognition was slow and due in part to critical acceptance outside of Italian literary circles. In Trieste, where he was born in 1861, Svevo was the head of an important industrial concern. Thus his practical life had a wider scope than that of the ordinary professional man of letters; this too may account for the delay in recognition, while the contacts he did have with contemporary writers may for that reason acquire sharper relevance (e.g., with James Joyce during his Trieste period). His first two novels came out in Trieste in 1892 and 1898 with extremely limited success; his major work, *The Confessions of Zeno*, first appeared when Svevo was sixty-two. He died five years later in 1928, as a consequence of an automobile accident. The shorter pieces of narrative were published posthumously as Svevo's reputation acquired world dimensions.

# This Indolence of Mine

From neither calendar nor clock can the present really be sought; calendars and clocks are consulted simply to establish one's relationship with the past or in order to move with some semblance of consciousness into the future. I and the things and people surrounding me constitute the true present.

Besides this, the present consists of various stages. Thus there is this very significant and very lengthy present stage: the abandonment of business. It has lasted for eight years. A touching inertia. Then there are some important events that break it up: the marriage of my daughter, for instance, an event long passed and one which is becoming part of the other drawn-out present, undisturbed—or perhaps renewed or, better, rectified—by her husband's death. The birth of my little grandson is distant now as well, because the real present as far as Umberto is concerned is my affection for him and his winning of it. He is not aware of this since he believes it a birthright. (Or, generally speaking, is that wee soul able to believe anything at all?) His present, and mine in relation to him, are actually his short, steady steps interrupted by painful moments of fear and relieved by the company of dolls when he cannot win help from his mother or me, his grandfather. My present is also Augusta (the poor woman!), reduced now to her animals—dogs, cats, and birds—and her eternal petty complaints to which she is not devoting energy enough to recover. She does the little bit prescribed by Dr. Raulli but refuses to listen to me, who by superhuman effort was able to overcome a similar tendency toward heart strain; nor does she see fit to listen to Carlo, our nephew (Guido's son), who has just finished the University and is therefore acquainted with the most up-to-date medicines.

*Translated by Ben Johnson.*

Unquestionably, a great part of my present has its origins in the pharmacy. I cannot recall exactly when this present began, but every now and then it has been intersected by medicines and new theories. Where is the time when once I believed I was fulfilling all my organism required—every evening gulping down a hearty dose of some compound of powdered licorice or those ordinary powdered or broth bromides? Now, with Carlo's help, I have at my disposal much better means for the struggle against disease. Carlo imparts all he knows; but I am not telling all I surmise because I am afraid that he does not agree with me and might with his objections demolish the castle which I sought with such effort and which gave me a measure of tranquillity, a security people at my age do not normally have. A real castle it is! Carlo believes that it is out of confidence in him that I accept all of his suggestions so readily. Tommyrot! I am quite aware that he knows a great deal; I am trying to pick it up, to put it to use—but with discretion. My arteries are not what they ought to be. About this there is no doubt. Last summer my blood pressure reached two hundred and twenty. I cannot say whether it was due to that or something else; at any rate I was very depressed at the time. The depression ended as soon as generous doses of iodine and another chemical, the name of which I never remember, reduced the pressure to a hundred and sixty, where it has remained till now. . . . (I have just now interrupted my writing for a moment in order to measure it at the machine I keep ever ready on my table. It is exactly a hundred and sixty!) In the past I always used to feel threatened by an apoplectic stroke which I honestly felt was coming on. In the presence of death I did not really become any kinder, because I was unable to stomach all those people who were not threatened by a stroke, and had the disgusting look of safe people who pity, commiserate with, and amuse themselves.

Guided by Carlo, I even cured some organs which in no way required help. It has to be understood that every one of my organs cannot help but feel fagged out after so many years of work, and that they profit from being assisted. I send them unasked-for aid. When disease strikes, the doctor is very apt to sigh: I've been called too late! For that reason it is better to look ahead. I cannot initiate cures for the liver when it shows no sign of malfunction; but even so, I must not lay myself open to an end like that of a son of a friend of mine who, one fine day, at the age of thirty-two and in full health, turned yellow as a melon with a violent attack of jaundice and then died within forty-eight hours. "He had never been sick," his poor father told me, "he was a giant, yet he had to die." Many giants finish badly. I have noticed this and I am quite happy not being a giant. But prudence is a fine thing. So every Monday I donate a pill to my liver, and this protects it from violent and sudden maladies, at least until the following Monday. I watch over my kidneys with periodic analyses, and until now they have shown no sign of malfunction. But I know that they can stand some help. My exclusively milk diet on Tuesdays affords me a certain security for the rest of the week. Wouldn't it be fine, while others—who never give a thought to their kidneys—keep them running merrily along, for me, sacrificing myself to them every week, to be suddenly rewarded by a surprise like that which befell poor Copler!

About five years ago I was disturbed by chronic bronchitis. It interfered with my sleep and from period to period had me jumping out of bed to spend several hours nightly sitting in an easy chair. The doctor did not see fit to tell me, but doubtless a cardiac weakness was involved. Raulli proceeded to prescribe that I give up smoking, that I lose weight, and that I eat very little meat. Inasmuch as giving up smoking was difficult, I sought to fulfill the prescription by renouncing all meat. But not even losing weight was easy. At the time I had a net weight of two hundred and seven pounds. In three years I succeeded in losing four and a half pounds, and at that rate, to reach the weight Raulli wanted, another eighteen years would have been called for. But it was a bit difficult to eat moderately when I was abstaining from meat.

And here I must confess that I really owe my loss of weight to Carlo. It was one of his first curative successes. He proposed that I forgo one of my three daily meals; and I resolved to sacrifice supper, which we Triestines take at eight in the evening unlike other Italians who have lunch at noon and dinner at seven. Every day I fast uninterruptedly for eighteen hours.

First of all, I slept better. I felt at once that my heart, no longer assisting in digestive work, could devote every beat to filling the veins, to carrying waste matter from the organism, and above all to nourishing the lungs. I, who had once suffered from terrible periods of insomnia—the great unsettlement of one longing for peace and who for that very reason loses it—I would lie there motionless, calmly awaiting the approach of warmth and sleep—a genuine parenthesis in an exhausting life. Sleep after a sumptuous dinner is entirely something else again: then the heart is occupied with digestion alone and its other duties are dismissed.

In the first place, it proved that I was better adapted to abstinence than to moderation. It was easier not to eat supper at all than to limit the amount of food at lunch and breakfast. At these times there were no limitations. Twice a day I could gorge myself. There was no harm in it because eighteen hours of autophagy followed. At first, the midday meal of *pasta asciutta* and vegetables was topped off with some eggs. Then I even gave these up, not because Raulli or Carlo asked me to, but in accordance with the judicious advice of a philosopher, Herbert Spencer, who discovered some law or other to the effect that organs which develop too fast—through overnourishment—are less strong than those taking a longer time to grow. The law naturally pertained to children, but I am convinced that returning to it is a step forward, that even a seventy-year-old child would do well to starve his organs rather than overnourish them. Carlo, moreover, agreed with my theory, and sometimes wanted others to believe that he himself had formulated it.

In this effort to renounce dinner, smoking was a tremendous boon. The smoker can fast more easily than others. A good smoke numbs whatever appetite there is. It is precisely to smoking that I believe I owe having been able to reduce my net weight to one hundred and seventy-six pounds. It was a great relief to smoke for hygienic reasons. I smoked a little more with this perfectly guiltless conscience. Fundamentally, health is a truly miraculous state. Brought about by the interworking of various organs whose functions we can only know imperfectly (as even Carlo admits, who has grasped the whole science), it derives from the belief that perfect health never exists. Otherwise its termination would be even more miraculous. Moving things ought to be able to move forever. Why not? Isn't this the law in Heaven, the same law as that enforced on earth? But I know that from birth onward diseases are predestined and prepared. From the very beginning some organs start out weaker than others, overexerting themselves and driving related organs to greater effort; and where there is exertion fatigue results, and from it, ultimately, death.

Because of that, and only because of that, a malady followed by death does not reveal any disorders in our constitutions. I am too ignorant to know whether at the end, up there in Heaven, as down here on earth, there exists the possibility of death and reproduction. I only know that some stars and even some planets have less complete movements than others. It must be that a planet which does not rotate on itself is either lame, blind, or humpbacked.

But among our organs is one that is the center, almost the sun in a solar system. Up until a few years ago this organ was thought to be the heart. At the moment everybody knows that our entire life is dependent upon the genital organs. Carlo turns up his nose at rejuvenation operations, but still he doffs his cap when the genitals are mentioned. He says: If the sexual organs could be rejuvenated they would naturally rejuvenate the whole organism. This was nothing new to me. I would have known that without his telling me. But it will never come to pass. It's impossible. God only knows what the effects of monkey glands are. Maybe a rejuvenated person upon seeing a beautiful woman will be driven to climb the nearest tree. (Even so, this is a pretty juvenile act.)

This I understand: Mother Nature is a maniac. That is to say, she has a mania for reproduction. She maintains life within an organism as long as there is hope of its reproducing itself. Then she kills it off, and does so in the most diverse ways because of her other mania of remaining mysterious. She does not wish to give herself away by always finding recourse in the same malady to do away with old folks—like a malady which might throw light upon our deaths, a little tumor always in the same place, for example.

I have always been very enterprising. Without resorting to an operation, I wanted to hoodwink Mother Nature and make her believe that I was still fit for reproduction; so I took a mistress. This was the least disturbing affair I have ever had in my life: first of all, I considered it neither a lapse of character nor a betrayal of Augusta. I should have felt a bit uneasy, but I regarded taking a mistress a decision equivalent to entering a pharmacy.

Then, of course, matters complicated themselves a little. It ended with my awareness that a whole person cannot be used as a medicine: besides, it is a complex medicine containing a substantial amount of poison. I was still not really old. It was an episode which occurred three years ago, when I was sixty-seven: I was not yet a very old man. Therefore my heart, which was an organ of secondary importance in the adventure and should not have had to enter it, ended by taking part. And it so happened that on some days even Augusta profited from my adventure and was caressed, fondled, and rewarded as she had been when I had had Carla. The curious thing was that it did not surprise her and that she was not even aware of the novelty. She inhabits her great calm and finds it natural that I occupy myself with her less than in the past; still our present inertia does not weaken the bonds between us, which are knotted with caresses and affectionate words. These caresses and affectionate words do not have to be repeated in order to endure, to exist anywhere, to remain always alive and always equally intimate, this bond between us. When, one day, in order to salve my conscience, I placed two fingers underneath her chin and gazed at length into her faithful eyes, she abandoned herself to me, offering up her lips: "You have always remained affectionate." At the moment

I was a little taken aback. Then, examining the past, I noticed that in fact I had never been so wanting in affection as to deny her my old love. I had even hugged her (a little distractedly) every evening before closing my eyes in sleep.

It was somewhat difficult to find the woman I sought. There was no one in the house suited to such a role; no more was I eager to sully my home. But I would have done so, since I had to hoodwink Mother Nature into believing that the moment for my final illness had not yet arrived—since there was the grand, the enormous task of finding one who would serve the purposes of an old man engaged in political economy. But, really, that was not the approach. The handsomest woman at home was Augusta herself. There was a little fourteen-year-old girl Augusta made use of for certain household chores. But I knew that if I were to accost this child Mother Nature would not have believed me and would have struck me down at once with one of those thunderbolts she always keeps at her disposal.

It is pointless to relate how I came to find Felicita. Out of sheer devotion to hygiene I used to go every day, to supply myself with cigarettes, some distance beyond Piazza Unità, and this called for a walk of more than a half hour. The clerk was an old woman, but the owner of the tobacco shop and one who spent occasional hours there supervising was actually Felicita, a girl about twenty-four years old. At the beginning I was of the impression that she had inherited the shop; much later I learned that she had bought it with her own money. It was there that I came to know her. We struck it off well at once. I liked her. She was a blonde who dressed in a variety of colors, in material that did not seem expensive to me but was always new and gaudy. She took pride in that beauty of hers: the small head puffed out at the sides with close-cropped, very curly hair, and the very erect and lovely little body which appeared to contain a staff within it arching a little backward. It was not long before I came to learn something of her liking for varied colors. At her house this taste was revealed all over the place. From time to time the house was not well heated, and once I took note of the colors she was wearing: she had a red kerchief bound around her head in the style of a peasant woman, a yellow brocaded shawl about her shoulders, a quilted apron in red, yellow and green over her blue skirt, and a pair of multicolored quilted slippers on her feet. She was a real oriental figurine; but her pale face was actually one from our parts, with its eyes that scrutin ed things and people to derive from them as much as possib e. A monthly allotment was established at the outset and, fr nkly, it was so high that I could not help comparing it with regret to the much lower allowances given before the war. And as early as the twentieth of the month Felicita (the dear girl) began to talk about the stipend that was falling due, thereby disturbing a good part of the month. She was sincere, transparent. I was less so; and she never learned that I had come to her after having studied medical texts.

But I soon lost sight of that fact. I must say that at the moment I long for that house, so completely rural in aspect except for a single room appointed in the good taste and luxury one would expect at the price, very soberly colored and dimly lighted—a background against which Felicita stood out like a multicolored blossom. She had a brother living in the same house: a good, hard-working electrician whose daily wages were more than enough. He was extremely skinny, but that had nothing to do with his not being married; rather, one could easily see, this was due to his economy. I spoke with him the times Felicita called him in to check the fuses in our room. I discovered that brother and sister were partners, about to make themselves some money. Felicita carried on a very serious life between the tobacconist's shop and the house, Gastone between the house and his workshop. Felicita must have been making more than Gastone but that did not matter, since—as I later learned—she apparently needed her brother's help. It was he who had organized the tobacco-shop business which was proving itself such a sound investment. He was so convinced that he was leading the life of an upright man that he spoke scornfully of the many workers who were frittering their earnings away with never a thought of tomorrow.

All in all we three got along rather well together. The

room, so soberly and meticulously kept, smacked of a doctor's consultation chamber. But only because Felicita was a slightly tart medicine that had to be bolted down without the palate's savoring it at its leisure. At the very beginning, somewhat before drawing up terms and in order to encourage me, she threw her arms around me and said: "I give you my word, I don't find you repulsive." It was said nicely enough because said so sweetly, but it gave me pause. I had never really thought of myself as being repulsive. On the contrary, I had believed that I was returning to love, from which I had long abstained through a misinterpretation of hygienic laws, in order to surrender, to offer myself up, to whomever wanted me. This would have been real hygienic practice, which was my aim, and in any other form it would have been incomplete and ineffectual. But notwithstanding the money I paid for the cure I did not dare explain to Felicita how I wanted her to be. And she, very frequently throwing herself at me, would spoil the cure with her complete naïveté: "Isn't it curious! I don't find you repulsive." One day, with the crudeness I can sink to on certain occasions, I murmured gently in her ear: "Isn't it curious! I don't find you repulsive either." This made her giggle so much that the cure was interrupted.

And off and on, in my mind, I even dare boast—to give myself a lift, feel more confident of myself, worthier, loftier, to forget that I have dedicated a part of my life to the task of making myself unrepulsive—I boast that Felicita during brief moments of our long relationship was even in love with me. But when I seek a genuine expression of her affection I find it not in the never-changing sweetness with which she invariably greeted me, nor in the maternal care with which she protected me from drafts, nor in her solicitude once when she covered me with one of her brother's overcoats and lent me an umbrella because a storm had blown up while we were together; but I remember this honest prattle of hers: "Oh, how I loathe you! How I *loathe* you!"

One day when as usual I was talking with Carlo about medicine, he remarked: "What you need is an affectionate girl given to gerontophilia." Who knows? I did not confess to Carlo, but perhaps I had once already found and then lost such a girl. Except that I do not believe that Felicita was a thoroughgoing gerontophile. She took me for too much money for me to think that she really loved me as I was.

She certainly was the most costly woman I have ever known in all my life. She quietly studied me with those cool, tender eyes of hers, often squinting the better to determine the extent to which I would allow myself to be fleeced. In the beginning, and for a long time thereafter, she was completely satisfied with her allowance, because I, not yet a slave of habit, intimated that I would refuse to spend more on her. On several occasions she tried to reach for my money, but withdrew her hand from my pocket in order not to expose herself to the risk of losing me. Once, though, she did bring it off. She got money out of me to buy a rather expensive fur piece, which I never laid eyes on. Another time she got me to pay for an entire Parisian ensemble and then let me see it: but for one even as blind as I was her varicolored clothes were unforgettable and I found that I had seen her in that suit before. She was an economy-minded woman who pretended caprice only because she thought that a man understood caprice in a woman more easily than avarice.

And now this is how against my wishes the relationship was broken off.

I had visited her at set hours twice a week. Then, one Tuesday after I had set out for her house it occurred to me midway there that I would be better off by myself. I returned to my study and quietly devoted myself to a recording of Beethoven's *Ninth Symphony*.

On Wednesday I should not have felt such a strong craving for Felicita, but it was really my avarice that drove me to her. I was paying her a substantial allowance and somehow, not receiving my just due, I finished by paying too much. One must remember that when I take a cure I am very conscientious in its application and resort to the greatest and most scientific exactitude. In the end, only in this way can it be determined whether the cure was good or bad.

As fast as my legs would carry me I was in that room which I believed to be *ours*. For the moment it belonged to another. Fat old Misceli, a man about my age, was sitting in an easy chair in a corner while Felicita lounged comfortably on the couch, concentrating on the flavor of a long and very choice cigarette—one which was not to be had in her shop. Essentially, it was the very same position in which Felicita and I found ourselves when we were left together, the only difference being that whereas Misceli was not smoking I joined Felicita in it.

"What may I do for you?" Felicita asked icily, studying the fingernails of the hand which was holding the cigarette aloft.

Words failed me. Then it became easier to speak because, to tell the truth, I did not feel the least resentment toward Misceli. This fat man, who was as old as I, looked considerably older because of his tremendous weight. He eyed me warily over the rim of the shiny spectacles he had perched on the tip of his nose. I always feel other old men to be older than I am.

"Oh, Misceli," I said forthrightly, fully resolved not to make a scene, "it's a long time since we've seen each other." And I extended my hand. He laid his ham of a hand in mine without returning my clasp. Still he said nothing. He was indeed showing himself to be older than I.

At that moment, with the objectivity that is precisely a wise man's, I understood perfectly that my position and Misceli's were identical. I felt that because of it we were in no position to resent each other. After all, our meeting here amounted to no more than an ordinary bumping-together on a sidewalk. However painful it may be, one continues on one's way mumbling a word of pardon.

With this thought, the gentleman I have always been re-formed within me. I even felt called upon to make Felicita's situation more tolerable. And I said to her: "Signorina, listen: I've got to have a hundred packets of well-selected 'sport' cigarettes because I have to make a gift. Would you see to it that they are soft, please? The tobacco shop is a little too far and I've dropped up here for a moment."

Felicita stopped staring at her nails and her attitude softened. She even rose and walked me to the door. In a low voice, with intense accents of reproach, she managed to say: "Why didn't you come yesterday?" And then, quickly: "And what have you come today for?"

I was offended. It was disgusting to see myself limited to fixed days at the price I was paying. I allowed myself immediate relief by giving vent to my pique: "I've only come here today to let you know that I don't want to see you any more and that we won't see each other again!"

She looked at me astonished, and to see me better stepped off, leaning way back for a moment. Quite frankly, she had struck an odd pose, but it was one that lent her a certain grace, that of a self-assured person capable of maintaining the most difficult equilibrium.

"As you like," she said, shrugging her shoulders. Then, to be sure she had understood me perfectly, just as she was opening the door, she asked me: "Then we don't see any more of each other?" And she searched my face.

"Naturally we don't see any more of each other," said I a little querulously.

I was starting down the stairs when fat old Misceli came bumbling to the door, yelling: "Wait! wait! I'm coming with you too. I've already told the Signorina how many 'sport' cigarettes I need. One hundred. Just like you."

We descended the stair together while Felicita closed the door after a long pause, a pause which gave me a certain amount of delight.

We went down the long slope that leads into Piazza Unità, slowly, careful where we placed our feet. Lumbering along on the slope he certainly appeared older than I. There was even a moment when he stumbled and nearly fell. I helped him right away. He did not thank me. He was panting a little, and we had not yet reached the foot of the slope. Because of that, and only because of that, he did not speak. This is borne out by the fact that when we reached the level area behind the town hall he loosened up and started talking: "I never smoke 'sports.' But they're preferred as a cigarette. I have to give a present to my carpenter. And then I want to buy the good ones which Signorina Felicita can get." Now that he was talking he could only go step by step. He stopped dead to rummage about in a trousers pocket. He pulled out a gold cigarette case, pressed a little button, and the case flew open: "Would you like one?" he asked. "They're denicotinized." I accepted one and also stopped, in order to light it. He stood there stock-still just to put the case back in his pocket. And I thought, *At least she could have given me a manlier rival.* In fact, I handled myself better than he both on the slope and on the flat area. Compared to him I was really a youngster. He even smoked denicotinized cigarettes, which are entirely flavorless. I was more a man because though I had always tried not to smoke I had never thought of stooping to the cowardice of denicotinized cigarettes.

As God would have it, we arrived at the gate of the Tergesteo, where we had to part. Misceli was now talking about other things: affairs in the Exchange in which he was very adept. He seemed a trifle excited to me, even a little distraught. Actually, it seemed as though he were speaking without listening to himself. I was not listening to him at all either; rather I was studying him, trying to discover exactly what he was *not* saying.

I did not want to break away from him without having tried better to find out what he was thinking. With this in mind I began by giving myself away completely. That is, I burst out with: "Felicita is nothing but a whore." Misceli showed himself in a new light: that of his embarrassment. His fat lower jaw began to move like that of a ruminant. (*Did he do this when he was uncertain as to what to say?*)

Then he said: "She doesn't seem so to me. She's got the best 'sports.'" He wanted to prolong this stupid comedy forever.

I became angry: "Then in other words you intend to continue seeing Signorina Felicita?"

Another pause. His jaw jutted out, swung to the left, returned to the right before fixing itself. Then, for the first time betraying an impulse to laugh, he said: "I'll be going back as soon as I need some 'sports' again."

I laughed too. But I wanted further explanation: "Well, why did you walk out on her today?"

He hesitated, and I detected signs of great sadness in his eyes, fixed darkly on the far end of the street: "I'm a little superstitious. When I'm interrupted in something I believe in recognizing immediately the hand of Providence, and I drop everything I'm doing. Once I was called to Berlin on important business, but I stopped over in Sessana because the train was held up there for several hours for some reason or other. I don't believe in forcing worldly things . . . especially at our age."

That was enough for me and I asked: "You didn't mind when you saw me getting 'sports' from Signorina Felicita too, did you?"

He shot back with such decisiveness that his jaw did not have time to swivel: "What difference should it make to me? Me jealous? Absolutely not! We two are old. We're old! It's all right for us to make love from time to time, but we mustn't become jealous because we are easily made to look ludicrous. We should never get jealous. Listen to me and don't ever let yourself seem jealous, because it would make you look foolish."

His words sounded friendly enough—just as they are written here on paper—but their tone was rather heavily saturated with anger and contempt. His fat face flaming, he approached me; being smaller than I, he looked up at me as though trying to find in my body the weakest point to strike. Why had he become angry with me while declaring that we should not be jealous? What could it have been that I had done to him? Maybe he was angry with me because I had held his train up at Sessana when he should have been arriving in Berlin.

But I was not jealous. I should, however, have liked to know how much he paid Felicita monthly. I felt that if I knew he paid more than I, as I thought he should, I would be satisfied.

But I did not have time to investigate. Suddenly, Misceli became gentler, and addressed himself to my discretion. His gentleness converted itself into a threat when he recalled that we were in each other's hands. I reassured him: I too was married and was aware of the importance of an imprudent word by either one of us.

"Oh," he said with an offhand gesture, "it's not because of my wife that I ask discretion. There are certain things which have not interested her for years. But I know that you too are under Dr. Raulli's care. He threatened to leave me if I didn't follow his prescriptions, if I drank just one glass of wine, if I smoked more than ten, even denicotinized, cigarettes a day, if I didn't give up . . . all the rest. He says that at our age a man's body maintains its equilibrium only because it can't decide what part must collapse. For that reason you shouldn't hint at the part because then the decision would be easy." He went on in a self-pitying mood. "When you come right down to it, it's simple to prescribe things for another person: Don't do this or that or the other. He might just as well say that one had better be resigned to living a few months less than to living like that."

Then he let up for a moment and used the time to extract some information about my own condition. I told him that I had once attained a blood pressure of two hundred and twenty, which pleased him enormously because his had reached only two hundred and ten. With one foot on the step that leads into the Tergesteo, he left with a friendly wave, adding: "Now, please, don't say a thing about it."

I was obsessed for some days by Raulli's fine rhetorical figure of an old man's body that continues to run because it does not know what part should collapse first. Of course when the old doctor spoke of "a part" he meant *organ*. And "equilibrium" also had its meaning for him. Raulli must have known what he was talking about. With us oldsters, health can only mean a gradual and simultaneous weakening of all organs. Heaven forbid that one of them fall behind, that is, remain too young! I suspect that their interdependence is capable of changing into a struggle and that the weak organs can be beaten up—with magnificent results on the general economy, one can imagine. Misceli's intervention must therefore have been desired by Providence, who guards my life and who even sent word as to how I should behave by way of that mouth with the wandering jaw.

And I returned, pensive, to my gramophone. In the *Ninth Symphony* I again found my organs working together and struggling. Working together during the first movements—the sort of working-together found in the scherzo when even, with two notes, the timpani are allowed to synthesize that which all the instruments are murmuring around them. The joy of the last movement seemed rebellion to me. Crude, with a strength which is violence, with light, brief moments of regret and hesitation. Not for nothing does the human voice, this least sensible of all sounds in nature, enter into the last movement. I admit that on other occasions I had interpreted this symphony otherwise—as the most intense representation of accord between the most divergent of forces, into which finally the human voice is also received and fused. But that day the symphony, played by the same records, appeared as I say.

"Farewell, Felicita," I whispered when the music had faded away. *I need not think of you any longer*. She was not worth risking a sudden collapse. There were so many medical theories in the world that it was hard to be governed by them. Those rascally doctors' only contribution was toward making life more difficult. The simplest of things are too complicated. To abstain from drinking alcohol is a prescription made from an evident truth. But even so it is known that alcohol at times has curative properties. Then why must I await the intervention of the doctor to offer me the comfort of this potent medicine? There is no doubt that death sometimes results from an organ's occasionally brief and sudden caprice or is the incidental and coincidental product of a variety of weaknesses. I mean that it would be momentary if it were not followed by death. Things must be so managed as to make the coincidence only momentary. So aid has to be at hand, ready even before the onset of cramps from excessive activity or a collapse due to inertia. Why should one wait for the doctor, who comes running merely to scribble out his bill? I alone am able to tell in time when I need something, by a feeling of discomfort. Unfortunately, doctors have not made a study of what can help in a case like that. For that reason, then, I take various things: a purgative with a wine chaser; and then I study myself. I might need something else: a glass of milk—but also a drop of digitalis. And all taken in the most minute quantities, as recommended by the great Hannemann. The mere presence of these minute quantities is enough to produce reactions necessary for the activation of life, just as though an organ, rather than nourished or stimulated, had to be reminded. Seeing a drop of calcium, it exclaims: "Oh, look! I'd forgotten. I've got to work."

This was what I had against Felicita. It was impossible to take her in doses.

In the evening Felicita's brother came over to visit me. On seeing him I was shaken with fear because Augusta herself showed him to my study. Fearing what he had to say to me, I was very happy when Augusta promptly withdrew.

He unknotted a bandanna from which he pulled a package: one hundred boxes of "sport" cigarettes. He broke them down into five stacks, each of twenty boxes; it was easy, therefore, to verify the quantity. Then he had me feel how soft every box was. They had been selected one by one from a large stock. He was sure I would be pleased.

Actually I was tremendously pleased, because after having been so frightened I was feeling completely at ease. I at once paid the hundred and sixty lire I owed him and cheerfully thanked him. Cheerfully, because I really wanted to laugh. A curious woman, Felicita; even though jilted, she was not neglecting her interest in the tobacco shop.

But the pale, lean man, after having jammed the lire he had received into his pocket, still made no move to leave. He did not seem Felicita's brother. I had seen him before, on other occasions, but better dressed. Now he was without a collar, and his clothes, though neat, were absolutely worn out. Strange that he felt he had to have a special hat for workdays: and the one he had was positively filthy and mis-shapen from long use.

He looked at me intently, hesitating to speak. It seemed that his look was rather dark, and the light that glowed in it, inviting me to guess what was on his mind, off-center. When he finally spoke his look became even more imploring, so imploring that it resulted in seeming to threaten me. Intense supplications border on threats. I can very well understand that certain peasants punish the images of saints they have prayed to by throwing them down beneath their beds.

Finally he said to me in a steady voice: "Felicita says we have reached the tenth of the month."

I looked at the calendar from which I tore away a sheet every day and said: "She's quite right. We *have* reached the tenth of the month. There's no doubt about it."

"But then," he spoke hesitantly, "you owe her for all the month."

A second before he spoke I understood why he had led me to look at the calendar. I believe I blushed the moment I discovered that between brother and sister everything was clear and sincere and honest in so far as money was con-cerned. The only thing that surprised me was the out-and-out request that I pay for the whole month. I even doubted whether I had to pay anything. In my relations with Felicita I had failed to keep very accurate accounts. But hadn't I al-ways paid in advance? and because of that didn't the last payment overlap this fraction of the month? And I sat there with my mouth somewhat agape having to look into those strange eyes, trying to determine whether they were implor-ing or threatening me. It is precisely the man of vast and long experience like myself who does not know how to be-have, because he is aware that by a single word of his, by a single deed, the most unforeseen events are liable to happen. One has only to peruse world history to learn that causes and effects can work themselves into the most peculiar rela-tions with each other. During my hesitation I took out my wallet and also counted and sorted out my money so as not to mistake a hundred-lire note for a five hundred. And when

I had the bills counted out I gave them to him. Thus everything I did was done with thought of gaining time through action. And I thought, *I'll pay now and I'll think about it later.*

Felicita's brother himself had ceased to think about it, and his eye, no longer fixed upon me, had lost all of its intensity. He put the money in a different pocket from the one in which he had deposited the hundred and sixty lire. He kept accounts and money separate. He bowed to me: "Good evening, Signor," and left. But he soon returned because he had forgotten another package similar to the one he had given me. By way of excusing himself for having come back he said to me: "This is another hundred boxes of 'sports' I have to deliver to another gentleman."

They were for poor Misceli, of course, who could not stand them either. I smoked all of mine, however, except for some boxes I gave to Fortunato, my chauffeur. When I have paid for something, sooner or later I finish by using it up. It is proof of a sense of thrift that is within me. And every time I had that taste of straw in my mouth I remembered Felicita and her brother more vividly. By thinking about it over and over I was able to remember with absolute certainty that I had in fact not paid the allowance in advance. After thinking I had been cheated by so much I was relieved to find out that they had been paid for only twenty days extra.

I think I must have returned to see Felicita once again before the twenty days had elapsed only because of my above-mentioned sense of economy: this sense of thrift which had even gotten me into accepting the "sports." I said to myself, *Now that I have paid I'd like to risk once more—for the last time—the danger of tipping off my organism to the part it ought to have collapse. Just once! It'll never know the difference.*

The door to her apartment opened just as I was about to ring. Startled in the darkness, I saw her pale, lovely little face, as though in a visor, clamped in a hat that covered her head back to her ears and the nape of her neck. A solitary blond curl stole from the hat down her forehead. I knew that at about this hour she was accustomed to go to the tobacco shop to supervise the more complicated part of her money-making enterprises. But I had hoped to induce her to wait for that short while I wanted to have with her.

In the dark she did not immediately recognize me. In a questioning tone she uttered a name, neither mine or Misceli's, which I could not make out. When she did recognize me she extended her hand without a trace of ill feeling, and a little inquisitively. I clasped her cold hand with both of mine and grew bold. She let her hand lie still but drew her head back. Never had that staff within her arched back so far: so much so that I felt like releasing her hand and seizing her by the waist if for no other reason than to steady her.

And that faraway face adorned with the single curl regarded me. Or was it actually looking at me? Wasn't it really looking at a problem which she had brought upon herself and which demanded a ready solution, immediately, there on those steps?

"It's impossible now," she said after a long pause. She was still looking at me. Then every shadow of hesitancy vanished. She stood there, that voluptuous body of hers holding its extremely perilous position, immobile, her little face wan and serious below the yellow ringlet; but slowly, just as though she were acting upon some serious resolution, she withdrew her hand.

"Yes!—it's impossible," she added. It was repeated to convince me that she was still considering the matter to see if perhaps there might be a way to content me, but apart from this repetition there was no other evidence that she was really looking into and thinking about it. She had already made her final decision.

And then she said to me: "You might return on the first of the month, if you wish . . . I'll see . . . I'll think about it."

It is only recently, only since I have set to paper this account of my love affair with Felicita that I have become objective enough to judge her and myself with sufficient justice. I found myself there asserting my rights to those few days due my subscription. She let me know instead that by my renunciation I had lost those rights. I believe that if she had proposed that I immediately enter a new subscription I would have suffered less. I am sure that I would not have run away. At the moment I was bent on love, and to tell the truth, at my age, it very much resembles the crocodile on dry land where, they say, he has to have a great deal of time to change directions. I would have paid for the whole month perhaps, even though resolved to make it the last time.

Instead, this way, she was making me angry. I could not find words; I hardly found air enough to breathe. I said: "Uff!" with the maximum of indignation. I was of the impression that I had said something, and even remained still for an instant, as if I thought that at my "uff," a cry that must have wounded her and given evidence of my deep-seated unhappiness, she would have replied. But neither she nor I had anything else to say. I started down the stairs. A few steps down, I turned to look at her again. Perhaps on her colorless face there was now some sign to belie such hardhearted selfishness, so cold and calculated. I did not see her face. She was completely absorbed in locking up the apartment, which must have remained unvisited for some hours. Once again I said: "Uff," but not so loudly as to be heard by her. I said it to all the world, to society, to our institutions, and to Mother Nature—all that had permitted me to find myself on that staircase, in that position.

It was my last love. Now that the whole adventure has adjusted itself to the past I no longer consider it so worthless, because Felicita—with that flax-colored hair of hers, her pallid face, slender nose, and inscrutable eyes, her disinclination to talk seldom revealing the iciness of her heart —Felicita is not unworthy of being regretted. But after her there was no room for another mistress. She had educated me. Up till then, whenever I happened to be with a woman for more than ten minutes I used to feel hope and desire surging in my heart. Of course I wanted to conceal both, but still my strongest wish was to let them grow so that I might feel more alive and have a sense of participating in life. In order to let hope and desire grow I had to express them in words and let them out. Who knows how many times I was laughed at? To the career of an old man to which I am now condemned, it was Felicita who educated me. I can hardly bring myself to realize that now in the field of love I am worth no more than what I pay.

My ugliness is ever before my eyes. This morning upon awakening I studied the position in which I found my mouth the moment I opened my eyes. My lower jaw lolled on the side I was lying on, and my dead and swollen tongue felt out of place.

I thought of Felicita, whom I very often think of with desire and hatred. At that moment I murmured: "She's right."

"Who's right?" demanded Augusta, who was dressing.

And I promptly replied: "A certain Misceli I ran into yesterday, who told me that he doesn't understand why one is born to live and grow old. He's right."

Thus I actually told her everything without compromising myself in the least.

And until now no one has ever taken Felicita's place. Nevertheless I seek to deceive Mother Nature, who is keeping her eye on me so as to liquidate me no sooner than it becomes apparent that I can no longer reproduce. With wise dosages in Hannemann's prescribed quantities I take a little of that medicine every day. I watch women passing by; I follow them with my eyes, seeking to discover in their legs something other than walking apparatus, so that I may again feel a craving to stop and fondle them. In this respect the dosages are becoming more measured than Hannemann or I should like. That is, I have to control my eyes lest they betray what they are looking for, and so it must be understood how rarely the medicine is of service. One may do without the caresses of others in order to attain a complete feeling, but it is impossible to feign indifference without running the risk of chilling one's heart. And having written this I can better understand my adventure with old Signora Dondi. I greeted her to do right by her and to make her aware of her beauty. The fate of old men is gallantry.

Never think that such ephemeral relations, entered into with the intention merely of rescuing oneself from death, do not leave their mark, do not contribute toward the adornment and troubling of one's life, like my affairs with Carla and Felicita. On rare occasions, because of the strong impression received, they reach the point of leaving an indelible memory.

I recall a girl who was seated opposite me in a tram. She left me with a memory. We reached a certain intimacy because I gave her a name: Amphora. She did not have a very striking face, but her eyes, luminous and rather round, stared at everything with great curiosity and something of a little girl's inquisitiveness. She might have been over twenty, but I would not have been surprised if she had playfully jerked the ropelike pigtail of the baby girl sitting next to her. I do not know whether it was because of a rare figure, or because her dress made her appear to have one, but from the waist up her slender body resembled an exquisite amphora placed upon her hips. And I was greatly taken by her breasts. The better to hoodwink Mother Nature, who had her eye on me, I thought, *Naturally I can't die yet because, if this girl wants me to, I've got to stand ready to reproduce.*

My face must have taken on a curious look as I gazed at that amphora. But I dismiss its having been that of a lecher, inasmuch as I was thinking of death. Still, others interpreted it as suppressed lust. As I later noticed, the girl, who must have been of a well-to-do family, was accompanied by a rather old maidservant who got off the tram with her. And it was this old woman who, when she passed by me, looked down and whispered: "Old lecher." She called me old. She was summoning death. I said to her: "You old fool." But she left without replying.

# LUIGI PIRANDELLO

## 1867–1936

> Before he emerged as one of the truly epoch-making
> dramatists of our century, Luigi Pirandello (1867-1936)
> had been mainly a novelist and a writer of short stories.
> The latter are now collected as *Stories for One Year,*
> *Novelle per un anno.* Quite a few of them were made
> into plays. I have chosen here *The Medals* and *War*
> not only for their intrinsic merits but also for the
> exemplary way in which they present, or imply, certain
> characteristic forms of relationship between individual
> people and Italian history. *A Character in Distress,* on
> the other hand, has obvious connections with the initial
> inspiration of Pirandello's most celebrated play, *Six*
> *Characters in Search of an Author.*

## A Character in Distress

It has for a long time been my habit to receive in audience,
every Sunday morning, the characters of my future stories.

Five hours it lasts, from eight to one.

Almost invariably I find myself in bad company.

I don't know why, but as a rule these audiences of mine
seem to be attended by the most disgruntled people in the
world, with whom it is a terrible strain to have to deal; either
they are afflicted with some strange malady, or else involved
in the most extraordinary circumstances.

Patiently I listen to all of them and question them politely. I make a note of their names and take particulars of

each of them; I keep a record of their feelings and aspirations. I must, however, add that, unfortunately for me, I am not easily satisfied. I can bear a lot, quite politely, too, but I don't like being fooled. Also, I always want to penetrate to the depths of their souls by long and exhaustive research.

Now, it has happened that more than one amongst them have taken exception to my questions, becoming sulky and obstreperously stubborn, perhaps because they thought I revel in robbing them of that earnestness which they invariably assume when they first introduce themselves to me.

Patiently, gently I endeavor to make them see and realize that my questions are not superfluous. It is easy to want to be this or that, but it remains to be seen whether we have the power to change into what we would like to be. If such power be lacking, then our pretensions cannot appear otherwise than ridiculous and futile.

Unfortunately, my characters refuse to recognize this. And then I pity them, for I am good-natured at heart. At the same time certain misfortunes cannot be pitied without provoking laughter.

Anyway, the characters of my stories go about the world, denouncing me as a cruel and heartless writer. What is needed is a sympathetic critic who would show how much there is of compassion behind that laughter.

But where are the sympathetic critics of today?

I must point out that at these interviews certain characters push their way in front of all others and assert themselves with such cheek and impudence that I am forced, at times, to dismiss them without delay. Later, many of them bitterly repent their display of temper and implore me to put right one or other of their faults in their make-up. Then I smile and tell them they must make amends for their original sin and wait until I have time and opportunity to return to them.

Amongst those who stand waiting at the back of the overcrowded room, some show signs of distress, some get cross and some get tired and go and knock at the door of some other author.

It happens quite frequently that I find in the works of many of my colleagues certain characters who had previously presented themselves to me; on the other hand, it has happened that I have spotted some who, not satisfied with the way I had dealt with them, refused to try and give a better account of themselves elsewhere.

I don't mind because as a rule two or three new ones present themselves to me every week. Often the crowd is such that I have to listen to more than one of them at the same time. But there comes a moment when my brain, divided and confused, revolts at this double and triple occupation, becomes exasperated and demands that they should talk one at a time, softly and quietly, or else go to hell.

I shall always remember the infinite resignation with which a poor old man, who had come a long distance to see me, awaited his turn. He was a teacher named Icilio Saporini. At the fall of the Roman Republic in 1849 he had been banished to America for composing a patriotic song. After forty-five years, when nearly eighty years old, he had come back to Italy to die. Exceedingly polite, his thin voice reminiscent of the buzz of a mosquito, he allowed everyone else to pass in front of him. At last, one day when I was still convalescent after a long illness, I saw him enter my room, all self-depreciation, with a timid smile on his lips.

"May I? . . . If you don't mind. . . ."

"Yes, do come in, my dear little old man." He had chosen the most suitable moment, and I made him die at once in a short story, called "Old Music."

This last Sunday I entered my study a little later than usual for the audience. A long novel, which somebody had given me, and which had been waiting for me more than a month to be read, kept me awake until three a.m. by the many thoughts aroused in me by one of the characters in the book—the only live one amongst so many colorless shadows.

It described a poor old man, a certain Doctor Fileno, who thought he had found an efficacious remedy for all human ills, an infallible recipe capable of bringing solace to himself and all mankind in case of any calamity whatever, public or private.

Actually it was more than a remedy or a recipe that Doctor Fileno had discovered; it was a method consisting in reading history books from morning till night and practicing looking at the present as though it were an event already buried in the archives of the past. By this method he had cured himself of all suffering and of all worry, and without having to die had found a stern, serene peace, imbued with that peculiar sadness which cemeteries would still preserve even if all men on earth were dead.

But Doctor Fileno had never even dreamt of drawing on the past standards for the present. He knew that it would have been waste of time, and stupid waste at that, for history is an idealized composition of elements selected by the historians according to their personal feelings, sympathies, antipathies, aspirations and opinions, preventing one from making use of this idealized composition, which keeps on moving, while its elements remain scattered and unruly. Nor did he ever dream of drawing on the present rules and forecasts for the future. Indeed, he was doing exactly the opposite. He was trying to project himself into an imaginary future in order to look at the present, and he succeeded in viewing it as if it were the past.

For instance, he had lost a daughter a few days before. A friend called to condole with him in his grief, but he found him already consoled as if that child had been dead for more than a hundred years. Although his grief was still recent, very recent, he had succeeded in relegating it to the past, pushing it back into time. This, however, did not prevent him from talking of his tragedy from the loftiest viewpoint and with a great sense of dignity.

Briefly, Doctor Fileno had invented a kind of inverted telescope for himself. He opened it out, not to look at the future, where he knew there would be nothing to see, but he tried to convince himself that by looking through it from the larger end through the smaller lens and by directing it to the present, all events would immediately become diminutive and distant. At the same time he was working at a book,

*The Philosophy of Distance*, which would undoubtedly have created a sensation.

While I was reading the novel, it became apparent to me that the author—completely absorbed in holding together one of the tritest stories—had found himself unable to understand this character, who in himself contained the germ of a real creation. But for a time the character had succeeded in escaping from the author, in cutting himself loose and superimposing himself vigorously upon the banal story of the book. Then all of a sudden, deformed and enfeebled, he had allowed himself to be bent to the exigencies of a wrong and silly ending.

My imagination aroused, I remained there for a long time in the stillness of the night, with the picture of this character before me. What a pity! There was enough material there to build a masterpiece, provided always that the author had not so miserably misunderstood his character and neglected him, and had made him the central figure of the story. All those artificialities which he had introduced might perhaps have transformed themselves, might have become alive too. A great sorrow and considerable resentment got hold of me because of that life which had remained so miserably unfulfilled.

On entering my study late on that particular morning, I found unusual confusion there, for that Doctor Fileno had already forced his way amongst my other waiting characters, who got angry and nasty and went for him, trying to push him back, to throw him out.

"Now then," I said. "Ladies and gentlemen, what is all this about? And you, Doctor Fileno, what do you want here? I have already wasted too much time on you. You don't belong to me. Leave me alone to look after my own characters. Go away!"

So deep and desperate a sorrow marred the face of Doctor Fileno that all the other characters felt sorry for him and retired.

"Do not send me away, please, do not send me away!

Grant me but five minutes if these ladies and gentlemen will permit, and let me explain, please!"

Perplexed, but moved to compassion, I asked him:

"Explain what? I am perfectly sure, dear doctor, that you deserved to have fallen into better hands, but what can I do for you now? I have already expressed my regrets, and that is all I can do."

"All you can do? By God, no!" burst out Doctor Fileno, while his whole body seemed to shake with indignation. "You say that, because I do not belong to you. Believe me, your neglect, your scorn would be less cruel than this passive pity, which, I am sorry to say, is unworthy of an artist. Nobody understands characters better than you; nobody knows better than you do that we are live beings, more alive than those of flesh and blood; perhaps less real, but more true. One comes into the world in various ways, dear sir, and you are well aware that nature uses the human imagination to carry on her creative work. Whosoever is born through this creative activity which resides in the spirit of man is ordained by nature to a life far superior to those who are born from the womb of woman. He who is born a character, who has the great gift of being born a live character, can even scorn death. He will never die. Man will die, the author will die—he is only the natural instrument of his creation—but the character remains immortal. To remain immortal does not require extraordinary gifts nor the accomplishment of miraculous deeds. Tell me, who was Sancho Panza? Tell me, who was Don Abbondio? Yet they have eternal life, because they are vital germs who had the luck of finding a fertile womb, a brain that knew how to raise and nurse them."

"Yes, dear doctor," I said. "This is all very well, but I still fail to see what you want from me."

"Oh, you fail to see? Have I perhaps come to the wrong place? Or am I loafing about the moon? What sort of a writer are you then? Dare you really say that you do not understand the horror of my tragedy? To have the inestimable privilege of being born a character—and in our times—

I mean in times so beset with demeaning difficulties, which hinder, deform and enfeeble human existence. To have the privilege of being born a live character, to have been ordained—even in my small way—to immortality and yet, just through bad luck, to have fallen into those hands, to be condemned to an iniquitous death, to be forced to live in that artificial world where I can neither breathe nor move because everything is faked, false, prearranged, protracted? Mere words and paper! Paper and words! A human being who finds himself involved in such conditions, and who cannot or will not subject himself to them, can free himself of them, and run away, but a poor character cannot—he must remain nailed to eternal martyrdom. Air, air, life!

"Just look at me . . . Fileno! . . . he has called me Fileno! . . . Do you really think my name should be Fileno? Idiot, idiot! Not even a name was he able to give me. Fileno! And why should he come to me, the author of *The Philosophy of Distance*, to make me end in such a miserable way and make me solve all that stupid muddle of his plot? Instead of Negroni, the solicitor, he had to force me to marry as her second husband that fool Graziella. Don't try to make excuses for him. These, my dear sir, are crimes which should be avenged with blood and tears. But what will happen now instead? Nothing. Silence. Or perhaps a few slating lines in two or three papers. Perhaps a critic will write: 'A pity about that poor Doctor Fileno! He was really a good character!' And there the whole thing will end. Condemned to death, that is what I am, I, the author of *The Philosophy of Distance*, which that idiot who is my author was not even able to get published at my expense. Terrible, sir, terrible! Don't let us think about it any more. To work, and quickly, dear sir. Rescue me at once, at once. Make me live, you who understand all the life that is in me."

At the conclusion of this passionate outburst, I could only answer with a long look at Doctor Fileno's face.

"You think it might upset my author?" he resumed anxiously. "You think it might upset him. But isn't it a legitimate proposal? Haven't you the undeniable right to make me your own and give me the life which that idiot has not been able to give me? It is your right, it is mine too—you do understand, don't you?"

"It may be your right, dear doctor," I answered. "It may be even a legitimate right, as you seem to believe. But I never do such things. It is useless for you to plead. I simply will not do it. Try someone else."

"And to whom can I apply if you . . ."

"I don't know. Perhaps you will find somebody who is perfectly convinced of the legitimacy of this right. Just a minute, dear Doctor Fileno, I have an idea. Are you or are you not the author of *The Philosophy of Distance?*"

"How could I not be?" the doctor burst out, jumping to his feet and placing his hand on his heart, as a sign that he was speaking the truth. "Of course I am. How dare you doubt it? Oh, I understand. It is always because of that murderer of mine. Unable to realize all that was to be got out of my discovery of the inverted telescope, he merely gave a brief résumé of my theories. . . ."

I put out my hand as he was getting too near me. Then I smiled and said:

"All right, all right! But why do you . . ."

"Why do I? . . ."

"Yes, why do you grumble at your author? Have you yourself been able to take advantage of your theory? This is precisely what I want to tell you. Let me explain. If you really believe in the virtue of your philosophy, even as I do, why do you not apply it to your own case. You are trying to find—and in our times—a writer amongst us who will give you immortality. But just read what all the most important critics say of us poor little contemporary writers. We are, and yet we are not, my dear doctor. Why not submit—as we are doing—the most important events, the most burning questions and the most marvelous modern works to the famous inverted telescope? My dear doctor, I think if you will do this you will not see anyone or anything any more. Therefore try to console yourself, or if you prefer, be satisfied with your lot; and let me now hold audience with my own poor characters, who may be bad, but are less extravagant in their ambitions."

# War

The passengers who had left Rome by the night express had had to stop until dawn at the small station of Fabriano in order to continue their journey by the small old-fashioned "local" joining the main line with Sulmona.

At dawn, in a stuffy and smoky second-class carriage in which five people had already spent the night, a bulky woman in deep mourning, was hoisted in—almost like a shapeless bundle. Behind her—puffing and moaning, followed her husband—a tiny man, thin and weakly, his face death-white, his eyes small and bright and looking shy and uneasy.

Having at last taken a seat he politely thanked the passengers who had helped his wife and who had made room for her; then he turned round to the woman trying to pull down the collar of her coat and politely inquired:

"Are you all right, dear?"

The wife, instead of answering, pulled up her collar again to her eyes, so as to hide her face.

"Nasty world," muttered the husband with a sad smile.

And he felt it his duty to explain to his traveling companions that the poor woman was to be pitied for the war was taking away from her her only son, a boy of twenty to whom both had devoted their entire life, even breaking up their home at Sulmona to follow him to Rome where he had to go as a student, then, allowing him to volunteer for war with an assurance, however, that at least for six months he would not be sent to the front and now, all of a sudden, receiving a wire saying that he was due to leave in three days' time and asking them to go and see him off.

The woman under the big coat was twisting and wriggling, at times growling like a wild animal, feeling certain that all those explanations would not have aroused even a shadow of sympathy from those people who—most likely—

were in the same plight as herself. One of them, who had been listening with particular attention, said:

"You should thank God that your son is only leaving now for the front. Mine has been sent there the first day of the war. He has already come back twice wounded and been sent back again to the front."

"What about me? I have two sons and three nephews at the front," said another passenger.

"Maybe, but in our case it is our *only* son," ventured the husband.

"What difference can it make? You may spoil your only son with excessive attentions, but you cannot love him more than you would all your other children if you had any. Paternal love is not like bread that can be broken into pieces and split amongst the children in equal shares. A father gives *all* his love to each one of his children without discrimination, whether it be one or ten, and if I am suffering now for my two sons, I am not suffering half for each of them but double. . . ."

"True . . . true . . ." sighed the embarrassed husband, "but suppose (of course we all hope it will never be your case) a father has two sons at the front and he loses one of them, there is still one left to console him . . . while . . ."

"Yes," answered the other, getting cross, "a son left to console him but also a son left for whom he must survive, while in the case of the father of an only son if the son dies the father can die too and put an end to his distress. Which of the two positions is the worse? Don't you see how my case would be worse than yours?"

"Nonsense," interrupted another traveler, a fat, red-faced man with bloodshot eyes of the palest gray.

He was panting. From his bulging eyes seemed to spurt inner violence of an uncontrolled vitality which his weakened body could hardly contain.

"Nonsense," he repeated, trying to cover his mouth with his hand so as to hide the two missing front teeth. "Nonsense. Do we give life to our children for our own benefit?"

The other travelers stared at him in distress. The one who had had his son at the front since the first day of the war sighed: "You are right. Our children do not belong to us, they belong to the Country. . . ."

"Bosh," retorted the fat traveler. "Do we think of the Country when we give life to our children? Our sons are born because . . . well, because they must be born and when they come to life they take our own life with them. This is the truth. We belong to them but they never belong to us. And when they reach twenty they are exactly what we were at their age. We too had a father and mother, but there were so many other things as well . . . girls, cigarettes, illusions, new ties . . . and the Country, of course, whose call we would have answered—when we were twenty—even if father and mother had said no. Now, at our age, the love of our Country is still great, of course, but stronger than it is the love for our children. Is there any one of us here who wouldn't gladly take his son's place at the front if he could?"

There was a silence all round, everybody nodding as to approve.

"Why then," continued the fat man, "shouldn't we consider the feelings of our children when they are twenty? Isn't it natural that at their age they should consider the love for their Country (I am speaking of decent boys, of course) even greater than the love for us? Isn't it natural that it should be so, as after all they must look upon us as upon old boys who cannot move any more and must stay at home? If Country exists, if Country is a natural necessity like bread, of which each of us must eat in order not to die of hunger, somebody must go to defend it. And our sons go, when they are twenty, and they don't want tears, because if they die, they died inflamed and happy (I am speaking, of course, of decent boys). Now, if one dies young and happy, without having the ugly sides of life, the boredom of it, the pettiness, the bitterness of disillusion . . . what more can we ask for him? Everyone should stop crying: everyone should laugh, as I do . . . or at least thank God—as I do—because my son, before dying, sent me a message saying that he was dying satisfied at having ended his life in the best way he could have wished. That is why, as you see, I do not even wear mourning. . . ."

He shook his light fawn coat as to show it; his livid lip over his missing teeth was trembling, his eyes were watery and motionless and soon after he ended with a shrill laugh which might well have been a sob.

"Quite so . . . quite so . . ." agreed the others.

The woman who, bundled in a corner under her coat, had been sitting and listening had——for the last three months ——tried to find in the words of her husband and her friends something to console her in her deep sorrow, something that might show her how a mother should resign herself to send her son not even to death but to a probable danger of life. Yet not a word had she found amongst the many which had been said . . . and her grief had been greater in seeing that nobody——as she thought——could share her feelings.

But now the words of the traveler amazed and almost stunned her. She suddenly realized that it wasn't the others who were wrong and could not understand her but herself who could not rise up to the same height of those fathers and mothers willing to resign themselves, without crying, not only to the departure of their sons but even to their death.

She lifted her head, she bent over from her corner trying to listen with great attention to the details which the fat man was giving to his companions about the way his son had fallen as a hero, for his King and his Country, happy and without regrets. It seemed to her that she had stumbled into a world she had never dreamt of, a world so far unknown to her and she was so pleased to hear everyone joining in congratulating that brave father who could so stoically speak of his child's death.

Then suddenly, just as if she had heard nothing of what had been said and almost as if waking up from a dream, she turned to the old man, asking him:

"Then . . . is your son really dead?"

Everybody stared at her. The old man, too, turned to look at her, fixing his great, bulging, horribly watery light gray eyes, deep in her face. For some little time he tried to answer, but words failed him. He looked and looked at her, almost as if only then——at that silly, incongruous question——

he had suddenly realized at last that his son was really dead
. . . gone forever . . . forever. His face contracted, became
horribly distorted, then he snatched in haste a handkerchief
from his pocket and, to the amazement of everyone, broke
into harrowing, heart-rending, uncontrollable sobs.

## The Medals

All that morning, Sciarame' had been pacing his little room
like a lion in a cage.

On more than one occasion Roro', his stepdaughter, had
peeped through the door to ask him:

"What are you looking for?"

Whereupon Sciarame', trying to hide his worry, had answered at first that he was searching for his stick.

"But there it is, can't you see it? There, in that corner."

And Roro' had handed it to him. Then, a little later, he
had asked for a handkerchief. Roro' had given him a clean
one, but still Sciarame' would not leave the room.

The truth was that Sciarame' was summoning up his courage to speak to his stepdaughter about something very important but, so far, he had failed. He had failed because he
was as shy of her as he had always been of his wife, now
dead for the last seven years, dead "from a broken heart"—
Roro' used to say—"due to her husband's stupidity."

A succession of bad years had forced Sciarame'—at one
time comfortably off—to sell first his small lemon and
orange orchards and then the house, so that, at sixty-eight
years of age, he had been compelled to turn a middleman,
selling on commission those very oranges and lemons which
were once his own.

Poor Sciarame'! He who had always looked upon middle-
men as thieves was now finding himself one of them; tramp-
ing from morning to night at his age, weak and ailing, dragging his swollen feet buried in a pair of ragged felt shoes,

fighting for a small commission which dealers would throw at him more as a charity than as a due.

Those who had known him before felt sorry for him. Yet everyone was certain that all these trials were more than made up for on national holidays when—dressed up in a faded red shirt, with the large handkerchief tied round his neck and the pointed hat well over his eyes—he would join the Garibaldian veterans in their procession, with his fine row of medals shining on his breast.

Seven medals!

And yet, when walking with his old companions behind the Garibaldian flag, he looked almost like a lost dog. He would constantly lift his left arm tugging at his beard or stroking his mustache, as though shy and anxious to hide those very medals of which he was so proud.

Many of his friends, seeing him pass by, would shout:

"Long live the Fatherland, Sciarame'! Long live Italy!"

Shy and smiling, he would lower his bald little eyes, answering in a low voice:

"Long live Italy! Hurrah! Hurrah!"

The headquarters of the Garibaldian Veterans' Society occupied a ground-floor room of the last shanty left in Sciarame's possession. A steep wooden staircase led to two rooms upstairs, one for his stepdaughter and one for himself. On the front door, half covered by a stray branch of jasmine gracefully stretching from Roro's window, was a large inscription in bold red lettering:

## GARIBALDIAN VETERANS' SOCIETY.

The room was scantily furnished: a large table, covered with a green cloth, specially reserved for the Council; a smaller table for the display of newspapers and magazines; an old and dusty bookcase stuffed with volumes mostly uncut. On the walls hung a life-size color-print of Garibaldi; a portrait of Mazzini—of smaller size; a portrait of Carlo Cattaneo—still smaller; and—surrounded by ribbons, paper lanterns and flags—a print commemorating the "Death of the Hero of the Two Worlds."

Every morning Roro', having tidied up the two rooms upstairs, would put on her famous flaming red blouse and would go down to the ground-floor room where, sitting by the door, she would talk to her neighbors while carrying on with her sewing. She was a beautiful girl, dark and healthy, and they called her "La Garibaldina."

It so happened that, that very day, Sciarame' had to ask his stepdaughter not to come down to that room any more and to remain upstairs instead. For Amilcare Bellone, the President of the Association, had complained to him, not because of this habit of Roro's who, after all, was mistress in her own home, but because of a certain young fellow, Rosalino La Rosa, who—with the excuse of coming to read the papers—would go there every morning and pretend to be a Garibaldian veteran when, in fact, he had merely fought in Greece against the Turks.

This La Rosa, rich and lazy, was so proud of his youthful adventure that it had almost become an obsession with him and he could speak of nothing else. One of the three companions who had fought with him—Gasperi—had been slightly wounded at Domokos and Rosalino spoke of this almost as though the wound had been his own. Tall, slender, with a long square-cut, reddish beard and a generous turned-up mustache which, if properly stretched, could easily have been tied into a knot at the back of his neck, Rosalino La Rosa was certainly a handsome young fellow.

It was not difficult to realize that his visits to the headquarters were not so much for the purpose of reading the papers as for the double purpose of letting everyone know that he was quite at home with the Garibaldians and of taking the opportunity for a little flirtation with Roro', the girl with the red blouse.

Sciarame' had noticed it too, but he also knew that Roro' was a level-headed girl and that the young man was comfortably off. Could he, in all consciousness, rule out the possibility of a profitable wedding for his stepdaughter? He was old and poor; what would happen to the girl if he died and she had not found a husband? Besides, he wasn't her real father and hadn't sufficient authority to forbid her a thing which he not only considered harmless but eventually profitable to her.

On the other hand, he could not say that the President was altogether wrong. These were family matters which it was wiser to keep away from the Veterans' Society. Neighbors were already gossiping, some of them speaking of an intrigue between La Rosa and Roro' under the shadow of the Society and which the President—rightly jealous of the Society's good name—could not allow. What was Sciarame' to do? How should he approach Roro' on the subject?

The poor old man had been puzzling himself for over an hour, when Roro' herself gave him the lead.

Wearing her flaming red blouse, she bounced into her stepfather's room:

"Still here? Are you or are you not going out this morning? I haven't even had an opportunity of tidying your room. I'm going downstairs."

"Wait . . . Roro' . . . listen," started Sciarame', mustering up his courage. "That's just what I wanted to tell you."

"What?"

"That you . . . well, you see . . . I mean, couldn't you . . . wouldn't you prefer to work here, upstairs in your room, rather than downstairs?"

"And may I ask why?"

"Well . . . well, you see, because . . . because downstairs, you see, the members . . ."

Roro' raised her eyebrows in surprise.

"A new idea is it?" Have the honorable gentlemen decided to pay you for the rent of the room, then?"

Sciarame' grinned, as though amused by Roro's remark.

"Of course," he said, "it's true that they don't . . . they don't pay for the room."

"Then what do they want?" asked Roro' haughtily. "Are they going to dictate terms in our house?"

"No! that has nothing to do with it!" Sciarame' tried to explain. "It was my own offer. . . ."

"Yes, but for the evenings only," agreed Roro'. "They

are free to do as they like in the evenings, since you had the bright idea of offering them a free shelter, here. I alone know how difficult it is for me to get to sleep with all that talking, shouting and mad singing going on downstairs! Now, on top of all this, they would want me . . ."

"It isn't you," Sciarame' interrupted, "not really you, my dear. . . ."

"I see!" said Roro' becoming serious. "I knew what you meant even before you began to speak. You can tell the honorable gentlemen to mind their own business and to let me look after my own; and if this doesn't suit them let them find another place and I shall not be sorry. In my house I meet whom I like. I have to ask nobody's permission but yours. Now tell me: have you by any chance lost trust in me?"

"Of course not, my dear! Of course not!"

"Then that's enough! I have nothing further to tell you."

And Roro', her face as red as her blouse, turned her shoulders on him and went downstairs, fuming with rage.

Sciarame' gulped, then, standing in the center of the room, he rubbed his lips, worried and angry with himself, with Roro' and with the veterans. Something he must do, but what? Better go out, perhaps. Some fresh air! In the open, who knows, some bright idea might occur to him.

Hobbling carefully down the stairs, one hand leaning on the wall and the other on the stick, dragging down one swollen foot after another and panting at each step, he crossed the ground-floor room, leaving the house without a word. Roro'—sitting at her usual place—was too fully absorbed in conversation with one of the neighbors to take any notice of him.

Oh, what a relief it would have been for him if that blessed child were married! A marriage with La Rosa was—all things considered—unlikely: first of all because Roro' was poor, and then because she was known as "La Garibaldina," while La Rosa's family wanted—for their lightheaded son—a steady, sensible young woman, without patriotic vagaries. Not that Roro' had ever had any such vagaries, but having got the name for them she was perhaps using it now, like a spider with his web, to entangle that young butterfly—La Rosa.

"After all, why not?" sighed Sciarame', thinking how entangled the butterfly seemed already to be.

In all fairness, how could he destroy that cobweb just now, merely to satisfy the honorable veterans who did not even pay any rent? And, after all, what was the President's grievance? He had complained that, in Greece, La Rosa had worn a red shirt. Silly jealousy! The red shirt on that young man's back was a sacrilege to the President's eyes: making him as wild as a bull. If it had been any other young man he could have gone to the Society to read the papers and Bellone would have taken no notice of him, but La Rosa. . . .

Deeply absorbed with his thoughts, Sciarame' reached the main square of the village and seated himself, as he did each day, at one of the small tables outside the café.

There he would stop for hours, waiting for someone to find him an odd job, and eventually falling asleep from boredom, never ordering anything, not even a glass of water with a taste of kummel. Yet the proprietor welcomed him, knowing that clients liked to hear his tales of Garibaldi and of his battles. Sciarame' would speak of them with touching sadness, shaking his head and half closing his bald little eyes. He would describe painful episodes, the dead, the wounded, without a trace of boasting, so that—in the end—those who had expected to be amused by his talk became gloomy and distressed at this little old man whose poverty and misery seemed to have killed even the enthusiasm and the fire of the past.

That morning one of the customers, seeing him more depressed than ever, had tried to cheer him up:

"Don't worry, Sciarame'! The King's birthday will soon be here: a fine chance for an airing to the old red shirt!"

Sciarame', without moving from his seat, had made a quick gesture with his hands as if to say that far different thoughts were in his head. He was about to rest his chin on the knob of his stick when he heard the President yelling his

name from across the piazza: "Sciarame', Sciarame'!"
Sciarame' jumped to his feet to inform him:

"I have told her. . . . I have told her all right!"

But Bellone, seizing him by the arm and advancing a fist
under his nose shouted:

"Liar! He is there again!"

"Who?"

"La Rosa."

"There?"

"Yes, and now I'll show you what I'll do with him. I'll
kick him out myself."

"For heaven's sake!" begged Sciarame', "don't start a
row. Let *me* go. I promise that he will never set foot in
there again. I thought Roro' would tell him. . . . But leave
it to me. . . ."

The President jeered at him; then, without releasing his
grip, he asked:

"Shall I tell you what you are?"

Sciarame' smiled bitterly, shrugging his shoulders.

"A blockhead?" he said. "I know it, but did you only find
it out now?"

And off he went, stooping, shaking his head, leaning
heavily on his stick.

When Roro'—sitting by the door—saw him approaching,
she made a hasty sign for La Rosa to move away and to sit
at the table covered with newspapers. In a stride La Rosa
was there, at once opening a magazine and engrossed in
reading it.

"Back so soon?" she asked her stepfather, trying to look
indifferent. "What's wrong?"

Sciarame' glanced first at La Rosa who, his elbows on the
table and his head sunk between his hands, was pretending
to read, and then turned to his stepdaughter:

"I had asked you to stop upstairs."

"And I had told you that in my house . . ." began Roro'.
But Sciarame' cut her short, raising his stick and pointing to
the staircase:

"Go upstairs and don't argue! I have a few words to say to Signor La Rosa."

"To me?" said the young man, as though falling from the clouds and pulling at his fine mustache. "To me?" he repeated.

He rose to his feet, and, moving close to Sciarame', stretched himself to his full height, making him look smaller than ever.

"Yes, to you," he stammered, "but pray, be seated. . . . All I wanted to tell you was . . . You can go, Roro'; leave us alone, please."

Rosalino La Rosa bent himself in two to bid Roro' good-by, and when she had gone Sciarame'—turning to him with a smile—began:

"I know you are a good fellow, my dear Don Rosalino. . . ."

"My deepest thanks!"

"No, it is true," resumed Sciarame', "and I, for one, feel honored . . ."

"My deepest thanks!"

"No, no, it is true, I tell you. I am deeply honored, my dear Don Rosalino, that you should come here to . . . to read the papers. But, well, how can I explain? I am the master here and yet I am not the master. You see: these are the Headquarters of the Society of Veterans and I have certain responsibilities toward my fellow members. . . . Perhaps you don't understand. . . ."

"No, I don't," said La Rosa abruptly.

"Well," continued Sciarame', "I will put it in another way; you are a good fellow who comes here to read the papers; as far as I am concerned you are welcome, but these papers . . . well, these papers, unfortunately, do not belong to me. . . . If they were mine . . . Why, you could have them all, of course! But as you are not a member . . ."

"Stop," shouted La Rosa, furious and raising his hand. "Stop. I knew you would say this; I was waiting for it. I am not a member, am I? And now answer this: Have I been to Greece, yes or no?"

"But of course you have been to Greece! Who would doubt it?"

"Very well! And now the red shirt: did I wear it, yes or no?"

"But of course you did," repeated Sciarame'.

"Therefore I have been to Greece, I have fought, I have come back. I have documents, mind you, Sciarame', written documents to prove all this. And now, then, according to you, what am I?"

"Why, you are a good fellow, a nice young man, I have already said so."

"Many thanks!" hissed La Rosa. "But that isn't what I want to know. According to you am I, or am I not, a Garibaldian?"

"A Garibaldian? Er . . . yes . . . why not?" replied Sciarame', quite dazed and not knowing where La Rosa was leading him to.

"And a veteran?" resumed the latter. "I am also a veteran because I am not dead and have come back. Is that right? And yet these veterans here do not allow me to come and read the papers of the Association because I am not a member, isn't that so? You said it yourself. Well, I'm going right away to find my three veteran comrades of Domokos and the four of us will, this very evening, make our formal application for membership."

"What? . . . What do you say?" replied Sciarame', opening his eyes in amazement. "You, a member here?"

"And why not?" asked Rosalino La Rosa, with a frown. "Aren't we worthy?"

"Yes, yes . . . I did not mean that. . . . Personally, I assure you, it would be an honor, a pleasure!" exclaimed Sciarame'. "But the others, you see . . . my . . . comrades . . ."

"I am not afraid of them, don't worry. I know that I am better entitled to be a member of this Association than someone else, do you understand, Sciarame'? And I will prove it, if they force me to do it."

Seizing him by the lapel of his coat, La Rosa gave him a good shaking; then, looking deep into his eyes, he added:

"Tonight, Sciarame', do you understand?"

Stunned and shivering, Sciarame' was left standing in the center of the room, scratching his head.

The Veterans' Association had only a little over a dozen members left, none of whom was a native of the village. Amilcare Bellone, the President, was a native of Brescia; Nardi and Navetta were from Ravenna, and in fact all of them were born in different parts of Italy, but had come to Sicily to trade in fruit or sulphur.

The Association had been formed by Bellone many years ago. At the news that Garibaldi himself was coming to Sicily to celebrate the independence of the island from foreign domination, the few Garibaldians living in the village had gathered at the café with the idea of discussing a joint trip to Palermo in order to meet—perhaps for the last time— their glorious Leader. Bellone's proposal to get together, there and then, a deputation of veterans who would—under their own flag—take part in the official procession had been greeted with genuine enthusiasm. Some of the customers at the café had brought to Bellone's notice Sciarame'—dozing as usual at one of the tables—introducing him as the old patriot of the village, a Garibaldian veteran, too. Bellone, warmed by the memory of his youthful enthusiasm and per- haps also by the wine, had gone to him, shaking him from his sleep and urging him to join the newly born Society. "Picciotto! Picciotto!" *

Enthusiasm was running high, everybody toasting and cheering. Sciarame'—amid the general shouting—had made an offer. To help the newly born Association he would al- low them to install their headquarters on the ground floor of his house, free of charge, at least temporarily, until they were able to pay their own rent. The offer had been accepted amidst general enthusiasm and from that day—forgetting that it had been merely a temporary arrangement—the vet- erans had stayed there for good, and paid no rent, while

---

* Nickname for the Sicilian volunteers, owing to their extreme youth.

Sciarame', in his turn, had saved the monthly contribution of three lire paid by the others toward the cost of news-papers, magazines, light, etc. Apart from them meeting in the evening to play cards, read the papers, talk politics or share a drink, these veterans were really giving him no trouble.

It was only now—after the President's request about Roro'—that Sciarame' had found himself between the ham-mer and the anvil; between an impulsive and noisy Presi-dent who would hear of no contradiction, and an obstinate girl who would listen to no reason.

"Mere children! Mere children!" shouted the President that evening, having read the application for membership from La Rosa and his friends. "Mere children, gentlemen, mere children! These brand-new red shirts of recent make at three lire a yard, have only been worn once in Greece and have been brought back as clean and spotless as if they had never been used. Sit down, sit down. We shall forgo all formalities. Let the meeting decide at once; let us get rid of these children right away, with a stroke of the pen! Sit down, sit down."

But the members—all except Sciarame'—had gathered round him, asking to see the application, as though unable to believe it, and firing questions at him, especially the fat and toothless Navetta who was slightly deaf and whose wooden leg—a kind of stump round which flapped the trouser—he dragged along with almost dull, repulsive thuds.

Bellone swept them back with his arms and resumed his seat at the conference table where, ringing the bell for si-lence, he began to read the application aloud with endless grimaces and with comic twisting of his nose and of his lips, which sent the audience into fits of laughter.

Sciarame' alone sat quiet, his chin resting on the knob of his stick, his eyes staring at the paraffin lamp.

Having finished reading the letter, the President became solemn and dignified. Sciarame', who had stood up to speak, was quickly called to order.

"Sit down!" shouted the President.

"The lamp is smoking," retorted Sciarame', humble.

"Let it smoke! Now, gentlemen, I consider that it is idle, almost humiliating for us even to discuss such a ridiculous application" (cheers). "By a unanimous vote we shall reject —with a mere stroke of the pen—this incredible . . . this unqualifiable . . . this. . . . How shall I call it! . . ." (Bursts of applause.)

Presently Nardi asked to be allowed to speak, saying that in his opinion it was necessary and imperative to state, once and for all, that Garibaldians were only and exclusively those who had actually followed Garibaldi. (Hear, hear! Hurrah! Well spoken!) Giuseppe Garibaldi, and nobody else.

"And nobody else, yes, nobody else!"

"And let us add . . ." said Navetta, suddenly springing from his seat, "let us add, gentlemen, that the . . . the, what do you call it? . . . the unfortunate war between Greece and . . . and, what's the name? . . . and Turkey cannot, must not be taken seriously, in view of the . . . yes, exactly, of the . . . the dreadful impression created by that nation which . . . which . . ."

"By that degenerate nation," interrupted the President, rising to his feet.

"That's the word. *Delgenerate, delgenerate,*" shouted Navetta amongst the general approval.

At this moment Sciarame', who had been listening from his seat, lifted his chin from the knob of his stick and raised a hand.

"May I? . . ." he asked timidly.

Everybody turned round, frowning, while the President could not help showing his disapproval.

"You? What have *you* to say?"

Poor Sciarame' felt lost, gulped and raised his hand once more.

"You see, I should like to point out that . . . when all's said and done . . . these . . . these four young men . . ."

"Bluffers!" snapped Bellone. "They are bluffers and nothing else. Why, would you try to stick up for them?"

"No," Sciarame' hastened to reply. "No . . . but you see, I should like to point out, as I was saying, that . . . when all's said and done they . . . they *have* fought, these four young men: they actually *have* been in the war . . . and have shown that they were brave and fearless . . . one of them, in fact, was even wounded . . . what more do you want? That they should have all been killed? If Garibaldi, our great Leader, was not there, it was merely because he was dead, but his son was there, and it seems to me that nobody better than he had the right to wear the red shirt and to allow it to be worn by those who followed him to Greece. Therefore . . ."

To his surprise, Sciarame' had so far been allowed to speak without interruptions but now he was beginning to feel less sure of himself and less confident at the ominous silence which greeted his words. He knew quite well what it meant. He was sure that his comrades—by remaining silent—were far from approving his arguments and merely daring him to go on in order to test his stupidity or his impudence, ready to attack him at the first ill-chosen word. He became panicky and tried to soften, little by little, the expression on his face and the tone of his voice. But soon, the words failed him as if he had said enough and the last word had been spoken in defense of those boys.

"And therefore, having regard to all this . . . I believe . . . I believe . . ."

"What do you believe?" the President interrupted at last, leaving his seat and going up to him.

"Trash! Trash!" shouted the others, also rising from their seats to hem him in, pulling him right and left and trying to convince him that he was sticking up for an unworthy cause. How could he say that those children were Garibaldians? He should be ashamed of himself—they said—for defending those four lazy rascals! Did he imagine that epics —real epics like that of Garibaldi—could have extensions and additions? Greece, he should know, had covered herself with the ridicule of the world.

They were all talking at the same time and poor Sciarame' was unable to answer them all. At random he stuck to what Nardi was saying and shouted:

"You say that the expedition was not a national one? But,

allow me, did Garibaldi, by any chance, fight exclusively for our independence? He also fought in America and even in France, always at the service of Humanity!"

"Will you be quiet, Sciarame'?" thundered Bellone at this point, with a loud bang of his fist on the conference table. "Don't make insulting comparisons! How dare you compare the Garibaldian epic with the farcical expedition to Greece? Shame! Shame! I know why you want to uphold those four buffoons, but we here tonight, you understand, with a unanimous decision will render you a service too by freeing you of a pest which threatens the honor of your family. The application of these fellows must be rejected without a single dissenting voice. Do you understand?"

"Allow me at least to stand aside . . ." begged Sciarame', joining his hands as if in prayer.

But such was their pressure and so loud were their shouts that poor Sciarame' at last agreed to cast his vote with theirs. The application was "unanimously" rejected.

Two days later, the following letter appeared in the local newspaper under the signature of Gaspari, the young fellow who had been wounded at Domokos:

NEW AND OLD GARIBALDIANS:

Sir,

In my own name and on behalf of my comrades La Rosa, Betti and Marcolini, I beg to inform you of a unanimous decision arrived at by the Garibaldian Veterans' Association in reply to our application for membership.

The Association has refused our application.

According to them, our red shirts are not authentic. Just so . . . And do you know why? Because—as we were neither born nor even babies when Giuseppe Garibaldi—the REAL the ONLY one (to use the words of the Association)—decided to fight for the freedom of the Fatherland, we, poor fellows, could not—together with our nurses and our mothers—follow him

at the time and we have made the mistake of following to the sacred land of the Hellenes, his son, who (it
would appear from the resolution of the above-praised
veterans) is not a Garibaldi. Moreover, we are held
responsible for the sad and humiliating end of the
Greco-Turkish war, as if we had not fought and won
at Domokos, leaving on the field the heroic Fratti and
several others.

You will therefore realize, sir, how difficult it is for
us to defend our Leader, as well as the great ideal
which made us answer his call, our fallen comrades
and the survivors, against the cruel offense embodied in
the unqualifiable decision of these Veterans; we have
no remedy because we are, unfortunately, faced by old
men obviously in their dotage. These words may seem
hard, Sir, but are justified by the fact that these men
have rejected our application while harboring amongst
their members, *a man who has not only never been a
Garibaldian and has never taken part in any actual
fighting, but actually wears a red shirt and pins to his
breast no less than seven medals which do not belong
to him but to his brother, heroically killed at Dijon.*

Having said this much, I deem it superfluous to
make any further comment on the Association's decision. I am ready to prove, with the support of undeniable evidence, all I have written above. If necessary,
I shall also give the name of this false Garibaldian
who even had the audacity of voting with the others
against our admission.

In the meantime, I beg to remain, Sir,

Yours, etc.

ALESSANDRO GASPARI.


The letter was followed by a short note by the Editor.


We have been aware for some considerable time
that one of the members of the Association of Garibaldi Veterans had never fought with Garibaldi or even
seen him. We have always refrained from revealing

this fact out of pity for an old man, but owing to the incredible step taken by the above-mentioned Association in refusing the application of Signor Gaspari and his brave companions who fought in Greece, we consider that the Association should at least give some satisfaction to these young men and safeguard its own reputation by urging the resignation of a member who appears to be totally unworthy of belonging to it.

The entire village was puzzled, everyone commenting on Gaspari's unexpected protest. Sciarame' was about to leave his home for the piazza, when Bellone—a copy of the paper in his hand—rushed to him, pushing him into a chair and holding the paper under his nose.

"Have you read it?" he asked. "Read this!"

"No . . . what . . . what has happened?" muttered Sciarame', unable to understand the outburst.

"Read! Read!" yelled Bellone, clenching his fists to control himself, and pacing the room like a lion.

Sciarame' fumbled for his glasses, placing them on the tip of his nose and wondering what he was supposed to read in that paper. Bellone came up to him, tearing it from his hands and pointing to the letter which appeared on the second page.

"Here! here! Read here!"

"Ah!" said the other sadly, after a quick glance at the headline and the signature. "Didn't I tell you?"

"Go on! go on! Read!" again yelled Bellone, more furious than ever.

Sciarame' began to read, at times knitting his brows, at times smoothing them out again, then staring with his mouth wide open as if staggered. The paper nearly fell from his hands. He grasped it more firmly bringing it closer to his eyes as though his sight had suddenly failed him. The President was now watching him, his eyes flaming, his arms folded, waiting for a protest, a denial or an explanation.

"What have you to say about it? Lift up your head! Look at me!"

Sciarame', his face deadly pale and his eyelids hanging

heavily over his weary eyes, shook his head slowly, unable to speak: he placed the paper on the table and brought a hand to his heart.

"Wait . . ." he finally said, more with his gesture than with his voice.

He tried hard to swallow, but his tongue was dry and swollen. His breathing had become heavy.

"I . . ." he feebly murmured, "I . . . I *was* there . . . at . . . at Calatafimi . . . and at . . . at . . . Palermo . . . at Milazzo . . . and in Calabria at . . . at Melito . . . then right up to . . . to Naples . . . and the Volturno. . . ."

"But how were you there? What proofs can you give?"

"Wait . . . I . . . together with my brother . . . I followed him with the donkey. . . ."

"What are you raving about? The medals, I want to know, whose are they? Yours or your brother's? Speak up!"

"I was . . . let me explain. . . . At Marsala . . . we were there together, my little brother Stefanuccio and I . . . I had been acting as a father to him. . . . He was barely fifteen, you see? He ran way from me when . . . when the glorious 'Thousand' landed there . . . to follow him, Garibaldi, along with the other volunteers. . . . I came home; I found my brother had gone. . . . So I hired a donkey . . . I made up my mind to bring Stefanuccio back. . . . I caught him up before he had reached Calatafimi. . . . At fifteen years of age of what good could he have been to the Leader, I ask you? . . . But he threatened to . . . to blow his own head off with an old rifle—twice his size—which they had given him, if I forced him to return. . . . Yes, his own head. . . . Then, listening to the advice of the other volunteers, I let the donkey free . . . for which I had to pay later on . . . and . . . and I decided to join them too."

"As a volunteer also? And did you fight?"

"I . . . I hadn't a rifle."

"And in fact you hadn't the courage?"

"No . . . no . . . I would have rather died than leave my brother."

"So you followed him."

"Yes, everywhere."

And Sciarame', feeling a shiver down his back, pressed his hand a little firmer against his heart.

"But the medals? The red shirt?" resumed Bellone, trembling with rage. "Whose are they? Yours or your brother's? Answer me!"

Sciarame' extended his arms without daring to lift his head; then he said:

"My brother was dead . . . and could not enjoy them any more . . . so I thought . . ."

"You decided to show them off, instead!" The President finished the sentence for him. "Oh, you wretched impostor! Cheat! I could spit at your face! You deserve to be . . . But I will have pity on you. Out you go from the Association; out you go, at once!"

"What? You want to turn me out of my own house?"

"No, we shall go away ourselves, right now! Have the plate removed! How blind I was not to see that a fool like you could never have seen Garibaldi—even at a distance!"

"Never seen him, you say?" shouted Sciarame' with a jerk. "Never seen him? I'll tell you whether I saw him or not! I even kissed his hands! I kissed them on the piazza Pretorio at Palermo, where he had set his camp."

"Shut up, scoundrel. I don't want to listen to you any longer. I don't want to see you any more! Remove the plate and heaven help you if I ever see you wearing the red shirt again."

He made for the door, but once more turned round to yell:

"Cheat! Cheat!"

Left alone, Sciarame' tried to rise to his feet, but his legs were unsteady and trembling. Clinging first to the table, then to the chair and to the railing, he carried himself heavily upstairs.

Roro', seeing him in such a state, gave a cry: but he motioned to her to be quiet: then, pointing to the chest of drawers in the room, he begged her in a half-choked voice:

"The papers?"

"What papers?" implored Roro', trying to help him.

"My papers . . . my brother's . . ." muttered Sciarame',

dragging himself to the chest of drawers. "Open it. . . . Let me look. . . ."

Roro' opened the drawer. Sciarame' laid a trembling hand on a bundle of soiled, faded documents tied together with a string, and then turned to his stepdaughter with lifeless eyes:

"Did you . . . did you show them to . . . to La Rosa?" he asked. At first Roro' could make no reply: then, anxious and scared, she said:

"He asked me to see them. . . . What harm have I done?"

Breaking into wild sobs, Sciarame' collapsed in her arms. With difficulty Roro' dragged him to the chair at the foot of the bed and made him sit down.

"Daddy! Daddy!" she implored. "What is it? What have I done? Why are you crying? What has happened?"

"Go . . . go away . . . leave me alone!" gasped Sciarame', choking. "And to think that I stood up for them . . . I alone . . . and this is their gratitude! I *was* there . . . with him. . . . He was only fifteen. . . . There was the donkey, too . . . then at the first shots . . . my legs . . . my legs. . . . No, I was not afraid. . . . And later at Milazzo . . . concealed amongst the vineyards . . ."

Roro' was watching him, unable to understand.

"Daddy . . . Daddy . . . what are you saying?"

But Sciarame', his eyes wide and lifeless, his face contorted, a hand pressed on his heart, no longer heard her words.

He was looking back, far back, into the past.

He really *had* followed him, that little brother of his to whom he had been a second father; he really *had* caught him up, on his donkey, before they had reached Calatafimi, imploring him with joined hands to come back home, and not to make him die of sorrow at the thought of leaving him alone in such grave danger. It had all been in vain, so that he had had to give way and little by little, fired by the general enthusiasm—he had himself followed the others. Then, when the first shots had been fired . . . No, no, even then he was never really sorry to have let the donkey go. Would he have ever gone back knowing that his young

brother was in the thick of a battle and perhaps on the verge
of being mercilessly killed? On the contrary, he had felt like
rushing to his help and throwing himself into the battle too,
but his legs, his legs had failed him. What can a poor man
do when he is no longer master of his legs? Nothing but
wait and suffer. God alone knew how much he had suffered.
He had suffered for two: for himself and for his brother.
. . . Then, when the battle was over, he had searched the
field trying to find his little Stefanuccio amongst the dead
and the wounded. . . . But no. . . . Stefanuccio was alive
and well! From that day, he had followed him everywhere,
first to Palermo, as far as Gibilrossa, where he had waited
for him, more dead than alive, for endless days: an eternity!
At Palermo, Stefanuccio—as a reward for his bravery—had
been allowed to join the Carabineers, a famous regiment
which was later almost annihilated in the battle of Milazzo.
It was really a miracle that he too—Sciarame'—had not
been killed on that day. Squatting in a vineyard he could
occasionally hear—on all sides—strange thuds among the
foliage; but never once had it dawned on him that they
might be bullets, when suddenly, amongst the branches of
the vines he was crouching against . . . Ah! that dreadful
hiss before the thud! Flattened on the ground, shivering
with fear, he had tried to move away, but in vain; and he
had stopped there, in agony, amid the deluge of bullets, facing death at every thud.

Who could dare to say that he had not known all the hor-
rors of war? Who could dare to say that the stories he was
so fond to relate had not been seen and lived by him? Yes,
he *had* been in the war even if he had not actually fought in
it. Back in his village, after Garibaldi's gift of the Two
Sicilies to King Victor-Emmanuel, he had been hailed as a
hero along with his brother Stefanuccio. As to the medals,
however, his brother alone had received them, but in a way
didn't they belong to them both? . . . Besides, he had never
boasted about them: when he had been asked to speak, he
had always talked on something he had actually seen, nothing else. Never—never indeed—would he have dreamt of
joining the Association had he not been almost forced to do

so on that eventful night at the café, when he had found himself a member almost against his will. He had recipro- cated the honor bestowed upon him (an honor of which he was really not altogether unworthy) by giving them shelter, rent free, during all those years. Yes, perhaps it was wrong to wear his brother's shirt and to decorate his breast with medals which—strictly speaking—were not his own; but, having once made the first step, how could he possibly with- draw? He simply had to keep on, being satisfied at the thought that—at all events—he was representing his poor little brother, now dead, killed in battle at Dijon, his poor little Stefanuccio who so well deserved those medals and yet had never been able to wear them at a single ceremony.

This—if a sin it was—had been his only one. Those new Garibaldians had been the cause of all the trouble; they had quarreled with the old ones; and *he* had been their victim, he who had stood up for them, one against them all. Ah, the ungrateful creatures! They had killed him!

Roro', frightened at the ghastly, lifeless expression of his face, rushed to the window shouting for help.

A few of the neighbors hurried to her assistance.

"What is it? What is it?"

At the sight of Sciarame', sunk in his chair, they stood still.

Two of them, bolder than the others, took him by his shoulders and feet, trying to lift him on his bed. They had only just laid him down when . . .

"God! . . ." said one.

"Look! . . ." said the other.

"Dead? . . ." asked someone from behind.

For a second Roro' was stunned, her wide eyes staring at him, helplessly. Then, turning to the neighbors who had answered her call, she muttered:

"God! . . . Dead? . . . Really *dead?*"

And, throwing herself over her stepfather's body, her head bent low and her arms stretched out over the corpse, she knelt by the bed.

"Forgive me, Daddy! Forgive me! . . ."

The neighbors were puzzled. Forgive her? Why? What

had she done? Why—in her sobs—was she speaking of papers and documents? What documents? They tore her away from the bed and dragged her into her own room. While some of them went to fetch the President others remained to watch beside the bed.

When the President arrived—dark and concerned—with Navetta, Nardi and the other members, old Sciarame' was lying on his little bed, wearing his red shirt, with the seven medals pinned to his breast.

The neighbors had thought it right to bury the old man in the red shirt of which he was so proud. It didn't belong to him? What then? Worse lies than this have been written on many graves. On with the medals! Let all seven of them be pinned to his breast!

Thud, thud, thud. Navetta—the man with the wooden leg—came near the corpse. For a while he stood by in silence, then turning to his comrades and in a hollow voice:

"Shall we take them off?" he said.

The President—who had retired to confabulate with the others in a corner of the room—called him with a sign of his hand. Then, shrugging his shoulders as if to show that he was merely expressing the opinion of his members, he ordered:

"Leave them on. . . . He is dead. . . ."

They gave him a magnificent funeral.

# ALDO PALAZZESCHI

## 1885–

After the fireworks of his early verse, Palazzeschi, who was born in Florence in 1885, settled on a career as writer of a very individual type of fiction. He transferred into it some of the bizarre mood of his poetry, increasingly mixing it with concrete visions of the world around him, particularly of his native Florence, in a light that is part humorous and part nostalgic. This is especially true of that collection of evocative pieces which he called "nineteenth-century engravings." (*Stampe dell'Ottocento*. It contains for instance that little masterpiece of irony and affection, "The English Ladies in Florence.") Working with his usual regularity much of the year in Venice, Palazzeschi has recently published his collected short stories, after himself preparing the revised definitive manuscript in long hand. My selection from these stories had earlier appeared in a book called *Il palio dei buffi* (approximately: "the race of the buffoons"), a title which could be descriptive of most Palazzeschi stories, and even of the major and most popular novels, *The Sisters Materassi* and *The Brothers Cuccoli*. Palazzeschi himself defines his *buffi* as "all those who, for some characteristic trait of character or natural peculiarity, are at variance with the general community of human beings; a variance which at times appears ludicrously humorous and at others tragically sad."

# Bistino and the Marquis

"Nunzia. You know what, Nunzia? I saw the Marquis."

"Ha!" Nunzia would reply, without turning away from the stove where she would be all intent on putting the last touch on lunch or supper; and meanwhile a neat and shiny white table, all ready beside the open window that looked out on the little garden, would be awaiting the two diners with open arms. The woman would show no curiosity about the encounter, but at times she would add more affably: "What did he say to you? What is he doing?" in a tone suggesting no inclination to listen for long to any news of that sort.

At times, Bistino, approaching the kitchen door half alarmed and upset as if he lacked the courage to enter, would say hastily, "You see, I saw him, I met him, I spoke to him," as though there were only one person in all the world to see, meet, and address, or as though no one else could interest him in the slightest. "A pleasure, I'm sure," Nunzia would answer dryly, waddling between stove and pantry.

It was amusing to see that hulking man, almost as tall as the door that made him duck instinctively as he approached the lintel in a stunned attitude of expectancy, and to see him like a huge baby follow the movements his wife executed in front of the stove which was almost as tall as she; indeed, she had to stand on tiptoe to see into the pot.

When they were side by side, Nunzia with her unruly forelock stood only a little higher than Bistino's elbow: they were a random couple and perhaps for this reason happy and perfect.

"Did he ask you anything?" she would add after a cold silence, at which her husband would stand stock-still and agape.

*Translated by Lowry Nelson, Jr.*

And unable to lie to his wife, he would answer cautiously, "I paid for his coffee. Coffee, and a pastry."

"So he was *hungry*, huh?"

After enunciating the word with a cruel edge, the woman would heave a long sigh.

"That's all the good that comes of those meetings. You can be sure he won't do the same for you." She was aware that her husband must have done even more.

Bistino felt disarmed, discouraged, wounded.

"You should understand. . . . What do you want? . . . What's there to be done? . . ." He stammered, trying to hide and excuse the impulse of his own heart, and at the same time to excuse the Marquis who had drunk the coffee and had eaten the pastry. It may be that he had pocketed a few lire which Bistino had kindly offered him on pretext of a loan.

And every now and then Nunzia, who loved her Bistino dearly, would say something that encouraged his recital, and he, like a river flooding its banks, would overflow.

"If you could only see him . . . if you could only see him . . ."

She encouraged him, but only to interrupt him and put obstacles in his way.

"Since he's to blame for his own troubles, let him do the crying." She made sententious declarations as if she were reading from the rolls of a universal, supreme law; and with them she braked her husband after giving him free rein. And he, just a big child, pink and fresh despite his fifty-five years, with blue eyes that smiled gently and boyishly, would come to a halt openmouthed: though able to master the woman physically, he felt mastered by her in spirit. That hardness, which became apparent only when the Marquis was brought up, proclaimed loudly and clearly her principles of life, the strength of virtue not to be toyed with. It was only in this one instance that she would rise up before you like a snake; for in every other there was no wife so attached and tender and, most of all proud, at the age of sixty, to have a fine husband with a jovial countenance, still strong and attractive.

Bistino was incapable of being persuaded that she felt no pity for a person for whom he felt so much; that compassion which good Christians should feel for all creatures without exception, and which he, on the other hand, felt only for one. He had just two affections: his wife, and the Marquis whom he was unable to forget. But it happened that his wife was too intelligent and aware not to weigh the disadvantages in giving full rein to that compassion and to that affection in his simple soul which she had never been able to overcome and which, indeed, she felt growing day by day.

So it was that in the little house of the two retired servants there were two divinities: one black, the Marquis become infernal; and the Countess, who had become celestial blue, twice over one might say, since after having been for eighty years an angel on earth, she had then been in paradise for five and had left an earnest of paradise to her faithful maid: that clean and respectable house, a check for ten lire a day, and lots and lots of other things. It was to be expected that she should give vent to all those stories and at all hours, and Bistino should stand there listening as children listen to their mothers telling fairy tales; though at bottom the Countess meant nothing to him, the Countess he had served for ten years; in fact, way down deep he disliked her, partly out of jealousy for his wife, but mostly because it was she who shoved his Marquis down into hell. He found her tiresome in the extreme, a real bore, with all her virtue; but he would be quite careful not to let on to Nunzia who, except on rare, very rare occasions and in moments of tenderness, would lend an ear to his recital. And he, on the other hand, could hardly find anyone to agree with him. How can you compare a woman who for eighty-six years had been a paragon of nobility and wisdom, austerity and modesty, of charity, with a man who had been a vessel of all vices, who, bequeathed an inheritance when very young, had ruined his own fortune and dissipated in the twinkling of an eye several small inheritances which destiny had showered on him to keep him on the edge of the abyss? And now at the age of seventy, he found himself reduced to begging, living off the niggardly alms of some distant relation, or a friend among those who had not snubbed him or turned their backs on him and were still disposed to listen to him a moment or two in the street or to read his letters. He was reduced to asking for a hundred or for fifty lire as a loan, only to find himself given on sufferance ten or five, and, by writing humiliating letters, granted subsidies that never came or that came much curtailed. If then he ventured to push his way up to the doors of his erstwhile friends, he found them inexorably barred; and descending the stairs empty-handed, clutching the fancy railing, supporting himself on the monumental balustrades, recovering in that atmosphere a shred of his lost pride and dignity, he would mutter ironically: *"Ou ils sont fatigués . . . ou ils sont indisposés . . . ou ils sont malades. Il faut vraiment dire que la race décline."* If it should happen then that good fortune allowed him to meet a charitable old friend who with good grace slipped fifty lire into his coat pocket, he would not think of hoarding it or paying it on account to the hotel keeper for his indebtedness, but would take a taxi, and after stopping and having it wait during his apéritif, he would have it convey him to one of the best restaurants. There he would shun the greetings of some old acquaintance by making a show of indifference, and the acquaintance would wonder, "Has he come into another inheritance?" Upon returning to his hotel, of the lowest category, getting out of the taxi once more (all of which incited the hotel keeper to fury, so that he reminded the Marquis at once and with ill grace of the unpaid bill), he would say to himself, giving the last lire to the driver, *"Ma vie est couteuse mais digne."*

How could Bistino speak of such a blackguard to Nunzia who cherished in her heart the memory of a sainted woman and kept her portrait in the pretty silver frame over the chest of drawers like a relic? Bistino, likewise, had a portrait of the Marquis when young, and what a handsome fellow, what a handsome gentleman! But he kept it hidden at the bottom of a chest, buried under a quantity of useless trash so that his wife would not be able to dig it out. That

portrait he must keep at the bottom of the chest and keep
it only for himself.

When at last Bistino decided to leave the Marquis, who
no longer had a house and was living from hand to mouth,
he should have had eighteen months' wages and ended up
with his pockets empty. He was taken on by the Countess
as a coachman. To the end of her days the Countess had
tenaciously kept a horse, asserting that there was no need
to go so fast to catch up with death; and though he had an
inborn devotion for horses, Bistino finally felt almost
ashamed at taking that old woman out with a horse in the
midst of automobiles. She was very insistent on the good
appearance of her servants, and wanted the coachman and
the butler to cut an ornamental, an impressive figure. And
the handsome coachman, who at the age of forty seemed
still a young man, so fresh he was, so robust, with such a
serene and manly bearing, pierced the heart of Nunzia who
until then had considered herself immune from such surprises.

Love took an odd course with that girl, who had not
known what to be in love meant before that day: she began
to cry. She would never, never hide her face and she would
begin to weep torrents, as if she were ashamed of being in
love: first of all, because of her age, but what really made
her uneasy and ashamed was loving a man who was too
handsome and six feet three. Tiny and thin as she was, she
loved that big man who looked like a hussar. She thought it
improper, dishonorable. She was seized with fits of crying
she could not withstand.

The Countess, aware of the woman's inward distress,
summoned her affectionately and received her confession
with an indulgent smile. The heart cannot be controlled,
and even at the age of forty-five, though tiny and thin, one
may fall in love with a hussar. She spoke openly with Bistino and concluded without delay by setting the day of the
marriage: in her house things were done according to law.
Bistino did not ask her to say it again; he felt lucky to

marry that little woman, not pretty, of indeterminate age, but one who, he felt, was well bolstered in the Countess's heart.

It was owing to the Countess that they possessed that pretty little house of four unencumbered rooms, with a little garden bordered by climbing roses, where Bistino delighted in growing lettuce, tomatoes, and fruit: "A real treasure," said those who went to see it, "a gem, a pippin." There were four rooms fully furnished, a fine bedroom, a sitting room, a kitchen, and another little room Nunzia kept ready to let to a student or a young lady, in case the income got too little to live on. But the income was sufficient, it was sufficient without scrimping, since the Countess had left her a pension of ten lire a day, and before she died she would every day pull something out of the cupboard drawer or would have her look for something in the closet drawer: here a bundle, there a bundle, something to wear, something of value: "Take it, Nunzia, put it away without being seen," so that her children would not see that she left too many things to her loving and faithful maid. And Nunzia had forty years of scrimping registered on the books of her savings account, all the money she had earned; she hadn't spent a cent for clothing. All the Countess's things fitted her well—she was a woman of her size. Dresses and lingerie, even shoes and stockings fitted her, and she had enough in reserve to last her a hundred years if the good Lord let her live that long. The little room was ready to be rented to a young lady or to a student, but for the time being that was not necessary; on the contrary, the income was more than sufficient, and for her the freedom of her house was worth more than what the young lady or the student might pay; she kept in reserve this expedient in case of need.

"If you could only see . . . if you could see his shoes . . . the shoes he wore!" The old valet remembered the closet in which, row on row, there had been forty pairs of shoes. "Greasy! . . . worn out . . . buttons missing from his jacket, and his stockings badly mended; he must mend them himself." He could see again the four closets in the dressing room, two on each side, all full of suits and coats of his master, for all hours, for all places, for all the occasions in the life of a man of society, an elegant man: a hundred shirts, two hundred ties! "If you had seen his collar and his shirt . . . and his cuffs, they seemed to have fringes they were so frayed, and with an inch of dirt at the seams."

The woman would nod and smile wryly, as if she were replying to every detail or giving him to understand, "Good, good, I'm glad to hear that."

"And do you know where he sleeps? In a hotel where they let in those women."

Nunzia, who continued to nod as if to say, "Good, good, I'm glad to hear that," would suddenly burst out:

"You won't take it into your head to go call on him?"

"What a thing to ask!" he would reply, alarmed, feeling threatened by that question. "You understand, they chase him away from all the houses because he doesn't have the money to pay his lodging. At the hotel he ought to pay three lire a night, but the hotel keeper gives him an advance of three hundred lire, puts him up in a hole without windows, and at night he has to get undressed with a tiny piece of candle, when he has that, and sometimes with nothing, in the dark; the owner took away the light bulb for fear he would stay up to read."

Forgetting for a moment those women, Nunzia would again start to nod as if to say, "Good, good!" It was good he had ended up in the dirt with swindlers; it was good he had ended up in the dark, both night and day: "Good, good!"

Bistino's youth was utterly bound up with the Marquis's life; he had been one of his peasants and at the age of fifteen he had been taken on as a stable boy. Then, as the Marquis realized little by little what stuff he was made of, he had become both groom and butler, a trusted aide, a secret and chivalrous secretary. For his master's existence Bistino knew how to provide everything, to have things ready for all contingencies, to foresee and to manage. He had traveled throughout Europe with him, but actually he had seen nothing except his master; all the servant knew of the world was its reflection through his master, his tastes, his habits and ideas, his manner of living, as if it were the most reasonable if not the only way, his clothes, his shoes, his possessions. The master, and the horses: the horses that had brought them together; out in the world he had eyes only for the horses, the horses on the famous boulevards, at the meets, at the most celebrated races. He had lived in so many hotels in so many cities, and he recalled them all together as in a running tournament without being able to focus on anything, or he remembered details which could only have struck his own particular fancy, which only he was capable of seizing upon. He spoke of them so ingeniously and so oddly, or in a way that made everything converge on so unusual and negligible a detail, that people could only wonder what he had in his head to say such stuff. He had seen all this, and the maids; in twenty-five years, how many maids! He could scarcely recall them all. Naturally, he ended up marrying one, not the prettiest but certainly the wisest; he could not have come to a different end, and he could not have ended better.

If Nunzia had known! She understood, naturally; she understood but she didn't want to admit it, and most of all she didn't want to hear it talked about. Better not to say a word for she was jealous and if he had merely alluded to it, she would have turned on him in a rage. The Marquis had been an inveterate lady-killer, notorious, a real Don Juan; the most beautiful women of the world of fashion had been his, and, like a well-rehearsed ensemble, where the mistress fell the maid was sure to fall in turn; it was a sort of obligation; two glances, a few words, and they would fall like ripe pears. Bistino had been the Don Juan of the maids, the most beautiful and famous in their own world, as the mistresses were in theirs. He too had been a most handsome youth. He retained the freshness and serenity of a man from the country, had become a polished servant, irreproachable, who knew how to ride and drive horses with superlative skill. Between master and servant there seemed to be an understanding and, down deep, a mutual pride, a mutual male satisfaction in ascertaining, each from his own position, certain things which a sly discreet smile or a pat on the back sufficed to reveal. And in that smile and in that touch of the hand lay hidden the words: "How inexhaustible life is, and how fine it is to be alive!" Could Bistino forget such things?

"If you could see him . . . withered, emaciated, yellow, bent, he no longer has the breath to speak; I say he's sick, he seems just half his size, you wouldn't even recognize him, he's lost all his old notions."

Then there were the Marquis's fits of ill temper: the loan sharks, the bills of exchange, the mortgages, the debts to be paid, the difficult or unsuccessful adventures, his impatient moods, his rages, all violent; and since he always had Bistino at hand, and only him, the servant took the place of family. Everything landed on his shoulders. Bistino was happy to be of service. The suits were not well kept, the shoes badly shined, the horses had not been inspected before leaving, errands were performed wrong. Shouting and bellowing from the Marquis till finally a shoe or a boot would hit him behind: wham! Instead of resenting them, he loved those intimate outbursts, those tirades, those rages; in those moments more than in any others he could feel what he meant to his master, what he was; he would feel much more attached and indispensable than when he was happy. When all was said and done, he felt that he was the only person who really liked his master. Fits and scenes meant affection, as did even the shoes thrown at him. Indeed as soon as he calmed down, the Marquis, who had a generous and noble heart underneath his thoughtlessness and indolence, would become expansive, cordial. He would become gay and witty again. He would feel disposed to show his remorse and forgiveness by giving Bistino money, a couple of ties, a package of cigarettes, whatever happened to be in his hands at the time. He would lay his hand on the servant's back in a friendly, confidential gesture. Those rages only confirmed their mutual attachment; a simple heart could not be wrong.

Sitting in the kitchen where his wife would be preparing lunch or supper, he could see all these things together again, and he would talk as if speaking to himself, finding no adequate way to express his feelings: "Poor fellow . . . He had every one of them!" What he meant to say was that all human passions had taken possession of him, had burned him: horses, gaming, women, sprees. At times he would go carousing and afterward fall limply into his arms, in a faint; and Bistino would have to put him to bed as if he were an infant.

"Poor fellow . . . He had them all. . . . He had all of them, every one," he would repeat, bemused.

"Poor fellow, my foot!" the woman would reply in order to rouse him. "He had them all, and now he's paying for them, every one. In this world you have to pay; don't worry, Saturday always comes." She would pour out the steaming soup and Bistino would draw near the table, pensive and troubled. "It comes sooner or later, rain or shine; somebody pays out and somebody takes in," she would mutter, putting the pot away under the stove: "Just one, and you pay for the lot."

One day Nunzia came out with a statement which Bistino found himself too weak to answer, so great was the joy that filled him. He couldn't believe it, and touched himself to make sure he was still there or that he wasn't dreaming:

"One of these Sundays we ought to invite your Marquis to dinner. It will take away some of his hunger, and he must feel his share of that."

The minute he recovered he lifted her up and carried her around the house, just as if she had been a cat or a dog or a baby; he even carried her into the garden, where the residents of the upper floors leaned out of their windows to watch, while she flapped and fluttered, flailing her legs and laughing convulsively:

"Let me go! Let me go!" she shrieked. "Let me go, you're hurting me! Leave me alone!"

But instead of setting her down, he continued running about and saying:

"He'll accept, you'll see, he'll come, I know he will, I'm sure of it, he'll be only too happy, I know. . . ."

She knew just how great a comfort she could give him,

and she was not able to resist. "We'll see what happens," she thought, "the world won't come tumbling down if we invite him to dinner." And when he had set her down she said, "That's what I say too: he'll come. With that big hungry mouth of his!"

The Marquis showed that he was grateful for the invitation, but without smiling; his mouth was no longer capable of smiling. And that Sunday at the hour set he arrived at the house of his former servant, where awaiting him was a modest dinner of which he partook sparingly. His fiber had been deeply shaken; he was no longer anything but a sick and defeated man—a mask. He showed himself to be grateful with complete naturalness, and, in his sad state, to be still a gentleman; indeed his manners were such that during the dinner, his hosts experienced a vague disappointment rather than the instinctive embarrassment of two former servants in the presence of one who had been their master.

Bistino watched him ecstatically, unable to believe his own eyes, forgetting to eat, and holding himself ready for what could not happen: a sign of joy on the old man's face, pale, hollow and exhausted. He would rouse himself only to offer the Marquis something, which would be refused gracefully and unsmilingly. Was he not happy to be there? "Marquis, sir; Marquis, sir," Bistino would repeat, half joyful and half afraid. The woman was watching. The Marquis would have preferred not to hear his title too often—in his present condition the title was a kind of stab—but he didn't dare show his discomfort. But he could not hide the sense of shame and tribulation caused by his clothes which gave no more than modest cover to the nakedness of body he would not wish to expose. The woman, deeply curious to know how this game she didn't understand would finally turn out, kept watching the two of them. She would look at the Marquis: "What a pretty mess your bad judgment has got you into!" Then she would look at her husband: "What can he want to see! What is it that gives pleasure to this big baby!" And gradually she felt herself possessed by a vague sense of pity for the guest and a lively tenderness for her husband. But such sensibilities she quickly intercepted and erased by stinging resentment and by a sort of remorse for having felt tenderness and pity.

After dinner the two men went out together. Nunzia remained at home because she was tired after preparing all that the invitation required, and then too, because she had to put everything back in place. Dinner had been served in the parlor, with due ceremony.

Once Bistino was alone with him, he would have liked his old master to rouse himself, to cheer up. He looked at him, offering him his soul, but he could not succeed in rousing him and cheering him up. The poor man, whether outside or in the house during dinner, held himself to a gloomy dearth of words. Most of all Bistino would have liked to bring the conversation around to the past, and he sought every pretext for doing so: to recall twenty-five years of a life they had shared, the trips, the adventures, the horses, the women, the sprees. . . . But it was clear that the other was not of the same inclination; the things that had once enflamed him seemed no longer even to exist, and he lit up only when he spoke of the present, of his wretched state, the effrontery of the base hotel keeper, the indecent lodging, the cousin in Siena who ought to send something regularly but sent nothing or too little. When he threatened to have himself committed to a home for the aged, his cousin had promised him a hundred and fifty lire a month to save the dignity of the family, and then would send him fifty, very rarely a hundred, claiming that the harvests had gone badly. A friend in Milan, very rich, would also send him something to help out every now and then, but long and frequent epistles were required. The others turned a deaf ear, used him rudely; no one undertook to receive him, to listen to him: *"Ou ils sont fatigués . . . ou ils sont indisposés . . . ou ils sont malades. La race décline."* Or they would offer him sums out of all proportion to the necessities of life. These were the subjects that would still make the old man light up, and to Bistino they were not of the slightest interest.

Once again husband and wife invited the Marquis for a second Sunday dinner, then a third and a fourth; till finally, when it became clear that they could invite him without altering their usual custom of serving in the kitchen, it was agreed that they invite him every Sunday. A good soup, a well-made broth (Nunzia's was excellent) pleased him most. For this he felt the deepest need and for this he showed real satisfaction and gratitude. Afterward he seemed cheered and contented; he would then be satisfied with just a few mouthfuls of something else, which he shoved down slowly, without the greediness natural to unstocked stomachs. "This will stick to your ribs," Nunzia would say with a note of irony which she was unable to overcome, while the poor fellow really felt it stick to his ribs. Other times, inviting him to eat some more, she would fashion an odd metaphor, "It's the mouth that carries the legs," proud of saying something paradoxical.

All this, until one Sunday, to the ineffable surprise and joy of Bistino, the Marquis, Lord knows why, right then and there began to laugh: "Ha! ha! ha! *cochon!*" he said to his old servant. "What can he be laughing at? He's going crazy," thought Nunzia, who had grown used to seeing him gloomy. "It's really the end of him; we'll have to call somebody to help tie him up." "Ha! ha! ha! *cochon!*" repeated the Marquis, pretending to poke Bistino in his stomach which he was clutching from laughter.

His unexpected glee was not madness, but wisdom clear and simple; and as Bistino was exploding with laughter, Nunzia thought, "They're going crazy, the both of them; they'll need the cage from the madhouse and a troop of orderlies to tie them up."

Then having recovered from leaden dejection, he began to talk, to talk about everything, about all subjects, big and little, but especially about the past, about the horses, the women—yes sir, even about the women. Growing more animated, he would repeat, "Ha! *cochon!*" The woman would keep saying to herself, "Just what I told you; he needed my broth to set him up, to bring back his strength." Bistino was blindly happy. He urged the Marquis on and reminded him of things with the eagerness of one who wants to hear all. At one point he stared at him in fear, afraid that in telling one of his intrigues the Marquis might blurt out one of Bistino's. Nunzia would have sprung for his eyes with her nails bared. But the Marquis was excellent, superb; he was wily, and however ruinous his condition, he had not forgotten how to manage shrewdly, so much so that the woman, when she was alone with her husband, ended up by confessing, "When all is said and done, these lubbers are amusing; when he's in good form your Marquis is quite pleasant." That was the reason he was invited on Thursdays too, then every day, and finally, after an arduous discussion in which the woman in the end had to give in, since the room was all ready and unoccupied and since the Marquis ate so little he cost no more than a dog, one fine day he was awaited at Bistino's house in the role of permanent guest. "We'll try it. . . . We'll see how it turns out," said Nunzia by way of conclusion.

He arrived wearing everything he owned: no handkerchief, no collar, no stockings. It was either because his clothes were in no condition to stand the transfer or because he wanted to avoid arousing the suspicions of the hotel keeper that he had brought nothing with him. Most likely he had made a clandestine exit under the very eyes of the hotel keeper to whom he owed four hundred lire. He needed mending to put him in a presentable state.

As soon as he was installed in the light and decent room, the poor man felt himself revive, just as that Sunday at the first spoonfuls of that restorative broth; and he pondered every way to avoid gambling away that new well-being which nothing in the world could have led him to expect. His upbringing and the logic of life would have suggested that he behave with delicacy and tact so sensitive that his weight would be felt as little as possible, as if he were not there. It was the only way, moreover, that he could save the last shred of personal dignity in the presence of his former servants, his benefactors. But logic is not always the rule in this life; indeed, most of the time it doesn't fit the lock which may be absurdly illogical.

As for Bistino, he deplored the fact that the Marquis accepted everything without a whisper. With the decency of the ruined master, he found everything to be good and well done; he never proffered an opinion, a wish, an order: "At your service, at your service, don't hold back, don't be shy; I have nothing to do, sir," Bistino would repeat, mortified and offended that he did not command. He could not be persuaded that the man whom he had obeyed for twenty-five years had forgotten how to command, and to command snappily according to his fashion, without delay or reticence. He felt that the former masher must suffer from this more than from anything else; and he looked at him disappointedly, as at dinner those first Sundays when he was not inclined to laugh and relive with his willing servant all those pleasant memories, to speak of a time and of a life that brought him pain. Every now and then Bistino would approach the door and listen; then he would say softly, in a stifled voice, "Sir, is there something you would like?"

It was as a man of the world and of experience, even in total decay, that the Marquis understood he had to respond. One morning a voice issued from his room, hoarse and angry, and a name was repeated incessantly: "Bistino! Bistino! Bistino!" Bistino jumped out of bed and ran half-naked to hear what his old master would have; while Nunzia sat bolt upright, rubbing her eyes, and wondered impatiently: "What's wrong with him? What does he want? Is he dying? Is he sick? What a way to call."

"Bistino!" shouted the Marquis; and Bistino responded by running, all agog, while still buttoning his underwear: "Here I am; coming; I'll be right there, sir."

"What did he want?" asked his wife to begin with. "What did he want, that's what I'd like to know."

"Nothing. He wanted his suit and shoes; he's going out early this morning, since it's a nice day; the sun . . ."

"Ha! His suit and shoes . . . and he calls you in that

lordly way? Was that the reason he woke us up and made you get out of bed?"

"You understand. . . . Let's face it, he's still a Marquis; no matter what you say, he's used to commanding, poor man. It's not his fault, he does it without realizing; he doesn't realize," he said glowingly.

"Ha! He doesn't realize . . . because he's still a Marquis"; she drew herself up threateningly. "Well then, I'll just see about making him realize, and after that I'll tell him who he is; and I'll tell you who you are too, answering him like that. A Marquis . . . A fine thing, yes, a fine thing, this Marquis of yours: today I'm telling him to leave, I'm giving him his walking papers."

Bistino threw himself to the knees of his wife who was incapable of understanding the sentiment that exhilarated him, saw him apparently confounded, and felt that inwardly he must be happy. He implored her to forgive the Marquis, not to send him away. In spite of all, from that day on the voice of a master was to be heard, louder and louder, issuing from the modest, quiet little room: "Bistino! On the double, by God! What are you doing, you dawdler? You sluggard! Are you there scratching your behind? Quick, you lazy oaf!" Shouts, orders, taunts, insults, threats. Now Nunzia was just watching the game, trying to understand, and said nothing. *"Je te f . . . à la porte!* Away with you!" shouted the Marquis. Touring about Europe, Bistino had learned not a word of any language, but when his master shouted he understood them all.

"Away with you? Where to?" thought the woman, disconcerted: "If there's anyone who ought to go, it's you, you alone, my dear Marquis, and with all the baggage you brought with you when you came." After the hubbub, she would have taken it into her head to show him the door. But her husband's face left her perplexed, and it made her withhold the cry of revolt which her countenance foretold as imminent. She had never seen him so happy. She wanted to wait a little longer and see just how things turned out. Then she intended to eject the lodger; that old fool of a Bistino would have his comeuppance and good cry over it.

But with Nunzia the Marquis was another man altogether.
The orders, the taunts and the threats were all confined,
with mathematical exactitude, to his room; and this gave
her even more to ponder. With her he was kind, full of
praise and compliments, bows, smiles, all courtesy and gen-
tlemanliness; like a real nobleman. The food was exquisite,
superb, excellent, and he would compare it to that of the
most famous chefs, who had been with the great families
whom she knew only by name, or by looks if she had seen
them at the Countess's: the chefs of duchesses, princesses,
marquises, and even that most famous of all, the chef of
Victor Emmanuel, who left to posterity a highly reputed
cookbook. He honored her as if he were the guest of some
great lady. And once in his room with Bistino: shouts,
scenes, foul words, and in the midst of them, cries of joy or
epic laughter. "But really, what a way to live," thought
Nunzia embattled between rebellion and flattery. And talking with her husband, she submitted in evidence this dis-
crepancy: "He does it with you because he knows he can.
With me you can rest assured he wouldn't do it. With me he
toes the line, the Marquis does. He knows he can do it, he
knows you, he knows you well and naturally he takes advantage of that. Look how he treats me." This put Bistino
in seventh heaven, because not only was he happy that the
Marquis treated him with his former confidence and intimacy, but also he was happy that the Marquis acted toward
his wife like a true gentleman of breeding, that he respected
her and treated her with consideration. And Bistino was
happy because this paralyzed her resentment. "Didn't I tell
you? You see what a fine gentleman he is, how he treats
you, huh? What breeding!" He told her these things incessantly. "We all get treated the way we deserve," she concluded, tossing her head, growing susceptible to the fact
and priding herself on it, striking a dignified pose, a demeanor that came easy to her since she had lived for forty
years by the side of an irreproachable woman. To put an
end to one of their squabbles he replied:

"Listen, Nunzia, if all of a sudden you heard the voice

of the Countess calling you, you'd climb out of the window to get down sooner and see what she wanted."

"That's not the half of it; and I'd only be doing my duty." Then she looked at him threateningly: "And you would put the Countess on the same footing as this starveling?"

"No, don't you see, money doesn't count. In some things it's the heart that counts. And if the Countess were dying of hunger, wouldn't you give her something to eat?"

"Why, I'd take it out of my own mouth to give to her." She would draw herself up: "Are you comparing the Countess to this chimpanzee?"

"Away with you!" shouted the Marquis in his room, *"Je te f . . . à la porte!* Away with you!" Bistino would take refuge in the garden; he didn't have the courage to go near his wife until a new order called him back and he made things up. Then the Marquis would put a hand on his shoulder and begin to laugh. "He acted like a bedraggled cat so that we would take him in, the sly old creature, and now that he has a toe-hold he makes demands, he takes it into his head to command, this sliver of a nobleman. His cheek was just what we needed. If he acted that way with me I'd tell him off."

But the changeable behavior of the guest, besides giving her something to think about, flattered her inwardly. "What do you expect? He's still a Marquis, no matter what you say; they're all alike, they're made that way, they're used to ordering. He doesn't even realize it."

One morning the Marquis said in a loud clear voice that he did not intend to live without a bell in his room. They were to supply it at once: he was not accustomed to shattering his vocal cords to call his servant. "The bell? A bell?" said Nunzia over and over, running through the house at the height of fury: "The bell?" Pausing, she stiffened from head to toe, arched like a sling-shot ready to let fly: "A bell?" Meanwhile Bistino, radiant, had run to the electrician to have it put in. "The bell? But will you tell me? In what world are we living?"

"You understand. He doesn't realize; if he did, he wouldn't do that. Do you really think he would?"

Bistino was laughing, doting on this novelty: "He does it without realizing!" "He doesn't realize he's no longer master," he meant to say. "He doesn't remember any more. They're all alike, they're made that way. I've known thousands. . . . But do you actually think he could stand it? A gentleman without a bell—now is that right? They're the sort who have the bell in hand from the time they open their eyes in the morning until nighttime when they close their eyes. I'm surprised he didn't ask for it before now, that he's been so long without one, that he was able to get along. Who knows how he suffered. A gentleman without a bell is unthinkable; as far as bells go, gentlemen have them in their blood."

And once the bell was there, the little room worked perfectly. "What are you waiting for, sluggard? On the double, you booby! How long does it take for you to answer? Don't you hear the bell, you glutton? Have you got peas in your ears?"

Bistino would run, bursting with laughter: "He doesn't realize, poor man, he doesn't realize, he doesn't remember any more," he would reflect at the height of bliss.

The Marquis had brought life back to that house where happiness, too secure and too even, had made it stagnant.

And with Nunzia, at dinner, what gallantry! It was an uninterrupted crescendo, flattery point-blank. What delightful figures of speech, what aristocratic subjects of conversation: bowing and scraping; all the chefs in history, and ladies of society. The poor kitchen would become a glittering drawing room: the duchesses, the marquises, the countesses, whom Nunzia had seen at her mistress's or whom she had heard talked about. He knew their stories and anecdotes; troubles, scandals, muddles: an inexhaustible repertory. Or if she didn't know them, she pretended to know them to keep up with the Marquis, like someone well able to do so, showing how well informed she was. All the clamor occurred in the room to which Bistino, having suddenly awakened to the sound of the bell, would run every morning to put himself at the disposal of the Marquis who now and then would express his disapproval and fly into his rages. Nunzia would turn over and continue to sleep: "Stupid creature, I'll make him change his tune." She paid less and less attention to what went on between the two of them, to the shouts and the taunts, not to mention the noise and the laughter, as if they were two boys who played at their games in a corner without causing any trouble. And one morning, Wham! Bistino felt a shoe on his behind. "Good!" his wife added, "Good and hard!" without even turning away from the stove where she was going about her business.

When this way of life had become normal, and Nunzia had grown used to it, the oddity of the situation caused her spirit to take another turn, in exactly the opposite direction. She began to want to go out with the two of them, to strut ostentatiously between them, and to frequent a café in the center of Florence, the Grande Italia in Piazza Vittorio Emanuele, where she might meet friends: a pensioner of the Guards and his wife, a letter carrier with his wife and a daughter who was engaged to a sergeant major (the poor things would have to wait ten years for a promotion so that they could get married); another sergeant came along with them; two ladies who rented rooms to big shots; more employees, senior officers, rich foreigners (and they too had much to tell); a streetcar conductor with his wife and four children who, with a mixture of mistrust and excessive impatience, were waiting for someone who was supposed to have left and who delayed in returning. And to introduce the Marquis to her new acquaintances: "This is the Marquis. He lives with us, we're together," as if to say, "Pay attention because we are folks way up the ladder." And they, who were unacquainted with the Almanach de Gotha, indeed were unaware it existed, at once looked at him diffidently, stroking their noses and exchanging glances. "Is he really a Marquis? Is he a real Marquis? Or shouldn't one say, as of diamonds, 'piece of glass'?" However much they would have liked to put him in his place, the aspect of the old man was not such to confirm their certainties. But then, because of the luster reflecting on them all, impressed as they were by a hyphenated name, and even more by certain reliable information circulating in the café, they all ended up by believing and by aspiring to his aristocratic company. "Isn't it, Marquis? Did you hear that, Marquis? Marquis, what do you think?" Nunzia would say repeatedly with great affability and every few words or so.

And what with the Marquis, she began now and then to hint at something about herself too, or to have people believe it of her. She did it in such a way that she started the rumor that if she were not actually titled, she was most certainly noble, or that at least her mother or her grandmother must have been. To tell the truth, neither of them had known but one coat of arms: the scythe to mow forage and the hoe to ready the ground for planting potatoes—at any rate, tools noble of their kind. But that they were on easy street this would hardly signify. She boasted noble acquaintances, recounted anecdotes and adventures in which there were always marquises and countesses, as if they were people of her circle. "Do you recall, Marquis?" It was understood that they were, in short, more or less noble, and a point was made of reserving them more and more space and doing them greater and greater honor. Bistino was happy and did nothing but laugh. Like a perfect servant, he made bows that could easily be mistaken for traditional aristocratic behavior by someone not well up on such matters.

As for the Marquis, who every morning in his room had to give the bell many noble rings, and every now and then to fly into most noble rages which he would willingly have dispensed with (Bistino, unaware that he was indulging in great luxury, was paying a cheap price for a master), he was not astonished at the woman's presumption. He understood her too, and lent himself at once to the game, showing to the ladies in the café what still remained of his real and ruined nobility.

There was no choice: from Siena came fifty lire a month, that was all. The harvests were getting worse and worse. And from Milan came nothing any more because he became vexed at writing his famous epistles. For a good soup, and a decent lodging, the Marquis had to manage some other way.

# RICCARDO BACCHELLI

1891–

Born at Bologna in 1891, Bacchelli has had as contin-
uous and full a literary career as any Italian writer in
our century. A sensitive and original poet in his early
youth, he later established his importance mainly as a
writer of fiction. A powerful stylist, Bacchelli is con-
sciously within that classic tradition of Italian narrative prose which has its major nineteenth-century model
in Manzoni's novel *The Betrothed*. Several of Bacchelli's
novels are historical like Manzoni's; his major work
*The Mill on the Po* has a nineteenth- and early-twen-
tieth-century background, while in a very recent instance Bacchelli has gone back to Roman days, with a
mixture of historical insight and free imagination *(The
Three Slaves of Julius Caesar,* 1958). A conscious classi-
cist, Bacchelli has in common with the early Italian
authors of *novelle* a taste for the anecdotal and sometimes humorous type of story-telling. The present selection is an example.

## The Fourth Wife

Gasparin Falocchio seemed fated to bury his wives. He had
married the first wife for love when he was twenty-five, and
it was a real sorrow for the whole of Romagnano Codifiume
in Emilia when she died.

It is a beautiful and prosperous place situated where
four wide white roads intersect and the new concrete bridge

with its slender, white arch joins the two banks of the river, replacing the old ferry. It is, in fact, called the Ponte del Traghetto, the "ferry bridge." The river is a tributary of the Reno, one of those slow-moving rivers of Lower Emilia whose beds can be shifted by the hand of man, so gradual is the gradient and so uncertain its course. In point of fact, thanks to the science of hydraulics, the engineers have been able to make the Reno flow into the sea instead of the Po, and, if they should change their minds, they would only have to change the river-bed once again.

At the crossroads stood the parish church. The baroque style of its comfortable lines, its cream-washed, unpretentious rural placidity, gave an impression of architectural somnolence, extraordinarily well suited to that quiet country background. Before it stretched a grassy graveyard, between two lines of iron fence posts that bordered the roads and a hawthorn hedge on the other, the countryside. It was an attractive field, neat and smooth with choice, tender grass on which the parish chickens grew fat. It was said that it had been made long ago by the inhabitants who wished to outdo those living on the other bank of the river who, for spite, had built their bell-tower twelve feet higher than that of Romagnano Codifiume. "We will make a field big enough to impound the whole of their parish," had said the lord-protector of Romagnano, a great Bolognese patrician whose escutcheon still stands on the church façade, despite the fact that his family has had to sell the extensive lands which it formerly possessed for many miles round Romagnano to the peasants, stewards and tenants.

All that remains now of such patrician families are their names, their coats of arms, a certain distinguished ring in the names of the farms in the neighborhood and, of course, the occasional incidents, two centuries of exchanges of cudgel blows and arquebus shots having failed to exhaust the quarrels between these two places. Under Pope Sixtus the Bolognese patricians had armed the country against the militia of the said Pope, who was not one for half measures. From those days some of the farms and wayside shrines and certain crossroads bear such names as "The Ill-bred," "The Evil Way," "The Sign of the Cross," "The Brawl," "The Day of the Dead," "The Brave Wench"; and there were "The Crucifix of the Dead Man" and "The Madonna of the Thieves," because in those parts there had been a wood and a large canefield which, before the irrigation system reached the valleys, served as a hideout for the bandits. Indeed the people of Romagnano delighted in boasting of being their descendants, but no outsider was allowed to allude to it, least of all those who lived on the other side of the river.

There had been a spot called *la Rotta* where the river once had made a terrible breach in the embankment, but now irrigation had raised the level of the marshes, the canefield was now given up to wheat and for some little time the wood had fallen to the ax without revealing secrets of any buried treasure. On every hand, right up to the neighboring embankment, high and green, and as far as the eye could see was hemp, grain and turf and festoons of vine on the elm trees, and poplars with their tops nodding daintily in the light, first to feel the wind and last to lose the rays of the sun as it set.

Gasparin Falocchio, a well-known dealer in hemp from his youthful days, had found his first wife at "The Brawl"; she was a solid, cheerful, amorous wench. They got married in the spring. "As happy as Gasparino and Zelmira" became almost a proverb in the district. She had a passion for horses and broke in the proudest and most unruly beasts with amazing skill and courage. By the exercise of this profession she earned as much as she wanted. They were prosperous years for hemp growing; Germans, English and finally Dutch were among the buyers. After three years they were even more in love with each other than they had been at the start. He lost her and the baby in childbirth.

"I feel I've no luck in marriage," said Gasparin Falocchio to the comforting priest and his condoling friends—"well, I suppose it was God's will that it should be so."

Then he appeared to give the matter no more thought. He rode his horses, made large deals in hemp, shouted hour upon hour in the market in his efforts to persuade contracting parties, ate and drank more than all his sensual companions, who themselves were wild drinkers. And, when the latter fell forward with their heads on the table, Gasparin Falocchio, shining with sweat, strong and massive, would remove his squattish body, as sturdy and muscular as a bull, from the table and bring off the best deal of the day at the expense of his competitors. Then when the loiterers finally left the inn, half-tipsy, he was already in his cart greeting them mockingly and laughing at their abuse and their insults.

He took his time, and slackening the reins, let fly with his own abuse, always the most highly colored and most pungent of the lot, and went off. Business and money were not enough; he had to have the last word in every dispute.

He used to go to Bologna every Saturday for the agricultural market; but all the women who were to be had for money did not console him for the loss of Zelmira of "The Brawl." He would sigh deeply as he thought of his poor late wife.

When a year had gone by, he took a second who lived at "The Madonna of the Thieves," the farm where they grew kidney beans and thieves found their hiding-places, said the people, and where the stoutest and toughest frames, male and female, of the district were to be found. "We need Gasparino," they said, so as to feel safe here at "The Madonna of the Thieves."

The girl was very dark and thin, her cheeks were bony, her hips narrow and her ardent bosom was deep. She had black, prophetic eyes, grave even when she laughed. Thin, yes, but what a frame! "Four wings and four bones jump the ditch," Gasparin would taunt her. "It's a riddle," and he would explain with reference to the medlar—which has four nuts and four sprays of flowers so that wind blows it far away from the tree.

"Come and make me fat then," the brazen wench would jeer back at him. "I'll do what I can," said Gasparin, laughing, and taking her at her word in the joy of his new marriage. To such an extent that within four years he had dispatched her. She was a woman of humble origins who suffered from silent rages, quite unable to give vent to her feelings in words; and she was obstinate. In one of these rages she died; there was nothing to be done. It is true that Gasparino lost several pounds of flesh in this adventure; but she lost her life. When the end was near, the wife said to a sister and a friend who had come to "The Madonna of the Thieves" to help her, "He was the only man who could get the better of me . . . It has happened to me . . . it's my turn to die, because I refuse to admit that I'm beaten." With these enigmatic words on her lips she died, exhausted, cursing Gasparin Falocchio and refusing to see him.

The battle, as I have said, lasted four years.

The priest who had brought the sacrament, after giving the absolution, met the husband kneeling outside his door, and despite the secrecy of the confession, could not refrain from exclaiming, "Oh, Gasparin, there are things . . . ? Have I heard the worst?" The penitent beat his breast so that the priest made the sign of the cross over him as if to exorcise him; then he made off.

The deceased woman's sister vowed that, since neither her father nor brothers had the courage to stab him, she would marry him and carry out a plan of revenge.

The widower was seriously reproved by the parish priest who was getting alarmed at the paganism that was going on; the whole district was out of hand, and few young women went to the altar without having previously conceived a child or two in the ditches or behind hedges. The widower, therefore, conscience-stricken by the priest's words, began to attend Mass every Sunday, instead of coming to confession once a year, at Easter.

One Sunday morning in August he encountered his sister-in-law in the middle of the long, spacious cemetery in the burning sunshine. She intended to say, "I want to marry you to be revenged!" when he said, "*You* here, handsome creature! That's how it is—some of us remain and those who must die, must!"

His glance and bearing was so insolent and sacrilegious that, experienced and bold as she was, she hastily put her handkerchief over her head in accordance with the injunction of the Apostle Saint Paul, who knew how amorous and tempting women can be, even to the tips of their hair, and half in a daze hastened into a church to hear Mass.

"But not even religion can be of any comfort to me," reflected Gasparin, mortified.

Then the war came and, while the other men went off amid the sobs of their wives and mothers, Gasparin contrived to stay at home, with a certificate of exemption, in connection with requisitioning jobs. It was not that he was afraid of death but too much in love with life.

Some time later he had to leave the district, being sent to Bologna and further away still to Palermo, always provided of course with his exemption certificate. He had no relations. He was almost forgotten in his own country.

He brought his third wife from outside along with his discharge when the war was over. They had already been living as man and wife, and the priest published the banns and gave the blessing. It was a winter's day. Gasparin felt he had allayed his restless ardor. She had, it was true, a few white hairs and panted a little when she had to hurry, but she remained as solid as an oak tree and complained of not having enough to do. The shops were full; no one had been selling hemp for five years. His wife was handsome and good. Perhaps the change of air had done her good, possibly Gasparin had been behaving sensibly. The priest was delighted. The Spanish influenza epidemic came and went. They escaped the first wave, but the poor woman, along with so many others, was a victim the second year.

Gasparin wept and despaired as if he had been the only one who had lost a handsome and good wife in these tragic circumstances.

By now he was nearer forty than thirty-five and no woman in the district would have him at any price. He buried them all! you could not blame them.

Gasparin Falocchio shook his head. The hemp trade was looking up again; the German market had restarted, his health was sound, money was coming in. But one thing poisoned his life despite the fact that he was becoming king of the hemp trade once more and the chief figure in the inns where the brokers did their business for miles around. It was that he, a cheerful man and of a gentle and easy disposition, having a good appetite and rich blood in his veins, should have, so to speak, "the evil eye," that fatal evil on which he prospered and of which his wives perished. He looked at his healthy flesh with a shudder of disgust as if it was unclean and macabre. He would wake up at night shivering. A widower in a bed which three dead women had slept in. He felt he always had one or other of them by his side. He took to drink, and in his dreams all three began to visit him, strangely merged into each other, and there he lay amid the writhing limbs of these cadaverous paramours.

Confession and penance availed him nothing. The local doctor advised him to give up drinking, but it only made matters worse. The doctor dabbled in literature and compared Gasparin Falocchio's torments with those of Mesenzio of antiquity who used to tie living men to corpses; and, as the poor man's nerves deteriorated, he betook himself to the chemist's, quoting *Hamlet*, "There are more things in heaven and earth, Horatio, then are dreamt of in your philosophy."

And Gasparin Falocchio, in despair and equally afraid of waking and sleeping, got it into his head that if—as in the fairy tales—he could only find a woman disposed to love him, he would be cured. But it was hopeless to try and find her in his own neighborhood or the places round about. He and his story were too well known. They refused him with the best excuses, they declined with smiles, but underneath those excuses and their country affability, he discerned their sinister forebodings. He could not blame them. To come to terms with fate is not particularly agreeable.

He had a serving-maid in his house; she was approaching forty, small, stringy, thin; her clear, cold eyes which expressed her strong will had won her the nickname of *la Bietta*—"The Mischief-maker"—among local people who have an intuitive understanding of these things. Normally she was buttoned up to the chin, taciturn, capable, self-reliant; but sometimes, when she was washing the clothes or the crockery, she would reveal her white, plump arms, which made a strange contrast with her dry, wrinkled face. Then Gasparin jokingly would inquire, "Does the rest correspond?" "More or less," *la Bietta* retorted, unperturbed. She had a slight limp—enough to intrigue and no more; it lent her movements an almost gay undulation, a gentle, animal gracefulness like that of a kid, which made one want to stroke her brow. Among ordinary people, who are as shrewd in this as in other matters, the slightly lame are particularly sought after in marriage. They are said to be healthy; they are received everywhere with great friendliness. They are all of an agreeable disposition and wonderful —to speak frankly—in bed. Indeed, the wise Montaigne quotes a salacious Italian proverb in their praise.

But in the present case, it did not do to look beyond her gait and color of her arms, for she was otherwise a wisp of a woman with a face like a dried bean.

There is, however, no accounting for the moods and surprises of nature and its choices. Gasparin was desperate; whether it was his faith that he could and desire that he should be cured, his need for a wife, whether it was the seductive gait of *la Bietta* that had made a spider's web in his mind without his knowledge, the fact remains that one morning he stood before her trembling and asked her if she would marry him. She quietly assented, sitting down on the edge of the fatal wedding-bed.

They got married; *la Bietta's* wrinkle still remained fixed and vertical between her eyebrows; she dressed as the lady of the house and made up, all in the interests of Gasparin, who began to recover, become serene and cease having nightmares, in a word to enjoy life once more. He would say to the priest, "There's nothing like women, reverend Father!" "In holy and sanctified marriage," the priest would add in assent, delighted to see him cured.

Gasparin shouted to the doctor and chemist a hundred

yards before he met them, in his sensual voice. "Throw your medicine and science into the river," so that in the end they got angry and avoided him. "If you stick it out, you win in the end," he said to the women who, despite his entreaties, had refused to console and cure him. And to bring home to them the nature of *la Bietta's* fortune, he rattled the money in his pockets and the charms on his massive silver watch-chain. He intended to draw up his will in her favor and made no secret of it.

His insolent and expansive happiness was beginning to arouse annoyance and jealousy among the people. Dislike and bitterness too. It did not escape their notice that his hair was turning white and that his wind was getting short. His enormous, indomitable vigor was shortening and consuming his life. They asked him if it was always the same in bed as it used to be. "Just the same!" he would reply boastfully, "Ask *la Bietta!*" "I didn't know him in those days," the little woman would reply with customary discretion. "But how is he now?" they insisted. "I don't believe he could be better," *la Bietta* retorted. "Poor creature," people said aloud —or in a whisper—"he'll be burying her within three months!"

Three months was not enough; seventeen months went by.

One spring morning, when the hawthorn hedge was in blossom and the tender poplars were showing their green leaves in the fresh, clear air, a large bier left the church. Someone was going to his eternal sleep in the peace of the fluvial earth of Emilia.

A widow, sad but not morbidly so, serious and composed, a dried-up lentil of a woman, whose slight limp lent her movements a cheerful, mysterious grace, was following the bier. The whole population, which now forgave him even his final insolent felicity, followed too.

"*La Bietta* has settled his hash," said the chemist, speaking out his thoughts.

The widow is now extremely rich. She enjoys her wealth, however, without squandering it and declares she has no more use for men. She is not troubled with dreams, possibly because she is very punctilious about having intercessory Masses said and seeing that Gasparin Falocchio's grave is properly cared for in the graveyard of Romagnano Codifiume.

# CORRADO ALVARO

## 1895–1955

Born in 1895 at San Luca in the province of Reggio
Calabria, Alvaro spent most of his life in Rome. He
fought in the first World War; his novel *Vent'anni*, reflecting that experience, though the product of a lyrical rather than a consistently narrative literary talent,
remains as one of the highly significant Italian books of
the period between the wars. Like Pirandello and others
after him, Alvaro conformed to the pattern of the
Southern writer who realized on the national scene the
gifts of a literary imagination characterized also by
strong native elements. In such fiction as his novelette
*People on the Aspromonte*, which is possibly his masterpiece, Alvaro realized a sort of fusion between local-
color writing and the resources of a sophisticated literary experience; in his case as in others the formula
"magic realism" has sometimes been used. A fabulous
element is recognizable even in the brief anecdote presented here. Alvaro participated fully in the intellectual life of his country also as an editor and an influ-
ential writer of journalistic prose. His death in 1955
was one of the most lamentable losses suffered by Italian letters since the war.

# The Ruby

The daily papers had recorded one of those news items that
keep a town in a buzz of excitement for a whole day and
finally make a circuit of the world. A ruby as big as a
hazel-nut, a famous stone, bearing a famous name, and said
to be of enormous value, had disappeared. An Indian
prince, on a visit to a North American city, had been wearing this jewel as an ornament. He had suddenly become
aware of his loss after a journey he had made in a taxi that
had set him down—incognito—at a hotel in the suburbs,
for he had managed to evade the attention of both his private bodyguard and the police. The flying-squad was mobi-
lized, the entire city awoke the following morning to a
knowledge of the loss, and right up to midday hundreds of
people cherished the hope of finding the celebrated stone
in their own street. One of those waves of optimism and
excitement had fallen on the town; the kind of feeling you
get when the opulence of one individual enriches everybody else's hopes. The prince had not been very forthcoming in his statement to the police, but it ruled out any
possibility that the lady accompanying him could have been
responsible for the loss. They were not, therefore, to try and
locate her. The taxi-driver came forward to testify that he
had driven the Indian wearing his precious turban, and
stated that he had deposited him and the lady in front of a
hotel in the suburbs. The lady was a European, and the only
thing that distinguished her was a magnificent diamond, the
size of a pea, which she wore in her left nostril after the
manner of certain wealthy Indians. This detail distracted
the attention of the public for a while from the missing
ruby and whetted their curiosity still more. The driver,
after making a thorough search of the interior of the vehicle, checked up on the "fares" he had driven during the
early hours of the morning in question; they had been a

business man, a foreigner whom he had taken down to the port and who was evidently sailing for Europe, and a woman. The foreigner, recognizable as an Italian, had emerged from one of the houses where emigrants lived in a colony; he had been wearing a pair of trousers of generous width such as are popular with emigrants, rough, thick-soled shoes of a type nowadays seen only among people of that social class, and a hard hat set above a thin, clean-shaven face, seamed with wrinkles. His luggage consisted of a heavy suitcase secured with stout cord and one other weighty box which appeared to be made of steel. He had embarked that same day, but any suspicion that might have alighted on him was immediately dispelled when it was realized that he had behaved as though he was riding in a taxi for the first time in his life. He had not managed to close the door properly and had hugged the front window all the time, possibly so as to avoid being suddenly jerked backward into the road, and he had gazed at the streets with the air of one who is leaving a town perhaps forever. The driver reserved his attention rather for the man who, on leaving the suburban hotel, had taken the taxi immediately after the prince and had given orders to be driven to the Italian workmen's quarter, at which point his place had been taken by the foreigner. The fare in question, of whom he had given a description and who must have been a local resident, was searched for in vain. Furthermore the fact that he had failed to answer the appeal published in the newspapers, offering a large reward, was a logical proof that it was not he who had got hold of the famous gem. How-ever, since the missing stone was world-famed and easily recognizable, it was hoped that one day or other it would come to light.

The emigrant, meantime, was on his way home to a coun-try town in Southern Italy after five years' absence and was ignorant of all this stir. He had with him the most unusual collections of odds and ends—even for an emigrant. A suitcase, made of artificial leather which he thought was real, contained his blue overalls, pressed and cleaned, twelve fountain-pens which he intended to sell to the peo-

ple of the district, forgetting that most of them were herdsmen and not more than half a dozen of the inhabitants
could put pen to paper. In addition, he had some crested
table services, a pair of hair-clippers which he had used on
his fellow-workers, a metal object whose function completely mystified him—it had the form of a pistol, but did
not fire—twelve squares of American cloth and some novel-
ties to impress and amuse his wife, son and friends. The
heavy part of his luggage was the somewhat battered steel
strong-box; the lock was operated by a combination, the
six-letter name, *Annina*. By way of ready cash he took a
thousand dollars, which included three hundred to be paid
back later to those from whom he had borrowed it for the
voyage. In his waistcoat pocket he carried a lump of red
crystal; it was many-faceted and as large as a walnut. He
had come across it by chance in the taxi that had taken him
down to the harbor, but he had no idea what it was for.
His fingers had felt it behind the seat-cushions. He kept it as
a lucky charm for the future; perhaps he would have it attached to his watch-chain as a pendant. It seemed odd that
it had no hole bored through it. It could not, therefore, be
one of those large stones which city ladies have on their
necklaces.

The various objects one picks up just before leaving a
foreign country are apt to acquire an extraordinary sou-
venir-value, giving one, as it were, a foretaste of distance
and nostalgia. It was just such an affection that our emigrant felt for this lump of crystal, so cool to the touch, as
translucent and clear as sugar candy.

He had established a small trade with all these different
acquisitions. The strong-box, now fixed against the wall,
the counter for his transactions, fountain-pens in a box,
crested table services, squares of American cloth on which
were depicted the Statue of Liberty and angels in the corners bearing the portraits of the founders of American Independence, each square embroidered with white and blue
stars—five long years he had patiently built up his collection against his eventual return; selecting whatever would
seem most of a novelty to the folk in a region like his own,

though he might have taken his choice from the shabby second hand goods that come from heaven knows where and go the rounds among the emigrant population.

So he who had started life as a day-laborer had now become a dealer in various wares. It had been the strong-box that had set him on that train of thought; he had taken to shopkeeping for no other reason. He had felt almost rich because all the money he had in his pockets was in foreign currency and would turn into a larger number of coins when he exchanged them. Mental calculations connected with this engrossed him at all sorts of odd moments. He felt a childish delight every time he fingered the red crystal in his pocket. He began to regard it as a kind of talisman. It became one of those useless objects we cherish all our lives and never have the strength of mind to get rid of, so that in the end they become part of ourselves and even family heirlooms. Whereas important things that we watch over or hide away disappear, objects of the kind referred to never get lost, and our minds hark back to them at intervals. A few days later, for example, the crystal reminded our emigrant of the day when he had embarked for home, the interior of the taxi, the streets which seemed to roll slowly up like a piece of drop-scenery at the end of a play and become distant memories.

He set up his shop in the upper part of the country-town inhabited by peasants and herdsmen. A fortnight after his arrival he had furnished the ground floor of a peasant's cottage with a long counter and shelves, where the blue packets of flour-paste and the blue muslin for housewives found a place, and on one side of the shop stood a cask of wine on a couple of trestles, and an earthenware jar of oil. The strong-box had been fixed against the wall, and he felt a great sense of pride when he opened it in the presence of his customers. In it reposed his account-ledger and the notebook containing a list of all the goods sold on tick that were to be paid for at harvest-time or after the animal fairs. Gradually his business got to look like any other business; it acquired its own peculiar smell, there were chalkmarks made on the wall by his wife—who could not write

—recording goods supplied on credit. His young son, however, who attended school, and was now beginning to be able to write customers' names in the register, sometimes took a turn in the shop and managed it quite expertly on hot afternoons when all trade had ceased except that in iced drinks for gentlemen recovering from their afternoon siesta.

Slowly, his wife's narrow, American-style slippers acquired more and more creases and she herself the complacent, meticulous air of a shopkeeper's wife. The supply of new material which her husband had brought home had finally ended up among the shop-soiled goods, and only the hard hat, looking almost new, was still left in the wardrobe. The squares of American cloth had been distributed as presents among the important customers; as for the fountain-pens, no one had wanted them. Someone had handled them roughly and the fragments still lay in the box. The shopkeeper, who was a boy at heart, often imagined that the pen nibs were of pure gold and he cherished them as a small boy cherishes tinfoil-wrapping off chocolates. He also hung on to an old newspaper printed in English. He had refused to part with it even when he was short of wrapping paper. Sometimes he would scrutinize it carefully and the advertisement illustrations would recall to him the people who smoked gold-tipped cigarettes, the street-boys, the gramophones, in fact all the life he had seen in the central parts of the city on the rare occasions of his visits there. As for the lump of crystal, he remembered it one day and gave it to his son who was celebrating his birthday with his friends. At that time, boys played a game which consisted in knocking down and conquering castles made of hazelnuts by throwing a heavier one at it; the usual procedure was to select a larger nut, make a small hole in it, patiently scrape out the kernel, then fill it with small lead pellets. The crystal missile was just the thing, it was heavy enough to carry to the mark. Another of the boys used a glass marble of the kind extracted from lemonade bottles, which had the advantage of being round. The shopkeeper's son claimed that his was more beautiful because it came from America and because it was red. He cherished it in the way that boys

do who never lose objects of that kind. As his father con-
templated this curiosity which had become his child's plaything, his mind would often dwell on the illusions he had
once entertained in the days when he traveled about the
world, and the world seemed to be filled with valuable
things that had been lost which the lucky ones found. That
was why he had always felt with his fingers under mat-
tresses of berths on steamers, behind leather cushions on
buses and coaches, according to where he happened to be.
But he had never found anything. Yes; there had been one
occasion. He had found five dollars in the street. It had been
raining that day, he remembered.

# GIOVANNI COMISSO

1895–

Comisso is one of the authentic and consistent literary
talents in contemporary Italy where his name has been
prominent for at least thirty years. Born in Venetia,
at Treviso, in 1895, he fought in the first World War
and later followed the poet Gabriele d'Annunzio in his
expedition for the conquest of the city of Fiume, an
experience partly recorded in an early book, *In the
Wind of the Adriatic.* He has practiced itinerant journalism with results that have permanent literary value.
He has attempted fiction of a larger scope, for example
in the novel *History of a Patrimony,* but his most
recent publication is the autobiographical *My House
in the Country,* a record of a farming experience from
the thirties through the war, successfully mixing a
sensuous poetic concreteness with an unobtrusive but
deeply perceptible sense of the historical times. My
selection is taken from a book of short stories titled
*Earthly Adventures.*

## Aminta

I can now confess the real reason that drew me to finish
my university studies at Siena. It was on account of Aminta.
This shepherd's name was given by mistake to a marvelous
girl. The common people of Siena often search in poetry

*Translated by Lowry Nelson, Jr.*

for names to give their children. There are farriers named
Narcissus or Fidelio, butchers named Zephyr or Apollo, not
to mention all the Lauras and Beatrices. To convince my
family I told them that life in Siena was cheap, that there
were no distractions (the whole city, collected and closed
in by a wall, seemed like a boarding school), that the teachers were excellent, and so in a short time I should be able
to graduate and begin to earn my living.

I had met Aminta in my own town the autumn before.
She arrived, smiling and elegant, in the company of a
friend of mine. He had persuaded her to run away; he
hoped to set up housekeeping. The only thing he knew was
how to play the violin; he found a job playing in a movie
theater. But in a week the bill at the hotel had grown enormous and it was impossible for them to pay it. After the
first days full of joy because of the novelty of being away
from her own town, which she had never left before,
Aminta had become downcast and seemed to suffer.

My friend came to me for advice. She thought constantly
about her mother and about Siena; she was certain that she
would be forgiven everything. I told him that the best solution was to send her away. She had become so pale that I
began to think that my friend made her go hungry. She
would cough occasionally, but I thought it was from the
cold.

One morning I met her on the street; she was anxious and
trembling, almost running in the direction of the station. My
friend had abandoned her without a penny; he had gone
off with his violin to seek his fortune, and had left her a
farewell note which she was holding tightly in her fingers.
She was going to the station where she thought she would
find him. The money I had on me would be sufficient to
take her as far as Siena. A train was waiting. She accepted,
leaning her head on my shoulder. She was pitiful, so de-
fenseless and so beautiful that the moment she left I regretted very much letting her go; and I made the promise
to myself more than to her, that I would go and find her
again.

The following year, toward the end of summer, I went

to Siena. Up from the valley of Fontebranda rose the harsh smell of tanneries. I didn't have her address; I knew only her given name. The city was small; I hoped to find her without delay.

It was pleasant to walk on the ramparts of the Fortress. From there you could take in at a glance the whole undulating sea of slopes, reddish or light brown, broken by cypress groves or by deep ravines. In the distance to the south the horizon is bounded by the bluish hills of Maremma, and everywhere the sky arches light and dry. The city with its towers and its churches rises lengthwise along the top of a hill and in the evening it is lit up with lights at every window, like a ship ready to sail. On the western rampart, which is the most sheltered from the wind, linger peaceable women and girls who have trouble breathing and who try hard to keep from coughing for fear of revealing their illness to passers-by. It was here one morning that I encountered Aminta. She was dressed lightly to make people think she was well. We exchanged glances, finding it difficult to recognize each other; then she blushed and her thin hand trembled. About him she asked me nothing. It was quickly agreed that we would meet every morning, take a walk perhaps, and visit her city. I saw that she needed to be enlivened and I suggested trips to the outlying countryside, as far as the distant villages she would point out to me, telling me their names. I walked her to her house in a narrow shaded street. In front of it there was a flower seller and I bought her a bouquet of mimosa. We met again the next morning, a morning with a touch of autumn. The cold wind whistled at the street corners, low clouds covered the towers and occasionally they would descend to fill the squares.

Now and then the sun would appear, but then suddenly it was like being immersed in fog. She was dressed lightly, with bare arms, and she carried a parasol. I felt sorry to see her numb with cold. I was looking for some place sheltered from the wind. She showed she was afraid of nothing, but her lips were purple. I hoped the sun would come out, but in vain. Dust rose up in eddies and followed us, the wet

vapor of the clouds was in a continual state of rising and
sinking, and we took refuge in a café in the park. Here not
only were the drinks unpleasant, but also there was a draft
through the door that would not stay shut. She began to
cough. She told me it was nothing; she tried to be gay, because she saw that I was worried about her. But I managed
to persuade her to return home. The flower seller had some
bouquets of tuberoses set out on his bench. Aminta liked
flowers with a strong smell and I bought her a bouquet. The
flower seller was polite and wanted to show us his garden.
It was a charming place, full of flowers, with a large arbor
loaded with grapes. From there one could enjoy the panorama of the whole city, up from the valley of Fontebranda.
The sun had returned and it beat down as on the seacoast.
There was no wind there. Since we had to give up our
walks, I suggested to Aminta that we spend the morning in
that garden where everything lay so delightfully open to us.
She consented, smiling at me, but I realized that her face
showed pain.

In that garden we spent long hours together. We would
pick large bunches of muscat grapes; we would contemplate
and gently touch the beautiful flowers whose proper names
the flower seller would tell us. She taught me the graces of
her dialect: *"Spicciola quel fiore"* (pluck that flower),
"There are two kinds of peaches, *duràcine e partitoie"*
(clingstone and free), "When spring water flows down in a
rush, filled with little air bubbles, we call it *mussante* and
not *torbida"* (foamy and not cloudy). And she took delight
in correcting my accent.

Down from Fontebranda came the squeals of stuck pigs
and the shouts of the boys at the slaughterhouse who briskly
and joyfully ran to the basin to wash the blood off their
arms. The sun glowed on the skins set out to dry on the
terraces of the tanneries and made the water sparkle in the
big tub where washerwomen were beating their clothes and
singing. Sitting on the little wall, she became responsive to
life around her and was filled with an immense eagerness,
and I followed her for fear she might not be able to hold on.

It seemed that my attentiveness made her so happy that

she forgot the illness she suffered. But perhaps it was not that: rather, it was she who made an effort to be gay, hoping that I would forget that she was ill. And she vainly looked for proof of having succeeded by offering me the handkerchief with which she held back her fits of coughing so that I might wipe the sweet juice of the muscat grapes from my mouth.

Tiring of my restrained friendliness, she decided to tell me her life story and to set before me her plans for the future, as if to wring from me out of pity that kiss I had never given her and which she desired as the last testimony of the life she felt ebbing.

Her father, partially crippled at work, had taken to drink. A younger brother had died a few months before. The evening of his death they gave the father some money to go buy oxygen. Instead, he came back drunk; and while the boy in his bed was seized with the death rattle, he lay stretched out on the sofa in the next room, singing and cursing him by turns. Her father's cruelty reached such a point that if her mother cooked her a beefsteak to give her a little strength, he would say, "Others eat beefsteak and I always eat beans. A fine meal they make!" Then Aminta would offer him the beefsteak and he would eat it without remorse. Her illness grew worse every day. Infallible but expensive medicines were prescribed for her, and the money at home was not even enough to buy food. To live, Aminta had to have recourse to her beauty, and for a glass of wine her father would bring home people of his acquaintance.

She had gone off with my friend thinking she could save herself. Now she had lost all hope. She told me, her gaze fixed on the loud and echoing steps of some soldiers who were going down the little street under the garden, that in a week she would be gone. She didn't want to tell me where; she alluded vaguely to an aunt in Leghorn, but I felt she was lying. She promised to write to me and explain. For an instant it seemed to me that I had caught the desperate violence of her decision. Besides, I recognized in her such boundless courage that it made me ashamed. But

I didn't want to believe. She continued to harken to the steps of the soldiers.

I didn't see her again. The city, hemmed in by its high walls, kept me entirely dedicated to my studies. I busily attended class and took a great quantity of notes. In the evening there was no other pastime than gaming. In Siena they gamble an enormous lot in the cafés, in clubs, and at home. Isolation or boredom grew more intense at gaming. Carnival came. One evening I was losing consistently, not because of luck but because I was distracted. The smoke, the little room were getting on my nerves, when from among the people standing around to watch, a classmate of mine smiled at me and, as if it were a trifle, asked me:

"Did you know that that girl who always used to come with you is dead?"

"Aminta?" I asked in the hope he was mistaken.

"Yes; Aminta. Strange, isn't it? She had a man's name."

I left the game without heeding the protests of the others, and ran outside. I went at once to her dismal street between old houses. The windows of her room were lit up with candles burning inside. The entrance breathed cold air that smelled of disinfectant. I didn't have the courage to go up. Near by some women were talking in a whisper and one of them seeing me go by said, as if to stop me:

"She's dead—the prettiest girl in this part of town."

At certain moments I was sure of being an outsider, when it was my duty to go see her. I went the next morning. At the flower seller's the women of that district raised money for a wreath. I bought some flowers with a strong smell, the ones she liked. The flower seller told me he was always surprised to see me with that girl who was so ill, and certain now that I would no longer be buying flowers for her, he asked an exorbitant price. Going up the cold and rickety stairs I thought of the pain she must have felt when she climbed them. Some women had paused at the landing; they recognized me and accompanied me like a relative. A little old woman said to me:

"My poor little Aminta always talked about you."

I went into the room. Everything was closed up. On four chairs the coffin lay open with her inside under a veil. The candles on both sides burned placidly. Her bed was gray and hard as a rock. The room was bare. Her mother had drawn near her head, and raised the veil:

"Tell me if she wasn't pretty, my Aminta."

I saw a swollen earth-colored face with a half-open mouth, and placed the flowers at her feet.

I did not want to look any more. I went out stunned, dismayed. I didn't know where to go. I entered the main street which was filled with people coming boldly toward me. The shop windows were full of cardboard masks, swollen, with half-open mouths. The crowd was immense, and they would look at me as if they all knew me, and smile. I took refuge in the University, in a regular class. The teacher spoke with a fine voice, assured and precise; he was taking pains to explain an interesting problem of procedure. I looked at his face which was heated because he put all his strength into it in his desire to convince us of a particular opinion concerning the problem. I watched him as if from another room, and it made me smile to see him put to such trouble. If I bent my head over my notebook pretending to take notes, it was rather that I was trying frantically to draw a swollen face with a half-open mouth.

# GUIDO PIOVENE

## 1907–

One of the outstanding Italian men of letters, Piovene was born at Vicenza in 1907 and studied under G. A. Borgese at the University of Milan. Both his literary career and his successful journalistic endeavors started in the early thirties. As a fiction writer he had his first important success in 1941 with *Letters of a Novice,* which renewed the classic form of the epistolary novel, while for its themes it could partly be related to the atmosphere of subtle religious preoccupation that seems typical of Piovene's native city. The troubled years that followed are partly reflected in the two novels *Pity against Pity* and *The False Redeemers.* The present selection is a "detachable" story contained in *Pity against Pity.* The high literary quality of his writing coupled with a capacity for observation and synthesis both quick and profound has made Piovene a major exponent of a type of cultured journalism which is one of the positive traditions of the Italian daily press. Outstanding examples are his reportage of intellectual life in France, and the book *De America,* the result of a long journey through the United States. His latest product of this type is the huge and highly successful *Italian Journey.*

# The Dressmaker's Daughter

Perhaps it is true that we and food have offended one another. A memory comes to my mind, and it's not for the first time. It has returned to distress me several times lately. Perhaps I am beginning to suffer hunger.

It is a very distant memory. My father worked in a furniture factory outside the city. He used to go out of the house at dawn, leaving us alone, my mother and me, until late in the evening. I had finished with the junior classes at primary school, and my memory begins with the holiday between two school years. I used to spend a great deal of the day with my mother, who earned money as a dressmaker and enjoyed a certain authority in the family as a result. We used to sit together by the window with the curtains drawn back. I helped her if I could, and if I couldn't, I let my gaze wander slowly from her hands to the street below. In this way, I grew accustomed to remaining silent.

I used to watch the customers ordering and trying on clothes as though it were a theatrical performance. My mother's most important customer was a society woman, the wife of an industrialist, who bought her wardrobe from the big fashion houses, but came to my mother to have last season's clothes altered and also to have copies made of models which my mother pirated from the most celebrated dressmakers with the aid of some employee.

This lady possessed a large wardrobe comprising a whole hierarchy of clothes. She had reached middle age, but her figure was still firm and her complexion fresh; she radiated warmth and vitality. Her face was full, her eyes were heavy-lidded, and she had curly hair and very white teeth—more than the usual number, it seemed to me, so that, sitting in my corner, I often used to count them as she spoke. But her

*Translated by Michael Bullock.*

whole body seemed somehow "fruitful," impetuously bearing flesh, words, and expressions of emotion. When she stripped for fittings, she did so in a triumphant manner, standing proudly in the center of the room as though in a position she had taken by storm. The transparent underclothing revealed her milk-white body on which were distributed large red patches, as though someone had slapped her with the palm of his hand.

She knew all about literature, paintings, feeding infants and bringing up children, and love affairs. She moved in high society and was passionately devoted to charity. Occasionally she brought her husband with her, a little fat man, who sat silently in the corner during the fittings. He and I ended by staring at one another from our seats without exchanging a word, like two shy animals.

Now this lady, noticing how attentively I used to watch her, wide-eyed and speechless, discovered that I was very aristocratic in appearance, quite out of keeping with my environment. She began, as though to test me, by inviting me to her house to play with her children, of whom she had five. She appeared amongst them, pink and white and triumphant, in a house like herself, full of well-upholstered furniture, crowded with flowers and leafy with potted plants. She led me with the children to a table on which stood a row of big plates of sweets. Then she took me aside and questioned me about my education. She thought it very regrettable that I attended the state school, where I could only pick up common ways and vulgar expressions.

From that day on, she visited my mother even more frequently than before. Sometimes she used to make me rise from my seat and then examine me as I stood before her in the shadow cast by her body, scarcely veiled by the transparent underclothes. Finally she shook her head as though in doubt about something. She inquired tactfully of my mother whether I might not be the fruit of some youthful love affair with a person of distinction. "Because," she added, "pretty girls are to be found in every milieu, but their hands and feet reveal their humble origins. This child, on the other hand, though one couldn't call her pretty, has hands and feet, wrists and ankles, that a lady might envy."

Then someone she met in society told her that hands and feet were nothing to judge by, because aristocratic hands and feet were to be met with amongst the common people, as could be seen in actresses. An infallible indication of breeding was the line of the neck, but this test was not decisive until maturity, when all the lines of the body had grown heavier. After this she scrutinized the line of my neck, which was long and thin. "It looks beautiful to me," she said, "but you are too young. We shan't know until you are grown up." Then she left me, apparently upset by not having any dependable guarantee as to the excellence of my pedigree.

One day she suggested to my mother that she send me to a boarding school at her own expense. My mother refused her offer, saying that she needed me and that my father would be against it. Thenceforth my benefactress, incited by this opposition, started to talk about me as though I were not merely an aristocratic being, but a miracle, a violation of the laws of nature, which had intended me to be beautiful, but common (as she spoke she turned her gaze on my mother, as though confirming the contrast between us). Nature, she said, would re-establish her supremacy, if I were not snatched once and for all from her fatal influence. She pointed out to my mother the crime she would be committing if she failed to take account of my refinement.

"The child differs too much from other girls of the same origin for her to be neglected in this way," she said. "I speak frankly, because I feel it is my duty to say this. A human life, the life of your daughter, is at stake. She could grow up to be a lady: it would be a terrible crime to paralyze her finer instincts, to hold her down through self-interest and false pride, when it would be so easy to place her in more suitable surroundings. At her age an example, a word, would be enough to ruin her." (The lady would have felt her arguments confirmed if she had known that my mother always referred to her as "that cow," thinking perhaps of her physical exuberance.)

She made these speeches during the fittings, often scantily

clad, and I listened to her inattentively from my corner, all the time gazing fixedly at her buttocks. Then she spoke once more of the boarding school to which she wished to send me, enumerating the nuns, all of them highly qualified, and quoting the names of several girls of good family who had received their schooling from them. Didn't my mother realize that it would be a stroke of luck, a godsend, if they would take me?

At each visit, she reminded my mother that her guilt toward me was increasing every minute. What would she reply when, some day, I asked her why she had missed such an opportunity? How would she dare to look me in the eyes, for the rest of her life, knowing the irreparable harm she had done me and burdened by my conscious reproach?

My mother, still reluctant, partly because she felt I would be unhappy, and partly because of an instinctive aversion to the people with whom I would have to mix, finally said: "I'm not convinced of it, but perhaps this is really a stroke of luck for you."

She suggested a compromise: I should go to the boarding school during the day, for school and recreation, but sleep at home, "as so many girls do," she said.

"But not at such a good school!" objected my benefactress. "In the first place, the nuns don't take day girls; it's a tradition, a rule; they wouldn't alter it, even if the girl were a princess. And they're quite right, because such a good school has to isolate the girls, transplant them into a different atmosphere, so to speak, where they will be protected from all disturbing influences. Why should you, of all people, want to make difficulties and lay down conditions? As though you were doing them a favor, whereas in reality . . ." She stopped there out of delicacy.

"I have little confidence in the effect of this education on Anna, if she is not removed from outside influences. Isn't that the whole object? You should help me, not put obstacles in the way." My mother remained obstinate.

Giving up hope of finding in my mother a disinterested ally against herself and the family into which I had been born, the lady became more explicit: "If Anna were about to marry a man of much higher social station than your own, and this man asked you to retire into the background, what would your conscience tell you to do?"

My mother gave way before this unforeseen argument, but she stood her ground on the matter of the boarding school. She never understood "the duty of parents to sacrifice everything, to disappear from the scene altogether if necessary, for the benefit of their children." Instead she clung positively fanatically to the iron bedstead in which I slept next to her own.

In the end my benefactress was compelled to give in, since she was resolved to save me at any price. She implored my mother, who looked at her with a mixture of obstinacy and deference, but she had to be content with extracting the maximum advantage from the meager concessions my mother was prepared to make. She persuaded the nuns to accept me as a day pupil, no doubt by representing me as an innocent victim whom it was their duty to save by combating my sordid environment.

I was delighted at the thought of going to a boarding school, among so many distinguished children, whom I imagined as being fair-haired. At the beginning of the school year my mother provided me with a beautiful new dress, so that I should not look out of place among my elegant companions. She now took my new position seriously and was determined that I should derive the full benefit from it. The vigilance with which she watched over my personal cleanliness and that of my aprons, and even my underclothes—as if I had to undress at school—became burdensome to me. Every morning she handed me with my books a packet containing bread and fruit, or bread and chocolate. As I was not a boarder I could not have lunch with the rest of the school but had to bring my food with me from home.

As she handed me the books and food, my mother always wore an expression of great seriousness, as though transferring to my shoulders the burden of responsibility which my benefactress had previously placed on hers. By the solemnity with which she handed me the books and food, she made me feel how great would be my guilt if I disappointed the woman who had come to my aid, and what a grave duty I was assuming, each morning as I left home, toward my parents, myself, and my destiny. Thus I used to leave home with the feeling of being weighed down by a crushing burden that robbed me of liberty and stupefied me; but, being docile and affectionate, I gave no further thought to this feeling and accepted it as natural.

Perhaps because of this unheeded weight, or perhaps because of the attitude of the nuns and my schoolmates, I did badly at school and remained well below the average. In reality I did not possess the gifts which the lady had attributed to me. My mother was right when she said: "Believe me, signora, she's just like any other girl." It was simply that my silence and reserve were mistaken for intelligence and sensibility. In actual fact, I had an affectionate nature and longed to be fondled.

After a year's trial my benefactress withdrew her financial support, blaming my failure on my mother for keeping me in my old environment. "This proves I was right," she said. "You would have it your own way, but it's all wasted effort if what is done in the morning is undone in the evening." So she left me to my fate and the state schools.

But first I endured a whole year of unhappiness in the boarding school, in the course of which I experienced something I had never suffered at home—a kind of hunger. To my schoolmates I was "the day girl," who neither slept nor ate with them, the lonely butt for their spitefulness. The nuns were hostile to me and made it clear that I was breathing that air only as a favor and, to judge by the results, pointlessly. They were quick and practical women, business women rather than women of religion. My slow ways, my childish reserve, and even my longing for affection and my desire to mix with the others, seemed to them an encumbrance and a sign of my lowly origin; the stricter ones among them regarded these as signs of a sinful disposition. They were forever admonishing me to be quicker and more practical and to free my heart from slothfulness.

The baseness of character which I discovered in almost

all the teaching staff, their thirst for popularity and approval from the little world within which their lives were confined, drove them to encourage the other children in their attitude to me, to incite them against me—even those who had not made up their minds about me. The moment they noticed my unpopularity they did their best to increase it, confirming unalterably the tendency to shut me out from the corporate life of the school. They drew attention to my scholastic deficiencies and supported the children in their judgment that I was "stupid." In this way I became more and more apathetic and taciturn.

At midday I used to eat my bread and fruit, or bread and chocolate, alone on a school bench, and it left me hungry. True hunger is always hunger for some other food, for other people's food. Such was my hunger. For this reason, now that hunger occupied my thoughts more than ever before, my life seemed entirely dominated, permeated by hunger. I used to want to sit with the others, to drink in their conversation, to sleep among them, to wash with them in the water of the wash-basins, to immerse myself in the steam from their soup. Sitting alone on my bench, I imagined them as elegant and with their faces veiled by the steam rising from their soup. This image of their beauty made me incapable of satisfying my hunger with bread, chocolate and fruit. When I returned home in the evening, exhausted, hungry within because I had not partaken of that soup nor inhaled that steam, weak from lack of the only food that appeared to me satisfying, I flung myself on the family stew. My hunger stilled at last, I found repose in my iron bedstead, from which I could hear the breathing of my parents. Going to sleep in that bed I cast off my obsessive longings, because here at least I felt that I belonged to someone.

The birthday of the mother superior was in April, and the nuns planned an entertainment for her. A theatrical performance would cost too much, so it was agreed that the youngest pupils should sing a chorus in the chapel after high mass. I was permitted to take part in this ceremony. We were to be enveloped in tulle veils to make us look like angels, and to wear a wreath of flowers on our heads. The veils were to be made up at the last moment, so as to keep the preparations hidden from the mother superior and not spoil the surprise for her. And as the girls had to stay up and do the work in secret at night and rise very early next morning, I was allowed to sleep those few hours at school. The previous evening, Roberta, one of the pupils, had had a big box of lilies of the valley brought from her garden.

Now before the work began, Roberta was running a slight temperature, which compelled her to retire to bed and withdraw from the festivities. She was slender and had long legs and hair so fair as to be almost white. She too was slow at school, but her backwardness, full of aristocratic disdain, inspired respect and, far from lowering her prestige, actually increased her domination over her schoolmates and the teachers. Whenever I recall her I feel within me a sensation of acid chill, accompanied by a scent like that of spring flowers with their slender stalks and pale green, shadowless leaves.

Twenty of us, with two nuns, set to work secretly in one of the classrooms after the bell had rung for lights out. The long strips of flimsy fabric clung to our knees; the lilies of the valley gave forth scent from their box on the teacher's desk, and this perfume mingled with the other, less pungent but more deeply ingrained, of warm young bodies none too well washed. I immersed myself in that atmosphere; I delighted in it and was full of excitement at being united with the others by the clouds of fabric, by breathing the same stuffy air, by the nimble work of the scissors and needles, by the crackle of the fabric as it was cut. For the first time I had managed to enter into the life of the school by night, and I was living in the ecstasy of at last belonging to the community. I was no longer hungry, I felt replete. When we approached the box to make the wreaths, the scent of the lilies of the valley so excited me that all of a sudden, breaking the deep silence, I started to jump and shout, uttering shrill meaningless cries. This was so surprising in a child who was always taciturn and apparently sullen that the others probably imagined I had suddenly gone mad. One of the teachers immediately seized my arm and hissed in my ear: "You idiot! Do you want to wake the mother superior and give everything away?" Then they all, pupils and teachers, shook their heads, and I heard the word "stupid." But I was happy and felt no humiliation.

After a few hours of sleep, we all washed in the washroom. I had slept and washed with the others and felt myself one of them. Then, having given the finishing touches to our handiwork, we dressed hurriedly a few minutes before high mass. We were all rather pale from lack of sleep, and all fasting because we had to receive communion. I had already put the wreath of lilies on my head and was on the point of putting on the veil, when the door opened and the girl who had been ill entered, tall and fair, followed by a nurse. Roberta, the nurse said, had recovered during the night, knew the words of the song by heart, and had asked to take part in the chorus. One of the nuns said: "Well, that's difficult. . . . There's no material left for another veil and all the lilies of the valley have been used up."

Roberta stood directly in front of us, but she did not look at us. Distant, full of natural fastidiousness, she reminded me exactly of the white highlight on a green leaf, or the cold sap that sets one's teeth on edge. She kept her very long eyelashes lowered over her near-sighted eyes. I felt that she dominated us, even the nun in charge—and to my undoing. For then the nun said: "Unless . . ."

I caught my breath.

"Unless one of the others gives up her place. Roberta has more right than lots of others. Wasn't it she who brought the flowers? And she's a boarder."

I felt everyone looking at me.

"Anna, you're a day girl . . ." went on the nun, giving me a stern look that detached me from the group. She paused for a moment, as though waiting for my spontaneous consent. When this was not forthcoming, as though annoyed by her own hesitations and once more energetic and practical, she cried: "Come along, hurry up, there's no time to lose."

I quickly took off the wreath and, without a word, handed

it to my schoolmate. I believe I stared at her wide-eyed. She did not look at me but took the wreath without speaking, as though it were the most natural thing in the world that it should be given to her. It had a pungent scent.

When we moved off to the church, I remained a little behind and tried to slip away, in order to shut myself up all alone in one of the classrooms. But I was stopped by the caretaker, who was carrying a packet in her hand.

"I was just looking for you, Anna. Your mother sends you this."

It was the usual package containing bread and a piece of chocolate. I had hoped that day, after singing with the others, to be allowed to eat lunch with them as well.

"Take it quickly into the classroom and then go to church," said the caretaker, and went away.

I went into the classroom and sat for a moment at my desk. I felt neither anger against my schoolmates, and teachers, nor desire for revenge; but I no longer wanted to share their meal. I was unmoved by the thought of them. Instead, I felt angry with the food which I held between my hands in its wrapping, and wanted to take vengeance on it.

The school had a little garden, damp, always in shadow, uncultivated, and used by no one, neither the sisters nor the children. It was visible from the playground, from which it was shut off by an iron gate that was always firmly closed to keep people out. But I remembered a corridor, deserted at that time of day, which ended in a window overlooking this abandoned garden. I raced along the corridor, swung myself over the window sill, and dropped into the garden. It was a square patch of tangled grass and plants, enclosed on three sides by walls, one of them windowless. Coldly and decisively, as though I were not obeying a fantastic impulse but carrying out some practical task that had been entrusted to me, I crossed the little garden to the blind wall. Close to it grew a few hydrangea bushes and an inky-green yew tree, which had littered the damp soil with its bright red berries.

I dug a hole in the earth with my hands, without any feeling of distaste, took the food from its wrapping, threw it into the hole, and covered it over. Then I trampled the earth over it with my feet. I hated the food and wanted to insult it. That was the only emotion left in me, the only action to which I felt impelled and in which I found any pleasure. My task completed, I climbed in through the window again and waited for mass to finish.

That is the memory which torments me in these days of fear and half hunger. I keep thinking of that yew tree and the damp earth beneath it. It sometimes seems to me as though a part of myself, forgotten while I went on living, had remained in that very spot, amongst those sunless plants. Two or three times I have awakened during the night with the feeling that my hands were covered with mud and I must wash them: as though I had gone out of myself during my sleep and returned to that garden to dig up the soil in search of the bread and the chocolate.

# ALBERTO MORAVIA

## 1907–

Born in Rome in 1907, Moravia became as famous as
any practicing novelist in Italy at the age of twenty-
two when he published his novel *Gli indifferenti* ("The
Age of Indifference" in the recent American version).
Against many odds, including those of the political
situation in Italy, he settled on a type of career that
has long been normal in England and France but in-
frequent in Italy among serious writers: that of the
routine fiction writer, with a recognizable world which
an adequate number of readers may reliably find ex-
ploited and enlarged with each new work. An envi-
ably systematic worker (he claims this is also an
antidote to boredom), Moravia had already achieved
considerable recognition by the time of World War II;
but it was after the war that his fame acquired world
dimensions, especially through the Italian vogue in
America to which he contributed substantially. I have
chosen here an example of what we may call his major
manner, which may eventually prove the most endur-
ing: the realistic-psychological study of situation and
drama based on the analysis of certain recurrent types
(e.g., the frustrated sensual lover). Moravia is also an
extremely interesting essayist, and has been for many
years the film critic of a leading Italian weekly.

## Bitter Honeymoon

They had chosen Anacapri for their honeymoon because Giacomo had been there a few months before and wanted to go back, taking his bride with him. His previous visit had been in the spring, and he remembered the clear, crisp air and the flowers alive with the hum of thousands of insects in the golden glow of the sun. But this time, immediately upon their arrival, everything seemed very different. The sultry dog-days of mid-August were upon them and steaming humidity overclouded the sky. Even on the heights of Anacapri, there was no trace of the crisp air, of flowers or the violet sea whose praises Giacomo had sung. The paths winding through the fields were covered with a layer of yellow dust, accumulated in the course of four months without rain, in which even gliding lizards left traces of their passage. Long before autumn was due, the leaves had begun to turn red and brown, and occasional whole trees had withered away for lack of water. Dust particles filled the motionless air and made the nostrils quiver, and the odors of meadows and sea had given way to those of scorched stones and dried dung. The water, which in the spring had taken its color from what seemed to be banks of violets floating just below the surface, was now a gray mass reflecting the melancholy, dazzling light brought by the *scirocco* which infested the sky.

"I don't think it's the least bit beautiful," Simona said on the day after their arrival, as they started along the path to the lighthouse. "I don't like it—no, not at all."

Giacomo, following several steps behind, did not answer. She had spoken in this plaintive and discontented tone of voice ever since they had emerged from their civil marriage in Rome, and he suspected that her prolonged ill-humor, mingled with an apparent physical repulsion, was not connected so much with the place as with his own person. She was complaining about Anacapri because she was not aware that her fundamental dissatisfaction was with her husband. Theirs was a love match to be sure, but one based rather on the will to love than on genuine feeling. There was good reason for his presentiment of trouble when, as he slipped the ring on her finger, he had read a flicker of regret and embarrassment on her face; for on their first night at Anacapri she had begged off, on the plea of fatigue and seasickness, from giving herself to him. On this, the second day of their marriage, she was just as much of a virgin as she had been before.

As she trudged wearily along, with a bag slung over one shoulder, between the dusty hedges, Giacomo looked at her with almost sorrowful intensity, hoping to take possession of her with a single piercing glance, as he had so often done with other women. But, as he realized right away, the piercing quality was lacking; his eyes fell with analytical affection upon her, but there was in them none of the transfiguring power of real passion. Although Simona was not tall, she had childishly long legs with slender thighs, rising to an indentation, almost a cleft at either side, visible under her shorts, where they were joined to the body. The whiteness of her legs was chaste, shiny and cold, she had a narrow waist and hips, and her only womanly feature, revealed when she turned around to speak to him, was the fullness of her low-swung breasts, which seemed like extraneous and burdensome weights, unsuited to her delicate frame. Similarly her thick, blond hair, although it was cut short, hung heavily over her neck. All of a sudden, as if she felt that she was being watched, she wheeled around and asked: "Why do you make me walk ahead of you?"

Giacomo saw the childishly innocent expression of her big blue eyes, her small, tilted nose and equally childishly rolled-back upper lip. Her face, too, he thought to himself, was a stranger to him, untouched by love.

"I'll go ahead, if you like," he said with resignation.

And he went by her, deliberately brushing her breast with his elbow to test his own desire. Then they went on walking, he ahead and she behind. The path wound about the summit of Monte Solaro, running along a wall of mossy stones with no masonry to hold them together and rows of vines strung out above them. On the other side there was a sheer descent, through uninhabited stretches of vineyard and olive grove, to the mist-covered gray sea. Only a solitary pine tree, halfway down the mountain, with its green crest floating in the air, recalled the idyllic purity of the landscape in its better days. Simona walked very slowly, lagging farther behind at every step. Finally she came to a halt and asked: "Have we far to go?"

"We've only just started," Giacomo said lightly. "At least an hour more."

"I can't bear it," she said ill-humoredly, looking at him as if she hoped he would propose giving up the walk altogether. He went back to her and put his arm around her waist.

"You can't bear the exertion or you can't bear me?"

"What do you mean, silly?" she countered with unexpected feeling. "I can't bear to go on walking, of course."

"Give me a kiss."

She adminstered a rapid peck on his cheek.

"It's so hot . . ." she murmured. "I wish we could go home."

"We must get to the lighthouse," Giacomo answered. "What's the point of going back? . . . We'll have a swim as soon as we arrive. It's a wonderful place, and the lighthouse is all pink and white. . . . Don't you want to see it?"

"Yes; but I'd like to fly there instead of walking."

"Let's talk," he suggested. "That way you won't notice the distance."

"But I have nothing to say," she protested, almost with tears in her voice.

Giacomo hesitated for a moment before replying:

"You know so much poetry by heart. Recite a poem, and I'll listen; then before you know it, we'll be there."

He could see that he had hit home, for she had a truly extraordinary memory for verse.

"What shall I recite?" she asked with childish vanity.

"A canto from Dante."

"Which one?"

"The third canto of the *Inferno*," Giacomo said at random.

Somewhat consoled, Simona walked on, once more ahead of him, beginning to recite:

> *"Per me si va nella città dolente:*
> *per me si va nell'eterno dolore:*
> *per me si va tra la perduta gente . . ."*

She recited mechanically and with as little expression as a schoolgirl, breathing hard because of the double effort required of her. As she walked doggedly along, she paused at the end of every line, without paying any attention to syntax or meaning, like a schoolgirl endowed with zeal rather than intelligence. Every now and then she turned appealingly around and shot him a fleeting look, yes, exactly like a schoolgirl, with the blue-and-white cap perched on her blond hair. After they had gone some way they reached a wall built all around a large villa. The wall was covered with ivy, and leafy oak branches grew out over it.

" '*E caddi, come l'uom, cui sonno piglia*,'" Simona said, winding up the third canto; then she turned around and asked: "Whose place is this?"

"It belonged to Axel Munthe," Giacomo answered; "but he's dead now."

"And what sort of a fellow was he?"

"A very shrewd sort indeed," said Giacomo. And, in order to amuse her, he added: "He was a doctor very fashionable in Rome at the turn of the century. If you'd like to know more about him, there's a story I've been told is absolutely true. . . . Would you like to hear it?"

"Yes; do tell me."

"Once a beautiful and frivolous society woman came to him with all sorts of imaginary ailments. Munthe listened patiently, examined her, and when he saw that there was nothing wrong, said: 'I know a sure cure, but you must do exactly what I say. . . . Go and look out of that open window ·and lean your elbows on the sill.' She obeyed, and

Munthe went after her and gave her a terrific kick in the
rear. Then he escorted her to the door and said: 'Three
times a week, and in a few months you'll be quite all
right.' "

Simona failed to laugh, and after a moment she said bitterly, looking at the wall: "That would be the cure for me."

Giacomo was struck by her mournful tone of voice.

"Why do you say that?" he asked, coming up to her.
"What's come into your head?"

"It's true. . . . I'm slightly mad, and you ought to treat
me exactly that way."

"What are you talking about?"

"About what happened last night," she said with startling
frankness.

"But last night you were tired and seasick."

"That wasn't it at all. I'm never seasick, and I wasn't
tired, either. I was afraid, that's all."

"Afraid of me?"

"No; afraid of the whole idea."

They walked on in silence. The wall curved, following the
path and hanging slightly over, as if it could hardly contain
the oak trees behind it. Then it came to an end, and in front
of them lay a grassy plateau, below which the mountainside
fell abruptly down to the arid and lonely promontories of
Rio. The plateau was covered with asphodels, whose pyram-
idal flowers were of a dusty rose, almost gray in color.
Giacomo picked some and handed them to his wife, saying:
"Look. How beautiful . . ."

She raised them to her nose, like a young girl on her way
to the altar, inhaling the fragrance of a lily. Perhaps she was
conscious of her virginal air, for she pressed close to him, in
something like an embrace, and whispered into one ear:
"Don't believe what I just told you. . . . I wasn't afraid. . . .
I'll just have to get used to the idea. . . . Tonight . . ."

"Tonight?" he repeated.

"You're so very dear to me," she murmured painfully,
adding a strictly conventional phrase, which she seemed to
have learned for the occasion, "Tonight I'll be yours."

She said these last words hurriedly, as if she were afraid

of the conventionality rather than the substance of them, and planted a hasty kiss on his cheek. It was the first time that she had ever told Giacomo that he was dear to her or anything like it, and he was tempted to take her in his arms. But she said in a loud voice: "Look! What's that down there on the sea?" And at the same time she eluded his grasp.

Giacomo looked in the direction at which she was pointing and saw a solitary sail emerging from the mist that hung over the water.

"A boat," he said testily.

She started walking again, at a quickened pace, as if she were afraid that he might try once more to embrace her. And as he saw her escape him he had a recurrent feeling of impotence, because he could not take immediate possession of his beloved.

"You won't do that to me tonight," he muttered between clenched teeth as he caught up with her.

And she answered, lowering her head without looking around: "It will be different tonight. . . ."

It was really hot—there was no doubt about that—and in the heavy air all round them there seemed to Giacomo to reside the same obstacle, the same impossibility that bogged down his relationship with his wife: the impossibility of a rainfall that would clear the air, the impossibility of love. He had a sensation of something like panic, when looking at her again he felt that his will to love was purely intellectual and did not involve his senses. Her figure was outlined quite precisely before him, but there was none of the halo around it in which love usually envelops the loved one's person. Impulsively he said: "Perhaps you shouldn't have married me."

Simona seemed to accept this statement as a basis for discussion, as if she had had the same thought without daring to come out with it.

"Why?" she asked.

Giacomo wanted to answer, "Because we don't really love each other," but although this was the thought in his mind, he expressed it in an entirely different manner. Simona was a Communist and had a job at Party headquarters. Giacomo was not a Communist at all; he claimed to attach no importance to his wife's political ideas, but they had a way of cropping up at the most unexpected moments as underlying motives for disagreement. And now he was astonished to hear himself say: "Because there is too great a difference of ideas between us."

"What sort of ideas do you mean?"

"Political ideas."

He realized, then, why her standoffishness had caused him to bring politics into the picture; it was with the hope of arousing a reaction to a point on which he knew her to be sensitive. And indeed she answered immediately: "That's not so. The truth is that I have certain ideas and you have none at all."

As soon as politics came up she assumed a self-sufficient, pedantic manner, quite the opposite of childish, which always threatened to infuriate him. He asked himself in all conscience whether his irritation stemmed from some latent anti-Communist feeling within himself, but quickly set his mind at rest on this score. He had no interest in politics whatsoever, and the only thing that bothered him was the fact that his wife did have such an interest.

"Well, whether or not it's a question of ideas," he said dryly, "there is *something* between us."

"What is it, then?"

"I don't know, but I can feel it."

After a second she said in the same irritating tone of voice: "I know quite well. It *is* a question of ideas. But I hope that some day you'll see things the way I do."

"Never."

"Why never?"

"I've told you so many times before. . . . First, because I don't want to be involved in politics of any kind, and, second, because I'm too much of an individualist."

Simona made no reply, but in such cases her silence was direr than spoken disapproval. Giacomo was overcome by a wave of sudden anger. He overtook her and seized her arm.

"All this is going to have very serious consequences some day," he shouted. "For instance, if a Communist government comes to power, and I say something against it, you'll inform on me."

"Why should you say anything against it?" she retorted. "You just said that you don't want to be involved in politics of any kind."

"Anything can happen."

"And then the Communists aren't in power. . . . Why worry about a situation that doesn't exist?"

It was true then, he thought to himself, since she didn't deny it, that she would inform on him. He gripped her arm tighter, almost wishing to hurt her.

"The truth is that you don't love me," he said.

"I wouldn't have married you except for love," she said clearly, and she looked straight at him, with her lower lip trembling. Her voice filled Giacomo with tenderness, and he drew her to him and kissed her. Simona was visibly affected by the kiss; her nostrils stiffened and she breathed hard, and although her arms hung down at her sides, she pressed her body against his.

"My spy," he said, drawing away and stroking her face. "My little spy."

"Why do you call me spy?" she asked, taking immediate offense.

"I was joking."

They walked on, but as he followed her Giacomo wondered whether he had meant the word as a joke after all. And what about his anger? Was that a joke too? He didn't know how he could have given way to such unreasonable anger and have made such even more unreasonable accusations, and yet he dimly understood that they were justified by Simona's behavior. Meanwhile, they had come to the other side of the mountain, and from the highest point of the path they looked down at an immense expanse of air, like a bottomless well. Five minutes later they had a view of all one side of the island, a long, green slope covered with scattered vines and prickly pears, and at the bottom, stretching out into the sea, the chalky promontory on which stood the lighthouse. The sweep of the view was tremendous, and the pink-and-white checked lighthouse, hung between sky and sea, seemed far away and no larger than a man's hand. Simona clapped her hands in delight.

"How perfectly lovely!" she exclaimed.

"I told you it was beautiful, and you wouldn't believe me."

"Forgive me," she said, patting his cheek. "You always know best and I'm very silly."

Before he could control himself, Giacomo said: "Does that go for politics too?"

"No; not for politics. But don't let's talk about that just now."

He was annoyed with himself for having fallen back into an argument, but at the same time he suffered a return of the left-out and jealous feeling that overcame him every time she made a dogmatic, almost religious reference to her political ideas.

"Why shouldn't we talk about it?" he said as gently as he could. "Perhaps if we talked about it, we might understand one another better."

Simona did not reply, and Giacomo walked on after her, in an extremely bad humor. Now he was the one to feel the heaviness and heat of the day, while Simona, intoxicated by the sight of the distant sea, shouted: "Let's run down the rest of the way. I can't wait to get into the water."

With her sling bag bobbing about on her shoulder, she began to run down the path, emitting shrill cries of joy. Giacomo saw that she was throwing her legs in all directions like an untrained colt. Suddenly the thought, "Tonight she'll be mine" floated through his head and quieted him. What could be the importance of belonging to a political party in comparison to that of the act of love, so ageless and so very human? Men had possessed women long before the existence of political parties or religions. And he was sure that in the moment when he possessed Simona he would drive out of her every allegiance except that of her love for him. Strengthened by this thought he ran after her, shouting in his turn: "Wait for me, Simona!"

She stopped to wait, flushed, quivering and bright-eyed. As he caught up with her he said pantingly: "Just now I began to feel very happy. I know that we're going to love one another."

"I know it too," she said, looking at him out of her innocent blue eyes.

Giacomo put one arm around her waist, catching her hand in his and compelling her to throw it over his shoulders. They walked on in this fashion, but Simona's eyes remained set on the water below. Giacomo, on the other hand, could not tear his thoughts away from the body he was holding so tightly. Simona was wearing a skimpy boy's jersey with a patch in the front. And her head was boyish in outline as well, with the unruly short hair falling over her cheeks. Yet her slender waist fitted into the curve of his arm with a womanly softness which seemed to foreshadow the complete surrender promised for the coming night. Suddenly he breathed into her ear: "You'll always be my little friend and comrade."

Simona's mind must have been on the lighthouse, and the word "comrade" came through to her alone, out of context, without the sentimental intonation that gave it Giacomo's intended meaning. For she answered with a smile: "We can't be comrades . . . at least, not until you see things the way I do. . . . But I'll be your wife."

So she was still thinking of the Party, Giacomo said to himself with excusable jealousy. The word "comrade" had for her no tender connotations, but only political significance. The Party continued to have a prior claim to her loyalty.

"I didn't mean it that way," he said disappointedly.

"I'm sorry," she said, hastening to correct herself. "That's what we call each other in the Party."

"I only meant that you'd be my lifelong companion."

"That's true," she said, lowering her head in embarrassment, as if she couldn't really accept the word except politically.

They dropped their arms and walked down the path with no link between them. As they proceeded, the lighthouse seemed to approach them, revealing its tower shape. The water beyond it had a metallic sheen, derived from the direct rays of the sun, while behind them the mountain seemed to grow higher, with a wall of red rock rising above the lower slope which they were now traversing. At the top was a summerhouse with a railing around it, in which they could distinguish two tiny human figures enjoying the view.

"That vantage-point is called La Migliara," Giacomo explained. "A few years ago an Anacapri girl threw herself down the mountain from it, but first she wound her braids around her head and over her eyes so as not to see what she was doing."

Simona tossed a look over her shoulder at the top of the mountain.

"Suicide is all wrong," she said.

Giacomo felt jealousy sting him again.

"Why?" he asked. "Does the Party forbid it?"

"Never mind about the Party." She looked out over the sea and thrust her face and chest forward as if to breathe in the breeze blowing in their direction. "Suicide's all wrong because life is beautiful and it's a joy to be alive."

Again Giacomo didn't really want to get into a political argument; he wanted to make a show of the serenity and detachment which he thoroughly believed were his. But again his annoyance carried him away.

"But T——" (this was the name of a Communist friend they had in common) "committed suicide, didn't he?"

"He did wrong," she said succinctly.

"Why so? He must have had some reason. What do you know?"

"I do know, though," she said obstinately. "He did wrong. It's our duty to live."

"Our duty?"

"Yes; duty."

"Who says so?"

"Nobody. It just is."

"I might just as well say that it's our duty to take our life if we feel it's not worth living. . . . Nobody says so. It just is."

"That's not true," she answered inflexibly. "We were made to live and not to die. . . . Only someone that's sick or in a morbid state of mind can think that life's not worth living."

"So you think that T—— was either sick or in a morbid state of mind, do you?"

"At the moment when he killed himself, yes, I do."

Giacomo was tempted to ask her if this was the Party line, as seemed to him evident from that stubborn note in her voice which annoyed him so greatly, but this time he managed to restrain himself. By now they had reached the bottom of the slope and were crossing a dry, flat area, covered with wood-spurge and prickly pears. Then the land turned into rock and they found themselves before the lighthouse, at the end of the path, which seemed like the end of all human habitation and the beginning of a new and lonely world of colorless chalk and stone. The lighthouse soared up above them as they plunged down among the boulders toward the sea. At a bend, they suddenly came upon a basin of green water, surrounded by rocky black cliffs, eroded by salt. Simona ran down to the cement landing and exclaimed: "Wonderful! Just what I was hoping for! Now we can swim. And we have it all to ourselves. We're quite alone."

She had no sooner spoken these words than a man's voice came out of the rocks: "Simona! What a pleasant surprise."

They turned around, and when a face followed the voice, Simona shouted: "Livio! Hello! Are you here too? What are you doing?"

The young man who emerged from the rocks was short and powerfully built, with broad shoulders. His head contrasted with this athletic body, for it was bald, with only a fringe of hair around the neck, and his flat face had a scholarly expression. The face of a ferret, Giacomo thought, taking an instant dislike to it, not exactly intelligent, but keen and treacherous. He knew the fellow by sight and was aware that he worked in Simona's office. Now Livio came into full view, pulling up his tight, faded red trunks.

"I'm doing the same thing you are, I suppose," he said by way of an answer.

Then Simona said something which gave Giacomo considerable satisfaction.

"That's not very likely. . . . Unless you've just got yourself married. . . . I'm here on my honeymoon. . . . Do you know my husband?"

"Yes; we know each other," Livio said easily, jumping down on to a big square stone and shaking Giacomo's hand so hard that the latter winced with pain as he echoed: "Yes, we've met in Rome." Livio then turned to Simona and added: "I'd heard something to the effect that you were about to marry. But you should have told the comrades. They want to share your joys."

He said all this in a colorless, businesslike voice, but one which was not necessarily devoid of feeling. Giacomo noticed that Simona was smiling and seemed to be waiting for Livio to go on, while Livio stood like a bronze statue on a stone pedestal, with his trunks pulled tightly over his voluminous pubis and all the muscles of his body standing out, and talked down to them. Giacomo felt as if he were somehow left out of their conversation, and drew away, all the while listening intently. They conversed for several minutes without moving, asking one another about various Party workers and where they had spent their vacations.

But Giacomo was struck less by what they said than by the tone in which they said it. What was this tone exactly, and why did it rub him the wrong way? There was a note of complicity in it, he concluded, a reference to some secret bond different from that of either friendship or family. For a moment he wondered if it weren't just what one would find between fellow employees in a bank or government office. But upon reflection, he realized that it was entirely different. It was . . . he searched for some time, groping for an exact definition . . . it was the tone of voice of two monks or two nuns meeting one another. And why then did it rub him the wrong way? Not because he disapproved of Livio's and Simona's political ideas; in the course of a rational discussion he might very well allow that these had some basis. No; there was nothing rational about his hostility; its cause was obscure even to himself and at times it seemed to be one with his jealousy, as if he were afraid that Simona would escape him through her Party connections.

As these thoughts ran through his mind, his face grew dark and discontented, so that when Simona joined him, all smiles, a moment later, she exclaimed in surprise: "What's wrong? Why are you unhappy?"

"Nothing . . . It's just the heat."

"Let's go in the water. . . . But first, where can we undress?"

"Just follow me. . . . This way."

He knew the place well, and now led Simona through a narrow passage among the rocks. Behind these rocks they stepped across some other lower ones and then went around a huge mass which sealed off a tiny beach of very fine, black sand at the foot of glistening, black rocky walls around a pool of shallow water filled with black seaweed. The effect was that of a room, with the sky for a ceiling, a watery floor and walls of stone.

"No swimming-bath can match this," Giacomo observed, looking around him.

"At last I can shed my clothes," said Simona with a sigh of relief.

She put her bag down on the sand and bent over to take out her bathing-suit, while, leaning against the rocks, Giacomo stripped himself in a second of his shirt and trousers. The sight of him stark naked caused her to give a nervous laugh.

"This is the sort of place to go swimming with no suits on, isn't it?" she said.

"Unfortunately, one can never manage to be alone," Giacomo replied, thinking of Livio.

He walked, still naked, with bare feet, over the cold sand in her direction, but she did not see him coming because she was pulling her jersey over her head. Her nakedness, he reflected, made her seem more virginal than ever. Her low-swung, round breasts had large rosy nipples, and a look of purity about them, as if they had never been offered to a masculine caress. Indeed, her virginal quality was so overwhelming that Giacomo did not dare press her to him as he had intended, but stood close by while she pulled her head out of the jersey. She shook back her ruffled hair and said in surprise: "What are you doing? Why don't you put on your trunks?"

"I'd like to make love right here and now," said Giacomo.

"On these rocks? Are you mad?"

"No. I'm not mad."

They were facing each other now, he entirely naked and she naked down to the waist. She crossed her arms over her breasts as if to support and protect them and said entreatingly: "Let's wait till tonight. . . . And meanwhile let's go swimming . . . please. . . ."

"Tonight you'll put me off again."

"No; it will be different tonight."

Giacomo walked silently away and proceeded to put on his trunks, while Simona, obviously relieved, hastily donned her two-piece suit. She shouted gaily: "I'm off for a swim! If you love me, you'll follow."

"Let's go in right here," Giacomo suggested.

Simona paused and stuck her white foot into the green and brown seaweed that choked the black water.

"This pool is too murky. . . . It's no more than a puddle. Let's go where we just came from."

"But we shan't be alone."

"Oh, we have plenty of time for that."

They went back to the basin, where Livio was taking a sun-bath on the cement landing, lying as still as if he were dead. Somehow this increased Giacomo's dislike of him. Yes; he was the sort of fellow that goes in for purposeful tanning, and then wanders about showing it off, wearing skimpy trunks designed to exhibit his virility as well. When Livio heard them coming he leaped to his feet and said: "Come on, Simona. Let's dive in and race over to that rock."

"You'll have to give me a handicap of at least a length," she said joyfully, forgetful of her husband.

"I'll give you three lengths, if you say so."

There it was, Giacomo could not help thinking, the same intimate, conspiratorial, clubby, Party manner, that tone of voice in which, despite their marriage, she had never spoken to him, and perhaps never would speak either. Sitting on a

flat rock, just above the landing, he watched his wife plunge
awkwardly in and then swim like a dark shadow under the
green water until she came out, with her blond head dripping.

"That was a real belly-flop," Livio shouted, making a perfect dive to join her. He too swam underwater, but for a
longer distance than Simona, so that he came out farther
away. Giacomo wondered if this "Party manner" weren't all
a product of his imagination, and if there hadn't been in the
past some more intimate personal relationship between
them. And he realized that this second hypothesis was, on
the whole, less disagreeable than the first. Then he said to
himself that if he were to mention any such suspicion to Simona she would be outraged and brand it as utterly "bourgeois," not to say "evil-minded and filthy." The moment
after he dismissed it as out of the question. No, they were
comrades, as she had said, and nothing more. What still
puzzled him was why he objected more to their being Party
comrades than to their being lovers. With a wavering effort
of goodwill, he said to himself that his jealousy was absurd,
and he must drive it out of his mind. . . . And all the while
he watched the two of them race across the dazzling green
water in the direction of a round rock which emerged at the
far end of the basin. Livio got there first, and, hoisting himself up on a protruding spur, shouted back at Simona: "I
win! You're all washed up!"

"Speak for yourself!" Simona retorted.

This was the sort of joking insult he and Simona should
have batted back and forth between them, Giacomo reflected. If they didn't joke that way on their honeymoon,
when would they ever do it? He got up decisively, ran several steps along the landing and went in after them. He
landed square on his stomach and was infuriated by the
pain. After swimming several strokes under water he came
up and started toward the rock where Livio and Simona
were sitting. They were close together, talking uninterruptedly, with their legs dangling. He didn't relish the sight; in
fact, it took away all the pleasure he should have felt from

plunging hot and dusty into the cool water. He swam angrily ahead, arrived at the rock breathless and said, hanging on to a ledge: "Do you know, this water's very, very cold."

"It seemed warm to me," said Simona, momentarily interrupting the conversation to shoot him a glance.

"I swam here in April," Livio put in; "it was cold then, I can tell you."

With a curiosity that seemed to Giacomo somewhat flirtatious, Simona asked him: "Were you all alone?"

"No. I came with Nella," Livio answered.

Giacomo was trying to clamber up on the rock, but the only place where he could get a solid grip was the one where Livio and Simona were sitting. They seemed to be oblivious of his struggles, and he preferred not to ask them to move over. Finally, he caught hold of a jutting piece of the rock studded with jagged points, one of which left a pain in the palm of his hand as if it had dug deep into the flesh. Just as he got himself into a sitting position, the other two, with a shout of "Let's race back!" dived into the water, showering him with spray. He looked furiously after them as they raced toward the shore. Only when he had regained his self-control did he plunge in and follow. Simona and Livio were sitting in the shelter of a cliff and Simona was opening a lunch-box that she had taken out of her bag.

"Let's have something to eat," she said to Giacomo as he approached them. "But we must share it with Livio. He says he meant to go back up the mountain, but in this heat it would be too ridiculous."

Without saying a word, Giacomo sat down in the rocks beside them. The contents of the lunch-box turned out to be scanty: some meat sandwiches, two hard-boiled eggs and a bottle of wine.

"Livio will have to be content with very little," Giacomo said gruffly.

"Don't worry," Livio answered gaily. "I'm a very abstemious fellow."

Simona seemed extremely happy as she sat with crossed legs, dividing the lunch. She gave a sandwich to each one of them, bit into her own, and asked Livio:

"Where did you get your tan?"

"On the Tiber," he replied.

"Your whole group is very river-minded, isn't it, Livio?" she asked between one bite and another.

"All except Regina. She scorns the river completely; says it isn't aristocratic enough for her."

The things they talked about were trivial and childish enough, Giacomo reflected. And yet there was a greater intimacy between them than between husband and wife.

"No matter how hard she tries, Regina will never be able to put her background behind her," Simona observed.

"Who is Regina?" asked Giacomo.

"Someone in our outfit . . . the daughter of a wealthy landowner . . . a very fine girl, really," Livio told him. "But wiping out an old trade-mark is no easy matter."

"And in this case, what trade-mark do you mean?"

"The bourgeois trade-mark."

"If you people ever get into power," Giacomo said impulsively, "you'll have to wipe that trade-mark out of millions of people."

"That's exactly what we'll do," Livio said with complete self-confidence. "That's our job, isn't it, Simona?"

Simona's mouth was full, but she nodded assent.

"The Italian bourgeoisie will be a tough nut to crack," Livio went on, "but we'll crack it, even if we have to kill off a large proportion in the process."

"There's a chance you may be killed off yourselves," said Giacomo.

"That's the risk we have to run in our profession," Livio retorted.

Giacomo noticed that Simona did not seem to go along with Livio's ruthlessness; at this last remark she frowned and uttered no word of approval. Livio must have been aware of this, for he brusquely changed the subject.

"Simona, you really should have told us you were getting married, you know. There are some things it's not fair to hide!"

There was a note of tenderness toward Giacomo in Simona's reply.

"We decided from one day to the next. . . . Only the legal witnesses were present. Even our own parents weren't in on it."

"You mean you didn't want them?"

"We didn't want them, and anyhow they might not have come. . . . Giacomo's father and mother didn't want him to marry me."

"Because you're too far to the left, is that it?"

"No," Giacomo interposed. "My people don't go in for politics at all. But my mother had her eye on a certain girl. . . ."

"They may not go in for politics, as you say," Livio said, after another mouthful, "but there are always political implications. How could it be otherwise? Politics gets into everything these days."

True enough, Giacomo thought to himself. Even into honeymoons and a newly-married couple's first embrace. Then, annoyed at his own train of thought, he held out the hard-boiled eggs to his companions.

"You two eat them," he said. "I'm not hungry."

"Be honest now," Livio said with a look of surprise on his face.

"Why aren't you hungry?" Simona asked him.

"That damned *scirocco,* I imagine."

Livio looked up at the cloudy sky.

"There'll be a storm before night. I can promise you that," he said.

Livio's conversation was made up of commonplaces and clichés, Giacomo reflected. But Simona seemed to like them. They conveyed more to her than his own attempts to express emotions that were difficult if not impossible to put into words. Meanwhile Simona, having finished her lunch, said: "Let's lie down for a sun-bath now."

"Will you be my pillow, Simona?" Livio asked, sliding toward her with the plain intention of putting his head on her lap.

For the first time Simona took her husband's presence into account.

"It's too hot for that, and you're too heavy."

And she looked at Giacomo out of the corner of her eyes as if to say: From now on, I won't let anyone do that but you. Giacomo's spirits soared, and he once more felt that there was a possibility of love between them. He got up and said: "Shall we go for a walk among the rocks?"

"Yes," she said promptly, following his example. And she added, to Livio: "See you later. . . . We're going to explore."

"Have a good time," Livio threw after them.

Simona led the way through the passage which her husband had shown her before. She made straight for the black beach, sat down at the foot of a rock and said: "Stretch out and put your head on my legs. . . . You'll be more comfortable that way."

Overcome by joy, Giacomo threw his arms around her and drew her to him. He gave her a kiss, and Simona returned it, blowing hard through her nose, almost as if she were suffering. When they had drawn apart, she repeated: "Stretch out, and we'll snatch a bit of sleep together."

She leaned her back against the rock, and Giacomo, his heart overflowing with love, lay down and put his head on her lap. He closed his eyes, and Simona began to stroke his face. With a hesitant and timid motion, she passed her hand over his cheeks, under his chin and up to the top of his head, where she ran her fingers through his hair. When Giacomo opened his eyes for a split second he saw that she was looking at him with childish intentness and curiosity. Meeting his glance, she bent over, placed a quick kiss on each of his eyes and told him to go to sleep. Giacomo closed his eyes again and gave himself up to enjoyment of the light touch of her tireless little hand until finally he dozed off. He slept for an indefinable length of time and woke up feeling chilled. Simona was sitting in the same position, with his head on her lap. Looking up, he saw the reason for his feeling so cold. The sky was filled with heavy, black storm clouds.

"How long have I been asleep?" he asked her.

"About an hour."

"And what about you?"

"I didn't sleep. I was looking at you."

"The sun's disappeared."

"Yes."

"There's going to be quite a rainstorm."

"Livio's gone," she said by way of an answer.

"Who is that Livio, anyhow?" Giacomo asked without moving.

"A Party comrade, a friend."

"I don't care for him."

"I know that," she said with a smile. "You made it pretty plain. As he was going away he pointed to you as you lay there asleep and said: 'What's the matter? Has he got it in for me?' "

"I haven't got it in for him. . . . But he has no manners. I'm on my honeymoon, and he acts as if it were his."

"He's a good fellow."

"You used to be in love with him. Admit it!"

She came out with a peal of innocent, silvery laughter.

"You must be crazy. I couldn't possibly fall in love with him. He doesn't appeal to me in the least."

"But the way you talked to one another . . ."

"He's a Party comrade," she repeated, "and that's the way we talk." She was silent, for a moment, and then said with unexpected bitterness: "He's unintelligent. That's why he doesn't appeal to me."

"He doesn't seem to me much more stupid than the next man."

"He said a lot of foolish things," she went on angrily, "That we'd kill people off, for instance. . . . He knows better and spoke that way just to show off. . . . But such loose talk is harmful to the Party."

"You're the one that's got it in for him now."

"No. I haven't got it in for him; but he had no business to talk that way." Then she added, more coolly, "As a matter of fact, he's of value to the Party, even if he isn't too bright. He's absolutely loyal; you could ask him to do anything."

"And what value have I?" Giacomo was bold enough to ask jokingly.

"You can't have any value, since you're not one of us."

Giacomo was displeased by this answer. He got up and looked at the lowering sky.

"We'd better get back home before it rains. What do you say?"

"Yes. I think we had better."

Giacomo hesitated for a moment, put his arm around her waist and asked softly: "When we get there, will you be mine . . . at last?"

She nodded, turning her head away in order not to meet his eyes. Feeling easier in his mind, Giacomo quickly got dressed. A few steps away, Simona pulled on her shorts and jersey and started to adjust her bag over her shoulder. But with a tender protectiveness such as he had not displayed on the way down, Giacomo said: "I'll carry that for you."

They started off. First they crossed the flatland, where the pale green branches of the prickly pears seemed to gleam discordantly against the dark sky. As they reached the beginning of the slope they turned around to look behind them. The pink-and-white lighthouse stood out against a majestic mass of black storm clouds rising from the horizon to invade that part of the sky which was still empty. These clouds, shaped like great rampant beasts, had smoking underbellies, and irregular fringes hung down from them over the sea, which was spottily darkening in some places, while in others it still shone like burnished lead in the sun. The fringes were gusts of rain, just beginning to comb the surface of the water. Meanwhile, a turbulent wind covered the prickly pears with yellow dust and a blinding stroke of lightning zigzagged diagonally across the sky from one point to another. After a long silence they heard the thunder—no clap, but rather a dull rumble within the clouds. Giacomo saw his wife pale and instinctively shrink toward him.

"Lightning scares me to death," she said, looking at him.

Giacomo raised his eyes to the half-clear, half-stormy sky.

"The storm isn't here yet," he said. "It's still over the sea. If we hurry, we may get home without a wetting."

"Let's hurry, then," she said, continuing to climb up the path.

The clouds, apparently driven by an increasingly power-ful wind, were spreading out over the sky with startling rapidity. Simona quickened her pace to almost a run, and Giacomo could not help teasing her.

"Afraid of lightning? What would the comrades say to that? A good Marxist like yourself shouldn't have any such fear."

"It's stronger than I am," she said in a childish voice, without turning around.

There were steps, first narrow and then wide, to facilitate the ascent of the lower part of the path, and higher up it rose in wide curves through groves of olive trees. Simona was a long way ahead; Giacomo could see her striding along fifty or sixty feet in front of him. At the top they paused to catch their breath and look around. Anacapri, momen-tarily at their backs, stood reassuringly behind a barrier of green, looking like an Arab city, with its terraces, campanile and gray-domed church. Giacomo pointed to the shrunken lighthouse on the promontory below, profiled against the threatening storm.

"Just think, we were right down there!" he murmured.

"I can't wait to be home," said Simona, perhaps with the thunder and lightning in mind. Then, meeting Giacomo's eyes, she added with hesitant coquetry: "What about you?"

"I agree," he answered in a low voice, with emotion.

The climb was over, and all they had to do now was fol-low the level path to their rented house, which was well this side of Anacapri. They walked by the wall around the Munthe villa, along a meadow planted with oak trees, and there, just round a bend, was the white wall of their house and the rusty iron gate in the shade of a carob tree with pods hanging all over it. The clouds were straight above them now, and it was as dark as evening. Simona hurriedly pushed open the gate and went on ahead without waiting for her husband to follow. Giacomo walked more slowly down the marble steps among the cactus plants. As he went, there was another rumble of thunder, louder this time, like an overturned wagon-load of stones rolling down a hill.

From inside the house Simona called back: "Shut the door tight!"

The house was on a hillside, set back among the trees, and consisted of four roughly furnished rooms. Giacomo made his way in amid almost complete darkness. There was no electric light, but oil lamps of various shapes and colors were lined up on the hall table. He lifted the glass off one of these, lit a match, touched it to the wick, put back the glass and entered the dining room. No one was there, but he could hear Simona moving in the room next to it. He did not wish to join her immediately, and, feeling thirsty, he poured himself out a glass of white wine. Finally, he picked up the lamp and went to the bedroom door. The bedroom, too, was almost dark. The window giving on to the garden was open, and through it, in what light was left among the shadows, he could make out the terrace surrounded by lemon trees planted in big pots. Simona, in a dressing gown, was tidying the still unmade bed. He set the lamp down on the bedside table and said: "Are you still afraid of the lightning?"

She was leaning over the bed, with one leg slightly raised, smoothing the sheet. Pulling herself up, she answered: "No. Now that I'm in the house I feel safer."

"And are you afraid of me?"

"I never was afraid of you."

Giacomo walked around the bed and took her into his arms. Standing beside the head of the bed, they exchanged a kiss. Giacomo undid the sash of Simona's dressing gown and it slipped down over her shoulders and hips to the floor. But Simona did not interrupt the kiss; indeed she prolonged it with an awkward eagerness, betrayed by her characteristic way of blowing through her nose. With sudden decisiveness, Giacomo let her go.

"Lie down, will you?" he said, hurriedly taking off his clothes.

Simona hesitated and then lay down on the bed. Giacomo was aware of being impelled by strictly animal feelings, as if he were not in a house, but in a dark cave—yes, as if he were a primitive man, moved by carnal appetite alone. Yet it was with a certain tenderness that he lay down beside his wife. She was facing the wall, but brusquely she turned around and pressed herself against him, snuggling into his arms. For a few minutes they lay there, motionless, then Giacomo began chastely and gently to caress her. He wanted to possess her on her own virginal terms, without bringing any of his masculine experience into play. His light caresses and the words he whispered through her hair into one ear were intended to calm her fears and lead her almost insensibly to give herself to him. He was not in a hurry and it seemed to him that his new policy of consideration and patience would win for him what his haste of the previous evening had failed to obtain. And by degrees he had the impression that, in response to his words and caresses, she was yielding not only her body, but also that inward part of her which had resisted him heretofore. Simona did not speak, but her breathing grew gradually heavier. All of a sudden, almost involuntarily, he gave way to a natural impulse and attempted to take her. Under the impact of his body, Simona seemed at first to surrender, then brusquely she rebelled and struggled to free herself. With a mixture of anger and submission she whispered: "I can't do it! I can't!"

Giacomo refused to heed her change of heart and tried to prevail over her by force. She defended herself with her feet and knees and hands, while he did everything to overcome her. In the combat their naked bodies were bathed in perspiration. Finally Giacomo lost his patience, leaped out of bed, and went into the bathroom, saying: "I'll be back in a minute."

Guided by a furious inspiration, he groped his way to the wash basin, took the razor blade he had used for shaving that morning and plunged it into the cushion of his thumb. He felt the cold blade cut through his skin, but had no pain. Then he put the blade back on the shelf and squeezed his thumb, which gave out an abundant flow of blood. He went back to the bedroom and threw himself upon his wife, rubbing his bloody thumb on the sheet between her legs. Then he shouted angrily: "You may not realize it, but you're no longer a virgin!"

Tremblingly she asked: "How do you know?"

"Just look!"

He took the lamp from the table and threw its light upon the bed. Simona was hunched up on the pillow, with her knees against her chin and her arms crossed over breasts. She looked down at the place where Giacomo had thrown the light and saw a long streak of red blood. Batting her eyelids in disgust, she said: "Are you sure?"

"Positive!"

But just at that moment her eyes traveled to the hand in which Giacomo was holding the lamp. Blood was streaming out of the cut in the cushion of his thumb. In a plaintive voice she cried out: "It's not my blood. It's yours! . . . You cut yourself on purpose."

Giacomo put the lamp back on the table and shouted in a rage: "That's the only blood I'll see tonight or any night to come. You're still a virgin and you always will be!"

"Why do you say that? What makes you so unkind?"

"That's the way it is," he answered. "You'll never be mine. Some part of you is hostile to me, and hostile it will remain."

"What part do you mean?"

"You're closer to that fool, Livio, than you are to me," he said, coming out with his jealousy at last. "That part of you which is close to Livio is hostile to me."

"That's not true."

"Yes; it is true. And it's equally true that if your Party came to power you'd inform on me. . . ."

"Who says so?"

"You said so yourself this morning, on the way to the lighthouse."

"I said nothing at all."

"Well, what would you do, then?"

She hesitated for a moment and then said:

"Why do you bring up such things at a time like this?"

"Because they prevent you from loving me and becoming my wife."

"I wouldn't inform on you," she said at last. "I'd leave you, that's all."

"But you're supposed to inform on your enemies," he shouted, angrier than ever. "It's your duty."

Still huddled up at the head of the bed, she burst into tears.

"Giacomo, why are you so unkind? . . . I'd kill myself. That's what I'd do."

Giacomo did not have the courage to remind her that on the way to the lighthouse she had branded suicide as morbid and absolutely inadmissible. After all, this contradiction was more flattering to him than an open declaration of love. Meanwhile, still in tears, she had got down from the bed and gone over to the open window. Giacomo lay on the bed, watching. She stood straight, with her head bent to the side and one arm raised against the frame. Suddenly the room was lit up, and every object in it, her naked, white body, the garden and the potted lemon trees around the terrace. There followed a metallic crack and a violent tremor which made the window and the walls of the room tremble. Simona gave a terrified cry, left the window and threw herself sobbing into her husband's arms. Giacomo pressed her to him, and almost immediately, while still weeping, she sought his embrace, he penetrated her body without any difficulty whatsoever. He had the feeling that a hidden flower, composed of only two petals, had opened—although still remaining invisible—to something that in the dark night of the flesh played the role of the sun. Nothing was settled, he reflected later on, but for the time being it was enough to know that she would kill herself for him.

# ELIO VITTORINI

## 1909–

The fusion between the Italian South and the literary *avant-garde* has found a culmination in the work of Elio Vittorini, who was born in Sicily in 1909 and has long been living in Milan. Vittorini was to some extent exposed to American influences, and has translated numerous important American works of fiction. He is an extreme example of what is roughly called a lyric as opposed to a narrative literary temperament: the structure of his dialogues and the emblematic quality of his characters are typical, and they have also influenced younger writers. An important influence has been exercised by Vittorini in Italy in his capacity as editor and literary adviser to publishing houses. His own books have been widely translated since World War II, particularly *Conversation in Sicily*, which had appeared in Italy shortly before the war and was published in this country in 1949 with a presentation by Ernest Hemingway. I have chosen here some of the narrative sections which are now part of a book, formed of re-edited and amplified older material, published recently by Vittorini under the title *Diary in Public*. (For a wider selection see *Italian Quarterly*, Fall 1957.)

# Stories from an Autobiography in Time of War

## 1. THE DESERT

"In the middle of the city was the desert."

We were playing cards, talking. Four men; we were smoking, and in our hands we held aces, kings, queens—jacks too.

"Did you say *in* the city? Right in the middle?"

"That's what I said: there was city to the north, city to the west, to the east, and also to the south. From the squares and from the streets the winds blew."

"And it was desert?"

"Desert. It was rock and dust, with a clump of wormwood here and there; just so—and no water—and crows."

"And lizards?"

"And lizards."

"And no lights at night?"

"No stars."

We looked at each other. A card was thrown on the table. Another was thrown, another, another, and another. The Neapolitan won.

"Well, was it very big?"

"No one knew. There were the bones of animals scattered about. Skulls with horns."

"A real desert."

"I've seen even the ruins of houses there."

"Human houses?"

"Human houses. Rooms."

"And how did you get there?"

"In a taxi. I took my luggage with me."

*Translated by Lowry Nelson, Jr.*

"And it was the desert?"

The Croatian set his cards down and raised his hands, and with his hands gripped his forehead. The rest of us kept our cards up, throwing nothing down. The queen of spades lay on the table.

"I can see it," said the Croatian. "The ruins and the tree stumps, and the tracks, and the ties, and the burnt skeletons of the trains."

We threw down our cards.

"Are you talking about another desert?"

"No, it's the same one."

"The earth has only one heart."

The Neapolitan spat and took the trick. He shook his head.

"We have one too where I come from," he said. "It has a rough wall around it, and not a blade of grass grows there, and people who pass by it cross themselves, and they call it the desert. It's among olive groves."

We lit up cigarettes again.

"I can see it," said the Croatian. "It's just like now, and it's the desert."

There was one who wasn't playing, the Spaniard, and he hadn't said a word. He was chewing tobacco, drawing it out in strands.

"The desert is deep."

What did he mean by that? We turned toward him and waited.

"It covers me," he went on. "I'm sitting here. I'm chewing tobacco. And I'll never be able to escape it!"

"Come now," said the Neapolitan.

He laughed—he alone, and heard only himself. The other stood up.

"Oh, the lovely desert of long ago!" he said.

And the others after him:

"The glittering sand."

"The enormous sun!"

"The days on the road, the long days!"

"The names of places to reach!"

"Oh, the lovely desert!"

## 2. CITIES OF THE WORLD

We loaded rocks and sand all day long, then we sat resting for a bit; it was night.

"Hum!" we said.

Lights were being lit on the mountainside, on the ocean too. We looked at each other, and higher up girls were passing by, and we kept saying "Hum!"

At one point the tall man said: "Alicante!" We spoke at last. "Alicante?"

"Sidney! Alicante!"

"Sidney too?"

"Cities of the world!"

Two girls passed by. They stopped.

"What?" one said to the other.

We pointed toward the lights.

"The city."

"Cities of the world."

They laughed, but stayed on. And the tall man said: "Manila, girls!"

They were caught. We pointed out to them the lights among the leaves, and the lights and leaves on the water, the night. "Cities of the world."

"And San Francisco!" cried the tall man.

We all began to shout.

"And Leghorn!"

"And Acapulco!"

And a little fellow: "Arquata Scrivia."

He was trembling, young in years, and we asked where he meant.

"I was there," said the little fellow. "It was in Persia."

Dead boats went by below us. "I was in Babylonia," said the oldest.

"In Babylonia?"

"In Babylonia. In Babylonia."

"That," observed the tall man, "was an ancient city."

"And am I not ancient enough? I was there in my youth," said the old man.

"But," said the tall man, "it's now lost."

"Everything is lost," answered the old man.

"It's underneath the sand," said the tall man. "It's been dead for centuries."

"Oh yes," answered the old man. "And it was beautiful!" He sighed. "It had such lights!"

### 3. BEING A WRITER

I think there is great humility in being a writer.

I see it as it was in my father, who was a farrier and wrote tragedies, and did not consider writing tragedies any better than shoeing horses. In fact, when he was shoeing horses he never allowed anyone to say: "Not that way; this way. You did it wrong." He looked with his blue eyes, and smiled or laughed; he shook his head. But when he wrote he took everybody's suggestion no matter what it was.

He listened to what anyone told him, and he didn't shake his head. He agreed. He was very humble in his writing. He said he took it from everybody. And out of his love of writing he tried to be humble in everything: to take from others in all things.

My grandmother laughed at what he wrote.

"What foolishness!" she would say.

And my mother the same. She laughed at him because of what he wrote.

Only my brothers and I did not laugh. I saw how he would redden, how he humbly bowed his head, and that way I learned. Once, for the sake of learning, I slipped out of the house with him.

Every now and then my father would do that: he would slip away from home to write in solitude. Once I followed him. We walked for eight days among the fields of capers, amid the white flowers of solitude, and would stop under a rock for a bit of shade. He with his blue eyes would write and I would learn, and when we returned my mother gave me a drubbing for the two of us.

My father, then, asked me to forgive him for the blows received on his account.

I remember how it was. I didn't reply.

Could I tell him that I forgave him?

And he said to me in a frightening voice: "Answer! Do you forgive me?" He seemed like the ghost of Hamlet's father desiring vengeance. It wasn't that he wanted forgiveness.

But that was the way I learned what writing is.

*More superb short story collections in Dell Laurel Editions.*

### SHORT STORY MASTERPIECES

Edited by Robert Penn Warren and Albert Erskine. The finest collection of modern short stories available by such masters as Hemingway, Faulkner, Fitzgerald, Steinbeck, Maugham, Joyce, Conrad, Thurber, Salinger and 26 others.
LX102, 75c

### THIRTEEN GREAT STORIES

Edited by Daniel Talbot. James Joyce, Saul Bellow, F. Scott Fitzgerald, Isaak Babel, Felipe Alfau, Luigi Pirandello and Joaquin Arderius are among the storytellers represented in this collection of the world's best modern short fiction.
LC165, 50c

## GREAT AMERICAN SHORT STORIES

Edited by Wallace and Mary Stegner. A century and a quarter of the finest American Short Stories, from Washington Irving to John O'Hara.
LC103, 50c

## GREAT FRENCH SHORT STORIES

Edited by Germaine Brée. From Mme. de La Fayette to Samuel Beckett, four centuries of superb French story-telling by such masters as Baudelaire, Balzac, Camus, Colette and Marcel Aymé. Several stories are here translated for the first time.
LC149, 50c

## GREAT ENGLISH SHORT STORIES

Selected and introduced by Christopher Isherwood. Superb stories by Mansfield, Maugham, Moore, Forster, Wells and many others.
LC102, 50c

## GREAT GERMAN SHORT STORIES

Edited by Stephen Spender. Kafka, Mann, von Kleist, Boell and 13 other outstanding short story writers of 19th and 20th century Germany are represented in brilliant modern translations.
LC148, 50c

## GREAT RUSSIAN SHORT STORIES

Edited by Norris Houghton. A collection of stories from the richest period of Russian literature, including works by Pushkin, Turgenev, Dostoyevsky, Tolstoy, Chekhov, Lermontov, Saltykov, Gorky and Andreyev.
LC110,  50c

## GREAT STORIES BY CHEKHOV

Edited by David H. Greene. Nine stories, including *Ward Number 6, My Life* and *The Kiss,* representing Chekhov early and late, brief and at length, and always at his best.
LC126,  50c

PB 19291
5